ALCHEMICAL HERMETICISM

"*Alchemical Hermeticism* is historically rich, philosophically profound, and a significant contribution to the corpus of modern alchemical and Hermetic literature. Pantano's writing is scholarly yet highly readable and contains penetrating insights into the collected primary materials. Here is the kind of scholarship that synthesizes biography, philosophical theory, and practical esotericism into a symphonic whole, and for that I consider it one of the most important releases of the year."

IKE BAKER, AUTHOR OF *A FORMLESS FIRE*

"*Alchemical Hermeticism*, skillfully researched and translated, offers a captivating glimpse into the Hermetic and alchemical world of Marco Daffi. Pantano presents Daffi's insightful essays and enlightening letters, along with an illuminating biography of this key Hermetic figure of the twentieth century. Daffi's unique perspective on Hermetic initiation promises to inspire, stimulate the imagination, and guide all dedicated seekers of the Great Work."

MARLENE SEVEN BREMNER, AUTHOR OF
HERMETIC PHILOSOPHY AND CREATIVE ALCHEMY

"A groundbreaking exploration of spiritual transformation and hidden wisdom. Guiding readers through the mysterious path of initiation, David Pantano masterfully uncovers the convergence of ancient mysteries and the alchemist's quest for divine perfection. With exceptional scholarship, Pantano brings to light the teachings of Marco Daffi, offering readers an unparalleled journey into the heart of mystical traditions."

GWENDOLYN TAUNTON, AUTHOR OF *THE PATH OF SHADOWS*

"Pantano's meticulous presentation of the Italic Hermetic traditions continues its upward trajectory with the addition of *Alchemical*

Hermeticism. Here the reader is immersed in some of the deepest—and I say this in all seriousness—once most secret aspects of Hermetic initiation. Daffi, like Kremmerz, is not an easy friend and guide for the journey but certainly a very reliable one. Drink slowly and deeply from these pages and join the ranks of the heroes."

MARK STAVISH, AUTHOR OF *THE PATH OF FREEMASONRY*

"What a fascinating book! David Pantano is to be commended for producing such an in-depth study of this esoteric pioneer. I particularly enjoyed the insights afforded by the biographical details of Ricciardelli's life, which serve to anchor the Baron's spiritual alter ego, Marco Daffi, in actuality."

GOMERY KIMBER, AUTHOR OF *THE NAZI ALCHEMIST*

"A gem for serious practitioners as well as for investigators of this occult knowledge, and a treasure trove of insights that opens a new door into the vast world of Italian and European occultism and magic from a Hermetic perspective. Pantano has once again made a precious contribution to the rediscovery of these authors and their influence on the world of the occult."

RUDOLF BERGER, FOUNDER AND HOST OF *THOTH-HERMES* PODCAST

"This book marks a significant advance in introducing the English-speaking world to the influential Italian Hermeticist Giuliano Kremmerz and the highly controversial milieu of Italian occultism."

CRISTIAN GUZZO, EDITOR AND TRANSLATOR OF
GIULIANO KREMMERZ'S BOOK *ANGELS AND DEMONS OF LOVE*

"Pantano has shone a spotlight on the immense depth and importance of Hermeticism as it was practiced in what can be called its homeland. Daffi's presentation of the use of symbols for inner and outer transformation places his Hermetic view squarely in the domain of initiatory practices, not simply limiting it to psychological insights."

JOHN R. WHITE, PH.D., COEDITOR OF
JUNGIAN ANALYSIS IN A WORLD ON FIRE

ALCHEMICAL HERMETICISM

The Secret Teachings of Marco Daffi on Initiation

DAVID PANTANO

Inner Traditions
Rochester, Vermont

Inner Traditions
One Park Street
Rochester, Vermont 05767
www.InnerTraditions.com

Text stock is SFI certified

The following text was originally published in Italian:
Foreword by Valerio Tomassini in issue #28-October 1987 of *Kemi-Hathor*, Milano.
"Alchemical Hermeticism" [Alchimia Ermetica] by Ricciardo Ricciardeli in *Ulisse* no 7, 1948.
"What is Magic for Those Who Cultivate It" [Che Cosa E La Magia Per I Suoi Cultori] by
    Giuseppe Tucci in *Scienze del Mistero* 1, no. 4, 1946.
"Doctrine of Initiation" [Neobuddhismo e l'Iniziazione] by Marco Daffi in *Iniziazione* 1,
    no. 4, December 1945 by S. Giovene.
"Commentary on the Mirror of Virgins" [Commento alla novella 'La Meravigliosa Storia
    dello Specchio delle Vergini] by Marco Daffi in *Elixir* no. 7, 2009 by Rebis Editions.
Dissertamina in 1980 by Edizioni Alkaest.
Epistolario Filosofico in 1980 by Edizioni Alkaest.
Epistolario Confidenziale by Giammaria Gonella.
"Giammaria Remembers" by Giammaria Gonella.
"Remembering Marco Daffi" by N. R. Ottaviano in 2015 on ekatlos.it.
"The Magical Baron" [R.R., Il Barone Mago] by Piero Fenili in *Elixir* no. 4, 2006 by Rebis
    Editions.
"The Voice" [La Voce] by Giammaria Gonella in *Elixir* no. 8, 2009 by Rebis Editions.
"Don Ricciardo" by Auri Campolonghi Gonella, in *Elixir* no. 8, 2009 by Rebis Editions.

Cataloging-in-Publication Data for this title is available from the Library of Congress

ISBN 978-1-64411-997-6 (print)
ISBN 978-1-64411-998-3 (ebook)

Printed and bound in the United States by Lake Book Manufacturing, LLC
The text stock is SFI certified. The Sustainable Forestry Initiative® program promotes
sustainable forest management.

10 9 8 7 6 5 4 3 2 1

Text design by Virgina Scott Bowman and layout by Kenleigh Manseau
This book was typeset in Garamond Premier Pro with Bodega Sans, Amster, and Futura Std
used as display typefaces

To send correspondence to the author of this book, mail a first-class letter to the author c/o
Inner Traditions • Bear & Company, One Park Street, Rochester, VT 05767, and we will
forward the communication.

Hermeticism is an intuition.

MARCO DAFFI

A Dante Alighieri.
Divinus Perfectionis Magister,
"per patria celeste, di stirpe angelico e filosopho poeticho"

MARSILIO FICINO,
SOPRA LA MONARCHIA DI DANTE (1468)

Contents

PART 1

The Philosophy of Hermetic Magic

Collected Works of Marco Daffi

◎◎◎

Foreword

Valerio Tomassini

One could say MÖRKÖHEKDAPH (Marco Daffi is the Italianized form) is a nonexistent person . . . an abstraction, belonging to the world of visions, magic, reincarnations, of the world that lurks in the dark chasms of the subconscious and not a natural person, rather an entity of the invisible world . . .

TRIAL OF THE MAGUS

For the few who are familiar with Marco Daffi's work, these notes will seem superfluous. I would simply like to point out his approach to the "Dry" path and the strictly technical aspects of his writings. Furthermore, to draw attention to clarifications he made on the Monadic Tetrad of the Kremmerzian four Hermetic bodies. In fact, some of his writings are "connected" to one or other "body," depending on the level that is entered in the vibration. It is well known that in ancient Egypt even the lowest body, that is, the Saturnian, has a sacred character and "name." Not so in modern society, notwithstanding the remnants of religious customs, such as giving the name of a saint to newborns at the time of baptism.

Subsequently, in the initiatic sphere, Marco Daffi revealed his inner names to a few disciples, namely: Dr. Elio.†

*This foreword was first published in issue no. 28 (October 1987) of *Kemi-Hathor*, the Milan-based bimonthly journal of alchemy and symbolic studies.
†Dr. Elio G. was a practicing physician from Genoa who for over thirty years was one of Daffi's closest collaborators up until the Baron's passing in 1969. See the note on p. 188.

- Saturnian—hylic name—Ricciardo Ricciardelli
- Lunar—astral name—Mörköhekdaph
- Mercurial—Hermetic name—Ei hm'sc Bêl
- Solar—numen-nomen—∿ ± △ ⩔

That which we have inherited in trust will not be disclosed, since written names do not exhaust their eonic individuality, lacking the *sigils*, or graphic power of the energy in question.

Moreover, the Hermetic doctrine of the numen-nomen (or soul name) can only be realized if the "separations" are fully "integrated" in an eonic sense of their respective "body."

Only at the end of a lunar cycle and what seemingly occurs as a laborious procedure will the adept come to know of their occult numen-nomen, as the substance of the phonic and energetic synthesis of the monadic tetrad.

ADDENDUM

If I may, I would like to add a brief afterword to this passage. The most important names connected with the monadic tetrad are the Mercurial and the Solar because they have a magnetic capacity to attract and ultimately influence similar energies and "intelligences." Based on this knowledge, the ancient Egyptian ritual to incarnate the souls of masters through sacred coitus was practiced in the temples. Hence the incarnation of evolved souls was never accidental, rather they responded to specific laws of operative magic.

The Lunar body as the condensation and vehicle of the higher Mercurial and Solar bodies has a (-) passive capacity. Within Isiac parameters of magic, the Lunar body (black astral) becomes a vehicle for magnetic operations up to the level of the Mercurial (white astral). It is another matter, however, at the Solar sphere, where within an Osirian evolution, the Lunar body is assimilated in ascension to higher levels of alchemical evolution.

In sum: everything that undergoes change belongs to the astral (*a-stereon*, "without fixity," "wandering") whereas, as the alchemical work teaches, when the solarization is at its peak the whole mass becomes fixed, no longer iridescent; *Rubedo* concludes the Great Work!

VALERIO TOMASSINI,
ROME

VALERIO TOMASSINI, born in Rome in 1952, is a writer who has contributed to *Kemi-Hathor*, the international journal on alchemy. He received initiation into the Fr+ Tm+ of Miriam, under Lehajah and subsequently under Rehael. Tomassini has long been dedicated to researching bioresonance and its therapeutic potential. His investigations into altered states of consciousness prompted several journeys to South America, where he studied and engaged with indigenous shamanic traditions, particularly those involving the use of psychoactive plants.

What is the Oracle of Delphi? The tetractys, the quadratic harmony according to which the Sirens sing.

IAMBLICHUS, ON THE PYTHAGOREAN WAY OF LIFE

Chastity . . . occurs in the human domain . . . only as an alternation between abstinence and eroticism. The alternation is comparable to that of the Sirenae, who emerge from the sea to breathe (= purification) and then dive back down to copulate (= satisfaction). The instinct of a fish, in its element. . . . In short, the Sirenae refer to the emergence of the divine principle from the astral sea ruled by elementals. Hence, the exercise of magical chastity must be considered as preparatory, in alternation with the perception and realization of the coeval state of divine love.

MARCO DAFFI, "ON CHASTITY," DISSERTAMINA

The avataric state is the relative culmination of an outward movement, a release from the physical body. Before realizing the avatar you will have to digest further experiences . . . after which you can begin to fix the humanimal complex and prepare for the transference to a future birth.

MARCO DAFFI, EPISTOLARIO FILOSOFICO

La Fenice

Introduction

Marco Daffi holds a distinguished position within the pantheon of magical heroes, having carved out a niche all his own, within the vast universe of Hermeticism for explorations of the inner planes through the agency of Hermetic initiation. Daffi's writings are testimony to audacious pilgrimages undertaken through the profound recesses of the psyche to transcend the common boundaries of consciousness. His experimentations illuminate experiences refined by the mortar and pestle of internal practices and confectioned in philosophical and spiritual representations.

More than merely putting pen to paper, Daffi's writings are symbolic of an internal journey along the hero's path of self-realization to uncover and ultimately transfigure the deeper strata of selfhood. In the final analysis, Daffi's opus bears witness to a profound search for identity and transcendence, culminating in a gnosis of majestic illumination and splendor. Nevertheless, when examined on their own merits they represent some of the most unique and perplexing writings within the contemporary field of Hermeticism.

Baron Ricciardo Ricciardelli (1900–1969) is better known by his initiatic name Marco Daffi. An aristocratic esotericist born at the turn of the twentieth century in Naples, his affinities gravitated more toward the feral lands of the Abruzzi, his adoptive residency in the mountainous regions east of Rome, where his family were *domi nobiles*—local aristocracy and proprietors of a venerable patrimony of fiefs, titles, and prestige.

It is not surprising, however, that Daffi is remembered more for his association with the Italian magus Giuliano Kremmerz and the notoriety surrounding a court case, known as the "Trial of the Magus," which catapulted his name to fame among Italians at the start of the Second World War. However, this fame was fleeting and ultimately evaporated into an oblivion that enveloped Ricciardelli for the rest of his terrestrial stay. That he is remembered more for a clamorous legal proceeding of scarce importance and not for the magisterial writings that bear his name—veritable investigations, based on firsthand research, into some of the more rarefied aspects of Hermetic philosophy and spiritual initiation—is a testament of the *profanum vulgus* that values the sensational over the substantive.

Upon further investigation, however, the Baron appears as a much more profound if not iconoclastic figure of Hermeticism, revered by the intellectual and scientific community frequenting the many academies, salons, and circles that surfaced in postwar Rome for his expansive erudition as honorary advisor to prestigious committees of scientific research on the paranormal as well as for his peculiar paranormal feats—testimonies of auguries, prophecies, spiritual walk-ins, and other forms of inner manifestations.

In the final decades up until his death, in 1969, Ricciardelli was engaged in the articulation of his Hermetic *Weltanschauung*, finding expression through numerous epistolary exchanges, essays, and articles written to individual seekers as well to a wider audience through journals specializing in parapsychology, esotericism, and metaphysics.

Throughout the 1950s and '60s, as Italy rode the wave of the postwar socioeconomic boom exemplified by Fellini's *La Dolce Vita*, the Baron was sought after as a lecturer at the prestigious Accademia Tiberina of Rome for his expertise on Western and Eastern disciplines of the spirit about which he lectured with an esoteric and somewhat eclectic bent, delivering talks on a wide range of specialized topics including the I Ching, the myth of Andromeda, Jainism, telepathy, divination, animal psychism, and dream interpretation, to name a few. However, until recent years, very little attention was afforded to his remarkable spiritual journeys, inner experiences replete with numinous visions and Pythagoras-like episodes of *anamnesis*, recalling past-life events with vivid clarity and detail that were rich with symbolic signification.

In the words of Giammaria Gonella (1926–2022), a contemporary Hermeticist, collaborator, and heir of Daffi's alchemical-Hermetic body of work, "the Baron was endowed with a refined numinous apperception operating at levels outside of the norm, exploring far-reaching depths of the astral realm, especially when illuminating on his 'Atlantean' darkness."*4 Daffi was entirely consumed with fulfilling the life purpose of his existence, which was the re-equilibration of his being through the exercise of spiritual asceticism aimed at purging his soul from the defilement of karmic retributions. That Daffi was able to elucidate his Hermetic philosophy in an organic and coherent manner was largely the result of referencing direct experiences gained through initiatory journeys throughout his more than forty-year spiritual pilgrimage practicing Magical Hermeticism from the mid-1920s to 1969.

The Baron pioneered investigations into the numinal or inter-dimensional aspects of consciousness through the vehicle of a Hermetic chain that he founded, directed, and calibrated over the decades, known variably as the Pharaonic Group, Andromeda Ring, and the Rite of Hamzur. By means of spiritual explorations with a small circle of like-minded *sodales*,† he undertook a veritable *descensus ad infernos* into the dark cavernous recesses of past-life regressions for purposes of Hermetic healing—aka *medicinae dei*—to re-equilibrate his defective personality that he believed impeded his (reincarnated) evolution from transgressions incurred in previous existences.

---

*Ricciardelli recalled several past lives, including Atlantean, Chaldean, and Phoenician incarnations. It was in a particular Phoenician incarnation as a priest to the Pharaoh that he received recurring visions of committing a grave transgression by misappropriating the Pharaoh's jewels from the temple, carrying off the Pharaoh's wife and fleeing to avoid capture. This transgression led, so he believed, to incurring a curse that blighted his soul and impeded his karmic emancipation in future incarnations.

†From Latin *sodalis* meaning comrade, referring to a *sodality* or *sodalitas*, brotherhood, or confraternity of initiants, such as the ancient sodalitas of the Pythagorean school of Kortona.

According to Giammaria, "The ritual of Hamzur, therefore, offers the postulant the opportunity to become aware of their particular state of equilibrium and consciousness (imprint for a future memory), so that 'in solitude' they are certain of the indispensable necessity of exercising the . . . initiatic process. The work not attempted in this lifetime becomes, necromantically, essential in death. . . . The dream is a mirror into the consciousness of the dreamer, but the dream only becomes valid when the dreamer knows how to 'awaken in it'—only then will they experience the specter of sacred representations . . . that is, if they succeed in getting this far."

In confidence, "don Ricciardo" (as he was reverently called) engaged in multiple forms of mantic experimentation, extending his willingness to investigate the practical applications of oracular modes of consciousness, especially by exercising his considerable mediumistic capabilities through divinatory instruments like the tarot, *I-Ching*, numerology, dream interpretation, past-life regressions, and astronology.

Vincenzo Nestler, the noted researcher on parapsychological phenomena, describes the Hermetic process in these terms: "this psychic ocean, in which there are no distinctions of space or time, nor past or future, by means of the Hermetic process of telepathic osmosis; extrasensory contacts and fusions of individuals occur in a transcendent unconscious state."

The Hermetic process is one and the same as the magical ritual—infused with cosmic symbols, rhythms, accents, and gestures, which Giammaria recounts: "The intrinsic validity of the ritual, as of every ritual, resides in the supporting structure of the magical action, that is, in the apotropaic functionality of the sacred representation, where the operator functions *sub specie lectionis** of the 'magical means, which alone and of itself is not magical, since the inflection of an accent is enough to

---

*The Latin phrase literally means "under the aspect of reading." The term is mainly used in the field of philology and refers to the way we consider a text or manuscript. When we observe a text "sub specie lectionis," we are analyzing its external form, the arrangement of words and handwriting, focusing on its external form, structure, and aspects. In other words, we are examining the text in its visible form, without delving into the meaning or context.

displace the phonic resonance, while the 'carmen' (incantation) remains *flatus vocis* when not correctly intonated or charged with feeling, leaving the whole ceremonial operation sterile. Furthermore, the ritual is like a declaration of love: if spoken in a contrived manner for purposes of convenience it sounds silly, merely a stereotype, whereas, if it is sincere it will flow with heartfelt results."

The emergence of individual mantic powers is rendered primarily through unconscious channels by means of an excursus of cosmogonic synergies catalyzed by ritualized actions that can cultivate a veritable *Harmonia Mundi* to connect, internalize, and assimilate the macrocosmic with the microcosmic, as affirmed in the famous verses of the *Tabula Smaragdina*. This harmonic convergence or *hermetica ratio* leavens the initiate's psyche *sub specie interioritatis*—precipitating a breakthrough, *mutatis mutandis*, or Hermetic transformation that simultaneously detaches from chains connecting to the profane world and opens the initiate's psyche to the reception of spiritual influences.* A radical change or *metanoia* occurs within the operator that for the sake of simplicity can be described as a transformation in perception from the external-inward to that of an internal-inward flow of consciousness through astral channels, from spirit to spirit and soul to soul.† As Daffi says in *Epistolario Filosofico*, "The transmission takes place through intuition and by vibration as in true love at first sight (not sensory illusions), in illuminations, from a passage, from a sentence, from a little book; and then the Guardian of the Threshold bars the road to the curious and the unwary. Whoever overcomes the barriers, I would also call them 'The Seven Angels of Dante's

---

*The reception of spiritual forces or fluids is marked throughout this book with a (–) to indicate receiving energies and (+) to mark the cultivation, development, or projection of spiritual energies and forces.

†"Virtues, which are arranged and divided into rays of the Absolute, are to be considered as CHANNELS and each channel through the plane of intrinsic subjective-existence of the trans-human being is imbued with relativity, and obscured like a lens that clouds (for example, the Plotinian conception of the progressive fading of the four worlds or planes down to the ground). In short: the two planes of intelligence and nature are united in a single one, and the meaning of that one black or dark astral plane, which is presented here, will be understood." See p. 168

Purgatory,' achieves an operational illumination and if they persevere, no obstacle will be able to oppose him in the Work of constitution or reconstitution. And then, only experience will tell if it is a false or genuine Remembrance." (p. 142–43)

Daffi affirms that the harmonic synergy (syzygy) of the initiate's monad-tetradic state (microcosmic *mens*) with the macrocosmic *spiritus* opens the magus to the investiture of initiatic powers, *sub specie Interioritatis*. By harnessing these powers, the magus cultivates "a Hermetic imagination endowed with oracular capacities" yielding symbolic representations through the form of inspirations, intuitions, ideas, dreams, visions, omens, and so on, to state but the most prevalent signs. As Daffi says in "What is Magic," "Magic diverges from metapsychics in considering the latent powers of man as cultivable according to traditional practices and rituals" (p. 52). In "The Sublimation of Mercury" (p. 104) he asserts that the convergence of the macro-micro union is the veritable juncture that leads to creation. This affirmation neatly corresponds with the Vichian proposition on truth making "*verum et factum convertuntur*"—truth is that which is made or created. The magus is such by exercising the power to make truths through the creative process. It is precisely this function of exercising inner powers to create forms that articulate truths and affect change that is the quality that differentiates and distinguishes the magical *artifex*. The classical Latin aphorism "*Verum esse ipsum factum*" (truth is itself made) was later taken up by Giambattista Vico in an early instance of constructive epistemology. The numinal is, in and of itself, a metaphysical entity (cause) and exerts power by resisting quantitative phenomenonization, thus not succumbing to its laws, but rather operates magically in an astral dimension with the activation of subtle forces reverberating through the paradigms of rituals, dreams, intuitions, imagery, and so forth.

Hermeticism is characterized by its predication of embracing an incarnational epistemology, one that investigates the tendency of truths to originate as ethereal causes and terminate in tetradic manifestations. As the titular messenger of the gods, Hermes represents the bridge linking the divine with the earthly (the metaphysical with the physical or unmanifest with the manifest). Similarly, Mercurius is attributed with the ability to readily transition between dimensions of consciousness brandishing a caduceus and vested with wings on his feet and on his casque symbolizing the swift motion or aerial flight by which Hermetic forces act. In the quaternary of creation, Daffi confirms this point: "The practice demonstrates how difficult it is to grasp the very mobile Hermes, to identify first and then fix—against cerebral ruminations—the lucid idea, the joyous intuition, flashed in a moment of distraction and demeanor alienated from the Saturnian part."

In epistemic terms, Hermeticism addresses the anomalous, outlier, supernormal, extraordinary, and rare occurrences more so than the central tendency, the repetitive or common event, and when invested with phantasmagory plays out at the antipodes of experiences. In "What Is Magic for Those Who Cultivate It?" Daffi elucidates the point: "Therefore, metapsychics is purely external in its methods, and judged from the magical point of view as an error: first in its claim that all supernormal phenomena, in order to be accepted as real and not illusory, must be repeated at the will of the experimenter, regardless of the particular circumstances of time, of psychic or physical states, and of the place where the subject operates; secondarily, by ignoring that the same phenomena originate from powers susceptible to development. Magic objectivizes personal psychological observation, framing the succession of inner experiences and the sequences of fluidic projections in a language that is better suited to using mythopoeic-inspired philosophical terms. Intuitive empiricism is subjective, attributed to the most gifted qualities that become science, with experimentation and with feedback: experimentation involving the occurrence of identical cause and effect among different practitioners who communicate their observations *a posteriori*, through the insightful observation of the smallest daily accents to which the usual attention is not particularly drawn, because the subtle connection, symbolized by Ariadne's thread, is missing" (p. 53).

It could be rightfully said that Marco Daffi, despite having bequeathed a precious literary inheritance of alchemical-Hermetic writings, was neither a "divulgator" nor a "vulgarizer" and least of all a "popularizer" of any sort. That his writings, although not easy or simple but of remarkable interest and useful for the spiritual seeker, are now better known and appreciated, we owe solely to the diligent commitment and financial investment of Giammaria. And it is equally undeniable that, in this context, he was not simply an acute witness to events, characters, and episodes in the deeply fragmented and fractious panorama that has always characterized Italian esotericism, but revealed a trace of an unquestionably significant message, of which precious aspects, not only at the historiographic level, are left to reflect upon.

In conclusion, Giammaria summarizes Daffi's contribution to Hermeticism in these terms: "we cannot doubt that beyond all other interests, Marco Daffi's heart and soul burned with passion and love for magical and alchemical Hermeticism, his true vocation . . . which he refers to as an 'intuition.'" Clearly, the passion and love burned both ways, as the Hermetic muses reciprocated with bestowing a veritable cornucopia of gifts under the guise of inspirations, intuitions, visions, enstasies, and other extraordinary experiences conveyed by the Magical Baron.

ENIGMA OF THE SPHINX, THE SIREN, AND THE MAGICAL HERO

Perhaps the most enigmatic mythological figures represented within Daffi's Hermetic bestiary are those of the sphinx and the siren. The sphinx, as Daffi mentions in the essay on the major arcana regarding the tenth card of the tarot, known as the Wheel of Fortune, Destiny, and Being, is the central figure displayed on the card and presides over two daimons constituting the opposing forces of evolution and devolution.

As such, the sphinx represents the nexus or resultant nodal point linking the opposing trajectories, ascendant and descendant, divine and animal, that tows on the fate of every man. Consequently, the mystery concealed within the guise of the sphinx centers around the mystes and the capacity to move their nodal point past liminal frontiers of what is human to either the devolved states of the humanimal or evolved toward the *heroic* which in ancient Roman terms is referred to as *vir*. In a historical/existential context, the differentiated man embodied Stoic-like virtues of integrity, dignity, and principled behavior. Moving the nodal point to a more evolved or emancipated manner yields a higher vibrational frequency that can manifest in manifold ways including those exemplary individuals whose auras radiate a brilliantly toned presence and/or exude celestial fragrances perceptible by those within (or outside of) their physical proximity. Likewise, those in harmonious communion with the differentiated man can sense the presence of the pristine numen radiating outward through incandescent channels and manifesting through symbolic representations, dreams, or associated imagery as in the memories recollected by Giammaria and Auri in their postmortem encounters with the "Voice of Marco Daffi."

Daffi qualifies the differentiated man using Cabalistic terms (Cosmic Adam) and by contrasting him in complementary yet inverse tendencies with the common man:

- risen and fallen
- synthesis and analysis
- integration and dissociation

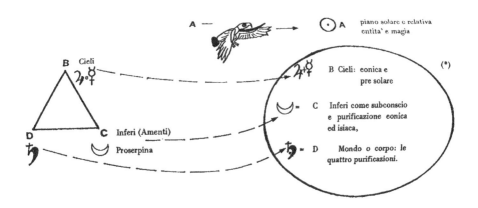

Argonaut of the tetradic monad: the Ibis in flight

The Sirenae

The commonly held notion of Sirens is as figments of the imagination and mythological creatures whose incantatory voices seduce unwary navigators to their peril, leaving a bounty of shipwrecked souls, as nearly happens to Ulysses in the *Odyssey*. In contrast, Daffi casts these enigmatic figures in a different light by reframing the image of Sirens as objects of fantasy, or as a reification or misplacement of truth like that described in the "Mirror of the Virgins," to a subject of being, that of an initiate or better yet an adept of initiation that has realized a transcendent state of Being.

In its essence, the term Sirenae encompasses a wide range of meanings and significance. However, within the scope of this tradition, and particularly in its most decisive interpretation, it denotes the archetypal psychonauts of classical times such as Orpheus, Ulysses, and Aeneas. In this context, the Sirenae symbolize the heroic figures who, through magical practices, transcend the ordinary by traversing a magical portal or initiatic wormhole. This journey allows them to explore a novel dimension of time, space, and causality, where the boundaries between past, present, and future dissolve into a myriad of specular representations.

The following section will delve into this figurative term from initiatic, ontological, and mythological perspectives and push the boundaries of meaning in relationship to the Baron's protean nature and corresponding *virtus* of anamnesis, thaumaturgy, and eonics.

In Greco-Roman mythology, the Sirenae are referred to as semidivine entities residing within the open seas. In the *Metamorphoses*, Ovid recounts the tale of the fisherman Glaucus who by a magical operation was purged of his mortal nature and transformed into a Siren. Dante in the *Paradiso* likens his own beatific transformation to Glaucus's metamorphosis into a Siren.

The common Homeric or Ovidian trope on the Siren as a mirage of specular reification—the fate of mistaking fantasy for reality—is repurposed here to represent the Hermetic perspective of the Siren as a spiritually integral initiate on an ascending evolutionary trajectory analogous with the figures of the Hermanubis rising and the Cynocephalus daemon of evolution recounted in "Symbolism on the Wheel of Becoming."

Two-tailed siren on the Tour Mélusine, Vouvant, France

The Siren is essentially a hybrid entity—partially human and partially chimeric creature—which in ontological terms manifests as a synthesis, the concrete affirmation of human and divine natures of the transcendent Self (transpersonal) through hyliac and astral mediums. Through a self-referencing allusion, Daffi calls this transcendent state, "pilot of the tetradic monad": the integration of the tetradic bodies of consciousness with the numen (monad) yielding a transcendent consciousness of Being.

Although similar in terminology, "pilot of the monadic tetrad" is not the same as "pilot of the tetradic monad." The fundamental distinction lies with the different natures separating the Siren (tetradic monad) from the avatar (monadic tetrad). The Siren assumes the individual consciousness rooted in its purely human *tetradic* dimension of a fragmented self (samsaric) on a journey to re-collect its numen (occult Self) and reconcile their constituent bodies (tetrad) into an integrated whole rooted in the numen. The second term, *avatara*, refers to individual consciousness centred within the transcendent or *monadic* dimension and whose quest or journey manifests within the tetradic bodies to assert itself for an underlying exalted purpose or mandate. This definition draws heavily upon the interpretation of the renowned passage from the Bhagavad Gita where Krishna boldly declares to a stupefied Arjuna, "in all times, whenever righteousness declines and darkness prevails, I will manifest to uphold the good and fight against evil."

The pilot refers to the particular state of consciousness realized by the dyadic Self, a synthesis of the conscious-unconscious monad (numen) affirmed through the tetradic Hermetic bodies. Likewise, the pilot refers to the initiatory operator navigating within astral seas and analogous with the Hermetic operation of V.I.T.R.I.O.L. (*visita interiora terrae rectificando invenies occultum lapiden*) in the *albedo opus* of alchemical Hermeticism. In this context, the Siren's hybrid nature—human and divine—can be characterized as the individual invested with internal powers that are asserted through human or extra-human channels. The divine aspect of the individual is understood as possessing the spiritual/transcendent dimension of consciousness (Solar + Mercurial + Lunar *principii*), the seven forms of illumination (*intelligentia*) with the ability through initiatic instruments to leverage spiritual disciplines and yield sacral representations, that manifest primarily through the aerial (*aeris*, वायु) and water elements (*aqua*, आप) and less frequently through the earth element (*terra*, पृथ्वी) on the somatic plane. The manifestation of sacral representations occurs by the invoking and downstreaming (↓) of spiritual forces (fluids) via human channels in the form of inspirations, visions, healing energies, and sacral representations, to name a few of the most common, as well as to elevate (↑) consciousness through transcendent channels in the form of astral voyages, anamnestic regressions, dreamscapes, and other meta-psychical experiences, while identity with the Self (numen) remains intact.

Similarily, in the *Thesaurus Medicinae Dei*, Daffi writes of transmitting metaphysical healing energies in these terms: the *Medicinae Dei* ritual is analogous to the transferring or lessening of the karma-fate on the ailing individual through administering the appropriate fluidic medium. With the efficacious evocation of the *Medicinae Dei* forces, the fluidic lavage—or purgation from the negative influence of the sickness—assists the ailing individual in a karmic way, where the healing fluids are transferred from the operator to the targeted party. The therapeutic action (of the numina) confers a means for the restoration and evolution of the ailing individual that purely terrestrial forces would lack; written in the conditional as (–), the collective karma-fate is defined as a state of heavy electromagnetic density that also prevents the evolved individual (initiate) or lesser ones from rising above the dense atmosphere in which they live and to which we often must submit.

Anamnesis (or Latin *reminiscentia*) refers to initiatory operations of excavating and elevating aspects of the innate or occult Self to the surface of consciousness through *psychurgic* techniques such as atavistic resurgences, avataric evocations, dreamscapes, and past-life regressions. As well, through the prism of lucid dreaming the operator is provided with a naked view of the occult Self, allowing for the direct experience of revealing and ultimately enucleating the occult Self into astral and somatic folds of consciousness. The conscious presence of the Self, of identification with the occult Self without deviation, in the Lunar and Saturnian planes occurs if the hyliac and the astral are not experienced as separate worlds, exclusive from each another, but as an unicum or fluidic continuum linking the triadic (Solar, Mercurial, Lunar) and the tetradic (Solar, Mercurial, Lunar, Saturnian) where $3 + 4 = 7$, resulting in possession of the seven vibrational forms of illumination.

From an ontological perspective, the Siren constitutes the integration of the tetradic bodies with its monadic root (numen) and the initiate's concrete synthesis of transcendent powers (divine) within their human constitution, exemplified by luminaries such as Mamo Rosar Amru,[*] Izar Bne Escur, Giuliano Kremmerz, and other lesser-known initiates of this august lineage. In auxiliary terms, it is not uncommon for the Siren

---

*Mamo Rosar Amru, the last pontiff of the Isiaic temple of Pompeii, refers to the principal egregore of the Myriam. Kremmerz, in his *La Scienza dei Magi* (Science of the Magi), vol. 2, writes a rather incomprehensible "Hermetic" story about Mamo and his role transfering the Isiac mysteries to the land of Parthenon (Naples, Campania) in the first centuries CE. See *The Hermetic Physician*, p. 8 for a summary of the story of Mamo and its esoteric implications.

to manifest with its astral double as the gender reversal or hermaphroditic vestiges (rebis) of the magical hero, that is, for the female heroine to manifest in the sacral representation as a Triton and as a Siren for the male hero. Daffi states in his *Diarum Hermeticum* that the search to locate and integrate his eternal female complement (astral double) and to restore karmic balance within his transcendent being was the life purpose underlying his terrestrial journey as an incomplete avatar.*

In coherence with the alchemical Hermetic tradition, the starting point of the opus assumes the individual in their natural human constitution and through initiation resolved with the conquest of integration with the transcendent consciousness of Being, leading to the great synthesis of human and divine nature into one, the Siren. Whereas the avatar assumes the descent or manifestation of a divine nature into a human form, in operational terms the fundamental difference between the two resides with the former being formed (*hominis faber*) and the later incarnated (*hominis creatus*).

Likewise, the Siren represents a figurative creature (initiate) whose actions take place—*uti piscem*—in the astral sea. As such, sirens emerge to the surface from the depths of the sea for purification (to breathe) and submerge back into the waters for copulation (eros), which parallels the binary alchemical process *solve et coagula* of man's transformation (cultivate, curate, incubate) into the higher ontological states of a *hero* or *vir*. Kremmerz states that the term *vir* is cognate with virgin or *vir agens*, the integral man of pure actions: "*Virgo* signifies *vir agens*, that is, man in action . . . in whose heart receives the Numen," that is, a man (or woman) who is placed in conditions of purity, taken in the magical and not in the moral sense, so that they become a *via electionis* as the Catholic Church refers to the Virgin Mary, and "In common with all of this, the teaching that not through pure contemplation or pure asceticism will truth become conquered but through the arcane transmutation yielding magical powers, that is solar ones, to the man who can elevate himself."

---

*Essay included in my forthcoming book *Hermetic Book of the Dead* (working title).

With this point, Daffi clearly draws a line of distinction between his teachings and the admonition made by his master Kremmerz who emphasized the value of chasteness = abstinence in sexual matters, as representing the proper preparatory conditions for the mystes or initiate to perform magical operations. Daffi seems to suggest that Kremmerz's teachings on chastity are regressive, repressive, moralistic, and ultimately self-limiting, hence not in keeping with Hermetic tradition. In stark contrast, Daffi suggests eros in the form of divine love (amor) is an initiatory *virtu* to cultivate as a preparatory means for the initiate to assert mastery over the elemental forces. Daffi replaces or rather supersedes the Kremmerzian teaching by constructing a finer and more evolved definition of chastity as representing a state of being or condition that integrates the dual negatives of purity and eros into one.

Furthermore, Daffi relates in highly enigmatic terms: "Alchemists represent her as the two-tailed alchemical siren . . . symbolizing two negatives!" which most certainly refers to the twin necessities, *respiration* and *copulation*, which in the profane sphere of the mystes represent unrequited desires (−) to fulfill horizontal yet divergent needs of vitality (respiration) and pleasure (copulation). However, when cultivated in an internal synthesis, the initiate transforms the two complimentary unrequited desires (−) into a positive virtu of self-realization (like when two negatives multiply into a positive [+]) by sublimating the fluids into the spiritual synthesis of amor (divine love) leading to the breakthrough of consciousness from the somatic to the eonic sphere that is the proper domain of the Siren. Eons are ethereal intelligences residing within the astral realm and accessed by initiates in altered states of consciousness. Daffi intimates these arcane operations in the article "Initiation," the first essay of *Epistolario Filosofico*: "Recourse to progressive means of purification up to a minimum of eonic perception of fluidic sensitivity. Entry into Isiac magic . . . after which the acquisition of a solar initiation, which at first is conditioned, as pre-solar, by the presence of one or more eons. In this series, there are found all the phases indicated by the alchemists, such as to whiten the *latona* that is to purify the body, the lunar, and so forth, cooking the lunar fluids, and so on" (see p. 137).

And seen purely from the perspective of a lunar body manifesting in an astral environment are figures to be understood as sacred representations appearing in dreams, visions, and apparitions—*sub specie interioritas.*

Here the initiate enters the land of visions. . . This is the sense of dreams of white light, those in which the Archetype of Healing or Asclepius shows himself to the dreamer—as Isis in Lucius' dream (in Apuleius' "Metamorphoses. The Golden Ass").

But the symbolic apparition of Asclepius if understood as a mirror postulation of archetypal consciousness, and considered as a masking of the Numen, as well as to the initiant unable to recognize himself in his own Self. Dramatizations can—according to one's own secret—be visional, both during waking life and in dreams. But you have to learn to see from Here—to die while alive, and to "live" after death, in the other realm.

Within the dream beyond the general modification there occurs the possibility of knowing the signs and figures. Both by night and day the activity of the initiate is in continuous *articulo mortis.* The day becomes night and the night day. The wheel of Fortune turns in the direction of an ebb and flow of consciousness as the heart muscle dilates and compresses. It can be said that all life—of the operator—is like this throbbing, since Mercury is extracted and re-merged with the body, it is re-extracted and replenished in an attempt and among re-tries to search always for deeper and interior meanings. Meanings that are increasingly clearer matrices of the things themselves.

This is the meaning behind the Figures! They appear according to the secrets hidden with the Operator—naturally!

And solitude ensures separation of control with contacting the Numen on the way to the ascension of that vibratory current that transmutes the situation by capturing its occult matrix. This requires a plasticity of detachment of the naked Diana *"sine robes"* by means of the Numen operating through Mercury. And the

Mirror or rather the Doubling is a symbol of this ability without which the awareness here is but pure utopia.*

Viewed from a purely initiatic lens—*sub specie interioritas*—and invested with Hermetic significance, the Sirenae refer to eons, astral entities of consciousness and precursors to the initiatic state of avatars. They are the eonic denizens of the astral plane on a path of accelerated evolution to a higher ontological state. In many ways the Sirenae could be characterized as navigators on a journey, as "Argonauts of the tetradic monad," "navigators of the Egyptian Amenti" (Duat), or the various spiritual helmsmen revealed by Dante in the *Divine Comedy* and parallel to the spiritual trajectories of heroes (h-eros), the likes of Aeneas or Dante, to shed the derivative larval atavism of their primitive humanimalism and to borrow some useful neologies from *il sommo poeta* (the supreme poet, attribute referring to Dante since the Renaissance) to "*trasumanar*" (transhumanize) and "*Nati a formar l'angelica farfalla*" (born to form the angelic butterfly).

The Sirenae represent a preliminary stage (body of light, glorious robe) in the chrysalis evolution of an initiate's transpersonal consciousness that is characterized by an inward journey to transcend finite selfness, whereas the Avatar is a later development of the Siren and assumes a passage or transference of consciousness from a higher plane to the terrestrial, that is, from a higher state of being to the human or to the horizontal transference from one individual to another.

The astral sea (plane) is favorable to this form of transformation due to the reduced fluidic density and greater mobility governing this environment. The ascetic initiate cultivates spiritual disciplines to facilitate transference and fix the center of his conscious being from the somatic to the astral plane. In such a transfer the historical-egocentric self fades with the emergence of the numinous astral self; hence the inherent value of shifting self-identity to a deeper dimensional root

---

*"Sul Rito di Hamzur," *Dagli Atti del Corpo dei Pari*, edited by Giammaria. Amenothes (private edition), 2006, p. 209.

and with it the revelation of the operator's astral name (nomen-numen).

To further underline this point, the contemporary esotericist Angelo Gentili elaborates: "We must keep in mind, for those who work in the intermediate astral field, that gray zone where there is a gradual awakening of previous existences or of past faculties of the psyche; the higher field is a symbol of the action consequential to the memory. Thus arises the Body of Glory, also called the Second Wood of Life and by alchemists the Philosopher's Stone. At this point the adept has conquered death as the Stone assumes the task of a receptacle for the Mercurial and Solar bodies, maintaining the continuity of consciousness and giving immortality."

Further to the excursus of findings informing the ontological and initiatic logos of the above explanation, we are able without equivocation to assert that:

Ricciardo Ricciardelli = Marco Daffi = Mörköhekdaph = Ei hm'sc Bêl = the Siren.

METEMPSYCHOSIS, REGENERATION, AND REINCARNATION

The initiatory vision closely integrates and merges the two theses, as:

primordial germs, given as a − (negative), that resolves into the integration of man as a construction of the + (positive).

In other terms:

Given the germs as Hermetically constructed into a "negative hemisphere" and a "positive hemisphere," resulting in the spherical perfection or "globe of Venus," ♀.

Philosophically, the alchemical scission of Being into two polarities:

(−) Saturnian body and Lunar body
(+) Mercurial body and Solar body

The positive hemisphere confers continuity and fixity—of consciousness—to Being.

Psychological and implicit proof is found in the oscillation of the human spirit between the

- undifferentiated—impersonal
- differentiated—personal.

Therefore, the alchemical Hermetic Work consists of arousing and taming the Beast (humanimal): the universal "metaphysical" drama on the alternation of consciousness is reflected in the animal series or – (negative) hemisphere and the light series or + (positive) hemisphere.

"The Work, if cultivated in a metaphysical sense, is one, and that is to say, it consists in the formation of the Second Wood of Life or Glorious Robe. This concept is confirmed by the hypothesis surrounding the immortality of the soul (and it is useful to note that esoterically this is not even exact because infinite are the planes of ascent, there are infinite levels of evolution toward the first principle) being a manifestation of the universal law of creation (and it is worth noting that Hermeticism is neither emanationist nor pantheistic, but creationist) is reproduced endlessly, at each stage of ascent or at each realization of transmutation that is intended to be performed by the operator or on others (symbolized by the powder of projection). The resulting fourth fluidic mental dimension magically 'kills' material forms and entire forces to resurrect them crowned and triumphant in the solar radiance."

Hence, Daffi affirms initiation as the onto-existential game changer by determining the souls of men as either those whose Being is integral or those whose soul is doomed to perish with their terrestrial death, absorbed into the great mass of spirit-matter and macerated by the greater macrocosmic monadic phagocytosis or the cannibalistic absorption (feeding) of the (dissolved soul) one into the All as related in the following passage: "with initiation, the contradictory positions on the speculation of becoming are resolved with the application of the synthesis."

The fully realized initiate or adept is defined in terms of consubstantivity with the One, that is, as a monadic constituent in the mosaic of the One-All—being one and the same, sovereign, and united with the One.

The initiate fully integrated with this principle of Being or numen is the vir, the magical hero whose identity in a Dantean sense "*trasumanar*" or transcends human nature by integration of his human nature with the transcendently divine consciousness and the capacity to lay dormant and to awaken, to recall this identity between incarnations. By employing this Dantean trope further, one could say that the Sirens circumvent the river of Lethe (oblivion, annihilation) by passing through the river of *Eunoe* (recollection, continuity). The Sirens (vessels of consciousness) are singular creatures, rarely seen but by *anamnesis of self-recollections*, are able to navigate through the murky astral seas to the shores of *identity preservation with the individualized essence* as aptly demonstrated by the oneiric hero Poliphilo in the enigmatic Renaissance novel *Hypnerotomachia Polifili*.

The soul becomes immortal when an evasion from the disintegration of the monadic unity of the Being entity on the Isiac plane is prevented with the formation of the "Second Wood of Life" (Glorious Body). In this sense, consciousness alone constitutes the identity of the entity-being. It is the phenomenon of consciousness and not that of historical-centered life that the setting and solution of the question must be reported. Hell is a state of consciousness in one's life! Of one's own personality! It is an unconsciousness-unawareness also of the subconscious.

The soul can inverse itself, if not initiated-integrated, to the same bestial and noted regress that is symbolized by death in hell and given eternal "punishment." Never will the soul be able to recover so much, albeit in such a minimal state of consciousness . . . indeed it will be absorbed and definitively confused, irretrievably, in another being (consciousness entity that ontologically will not be able to destroy it, but will absorb it, confuse the consciousness into one of the other being-entities with another history).

The possibilities vary:

Metempsychosis on the part of regressing souls toward lower states of being

Regeneration by the part of monad-souls in unconscious reconstruction of the analogous state

Reincarnation by the integrating or integrated soul

The similarity between the animal egg and the formation of the initiatic egg is evident. The two mobile principles are the Mercurial and the Lunar, analogous to those of the alchemists, which are transmuted under the occult fire and in incubation give rise to the new being; while externally the shell and coverings represent Saturnian (the yolk = Mercurial body, albumen = Lunar body) as the fixed elements that do not change with incubation.

Also here in the ternary operations, the shell and coatings adhering to it can be fused together and assume the complex as an active force as a vehicle of the heat of incubation (artificial or natural) by which the two negatives (Mercurial and Lunar) are transformed.

In a certain sense, the albumen can be understood by the black negative (unconscious) as it generates fixed effects in the body, bones, and so on, and the yolk for the white negative (consciousness) since it cultivates life to the moving parts, so to speak, of it (*Marco Daffi e la sua opera*, p. 75).

OVERVIEW OF THE CONTENTS

The essays included in part 1 of this volume cover a thirty-year span—from the mid-1940s to the late 1960s—on some of the more unique and unusual subject matter within the vast field of alchemical Hermeticism. Throughout, Daffi elucidates firsthand accounts of "initiatory experiences" by recalling images, seemingly archetypal in nature, and when

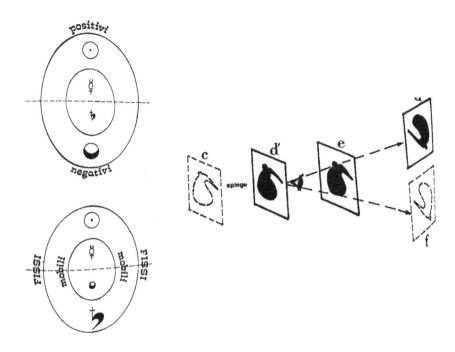

Left: Formation of the initiatic egg.
Right: The dyadic structure of Being represented as a polarity
consisting of a Negative hemisphere (black astral)
and a Positive hemisphere (white astral).

amalgamated one with the other and integrated into a whole, constitute a complete Hermetic vision brought to light by Daffi's unorthodox
exegesis and mythopoeic philosophical style. It is precisely experiences
drawn from "inner visions" that constitute the foundation of this volume and that can be defined as "operational," because they attest to
crossings of numinous thresholds in a clear and lucid manner, where
a singular aspect of the Hermetic *logos* emerges—not conditioned by
temporal or spatial events, but which in a Hermetic sense prefigures
them. Invariably the writings speak of Daffi's "inner laboratory," the
Hermetic forge that he fashioned and whose universal imageries are ripe
for meditation by the perspicuous meditator. In fact, the "figures" of
which the stanzas are *pictae*, rather than along the lines of images in the
Brunian sense, are to be seen as *scripta muralia* of phases, of events, of
the complex alchemical-Hermetic psychodrama.

The volume is organized into four parts. The first explores the principal doctrinal *themas* of Marco Daffi's Hermetic worldview, centered on original topics, rich in personal insights of considerable esoteric value, supported by a relevant experiential praxis and configured by the noble esotericist in essays of rare value. The few true followers of Hermeticism are offered a glimpse into a far-reaching spiritual horizon, supported by a broad erudition and a disentangled interiority by this pilot of the tetradic worlds. There is little in the canon of contemporary Hermetic literature to compare with this work.

The second part consists of correspondence with Daffi. Two volumes were produced by Giammaria documenting their epistolary ruminations on the Hermetic arts. These were released in limited quantities in 1978 by Edizioni Alkaest of Genova, a publishing house specializing in Hermeticism. These editions swiftly sold out, becoming a sought-after rarity among collectors.

The third part outlines the human aspects of the august figure known as Ricciardo Ricciardelli. It is not limited to mere biographical or historical perspectives but rather is a more expansive and fundamental investigation into the psycho-graphical strata underlying his initiatic and human guises seen through a collection of portraits and reminiscences written by various initiates, artists, and scholars who knew the magical Baron. The material found in this section offers an accessible gateway for those not familiar with this Adept: Marco Daffi, the interior and anterior personality of Baron Ricciardo Ricciardelli.

The fourth part departs from the biographical and concentrates on the magical legacy that Daffi left behind. This brings in voices from a wider circle, and traces the path of Daffi's ideas as explored by others.

1

The Philosophy of Hermetic Magic

Collected Works of Marco Daffi

Prologue to Part One

The first part of this book groups a collection of essays written for *Ulisse* (Ulysses), the 1948 journal of the Milan-based international review of culture dedicated to magic and science. The leading essay "Alchemical Hermeticism," which first appeared as the keynote article in a special issue (no. 7), introduces the central themes and motifs underlying Marco Daffi's vision of a gnostic form of Hermeticism. By appealing to a broader and generally more popular audience than previously addressed on the subject matter, it offers a relatively accessible conduit for the unfamiliar reader to become acquainted with the Baron's Hermetic worldview. The article begins by framing Hermeticism in its proper context not as a particular style of poetry—Hermetic poetry was popular in Europe at that time—but rather as a special branch of knowledge that tackles the fundamental questions confronting man's position within the cosmos and the means available through the art of transformation, including alchemy and specifically Alchemical Hermeticism, to participate within it. Hermeticism is presented here as the hermeneutic art of deriving the essence of things by internalizing or sublimating symbols, ideas, or images via the operator's consciousness to the universal ground of the spiritus, where they can effect change through the conjunction of the micro and macro worlds. Also, it is framed as a path of initiation leading toward a gnosis or inner ladder of transcendence so as to realize a veritable integration with the divine (metaphysical sources), accessible through portals of consciousness at the root or principle of being, the numen.

Daffi defines Hermeticism according to its alchemical variant as a symbolic science that penetrates the ideographic forms of the universe and parallels modern mathematical formulations that seek to decode the structure of the universe and reveal its occult laws, which, in his words, represent the highest expression of absolute truths that the human mind has imagined. Knowledge of applying these hermeneutic tools is crucial for the Hermeticist to fully integrate the disparate components of his tetradic being under the auspices of consciousness. Daffi affirms: "The tetradic principle, like all symbols, has innumerable meanings. Here are but two:

- quaternary structure of the body and the physical world to which is added purity, subtle intuition of justice, truth, and goodness emanating from a higher plane;
- integration of the four principles that make up the human body within the possibilities of the five senses with the complex of subtle powers of extra-normal intuition."

In addition he asserts, "If gnosis (alchemical Hermeticism) can be considered a science, synthesis, and mother of an exact or particular science, then it should generate a method that governs the intellectual penetration (Mercury-Hermes) that gifts the flash of genius to . . . those who are sensitive to the perception of the mysterious tendencies of the universe or the world; and, captured by the invisible self-supporting radar, granting the right direction to those currents of renewal and human transformation."

For the Hermeticist, the de-codification of life's mysteries by the subsequent grounding of symbolic representations—signs, images, ideas—in their epistemological essence (numen) is correlative to developing their mercurial capacities. The Hermeticist wrestles with philosophical investigations not merely as an intellectual exercise but as part of a Hermetic semiosis. Hermetic semiosis* is rooted in an epistemology that privileges thought-by-images, mnemonics, and silence. Thought begins with imagery and indeed even in its most reflective and refined

---

*Semiosis comes from the Latin *seminare*, meaning to sow.

states, thinking is done in and through images. Thus, the centrality of visualization in the Hermetic epistemology. The use of strange, primordial images rather than the refined classical ones is a sign of direction; that is, the decomposition of signs, ideas, or images is conducted in order to visualize its primitive originary essence and to experience the auscultation of the originary silence that engulfs it. The purpose of Hermetic semiosis is to internalize and sublimate meanings and significations that germinate into vectors of light to illuminate their conscious filament. The initiate is seen as a filament of light within a vast spectrum of light that relativizes in the human form as consciousness of the Self. Hence for the Hermeticist, knowledge of one's singular place in this world and within this cosmos of forces is central to pursuing philosophical investigations. It includes understanding the underlying structure of the world, the macro-micro interconnectivity resonating as *Harmonia Mundi*, the seven forms of intelligence or principles of light, and the application of the triadic law of creation within the manifestation of the quaternary.

In a somewhat more direct and lapidary manner, these teachings were made public by a circle of Hermetic aspirants known as the "Corpo dei Pari" (Corps of Peers) and led by Giammaria, who in the late 1960s posted manifestos on the walls around the city of Genoa and the Italian Riviera, declaring: "From the UNIVERSE to the Microcosm, Man, understood as Adam Kadmon, or Cosmic Man, comprises all the forces within the universe. On this basis, the binary of opposites: FIXED and MOBILE, POSITIVE and NEGATIVE are understood as the existential themes facing man, which include the elemental, intellectual, and archetypal qualities commonly represented by the three great 'Eonic numbers': the FOUR, the SEVEN and the TWELVE."

Incantation of the Corpo dei Pari

SEVEN from TWELVE,
ONE into FOUR,
vanquished, dispersed, and abandoned . . .
their Way is not of

the Consecrated!
for
they have
conquered their Investiture,
no longer Mystes,
are rendered Adepts.

With the sublimation and subsequent cultivation of Mercury there develops the fluid apperception of Hermetic insights by strengthening the analogies existing between Man, characterized as a Microcosm and the World, understood as the Macrocosm, and the ensuing relationship is like that which occurs with the internalization of a mandala. "How from the darkness of the Primordial Matrix of Potential Creation emerges Thoughts, Archetypes of the world, the Logos of the Platonic and Neoplatonic philosophy, passed on as a gift to Christianity with the Gospel of JOHN, which from the darkness of the mind in silence emerges suddenly, arcane, often paradoxical and irrational, the solution to a problem that has tormented us for a long time, the intuition of the right approach to guide research, the precise formula of a clause, of a legal act."

WHAT IS MAGIC FOR THOSE
WHO CULTIVATE IT?

Following this is an article extracted from the journal *Scienze del Mistero*, the revelatory content of which constitutes a rare gem and unexpected find among Daffi's publications, many of which are still unknown. The journal, although short-lived, published only thirteen issues between 1946 and 1947 and was noted, above all, for its editor, the renowned adventurer and scholar of Tibetan and Asiatic studies, Dr. Giuseppe Tucci. It begins with the most basic definition of true magic as *applied intelligence in its seven forms of illumination and manifestation*, based on the cultivation of latent powers through the application of occult laws that regulate reality in its tetradic dimensions. Daffi offers a lucid account of the Ars

Magia as evinced in the tradition of Marsilio Ficino, Giordano Bruno, and especially that of his mentor Giuliano Kremmerz and the magic of the Fraternity of Myriam.

DOCTRINE OF INITIATION AND NEO-BUDDHISM

Published just months after the end of the war in 1945, from one of the first issues of the Kremmerzian-inspired journal *Iniziazione*, the "Doctrine of Initiation and Neo-Buddhism" in chapter 5 skillfully contrasts the perennial Western tradition of magical Hermeticism with the vagaries of neo-Buddhism. Daffi takes a strong stand and makes a vigorous case for Westerners to follow a path of initiation based on Occidental inner traditions and to shun the seduction and appeals of alienating forms of Eastern spirituality.

COMMENTARY ON "THE MIRROR OF THE VIRGINS"

This essay is a masterful exegesis on the magnetic nature of Eros set in the background of the classic Persian novel *A Thousand and One Nights*. Daffi digresses on the esoteric teachings of integrity and human dignity underlying the ethical imperatives of this infamous story. Eros is explained as a magnetic power circuit of polarized forces, referred to as fluids (+ −) within the occult selves—that is, as a function of the heightened polar-magnetic forces aroused and cultivated by the astral complementarity embodied by the male and female principles within the respective personalities of the eroticized couple. Although engendered initially in an unconscious state between the beloved, over time and with art, Eros manifests in all four bodies— most notably through percolating currents of strong desires for union between the couple.

The lesson of Narcissus jumps to mind with the teaching on illusions underlying perceived imagery: "When we speak of the mirror, we must understand the incapacity, the impotence of those who look at it to see themselves without mediation. The reflected image is not free in itself, but repeats the gestures of those who mirror themselves. The reflected image expresses, therefore, the mirror, the dialectic of knowledge, the continuous recirculation of the vision in remembering that it, in and of itself, does not exist, instead, only the operator exists . . . such is the case that the protagonists here as with the humanimal in daily life . . . are those who look at the mirror, but do not even remotely envision that in reality there exists another or true self (numen), independent of the reflected image."

He continues, "The alchemical-Hermetic operator must not create distinctions, let alone fallacious divisions, such as to hasten the alienation between man and his world, being in fact, extraneous external events, estranged to those alienated and who witness life as a helpless sleeper—no longer such, but an expression of their interior self, a macrocosmic reflection of their microcosm. *A fortiori* they will continue the extraction of this 'secret' with pertinacity, discovering there and more subtly the symbolism of the world in themself."

When there is harmonic alliance the presence of the numen can be sensed through indirect channels like a recollection or an associated image or as with the case of Giammaria and Auri through the postmortem voice of Marco Daffi.

DISSERTAMINA—DISSERTATIONS ON HERMETICISM

The subject of the last chapter in this part is a series of short dissertations on Hermetic and related subjects. Giammaria states the material found in the Dissertamina (Dissertations) was developed within Marco Daffi's laboratory with the intent to establish, for future memory, themes related to the alchemical-Hermetic oratory, and which subsequently were elaborated further in a more systematic and detailed manner in the *Epistolari*. Giammaria states, "The following are essays developed by OURS,* after an initial '[just] between us' approach to the related issues, and which became a veritable 'Dissertamina.'"

---

*Giammaria refers to Daffi with the third-person impersonal pronoun *Ours*.

The *Dissertamina* are a series of essays written in an unpolished manner that address the meta-themes underlying the ontology of the universe (Reality) seen through the eye of initiation. The monadic ontology of the universe is the fundamental aspect underlying the laws of duality: the binomial aspects (unconscious-conscious unity of the Monad) are rooted within the synthesis of the Monad and that of the one Being. Being constitutes the (+) value of consciousness represented by the stream of light (consciousness). Whereas the Monad comprises the undifferentiated totality of the unconscious or (–) occult base subsuming the continuity of Being throughout the cycles of "(–) sleep in death" and "(+) consciousness in life."

Seen through this lens the ontology of Reality comes to light by means of a series of existences or physical groupings based on the same Monad-Being composition or fragmentation from the "mosaic of the One," into a negative unconscious Monad that integrates with fragments of consciousness that is explained as the (+) positive constituent underlying Being. Within this perspective, the Self, as commonly understood, is not the true essence, rather the "Monad" is seen as the primordial and universal substratum (–) feeding the continuity of life and death.

The quaternary (tetrad) is a conceptual framework useful for explaining the unity of Being manifesting across multiple states and understood as the unity behind the plurification of the Monad.

Kremmerzian teachings divide Being into four bodies. Kremmerz elucidates this concept in the following passage.

Man must be considered as a being that contains within himself the four elements that constitute the universe. The names that magic gives to these four constituent elements are traditional and borrowed from mythologies:

1. Saturnian body—a sensitive and concrete body—flesh, bone, connective tissue;
2. Lunar body—a more subtle emanation from the former and constituting its graver sensibility—nerves, nerve clusters, brain;

3. Mercurial body—a more complete individuality emanating from the previous two and constituting mentality or intelligence;

4. Solar body—a luminous, intellectual principle, a participant in universal life and therefore an inexhaustible source of both spiritual and corporal vitality. The divine individuality, which manifests itself in man only through the Mercurial body, which in its turn manifests through the Lunar and from this to the Saturnian.

The novice must understand that this division is purely made, so to speak, in a concrete way, but that it does not really exist in man, because these four bodies are interpenetrated in such a way that every cell, every atom of the physical body contains the other three rudimentarily or atomically.

From a Hermetic perspective the quaternary structure of Being represents the foundation of reality within the matrix of creation. In the essays "On Chastity," "The Sublimation of Mercury," and "Principle of Mercury," creation is examined from multiple viewpoints and facets of the Great Work. The manifestation of creation is correlated with the purificatory evolution of consciousness attained by the operator to effectively "dispense with" and "transcend," with the exercise of "free will," the fatal conjunctions linking the future with the past and the past with the future, to the auspicious influences of the zodiacal calendar on seasons, days, and hours.

When expressed in ontological terms the Monadic-Being principle underpins the constitution of bipolar laws:

Negative of Being = Monad (−)
Positive of Being = Quaternary (four bodies) (+)

Hence, the unconscious is considered negative "monad," and it establishes the continuity of Being in the sleeps of the dead and in the vigils of the living, through the series of existences or physical groupings on the basis of the same monad fragment of the "mosaic of the Ego."

In ontological terms the Monad comprises the negative (−) and Being the positive (+), which in synthesis constitutes the Hermetic matrix of creation and hence the spherical perfection represented by the "globe of Venus" (♀)!

As Daffi states in the opening essay, "On the Symbolism of the Wheel of Becoming," initiation sets a solid platform on which sits the figure of the sphinx and its attendant binary representations of negative or daimon of the Fall symbolized by a horned demon and its complimentary opposite, the positive or ascendent daimon represented by a cynocephalus carrying the caduceus, which in deeper analysis refers to the complementary yet inverse tendencies of initiation to reconcile positive and negative, descending and ascending, good and evil, which in its ultimate synthesis reveals the Cosmic Adam. Standing at the crossroads between the universal forces of dissolution and constitution is the *rara avis* known as Adam Kadmon, the Cosmic Man, which the Renaissance philosopher-magus Pico della Mirandola refers to as *de hominis dignitas* representing the supreme universal synthesis—the *umbilicus mundi*—uniting the negative or receiving forces of the Monad with the positive or creating forces of Being.

Sermones ad Vivos
Giammaria

After the passing of Giuliano Kremmerz, Marco Daffi became the foremost initiate, at a master's level, who, inspired by the vision disclosed by Kremmerz himself, carried forward the idea of Hermetic medicine and penetrated the most hidden aspects of the operative themes of Hermetic philosophy with his studies on alchemy, divination (manticism), and the I Ching.

In fact, his writings prior to the 1950s (see his *Introduction to Manticism*, *The Avatars*, *Life of Kremmerz*, *History of the Miriam*, and *Critical Notes to the Historical Papers*) are by the hand and head of Baron Ricciardelli, whereas the later ones (see *Solve and Coagula*, *Thesaurus Medicinae Dei*, *Tables and Commentary*) are from the hand of one whose head gradually escaped from the influence of Kremmerz's thought (see his letter dated March 23, 1963, p. 175 in the "Epistolario Confidenziale") by expressing himself through the voice of Marco Daffi. The essay on "Alchemical Hermeticism" of 1948 (from the journal *Ulisse*) offers a glimpse of his character, at that time, whose vision was changing, after we met and worked together, so much so that in the later years of his life, while the distinction between magic and alchemy was by now quite clear to him (as evidenced in the "Epistolario Filosofico"), even his ideas on reincarnation began to waver, through his opening up to a nontemporal or nonhistorical "extension," that is, "*in interior parte hominis*," and that was affected by my observations and down-to-earth reasoning about the idea of reincarnation not squaring with the increase of human beings over the centuries.

On the other hand, while the first authentic essays employing the term "alchemical Hermeticism," in printed format, can be traced back to Daffi, however, credit should be given to Kremmerz for its coinage and application, with the intent, however, failed, of founding the Fraternity of Miriam, to demonstrate the practical applicability of natural magic in terms of therapeutics, and distinct from the "paranormal," all under the banner of intentional action.

It is a fact that neither Daffi nor Kremmerz had a precise notion of the paranormal, which is still in this world and of this world. It seems he wishes not to discredit Kremmerz by the re-dimensioning of Ciro Formisano as a therapeut, haloed with magism, contextualized within Neapolitan-Egyptian initiatory esotericism, but in name only, and related like he is to other figures of the "Neapolitan school," who are all outside of the alchemical orbit. The facts are what they are.

Ricciardelli in the 1960s

Alchemical Hermeticism

Articles from *Ulisse*

Ulisse: Rivista di cultura internazionale (Ulysses: International
magazine of culture), year 2, vol. 2, issue 7,
Rome (October 1948): 15–22.

The term *Hermeticism* evokes in the mind of readers a school or method of poetry. However, before poetic Hermeticism, there was another Hermeticism: the alchemical one. Alchemical Hermeticism is, first of all, a science of symbols, that is, a teaching designed to penetrate the ideographic value of the various symbols, whether artistic, religious, or of sects and groups (for example Masonic symbolisms).

The mathematical symbols of the Pythagorean tradition are regarded highly by the Hermeticists to the extent that they consider themselves heirs of the Pythagorean method. And in the same token, it is looked upon with an eye interested more in modern mathematical concepts on the structure of the universe that in the future could be absorbed by neo-Pythagorean symbology, but which, now, gives confirmation to the mathematical symbol as the highest form of expression of the true and of the absolute that the human mind has devised.

HERMETICISM

Alchemical Hermeticism begins by positing to scholars the problem of Being, represented by the two principles of creation—*positive* and *negative*—antithetical terms that are reflected in the alternation of light and shadow, of dry and of humid, of warm and cold, movement and stasis, agent and recipient; this antithesis and alternation can be conveniently summed up in a single word: *vibration*, which—utilizing the same science of radiation and electromagnetic waves—confirms the origin of the Universe.

The term *Hermeticism* was adopted, indeed coined, by Dr. Ciro Formisano, born in 1861 at Portici and dying in 1930 at Beausoleil, France, who wrote of magic and occultism, especially in its practical application, beginning in 1892 at Naples under the pseudonym of Giuliano Kremmerz, and in the years between 1892 and 1912 where he exercised most of his activities as a proponent and a writer of Hermeticism. Voluntarily exiled to the French Riviera, he continued to write, and in his *Dialogues on Hermeticism*, which remained incomplete under the broader plan that was devised, with two of the dialogues published after his death, and especially in the preface to those dialogues, we can find his spiritual testament and perhaps the best synthesis of his thought.

Before him, the term *Hermeticism* was never mentioned in any lexicon, whether in Italian or in another language; in fact, the Hermeticisms of previous centuries (for example, Pernetty) speak always of Hermetic philosophy and not of Hermeticism. In his last work, Kremmerz points out that in the Italian dictionary, at the time he was writing, there were only the words *herma*, meaning a column with a two-faced bust, and the adjective *hermetic* or the derived adverb *hermetically*, which indicate an absolute and impermeable closure, wherein the translation of a thing or an attribute as sealed, secreted, and reserved to the maximum.

What is the precise origin of this word? We read in the Zingarelli edition of 1943 (page 461): "HERMETIC—of Hermes Trismegistus; Egyptian divinity to whom the invention of the science of alchemy was attributed. Perfectly enclosed (as in the fused vases of Hermes, where the glass is sealed shut with the same liquefied glass)." Let's put aside the luminosity of ampoules or, as we would modernly say, of filaments, and note how the words *hermeticism, hermetically, hermetic* associate the idea of the ancient deity Hermes (Hermes of the Greeks) with the idea of a reservoir, of a mental enclosure.

Hermes, god of inventive intelligence among the Egyptians, becomes in the pagan esoteric practice of *Romanitas*, the god of commerce and thieves, under the name of Mercury, which is also the name of quicksilver, of the *hydragentum*; the liquid metal, always mobile, iridescent, and divisible, which, by extreme ease, varies in volume with the variation of temperature.

SYMBOLISM: TRINITARIAN LAW

Therefore, in the symbolic and esoteric occultation of the ancient sanctuaries (united together in an *international* setting that has little to envy of the modern, whether overt or secret), the significance was quite different.

To begin with, esoterically, *commerce* was not the vulgar one of goods and products, or slaves, but rather trade with the invisible world of sensations and perceptions different from the common; that world was by no means a Hugo-esque president at the court of miracles, but the divine thief of knowledge, perfectly identical to Prometheus, who was tied to a cliff in the Caucasus and tortured by a vulture that devoured his liver, so punished for stealing the sacred fire of gnosis. Finally, the Hermetic reserve is not at all the mutism of the poor in spirit or the pseudo-diplomatic silence of the proud who dispense with avarice their precious speech with the economy of their vocal cords, but of the *silentium*, the one symbolized by monks in convents with two arms crossed, and therefore essentially referable to the quiet and inner isolation, even if the laryngeal silence can be considered a healthy and accessory integration of spiritual isolation.

The mobility of Hermes, of the spiritual mercury, makes us reflect practically on the analogies between man, defined as a microcosm of the alchemical-Hermetic tradition (the mandala of the Indians), and the world, understood as a macrocosm (Adam Kadmon of the Cabala).

How from the darkness of the primordial matrix or potential creation emerges thought, the archetype of the world, the Logos of Platonic and Neoplatonic philosophy, passed on as a gift to Christianity with the Gospel of John, so from the darkness of the mind in silence emerges suddenly, arcane, often paradoxical and irrational, the solution to a problem that has tormented our mind for a long time, the intuition of the right approach to guide research, the precise formula of a clause, of a legal act, the awareness of a mistake that inadvertently we were commenting on.

Hermeticism is an anti-materialist practice par excellence, that does not consider thought as arising from the activity of gray cells based on external stimuli or bodily needs, but considers it as a demonstration and at the same time a grand synthesis of the trinitarian law that governs the universe and that through the great merit of primitive Christianity was passed down with the Nicene Creed to civilized men. The law can be summarized as:

(*a*) *active*, that is, the conscious and unconscious mental motion of man or the inspiration that through his highest part comes from the divine plane, or in any case from a higher dimension;

(*b*) *first negative*, that is, the occult understood here as passive or as a matrix: the astral plane as generally understood; and

(*c*) *second negative*, that is, the psychophysical complex intended as a receiving apparatus that perfects the thinking act, bringing it to the logical, linguistic, and formal conscience of man.

According to the precepts of Hermeticism, thought is considered analogous to a mathematical triangulation: the invocation rises to the higher dimensions, the matrix, and descends from it to form three bodies with the rational part of being.

Artists and thinkers understand this law with the formulation of a mental request and the placing of oneself in a state of silence to receive the clear answer in their mind; it is of course an empirical procedure that believes that the answer comes exclusively from the subconscious, while it is a radar of being, which involves a larger unit than the simple individual.

This triangle can be high or low, it can be regular or irregular; this means that the sphere to which the motion of Being addresses itself may be more or less elevated, and consequently more or less clear; but the general principle is not impaired. Logical deduction and purity are the basis of every Hermetic practice, in its scientifically modernized pagan conception. The purity and premise of balance, of that equilibrium, that ancient magism, which is the legitimate ancestor of alchemical Hermeticism, is depicted with a five-pointed star, the same heraldry that protects Italy. The five points, like all symbols, have innumerable meanings. Here are but two:

(*a*) A quaternary structure of the body and the physical world to which is added purity, subtle intuition of justice, truth, and goodness emanating from a higher plane;

(*b*) An integration of the four principles that make up the human body integrated within the possibilities of the five senses with the complex of subtle powers of extra-normal intuition.

In Hermeticism, there are four components of the human body and of Being:

1. the physical body, the *earth* of alchemists, corresponding to Saturn of pagan symbolism;
2. the Lunar body, the water of the alchemists, Diana or Latona in pagan symbolism, representing the magnetic complex and the inferior fluid of the body, the one that condenses in ectoplasms;
3. the Mercurial body, the *air* of the alchemists, corresponding to Mercury of pagan symbology, the psyche or intelligence, superior fluid that participates in time itself and is embodied by the qualities of the Lunar body as well as the qualities of the last body; and
4. the Solar body, *fire*, the ahistorical being, the substantial germ of being, the true personality reproduced in the cycle of rebirths.

IN DEFENSE OF ALCHEMY

The ancient alchemists are still considered utopians, naive, who with the mirage of making money lost time and fortune, accumulating in their manuscripts very strange recipes in which, for example, the pounded snail was to combine with the "lunar fluids," or the "stellar essence" with a mysterious vegetable, the "moly herb" that no Linnaeus has ever been able to classify.

In their utopia—it should be added—as well as having no scientific basis, and based solely on the superstitions of the time, they, who intended to manufacture pure gold to be placed in safe vaults, were greatly hampered by the lack of knowledge that for us moderns is elementary; they—continuing on—were not even aware of a vague intuition of the numerous variety of bodies in creation (what later became the 92 elements of chemical science, and remained fixed on the vainest observations, which is common among savages and primitives in general, namely that the elements are four, that is, the aforementioned earth, air, water, and fire, the latter adored as a lightning god among those primitives who ignore the manner of producing fire at will. However—and in conclusion—their confused and utopian research gave rise to the interest in metalurgical research and knowledge of the bodies that later, with their dream vanished, produced the chemical science from the enormous mass of empirically derived material that was used by alchemists.

Now, to be able to rehabilitate the alchemists, to realize the true nature of alchemy and to understand that it did not consist solely of the anxious attempt to manufacture gold, it is necessary to have at least a summary idea of the nature of the integral science of gnosis, that is, of true traditional occultism.

Indeed, strictly speaking, it would be enough to carefully read the alchemical writings to see at first sight that the alchemists camouflaged with a rather coarse veil the true nature of their research: in fact, at every turn they were quick to protest that "our gold is not that of the vulgar"; that "our fire is of a spiritual nature," that "our stove or athanor is not found in commerce and is not made with common materials"; and display their contempt toward the "charcoal burners" whom they declare not to be true alchemists—very strange thing if they, that is, the true alchemists, had been precisely those that the historians of chemistry have imagined. Therefore, by the explicit declaration of the best and most authoritative texts of alchemy, the alchemists are not "coal or wood burners," they are not in search of vulgar gold, that is, of the metallic gold: they use furnaces and materials that are not found in the marketplace.

The same strangeness and contradictory nature of their recipes, the impossibility itself of understanding whatever might have existed in certain nonexistent materials in the world of nature, all suggest that, just as it was established with criticism by Valli on the Fedeli d'Amore and their impossible *women*, for their strange *loves*, for their strange *deaths* and amorous transports, "*the alchemical recipes and precepts have been nothing but conventional and analogical jargon to mask the initiatic and Gnostic nature of the true science of alchemy.*"

Now, therefore, the alchemists—to be properly understood—must be contextualized within the society and the initiatic groups of the time: which coincides with the thriving ferment of vitality and thought of that epoch, which, over about three centuries, from 1000 to 1300 CE, concludes the cycle of late *Romanitas* in its extreme ecumenical-canonical formulation of the Roman Church.

Alchemy is, therefore, to be considered an initiatic movement and proposes or proposed the teaching of the Great Art in the external forms of naturalistic research. Let us never forget, in the interpretation of this movement, that in the age in which alchemy arose an obscure anti-cultist reaction prevailed that forced all the other movements of the time to disguise themselves in a more or less skillful and fortunate way, or at other times decidedly unfortunate, as it was for the Albigensians and the Templars.

GNOSIS

Hence, it is worthwhile to reflect on such a camouflage, in order to answer the question of whether the alchemists were *empirical* and *scientific* in their research.

Gnosis and integral science, and the eternal and immortal wisdom that elected spirits reach or arrive at sooner or later in their transformations, as such, is a science not only for itself but for its methodology; this means that all human knowledge is potentially contained within it.

On the rigorous experimental value of gnostic research, today modernly understood by us as Hermetic, all practitioners end up agreeing, as alchemists and gnostics have always found themselves unanimously in agreement. The difficulty of laymen in understanding the scientific character of Gnosis lies in the fact that being the subject of the experiment, and at the same time the object (the vase or athanor of the alchemists) in the human person, requires a subtle penetration and a profound spirit of observation, symbolized by Ariadne's thread in the literary tradition of paganism, to reconnect all those facts or intuitions or perceptions that, if studied in isolation, and often deformed by popular beliefs, are believed to be pure superstition.

Finally, this experimental methodology explicitly requires freedom (which in the European West refers to *democratic freedom*) to carry out all research, both intimate and collective, without fear of pressures or monopolistic harassment of faiths or sects.

It is no coincidence that Kremmerz proposed, fifty-six years ago, renewed research to shed light on the Great Art, to scholars and those tormented by the need to know. He pointed out to them how the immense patrimony of popular superstition, divination, and the knowledge of gypsies and fortune tellers, of sectarian and religious symbology, of exorcism and mystical practices (or believed as such) of the various faiths are an enormous heap of raw, semi-realized, elaborate material, but all to be sorted out, to be cleansed, to be classified for rational use.

Thus, for example, the tables handed down by tradition, or intuited or *seen* by psychics or seers (real or considered as such), which indicate the good and beneficial days, the negative or ominous, or even harmful, and the indifferent ones, as well the general influences from various periods of the year on illnesses, on collective events, and so on. It is clear, these indications require experience and controls based on extensive statistical observation of materials and must be conducted with scientific rigour.

If Gnosis (alchemical Hermeticism) is to be considered a science, synthesis, and mother of an exact or particular science, then it should generate a method and also govern the intellectual penetration (Mercury-Hermes) that gifts the flash of genius to inventors, discoverers, scientists, founders of organizations and religions, political and social movements, and also to those leaders or those promoters who are *sensitive* to the perception of the mysterious tendencies of the universe or the world; which, captured as from the invisible radio waves, give the right direction to these currents of renewal and human transformation.

The prophet Muhammad, who was undoubtedly a mystic, is the most convincing example of this, as it is clear that the Koran was almost entirely written by him in a state of mediumistic inspiration.

Now, it is a fact that being an expression of the universal law (God), the Gnosis must necessarily follow this law itself, in the alternation of light and shadow. If we take as a shadow the periods in which the Gnosis is enclosed in a small number of scholars and in which the transmission, *discovered* in its laws and practices, takes place in *classical* form, that is to say, closed without any visible symbol or association that is its expression, then conversely, we must take it as a light in the periods in which the Gnosis permeates states and religions and castes and schools and groups. I dare hope that the reader will kindly consider reliable, or through a hypothesis of convenience, the point of view that the periods of renewal, whether social, religious, philosophical, juridical, political, scientific, literary, and so on, correspond in their positive part to the eruption of the Gnosis from the closed sanctuaries; we must also understand it only as an exact method of seeking and expressing the true and the good.

In manifesting itself to the public, the truth is cloaked; it must necessarily be wrapped in a veil or, if preferred, it must express itself in a relative and not absolute language. It follows that the manifestation of Gnosis is at the same time a veil and a practical realization, that is, it is relative. In reality, the myth of Midas occurs every time real initiates reveal their knowledge for mature or maturing souls.

Irradiation of thought springs from revelation, and the profane or immature man grasps—if he's capable of it—the practical application that derives from the new form of thought emanating from initiates, and perhaps joins them in the exterior application; or even unsuccessfully tries to imitate them, as the "coal burners" did, that is, the false alchemists ironized by the masters of the art; true alchemists, however, pursue a fundamentally organic method of research that, for example, occurs with radioactivity waves, to use a modern phrase, generating in themselves renewal and progress.

SUMMARY OF THE ALCHEMICAL THESIS

We will now try to provide a general outline of the alchemical thesis. There are four elements to be understood as the four eternal principles of the universe:

First, a primordial and primogenial principle: fire, first principle, Sun, intended metallurgically as gold; equivalent to the Neoplatonic One, the Egyptian Osiris, and to God the Father of Christianity.

Second, a derivative principle, similar to the previous one, but attenuated in the relativity of the realization; the intelligence principle taken as a *child* of the first principle: air, dove, Holy Spirit, Egyptian Horus, equivalent to the Platonic-Christian Logos, understood metallurgically as Mercury.

Third, a general natural principle, feminine and passive, changing, plastic, a point of transmission and realization, a fertilizing water subject to the tides and the seasons, also called Luna, receiving the force of the realization and therefore from the Matrix, Great Mother, Madonna, Isis, equivalent to the soul of the Neoplatonic nature and metallurgically understood as Copper.

Fourth, a principle resulting from the action of the other three and their condensations, represented by the physical world, earth, and understood metallurgically as lead and astrologically as Saturn.

Alchemical Hermeticism postulates the structure of man as a *microcosm* that is perfectly analogous to the *macrocosm*, and with this it postulates the structure (vulgarly but incorrectly understood as divided) into four bodies corresponding to the said principles, namely,

1. the Solar body or numen;
2. the Mercurial body or intelligence;
3. the Lunar body or magnetism;
4. the Saturnian or physical body.

Alchemy, therefore, can be reduced to the metallurgical symbolism of a will and an ardor to ascend (fire, Sun, Red Lion, solvent) which expresses itself as a radiative wave that acts on the complex of the human person determining a reaction, a boiling (boiling = alchemical cooking) in the being of the practitioner himself, either as a subject of the work (Heracles-Theseus-artist-Mars) or as an object (vessel-athanor-alchemical oven-crucible-still). This leads to the negativity that must manifest itself in the Hermeticist, symbolized by the black color of the alchemical crow that, in other terms, designates a crisis of conscience and detachment that the operator also suffers due to the practical applications attempted by the practitioner; a gradual clarification of the psyche follows, a state of quiescence symbolized by the color white; as the white turns red and the Red Lion appears, that is to say, as the penetrative and constructive power is consolidated. The various colors of the rainbow, which according to the alchemists of the Work are nothing other than the different forms of intelligence in the sevenfold universal division—as well as in the masterful Kremmerzian classification—must be experienced by the mystes.

The correspondences are shown with the seven days of the week:

- Sunday: Sol and movement; metal: gold; color: red.
- Monday: Luna and the matrix of forms; creation of the changing nature; metal: silver; color: blue or indigo.
- Tuesday: Mars and strength; metal: iron; color: orange, but here naturally with a different meaning than from the color orange of the alchemical work, of which we will discuss.
- Wednesday: Mercury and intelligence; metal: mercury; color: yellow.
- Thursday: Jupiter and goodness; both as a deity and as a planet, a symbol of the fairness of justice; metal: tin; color: light blue.
- Friday: Venus; the force of universal attraction as recounted by Lucretius in *De Rerum Natura*; love and realized form; metal: copper; color: green.
- Saturday: Saturn or Sabbath; the mysterious day for the gatherings of demons and witches; English Satur(n)day, the day of descent into the relative, purification, the discharge of waste; metal: lead; color: purple (see the vestments of the Catholic Church).

The Work, if in a metaphysical sense, is one, and that is to say, it consists in the formation of the Second Wood of Life or Glorious Robe,* whose concept is realized by the immortality of the soul (and it is useful to note that esoterically this is not even exact because infinite are the planes of ascent, and there are infinite works of evolution toward the first principle), being a manifestation of the universal law of creation.

It is worth noting that Hermeticism is neither emanationist nor pantheistic, but creationist and reproduced endlessly at each stage of *ascent* or at each realization of transmutation intended to be performed by the operator or on others (symbolized by the powder of projection).

ON THE WORK AND THOUGHT OF GIULIANO KREMMERZ

Historically, alchemical Hermeticism, as we have said, was brought to light by Kremmerz in his forty-year-long vocation as apostle and miracle worker, between 1892 and 1930, the year of his death. He chose the field of medicine as the one that least lends itself to the unleashing of human passions, while warning that alchemical magic or Hermeticism lends itself to all possible applications. He founded Hermetic academies in Naples, Milan, Rome, and Bari; the last two closed because they were falsely and artfully confused with Masonic lodges, between 1924 and 1926.

The generous attempt to practice Hermetic medicine for free by Kremmerz led to the application, by groups, of powers that he himself radiated; therapeutic results were also those that did not directly issue from him, but by necessity were from the narrow scope of contact with him and his teachings.

Kremmerz was a true alchemist, and never tired of repeating that he could cure a headache by concentrating forces in a group or chain of fraternal friends with beneficial intention, instead of proselytizing

---

*[Or Glorious Body; refers to the alchemical Body of Light.—*Trans.*]

like Simon Magus, or doing miracles with magnetization, or being a surgeon, past, present, or future.

This is to say that Kremmerz led us to understand that from the same exercise of powers and of the will directed toward a beneficial therapeutical end sprang the development of psychic powers in the practitioners. Therefore, alchemical Hermeticism differs from other organizations or associations that deal with things of the occult and does not limit itself to the external study of the phenomenon but rather prefers the slow, incremental development of actual faculties that all of us potentially have.

Unfortunately, his teachings (symbolized by a truth that was immediately eclipsed by relativism) were misrepresented almost at the very moment in which he offered them. The Hermetic academies soon became cenacles of discerning scholars, who in a pseudo-religious form reread and commented on the writings and councils of the master in a theological manner.

Today, there are some centers that have taken the name of Hermetic or Kremmerzian academies; but, while I do not question the honesty of the intentions of their leaders, I have the duty, having had the honor of direct dialogues with the late Ciro Formisano, to publicly declare that *none of these groups or associations is a legitimate repository of the Hermetic-alchemical tradition.* Instead, I know individuals who, not constituted in societies or circles, follow on their own the application of Kremmerzian methods.

They alone can consider themselves the perpetuators of Hermeticism, and if I may be allowed, I would express the hope that those who are mature in their studies and endowed with strength and purity of spirit will rise soon, reactivate the torch ignited by Kremmerz, and resume his journey not only in the field of medicine, but in the wider one of social activity and fraternity.

What Is Magic for Those
Who Cultivate It

This article, credited to Ricciardo Ricciardelli, first appeared in
Scienze del Mistero (The Sciences of Mystery and the
Mystery of Sciences) 1, no. 4, February 28, 1946,
a bimonthly journal edited by Giuseppe Tucci.

Magic has in common with metapsychics* the idea that man has in himself the possibility to tap into and harness certain forms of energy, and with religion the idea that these forces derive from a spiritual or superior plane or at least one different from the physical one of the common senses.

Like metapsychics, magic considers a phenomenon, however it presents itself, as usable, without predetermined exclusion of objectives; and like religion it is concerned with the *legitimacy* of the source from which latent or occult powers emanate. Magic therefore combats and condemns sorcery as religion combats and condemns it, recognizing it as an illegitimate use of powers. The fall of angels and then of man appeared as a religious doctrine first, the fall being from the immediate contact with the divine to an inferior, lower, or infernal state in which grace and knowledge are lost. Sorcery claims to operate on man without the basis of a necessary catharsis.† This claim, by specifying an entire plane of projection and irradiation, inevitably leads to evoking the "fallen angels" whether they themselves are taken to be impure entities or emanations from the darkest parts of being. Therefore, magic concurs with religion in considering "diabolical" practices not enlightened by absolute disinterest.

Magic diverges from metapsychics in considering the latent powers of man as cultivable according to traditional practices and rituals. Therefore, metapsychics is purely external in its methods, and is judged from the magical point of view as being an error: first in the claim that all supernormal phenomena, to be accepted as real and not illusory, must be repeated at the will of the experimenters, regardless of the

---

*[Metapsychics, not to be confused with metaphysics, refers to occult practices related to psychisms or transpsychisms such as mediumship, telepathy, or telekinesis. The term was coined in the early 1900s by Charles Richet, a French physiologist and Nobel laureate, and was popular in Europe from after World War II until the 1970s, when it was replaced with the terms paranormal and parapsychology. Baron Ricciardelli (Marco Daffi) was an honorary member of the Italian Associazione di Metapsichica (Association of Metapsychics) after the war up until his death in 1969.—*Trans.*]

†[In contrast to the advanced initiate who has purified his soul by a catharsis (ascetic practice) to separate pure material from the dross.—*Trans.*]

particular components of time, of psychic or physical states, and of the place where the subject is; second, in ignoring that the same phenomena originate from powers susceptible to development.

Magic objectivizes personal psychological observation, framing the succession of inner experiences and the sequences of fluidic projections in a language that is better suited to mytho-philosophical terms.

Intuitive empiricism is subjective, attributed to the most gifted, and becomes science with experimentation and with feedback: experimentation with the repetition of identical cause and effect in different practitioners who communicate their observations a posteriori; experimentation through the insightful observation of the smallest daily details on which the usual attention is not particularly drawn, because the subtle connection that is symbolized by Ariadne's thread is missing; and acknowledgment from traditional texts that through the observation of necessary controls the phenomena themselves will constantly and universally be reproduced.

Magic classifies its operations according to the double sphere of radiations and correlative apperceptions and sensations.

Natural magic (also called "Isiaic" from the goddess Isis, taken as a symbol of one who is passive, of a receptor who does not create by themselves) is based on a principle similar to that which acts in mediumistic sessions and in praying religious collectives: that of the strengthening of spiritual chains of the soul, which is electrostatically equivalent to the union of a complex of elements, batteries, or accumulators that arrive at results that the single battery or element cannot achieve. Therefore, a complex (chain) of operators engaging in natural magic, connected to each other, can accumulate enough energy to be used for the benefit of that participant who is deficient. In a magical chain, both the receiving sick subject and the transmitting subject—as a collector of the irradiations of all the participants, including his personal ones—are to be considered deficient.

It goes without saying that deep humility is indispensable for the head of the chain (leader) to be able to effectively transmit these energies.

Humility and moral virtue thus take on a scientific body in their magical application with the objective ascertainment of the insufficiency of one or the other for the purpose of healing. This is to neutralize the possibly prestigious side of magical achievements that would be easy to mention in an individual who is not very evolved and has little self-control, the pride of operational self-sufficiency, equally antithetical to both religious and magical assumptions.

From supplying energy to the individual who is deficient in energy, we move on to those applications in magical therapeutics that consist in transferring additional and homologous energy to a medicine: that is, in jargon, "valorizing" the medicines themselves.

This is the premise of the whole doctrine, about which we only mention that which relates to the analogies between the forms and origins of the herbs, plants, and minerals from which the medicinal substances are extracted and their possible therapeutic applications.

The so-called "solar" or higher magic (from the name of the god Osiris taken as a symbol of the active creative force) begins to manifest itself in the individual subject who manages to release certain radiations by himself, no longer required by telluric forces, but classified as coming from the superior (divine) plane or homologous to them. The saints and mystics endowed with powers, such as Giovanni Bosco, or the living Franciscan Padre Pio da Pietralcina, of the convent of San Giovanni Rotondo (Foggia), fall within the solar type of manifestations.

There isn't a clear-cut difference between the two magics, as radiations intertwine and intersect in the cosmos. Therefore, there are certain ceremonies involving the collective aspect of Hermetic chains that have the ability to empower solar states; and other rituals that empower the individual's nature, fostering solar-type developmental states, and activating the natural energies within a chain.

Of noteworthy consideration is that the transference from natural to solar magic occurs particularly in prayer. Prayers repeated for years, decades, even centuries end up integrating their primitive natural force and can assume an automatic virtuality in their own right; the magical explanation is that the invocation determines an astral or fluid imprint that, as it deepens, becomes operative in itself with the simple liturgical evocation.

In superstition, traditional classical magic distinguishes the foundation of truth handed down from arbitrary interpolations and from inventions mixed and confused with it to the point of deformation.

Of that foundation of truth, superstition is taken into account as a witness of magic, in the same way that the Jews are held in account as witnesses of truth for Christian revelation.

Henceforth, alchemical and magical language must be interpreted in the same way as the modern notions of psychology, introspection, and ultra-physics. In general, it should be noted that all the involved phrasebook based on plants, metals, colors, stoves, decantations, concoctions, is not for nothing, in its original intention, a metallurgical and climatological language, but symbolism of profound interior experiences due to changes—at times radical changes in psychophysical states—which in many magical experiences become evident, as in ascertained bilocations equal to those occurring in the great mystics, and, in our argument, precisely to the aforementioned two [Bosco and Pio].

The magical secret is comparable, almost literally, to the professional secret of a chemical laboratory whose keys to the cabinet storing poisons are not given to the firstcomer. Throughout history, the mystical secret has guarded its underlying rationale. In the past, the utilization of occult energies by those outside esoteric circles was condemned as diabolism and heresy. Even in contemporary times, official medicine recognizes *per se* that there are no diseases, *but only individuals who are sick*. This acknowledgement exposes the limitations of therapeutic generalizations, which, despite remarkable and moderate successes, still leave a large margin of ineffectiveness. Consequently, stringent penalties loom over "healers" who, considering precisely not the disease, but the patient, direct their beneficial influence towards the sickened individual and their corresponding vital energy.

The evolution of magic as a practice varies to the extent that man varies in the course of his development and evolution. There is a magic that makes man—and not man abstractly considered, but individual men in their various stages of development—the laboratory and the forge of hyperphysical energy, and conditioned by the human material that from time to time arranges it and practices it, and this explains how periods alternate between reduced, medium, or large activity, and periods of stasis. The point is the development or evolution of magical practices varies throughout the ages.

Its patrimony is the universal law of nature and of the universe, gradually rediscovered or reactivated or intensified by those who tread on its path.

The Doctrine of Initiation and Neo-Buddhism

This article first appeared in *Iniziazione: Rivista Mensile di Studi Esoterici* (Initiation: monthly review of esoteric studies) 1, no. 4, December 1945.

With the sympathetic and confraternal resumption of initiatic and spiritualistic studies in Italy, after the black-shirted oppression, we are witnessing the renewal of pseudo-Buddhist and Orientalizing propaganda coming from a Theosophical background.

In recent times, "Buddha centers" have acquired notoriety that, according to their programs, made known to the public, aim to disseminate Buddhist teachings for the salvation of Europe and the world.

In the second issue of *Initiation* (October 1945), a short yet provocative article was published in which our Western wisdom is affirmed by showing the damage of contamination from the degenerative forms of Eastern thought. The conviction, as put forward by the Theosophists and pseudo-neo-Buddhists, that original Buddhism proclaims is that truth propagated *pro salute populi* constitutes a philosophical and historical error.

Buddhism in present-day India has practically disappeared; its best elements have been absorbed into Hindu consciousness and subsequent schools. In its pure exoteric form, the Lesser Vehicle (*Hinayana*) survives in the monasteries of Ceylon. Its occultist Lamaist form has been developed in Tibet where it absorbed a whole series of ideas and practices that have nothing to do with original Buddhism.

Originally Buddhism was, in Sakyamuni's preaching, a reaction against the exaggerations of a faith that had crossed over from the primitive simplicity of the Vedas into a series of idolatries and animal cults, a superstitious background stemming from the Dravidian aboriginal race that was in contrast with the bearers of the torch of divine fire, of the initial consortial light of Zoroastrianism. Against such a degenerate faith and against the nebulosity of sacred texts he disseminated a method of concentration and contemplation that would, he believed, lead men to the solution of the problem of being.

Was Gautama Buddha an initiate?

If you pose such a question we can only answer by conjecture, as it is difficult to separate reality from legend.

With the matter of esotericism, both the deniers and the affirmers of an initiatory substance of the man or the movement can claim to be right.

Indeed, it is possible to argue that the Buddha hid his initial and occult thought under the veil of popular preaching and, on the other hand, it can be argued that he was a simple mystic, a Saint Francis of India whose thought indulged the average consciousness of his time and that it would gain a rapid propaganda triumph.

The Buddhists of the "Lesser Vehicle," disdainfully rejecting any hypothesis of esotericism, declare that the Buddhist doctrine is entirely and only in the popular preaching and methods of asceticism of the Sublime Eightfold Path; the Buddhists of the "Greater Vehicle" maintain that the popular revelation was one of the manifestations of the Buddha and that he lives again in the form of a hypostasis in the incarnations and in the lamaistic doctrines.

In our opinion, the conflict between the two schools can enlighten those who want to investigate the relationship between initiatory consciousness and Buddhist doctrine.

According to the monks of the Pali canon, nirvana is associated with nothingness, the annihilation of being in a mysterious primordial ocean, or at least a pure negation. For lamas, nirvana is a higher form of spirituality, a purifying state of being that is illuminated by the vision of the absolute.

This polemic, which is also clearly evident in recent vulgarizations (see the *Buddhist Catechism* published by the same publishing house as this magazine) seems to us more in keeping with the originally negative character of Buddhism. Buddha was a negator of Brahmanic superstitions and deistic beliefs, and, pushed by the inquisitive impulse, he went beyond the limits that could be ascribed to his negation and arrived at the concept of the goals of existence and elevation as a negation of the visible and the penetrable.

With the purifying function of the degenerate Brahmanism exhausted, I rediscovered Vedantism in more appropriate philosophical forms; having reached with the school of Saiva Siddhanta a near identity with Pythagorean speculation, the purely negative conception of evolution, was overcome. And while the monks of Ceylon re-masticated the negative forums of the original preaching in the silence of their cloisters, the philosophers of neo-Buddhism headed by Nagarjuna, despite the narrowness of their ontological impositions, applied themselves to rectifying negative becoming into a positive becoming. All Tibetan esotericism is grafted onto this.

Whatever judgment made on the original personality of Sakyamuni, the fact remains that the doctrine was born or was revealed incompletely, and only after several centuries, and with differences that still last today, were the gaps filled. In contrast, initiates—and in particular we of the Italian alchemical-Hermetic school—prefer to recognize the full orthodox validity of the doctrines and schools that explicitly affirm man's positive development in his solar evolution to a state of potentiality that does not cancel the personality but rather makes it act in accordance with natural laws, which are not violated but transformed in their application toward ascending or descending realizations.

The struggles and the wars of love, trading, and wealth are conceived by our initiatic schools as a reality not to be annulled by selfless pacifism, chastity and renunciation, poverty, or mystical mediums through which the initiatory secret of an arcane approach provides visual perspectives. The resulting fourth fluidic mental dimension magically "kills" material forms and entire forces in order to resurrect them crowned and triumphant in their solar radiance.

Both Eastern and Western initiatory schools agree with this statement.

The quasi-Pythagoreans in Kashmir, Zoroastrians, original Taoists, Vedantists, and the elaborate traditions of Tantric theory and practice seamlessly align with the philosophies of Sufis and the Knights of the (sweet) new style*—be they Persian, Italian, or Provençal. This unity

---

*[Sweet new style or *dolce stil novo* was a new genre of poetry written in the vernacular and concentrated within a circle of early Renaissance Tuscan poets known as the Fedeli d'Amore. This circle, including Dante, Guido Cavalcanti, Cino da Pistoia, and Petrarch, among others, practiced a form of initation related to sublimating the female element to achieve states of gnostic ecstasy. Politically, these poets were known for extolling Imperial and Chivalrous agendas and siding with Ghibelline forces, which placed them in opposition to the Guelf factions throughout Italy.—*Trans.*]

across traditions persists to Pythagoreans, neo-Platonists, Templars, alchemists, and modern Hermeticists alike.

In common with all of this, the teaching is that not through pure contemplation or pure asceticism will truth become conquered but through the arcane transmutation that gives magical powers, that is, solar ones, to the man who elevates himself. Therefore, initiatic associations are not conceived as parties or sects to which the adherents must justify their absence with forms or formulas. All formularies are exteriorized and profaned. As a true head of the spiritual chain, he or she must be able to find directly in the astral plane the alchemical credentials of the aspirant.

For this reason, we Hermeticists vigorously reject the propaganda claims of neo-Buddhism that, in the profane interpretation of Oriental conventional forms, repeat the motifs of the dewy mysticism that both the West and the East have for the most part digested.

Commentary on "The Mirror of the Virgins"

All initiatic occultations have multiple meanings; therefore it has been said that the same symbol may have 4 or 44 or 4,444 different significations. And this also applies to that splendid occultation inscribed in the collection of *A Thousand and One Nights* under the title "The Marvelous Story of the Mirror of the Virgins." We will touch only on some of the meanings behind the luxurious appearance of the content—as the covering is so light that it is not convenient to go beyond a certain sign. And we will try, in commenting, to follow the progress of the story to make it easier to understand.

It remains clear, from a little in-depth examination, that the story does not have a particular moral significance, given its fantastic content; one could think of it as praising virginity, understood as moral purity, and this may be one of the external and profane aspects of the interpretation as far as the figure of that womanizing, lustful, and good-for-nothing sultan goes, who almost receives a reward for his idleness and his erotic feats by conquering the virgin Latifah. However, he does not seem to constitute an example of moral edification, for what could be the moral substratum of such an interpretation, that is, the contrition of a womanizer who converts from an

*["The Marvelous Story of the Mirror of the Virgins" is an extract from the book *A Thousand and One Nights*. A liberal translation of the short story is from the French version of J. C. Mardrus, "Histoire merveilleuse du miroir des vierges," in *Le Livre des mille nuits et une nuit*, vol. 11 (Paris, 1902), 129–74.—*Trans.*]

external sensist to the expression of true love for the eighteen-carat virgin is not a wholesome picture at all.

In fact, we are not told, for example, that Sultan Zein has liquidated his harem, or at least his concubines, to devote himself exclusively to his latest bride. If the purpose of a virgin, on the other hand, which the Elder of the Islands was in search of, was for material reasons, it is not clear why there was "difficulty" for the mirror to find one, since, evidently, to inspect a girl there must have been even at the time of the *Thousand and One Nights*, medical experts, who were also barbers, and could have expeditiously investigated these types of cases.

The weak side of the material explanation is highlighted by the question: Why would the Elder request prior examination by the mirror? It would have been more worth their while to have proceeded by selection with the usual methods and then, if the goods had not corresponded to the required quality, to rescind the contract like any other trader for damaged goods. And besides, it is not credible that of all the fifteen-year-old girls of three populous districts there was not at least one virgin!

Esoterically, it is certain that the story wants first to point out the difficulty of selection, presented precisely by finding a single virgin in the whole of the East; this, of course, is to be taken in a relative and symbolic sense regarding the difficulty of finding a person who fulfills the requirement. But what then will the requirement be, if we do not limit ourselves to the literal-material meaning of the story?

We refer to the interpretation of the virgin given by Kremmerz in *The Hermetic Door*, where he writes that *virgo* signifies *vir agens*, that is, man in action. This means that a *virgin*, in the initiatory sense, is a man or woman, who can also be married, whose heart receives the numen, that is, a man or woman who is placed in certain conditions of purity, taken in the magical sense and not in the moral sense, so that they become a *vas electionis* that the Catholic liturgy gives as an attribute of the Virgin Mary.

Having posed the question in these terms, we begin to understand the difficulty of selection and we see that the required age of fifteen years is nothing more than a symbolic value given by the multiplication of 3 × 5—three by five, three being the symbolic number inscribed on the papal tiara, the Triregnum.

In the Emerald Tablet, Hermes Trismegistus claims to possess three parts of the wisdom of the world. We can understand these three parts as knowledge:

1. of the lower or elementary worlds of all underwordly fluidic entities and concretions;
2. of the human world and its equivalent eonic occult world under the domain of fluidic currents and concretions of individuals and collectivities; and
3. of the superior or divine world, both as a reading of the absolute values of the numbers and divine words and names, and as knowledge and evocative power of solar intelligences and entities of the same degree.

Hence, the three worlds: the underworld, the human and eonic world, the divine world.

A woman endowed with the assertive qualities to navigate these three realms will attain perfection. And this arduous attitude of hers must be multiplied by five, as the quinary symbolizes not only the fifth essence but also sapiential fixity (symbolized, in fact, by the *five-pointed star* emblem of magic, as can also be seen from the biblical legend of the Magi guided by a five-pointed star).

Therefore, the perfect woman is an adolescent of fifteen years: a *fifteen-year-old*, because she embodies all the powers inherent in the planes of knowledge; an *adolescent*, because the sacred science of the occult transformation of Being renders eternal youth. Adolescence, therefore, also applies to a state of mind comparable to that age of man and woman in which at the maximum the receptive capacity, common to invisible sensations, is enhanced.

With this premise, let us follow the story.

◎◎◎

Zein, the lustful protagonist, represents the common man prey to material sensations. He must rediscover in his writings or in the work that he usually neglects to delve into, as Zein neglected to read, before his state of emergency, the annals of his reign.

Zein must excavate the ground with manual work to find an underground treasure, and this supports the Hermetic motto that sound, when translated into language, *descends into the depths of the earth and with patient refinement one will come to discover the occult philosopher's stone and spagyric medicine.** The effort of breaking the dead bolt and opening the doors indicates the difficulty of penetrating into wisdom; in fact, Kremmerz states that *the door of wisdom is indeed small.*

The underground rooms symbolize the various phases of the alchemical work; the different colors represent the various colors of alchemical work, dominated by white, which is the primary—zodiac—phase of transmutation.

The gold in the first room is alternately in powder and coins. Powdered gold indicates the raw material, that is, the man who, in purging himself, is worthy of giving rise to alchemical gold within himself. The minted gold symbolizes the solar operation brought to completion.

The second room refers to the iterative process of reaching the alchemical heaven with the reappearance of the color green and other colors. It also indicates the completion of the work with the symbolism of the material of which the six adolescents are made: the diamond, which is superior to gold as a value (the diamond being a stone, and thus symbolic of the completion of the philosopher's stone or manufacture of the elixir, that is, of the possibility of importing magical transmutation outside the operator).

Zein's late father is unable to complete the collection of the seven adolescents and commits his son to completing it. He is the initiate who

---

*[The perspicacious reader will note that RR analogously references the alchemical motto V.I.T.R.I.O.L. (*Visita Interiora Terrae Rectificando Invenies Occultum Lapidem*) meaning "Visit the interior of the earth, and by purifying, you will find the hidden stone also known as the universal medicine."—*Trans.*]

has not reached the completion of the work and who is *subject to death*, having first to purify himself with the negative receptivity of alchemical black in order to achieve perfection.

The seven adolescents, one of which is missing, are the seven forms of intelligence, the perfecting nature of the seven astrological planets in the experience of the seven forms of being or existence, in the balancing and strengthening of all seven branches of the potentialities of being.

The missing seventh adolescent also symbolizes an arcane means of transmutation, the power of love that can do all in this world.

Zein embarks on the quest only after thoroughly exploring the depths of his inner self. Following a profound self-examination, which involves metaphorically digging into the underground and uncovering hidden treasures in the basement, Zein discovers a warning from his father. The message conveys that he cannot reach the seventh adolescent without the assistance of the servant Mubarak.

Why would he allow a servant, and only him, to provide the necessary assistance to reach the seventh adolescent?

To understand this, one must penetrate the alchemical symbol, where it is said that to reach wisdom one must capture the fugitive servant (because he left Basra or fled to Cairo, but it seems that his escape did not take place, in contrast with the deceased sultan).

The fact is a little strange: Why would the sultan tolerate that one of his slaves has escaped to Cairo, and has also enriched himself and become a rich merchant? The incongruity is all symbolic. The sultan-father dies after Mubarak goes away, and commits his son to find him; it seems that he knew the way to find the Hermetic operator who for whatever reason has lost Ariadne's thread, and has lost the guidance of Mercury (in fact Mubarak indicates Mercury, both with the symbolism of the flight and with the symbolism of the merchant he has become—merchants are under the protection of Mercury). And his exclamation on seeing Zein: "Praise be to Allah, for allowing the meeting between the Master and the Slave!" is symptomatic.

Zein, the solar virtue of the adept, must reunite with Mubarak-Mercury to proceed united and ultimately attain the quintessential wisdom.

Mubarak, therefore, is a fugitive servant tracked down and alchemically fixed; but in this fixing he keeps his personality distinct from Sultan Zein; this is symbolized by the liberation that Zein gives him from the bonds of slavery (the liberation of Mubarak is comparable to the Nicene Trinitarian statement that Jesus, the Son, despite being consubstantial and coeval with his Father, is distinct from him and remains so).

Therefore, Mubarak tells Zein that only the Elder of the Three Islands can give him the diamond teenager, that is, wisdom.

But, what does the Elder of the Three Islands symbolize?

The meaning is twofold: the Elder is an initiatic symbol of the wisdom teaching of initiatory colleges and also of the initiating master. In fact, he is on three islands: there are three, because there are three parts to the world of wisdom, as we have observed with the age of adolescents that the Elder requests from Zein. This wisdom is to be found on the islands, that is, to reach them you have to cross a lake by water.

This lake is very similar to the infernal lake of the Stygian swamp that Dante must cross with Virgil to reach the city of Dite, which is very similar to the Palazzo del Vecchio, and is also guarded by angels and not by infernal creatures.

But let's take a closer look at the details of the contact between these travelers and the Elder of the Three Islands.

The two find themselves at the foot of a rocky wall, and Mubarak, by reading a magical parchment, succeeds with opening a passage through the mountain.

Three things are symbolized here: the function of ritual in magic, the narrowness of the initiatory path, and the separation of the cliff.

In fact, without the aid of a rule of thumb, the sensory opacity represented by the rocky wall cannot be explained. The Hermetic door, says Kremmerz, is very narrow, and the object of the Great Work involves the emergence of an occult self that assumes a personality of itself that is able to dominate the vessel, or physical body, which he did to the extent that an Italian alchemist gave himself the nickname of Rupescissa,* wanting in the name to affirm the actual fulfillment in itself of the Great Work of alchemical separation.

The lake, there is no doubt, symbolizes the Mercurial lake, that is the solution of the dense principle of the Hermetic tradition, a lake that must be crossed on a boat driven by the initiate.

The boat is made of red wood; its solar color indicates that it is necessary, for the formation of the Second Wood of Life, that the color red, or alchemical gold, emerges.

The master tree is made of amber; amber is a concretion of congealed liquid, and is yellow in color. In fact, in the *Opera Alchimica* the master tree is a martial symbol of the transmuting force of ammonia, and also the silk threads of the robe indicate a spun material from the arcane silkworm of the Great Work.

The boat suddenly emerges, and, appropriately, the mystic, after long efforts and disappointments, sees the creation of Janus's bark (which was then "changed" to Peter's barque).

The elephant boatman symbolizes the wisdom that must guide the operator, as the god Ganesha in India, similar to the Egyptian Thoth, is represented by the figure of an elephant.

Zein must not move, nor speak: the operator must not profane his own operations with excessive talk and must not worry about whatever the phenomenon, that is, the reaction, that is about to take place in him, otherwise the Work will be interrupted and the boat wrecked— a symbol of the real danger of death that can happen to the unwary operator.

Once on the shore, the two walk along a path paved with multicolored gems, which means that in the Great Work all the colors of the rainbow are revealed successively, that is, all the forms of intelligence must be lived and traversed by the mystic in the initiatory experience.

---

*[Giovanni di Rupescissa, born in Marcolès, circa 1310, died in Avignon, 1365. In Occitan his name is Joan de Rocatalhada, Jean de Roquetaillade; in Italian, *rupescissa* literally means "to break into two."—*Trans.*]

The four threads of yellow silk, with which the postulants gird themselves before evoking the Elder, represent the four Hermetic bodies.

Zein must not move from the center of the prayer mat: the initiate must stay within the limits with respect to the master in order not to be involuntarily dissolved.

As soon as Mubarak begins to recite the invocatory formula, there is a darkening of the skies with thunder: the alchemical black is constantly manifested in all phases of the Work, and Mubarak persuades Zein that he fears bad omens from that storm. In fact, the alchemical texts do not recall anything other than the black color (in modern terms we would suggest there is a spiritual crisis, with the reaction of the environment and an anguish full of imminent deaths, which are not only good but necessary signs, as precipitated by the color orange, which follows in the operations without the completion of the black color occurring, and indicates imperfection of the Work and results in having to start all over again, that is, one must be wary of false clairvoyant or mental impressions that arise without control in the alchemical black phase).

The Elder, therefore, introduces himself to Zein and asks him for his fifteen-year-old virgin adolescent in exchange for the diamond adolescent.

We have already learned of the symbolic meaning of the fifteen-year-old virgin and of the Elder of the Three Islands, which represents both the master and the continuity of the initiatic teachings that is handed down from generation to generation.

We have already observed how Zein-father and Zein-son are the same person, that is, the initiate suffers a *death* after the first part of the traveled path. This death is essentially a crisis of detachment from the teacher. The culminating crisis of the *nero alchimico* and the detachment from the teacher is a detachment that is naturally apparent, but which the disciple believes to be definitive. In this crisis of despair, he forgets the symbology of the comet, that is, of the cyclicity of wisdom that cannot be traveled in a single stage, and believes in a definitive detachment from the master, and this is a reference to initiatory death in one of the most important of its meanings.

This crisis of detachment can often coincide with the possibility of death and therefore the form in which the Elder (the master) heals Zein as his ancient protégé and the son of his protégé symbolizes the real joy of the master when he finds his ancient disciple, by necessity, also in the shoes of a new incarnation, and he gives him the exegesis of the path traveled to rediscover the sapiential path.

But what is the occult meaning of the virginity required by the Elder as an essential requisite of the adolescent? And why does the Elder forbid the direct inspection, but he hands Zein the magic mirror, that infallible proof of the genital consistency of the girl under examination?

The virginity required by the Elder is the astral one, that is, that complex of elite qualities that make a woman evolvable, and that makes her capable of being transformed from a common woman to one that is integrated. Zein must not look at the adolescent directly, but through the magical mirror, that is to say, that magical virginity is something very different from morality or excellent physical qualities. These virtues must also be harmonized with the occult qualities—which is why the Elder says that the adolescent must be beautiful—but that does not contribute solely to the susceptibility to occult evolution. Basically, true beauty and occult susceptibility coincide: a competent initiate knows how to distinguish purely carnal beauty from spiritual ambition.

But the general public is more attracted by the crass *sex appeal* of purely material beauty, and therefore it is necessary to emphasize the distinction that sums up beauty, an attribute seen generically from the physical side, with occult harmony. The magic mirror, therefore, symbolizes the spectral examination of a woman's astrality to verify her state of purity and susceptibility.

We will not fail to note a subtle psychological teaching in the fair adolescent compared to Latifah's demeanor. True modesty is not ashamed of itself: Latifah serenely fixes her pure gaze on men that she is seeing for the first time.

And here there could be an even further occult symbology: the common woman widens her gaze beyond herself and is prey to the passions of the flesh; the pupil fixes his gaze forward and upward reflecting the images of the occult world.

The dervish Abu Bakr, in whose company we find Latifah, serves as a symbol of the untamed aspects of the common people, akin to a dog that needs appeasement or taming. Yet, this also signifies that valuable pearls can be found within a seemingly raw oyster. In a similar vein, Latifah is discovered amidst the repulsive exterior of the dervish, suggesting hidden qualities or treasures within.

In displaying and handing over the adolescent Latifah to the Elder, we witness a double beneficent deception: Zein simulates a wedding with Latifah, and the Elder pretends to take Zein's bride away.

What is the hidden explanation of this arcana?

From a moral standpoint, there is no doubt that Zein would have appeared correct if he had soon declared to Latifah the true nature of their relationship, and there is no doubt that the Elder appears more cruel than necessary in taking the adolescent, if in fact he planned to return her not intact.

But in occult psychology is it possible to reveal the mystery of the subject before one has understood it? Evidently not, and therefore he must resort to some pitiful deception.

The sphinx, in esoteric interpretation, has the persuasive face of a woman to attract and conquer, the robust body of a lion, and sharp claws to grasp, hold, and tear apart if necessary.

The apparent nuptials of Zein and Latifah symbolize the human embodiment of the magus, and in the sort of masking of the deeper relationship of arcane love under the guise of profane love. It is not possible to unveil the mystery, in order not to determine a reaction that would remove the subject before the fluidic taking possession has taken place; on the other hand, it is impossible not to reveal a love, under penalty of it being misunderstood.

The separation of two apparent spouses, but who already love each other, symbolizes the detachment from every human form of greed for attachment. By dying to human love, they unexpectedly succumb to arcane love. And the delivery of Latifah to the Elder can also be understood historically by the delivery of a vestal to the initiatory college, the vestal virgin in which the pontiff Maximus said: "*Ego te amata capio*," that is, "I take you, O beloved!"

The subtlest symbology of this wonderful story is disclosed in the ending.

Zein, flattered to find a diamond teenager, finds Latifah in the flesh and blood on the pedestal!

Zein, having separated from Latifah, believes he understands that love with her is now forbidden to him, and so he turns his wishes to the credulous diamond adolescent. That is, he believes that everything leads to a transposition onto the astral plane for the virtue of the beloved, and whereby he unexpectedly finds himself in contact with the magical lady. And here lies that special veil of Isis that no mortal has ever been able to lift.

And with that the story ends.

The story must be read and reread until it is possible to penetrate its profound and true meaning. And don't believe pure fantasy: there are real facts revealed, concrete operations, verifiable research that only those who are familiar with the Great Art can fully understand.

We close the commentary with the wish of the reader to arrive at a degree of knowledge that fully reflects the subtle and profound beauty of the Oriental tale.

Dissertamina

Dissertations on Hermeticism

The collection of dissertations on Hermeticism and other diverse and unusual topics by Marco Daffi, Genoa: Edizioni ALKAEST, 1978.

INTRODUCTION

Giammaria

When Marco Daffi took me aside in his laboratory, we agreed that, for future memory, I would be taking notes on themes from his oratory, and would reserve the possibility of developing them, at my future convenience, in one or another place. From these notes came the *Dissertamina*.

But like the activity in the laboratory, a short time later, it determined itself, in a well-defined manner, so that the themes were further developed in the *Epistolari*.

Despite the obvious lightness of the text, the evident literary disengagement, the natural limitations of concept and form, sketches such as the *Dissertamina* exude ideas that won't disappoint the attentive reader, while extracting fissile secretions* from the meditations of the mystes.

The monograph, moreover, in the appendix, on "The Sublimation of Mercury,"[see page 104] is after the period of the *Dissertamina*, although the subject matter reveals a similar committed operation, and suggests fertile juices, in form and substance, of the emblematic and masterful temperament that is Marco Daffi.

G.M.G.

ON THE SYMBOLISM OF THE WHEEL OF BECOMING

The "Wheel of Fortune," also called the tenth trump (X) of the Tarot, from the Book of Thoth,† depicts:

---

*[Fissile secretions signify the alchemical process wherein internal energies, such as fluids and secretions, undergo transformation into subtler forces via a process of separation and rarefaction. In physics, it denotes the splitting of an atom's nucleus into lighter nuclei, accompanied by the liberation of energy. In biology, it refers to the division of an organism into new organisms as part of the reproductive process.—*Trans.*]

†[Reference is made here to the Corpus Hermeticum, with a particular focus on Etteilla's *Livre de Thot Tarot* (ca. 1789).—*Trans*].

- a solid platform on which the sphinx is seated;
- further down, a wide wheel, hinged on a mobile axis, flanked by two supports to maintain its desired elevation;
- to the right, in opposition, the genii-monsters representing good and evil—the adversaries,
- a horned demon descending, with its head down, wielding a sort of pitchfork with its left hand; it twists its shaky, scaly legs behind the wheel; and
- on the ascendant there is a cynocephalus, whose head has nearly reached the platform and whose right hand clutches a caduceus.

At the top, there is the Egyptian sphinx, emblem of the absolute manifestation of the Word, the inextinguishable power of creation, summarizing in its synthetic representation the six sacred animals of the Cabala, figurative of the four letters of the incommunicable Divine Name.*

---

*[In the Cabalistic tradition, the six sacred animals are the Lion, Ox, Eagle, Human, Owl, and Serpent. These animals are associated with various aspects of divine attributes and spiritual symbolism. The four letters of the incommunicable Divine Name, often referred to as the Tetragrammaton, are represented by the Hebrew letters Yod, He, Vav, and He (YHWH). Each letter carries profound significance and symbolizes different aspects of the divine nature and attributes within cabalistic teachings.—*Trans.*]

The image of Typhon, which descends on the left, symbolizes the inward journey of the Word, its archetypes and submultiples, which absorb into matter, sunken by their weight and thereby propelling the wheel to move.

On the right is the figure of Hermanubis rising, a symbol of ascension, of the evolution to the progressive forms of the same matter moved by the spirit and therefore the return of the submultiples to the inexorable mother-unity, from which they have emanated.

Hence, on one side, the demon of involution, which with the sneer of the fall has not completely lost its human appearance, homologous to the divine impropriety, and not completely out of place with the horns of rebellion, egotism, or pride.

On the other side, there is the demon of evolution, who ascends with the caduceus of science and balance and is about to climb the platform of the sphinx. Preserved on his face is the infamous stigmata of animality as a symbol of the lower realm from where he emerges.

The two monstrous profiles, in the final analysis, indicate one and the same figure, Cosmic Adam in its complementary dualities or inverse tendencies:

fallen and risen
analysis and synthesis
dissociation and integration

ON THE REALITY OF THE INDIVIDUAL SOUL

Through synthesis, initiation reconciles the conflicting stances regarding the concept of becoming.

Specifically, one viewpoint asserts the eternal essence of the individual soul, while the opposing perspective highlights its transience, emphasizing the supremacy of the universal soul or principle, which absorbs it.

The initiatory vision closely integrates and merges the two theses, as primordial germs, given as a (−) (negative), whereby there derives the integration of man as a construction of the (+) (positive).

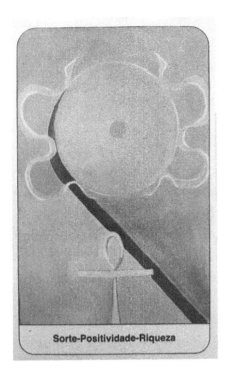

Sorte-Positividade-Riqueza

The Wheel of Fortune from the Tarot designed by Auri Campolonghi Gonella, based on Marco Daffi's *The Tarot According to the Mensa Isiaca and the I Ching*, where the figures of the Major Arcana of the Tarot are connected with images found in the "Mensa Isiaca" from the Egyptian Museum in Turin.

In other terms: given the germs as hermetically constructed into a "negative hemisphere" and a "positive hemisphere," the result is the spherical perfection or "globe of Venus" (♀).

Philosophically, the alchemical splitting (division) of Being yields two polarities:

(−) Saturnian body and Lunar body
(+) Mercurial body and Solar body

This division finds reflection in its "sacred representation," where the tangible negative hemisphere (− embodying Saturnian and lunar elements upon detachment from the Father) begets the positive hemisphere (imbued with Mercurial and Solar elements) through the cyclical initiation and transmutation of alchemical forms.

The positive hemisphere confers continuity and fixity of consciousness to being.

There is psychological and implicit evidence in the oscillation of the human spirit between the:

undifferentiated—impersonal,
differentiated—personal.

In fact, man when seen from an "infernal" state of passion appears as "another"—so much so that, after the outburst, even in the awareness of being extrinsic, from an individual point of view, always remains "himself," even though he has the feeling of being another.

The fact is that the Self, with passion vented, resumes its dominance; on the one hand, it stands out, and on the other, it incorporates the fatality of the accomplished act while repudiating its genesis, that is, from the succubus. Therefore, in the alchemical-Hermetic Work—which consists in arousing and taming the Beast—the universal "metaphysical" drama of the alternation of consciousness is reflected of the animal series or (–) (negative) hemisphere and the life series or (+) (positive) hemisphere,

Moreover, the participation in any type of animistic chain—empirical, scientific, religious, initiatory—automatically divides Being in a specific order and modality and object.

The community determines the collective psyche as the prerequisite for the type of common man. While outside the bonds of union, the individual soul is free from the possession of the collective entity. It is with this sense that we can explain actions performed by individuals in conditions of complete autonomy, which stand in stark contrast to previous actions or precedents yet stemming from the same autonomy inherent in the possession of the individual psyche within the collective.

On occasions, on the other hand, a real addition of physical-magnetic energy is developed, parallel to the conception of the activities to be performed in the imagination of the individual psyche, which is strengthened in those who physically perform the actions themselves.

Here life is strengthened for those who are self-possessed within the "Mosaic"!

ON THE HYMN TO THE
MOTHER OF THE GODS*

Attis is nothing other than the substance of the generating and creating intellect, which prides itself on all things to the extreme limits of matter and contains within itself all the principles and causes of forms joined to matter; nature, which for the exuberance of its creative power descends from the sky to the earth, such is Attis.

Without the root causes, Becoming is not possible.

By virtue of what resolves the multiplication of the species? What is the difference between the masculine and the feminine? How do beings differ into certain forms within their own species, if there weren't any post-mortem and post-mortemed principles as a model? The forms "exist actually before potentially!"

. . . in the field of material things? No, because this is the last.

Causes are outside of matter. Together with these the soul has existence and together it proceeds. It has assumed the principles of the forms—as a mirror welcomes images of things and in turn according to nature, bodies are formed.

Nature is the matrix which creates bodies to the extent that, taken in its universal aspect, it is the creator of the whole. The individual nature is the creator of each of the beings composed of parts.

Forms exist in nature potentially and not actively and also potentially in the soul, but in the sense that they are more distinct, so that they can be recognized.

On what will we base our affirmations on the eternity of the world?

Also, for the forms joined to matter, it initiates an immaterial first cause, which precedes it.

Attis is the cause that descends to the limits of matter.

---

*[Emperor Julian's "Hymn to the Mother of Gods" is a Neoplatonic analysis of the deity Attis, a youth who was the lover of Cybele, the Great Mother of the Gods. In a frenzy caused by a jealous lover, the hermaphroditic Agdistis, Attis castrated himself and died, but Zeus allowed his body to not decay. As a deity, he was associated with solar rebirth, vegetation, and according to Julian, Nature itself.—*Trans.*]

Who is the mother of the gods? She is the Virgin without mother, who has her throne beside Zeus and the Mother of all the gods endowed with intellect.

It's a unique aspect of providence; Attis was conceived through love devoid of passion. The assertion is that Attis doesn't contend with any other entity except with her, indicating that this creative force simultaneously seeks the preservation of what is uniform while also shunning indulgence toward the world of material forms.

This teaches the myth, when it mentions that the Mother of the Gods exhorted Attis to serve her alone and not to leave her to love someone else.

Instead, Attis insisted on lowering himself to the external limits of matter. But his unlimited drive had to stop and end. And how does one understand this emasculation?

And to arrest with the unlimited push.*

The generation was held back within the limits of the forms; this was made possible by the madness of Attis, who having shied away from the right measure, came to lose his vigor and his dominion.

Attis again is brought back to the Mother of the gods after the evasion.

To arrest the unlimited thrust, the purpose of the purification was the ascension of the Soul.

Attis—the cause that descends to the limits of matter.

THE QUATERNARY IN GENERATION

The quaternary of natural creation represents the phase of attraction between the two pairs of polarity. Hence, the four principles are in a

---

*[Daffi here references the larger philosophical concept involving Theogony, Cosmology, and the primary force of creation, where the primordial emanation or unlimited push is in continuous motion (infinite), and is arrested in the Cosmos by the mythologized force of Attis, which is characterized by harnessing fragments or filaments of energy from this unlimited push for the creation of new beings and forms of life. Attis provides finitude (separateness) to the universal flow of energy (infinite push of creation).—*Trans.*]

non-volitionary creative mixed phase—and equally so—in the common man, which is the typical expression of creation.

Without thereby disregarding that man is at the top of the evolutionary hierarchy of beings in the animal series, but rather referring to his evolution within the sphere of nature, as it is not yet modified in its structure, and that remains subject to an involitionary (regressive) primordial inclination, that is, to the world of the archetypes, and first of all, the archetype of the species and (human) generation.

That is to say, that in man the four bodies are bound by the law of attraction of opposites, which gives rise and inspiration to the creation and the organic constitution of the human being.

And by natural occultation in the "recipient" the two positives are virtually hidden in the two passive (bodies).

The manifestations of the divine occult powers, whose category may include "miracles," always have a lunar magnetic base. It is—always—only through manifestations of the lunar body of mediums or ecstatics that the existence of a "metaphysical" principle is manifested.

And only through intelligence is the mercurial principle determined.

This practice demonstrates the challenge of capturing the elusive Hermes—to initially recognize and then fix, amidst cerebral rumination, the clear idea and joyful intuition that arise in a fleeting moment of distraction, diverging from the Saturnian disposition.

The physical body—considered a prison by mystics and alchemists—generally and ordinarily is the expression of the prevalence of

the negative on the positive and
the involution on the evolution.

The process of involution unites in a single amalgam the four principles and expresses the Adamic archetype in the likeness of man. Though he perceives himself as fashioned in the divine image, he truly represents an image of creation, specifically, the divine incarnation! To unravel the process of evolution, a resolution of the four principles is required to dissolve the natural amalgam and transfer the *similia simillimis*:

- similar positives: Father-Son and Sun-Mercury
- similar negatives: Matrix-Nature and Moon-Saturn

The work progresses in alignment with the law of bipolar splitting, aligning like to like elements on the positive pole and like to like on the negative pole to form two magnetic centers within Being.

The two figures of the Wheel of Fortune are symbolic of this.

- descending Mercury (involution)
- ascending Mercury (evolution)

The philosophical basis of alchemical work is . . . Mercury! O how restricted is divine intelligence; that is, born, from the contrast between the eclipsed sun and the moon that made it, filters out a quiddity, and which must free itself from the destination of Being conditioned to nature in all aspects and every structure, to regain its primordial function—free to fixate itself at will—and fit to be seated beside the Father-Sun.

Hence the mystery of human generation and regeneration. The world of natural generation is an unlimited thrust because it is the work of the Word* and this is a willful thrust as well as a physiological and psychological act.

In this order of ideas resides the myth of the emasculation of the god Attis.†

The emasculation, that is, the arrest of the unlimited thrust, is essential to initiation.

ON CHASTITY

Chastity, as a cerebral exercise, is more than a matter of abstinence and can be considered as an intuition about the principle of limiting the

---

*See the Indian Purusha.
†See Emperor Julian.

ever-expanding universe. As the son is increasingly absorbed by the Father,* the more it is suppressed, curbing the boundless expansion until it eventually reaches a diminished state.

The vision of the image is substituted for obedience to the archetype.

Naturally, intermediate phases are determined and characterized by the vague consciousness of the image and its indirect vision.

The expression "chastity" has a purely mental and philosophical value; the practitioner and the initiate are free in their relationship choices since it does not affect the human to act or abstain against the plan of "divine love"!

However, the principle holds that the initiate must remain within the integral possession and dominion of his faculties; hence not to castrate oneself.

This highlights why the alchemical work is the work of complete creation. Neither determines any opposition between the operator and the first† principle since this is, by nature, not specifically voluntary,† but rather acts through the materialization in man as it is realized by the + (positive attribute) of the human monad.

According to statements made by Kremmerz:

1. "Chastity must be absolute, in divine magic, so that the higher intelligences do not distance themselves from the operator."‡
2. "Chastity is an act of abstinence from sexual generation."#

The term *chastity* is used improperly, which easily induces misunderstanding if understood to the letter. That, on the other hand, it must rightly take itself in a symbolic sense, and to penetrate hermetically is proved by the fact of non-abstinence from the activity generated by initiates and of Kremmerz himself!

---

*Meaning of the Resurrection.
†It is the symbol of the infinite and quiet flow of the Tao and the impassivity of the One in Plotinus.
‡See Introduction to Kremmerz's *La Scienza dei Magi* (Science of the Magi).
#As detailed in the *Corpus Hermeticum*.

The Catholic Church, in its concept of the sacramental "chaste union," matrimony by canon law, in antithesis to the lustful one of venereal delight or outside of sacramental parameters, confusedly overshadows and profanely contrasts divine love with earthly love. According to the theology that pushes the canonical doctrine to the extreme, which is misleading from every physiological and natural consideration, the perfect conjugal state should consist in sexual abstinence that is only interrupted by the strictly necessary and sufficient needs for the fertilization of the maternal egg. That is to say: divine love as a rule and earthly love for social purposes conforms with the evangelical precept: "increase and multiply."

The Church of Rome points to a form of love to be developed and made to last as long as possible; in other words, materially following in the footsteps of the ancient pagan tradition, which presents the generative act as an impurity impoverishing the divine part of love.

Kremmerz* uses the word "chastity" in a meaning that is somewhat ambiguously related to the church—directed toward disciples who are Myriamists, prioritizing the control of passions. However, in reality, chastity denotes a condition that fosters earthly love for the sake of the divine: it is a state where instead of embracing divine love, one adheres to and fulfills earthly desires through fornication.

He explicitly stated, "Do they desire to believe in the purity of white doves? . . . Then, I've fulfilled their wishes!"

Eroticism is considered a confusion of concepts that adapt divine love; but when it is used well and intelligently, such as in the sense of a magnetic physical occultation, it has a highly effective potentiality. The folly of abstinence, as advocated by religious figures, which purportedly leads to the "atrophy" of the sexual function, is evident when considering that the initiate requires their virile attributes to be intact and functional.

Even the keen observation of the phenomenon of love itself reveals a secret. Love transcending mere physical desire is chaste.

---

*By express declaration *ad personam* in the year 1929 at Beausoleil, France.

The image of the beloved woman is not just any woman, but that of the Madonna. The poets of the *Dolce Stil Novo*, fully aware of the profound spiritual significance of the name "Madonna," employed this sacred symbol to elevate their beloved beyond earthly confines to a divine ideal.

At this level of love the first glimpse bestows upon the eyes a sweetness that reaches the depths of the soul. Not of carnal possession, but through the merging and union of souls. Eroticism and erotic possession serve as pillars of this union. Hence, within every instance of "chaste" love, the divine spark thrives, rendering the lovers in a state of grace and purity.

The practice of deferring carnal conjunction to the first night of marriage suggests a hidden law that the copulation must be a ritual. The allure of the Catholic ritual among the masses is also influenced by the remnants of a culture centered on the consummation of marriage. However, canonical distortions and the neglect of wisdom have undermined the ritual's intended purpose from the outset. The holistic nature of love, often overlooked, is in fact ignored. The Church's focus solely on procreation reinforces this perspective.

On the other hand, the Catholic ritual has safeguarded the principle that the sexual union must be homologous to divine love and ceremonially completed. For its part, the pagan tradition overshadows the ritual as a means of preserving the purity and therefore of divine love, in the succession of the Venerean action. Furthermore, the tradition of Bacchanals was carried out with this sense of ritual union *sine filiis*, as well as that of the Baltic unions at the summer solstice.

Therefore, the Lunar astral plane, wherein the monads undergo the process of incarnation, is conditioned and resembles an ocean. Within its pelagic depths, nearly indistinguishable and post-mortem monads navigate based on their varying specific gravities, be they major or minor.

The act of love that attracts them, in turn, can vary in its purity, ranging from the utmost refinement of incarnative evocation, exemplified by the conception of Krishna, by the Virgin Devaki, and by that of Jesus by the Virgin Mary.

Conversely, in the most profound union, where the two individuals of the humanimal couple meld into a single form devoid of spiritual enlightenment, the attraction that arises mirrors the union of their two spirits. Nor are degenerate unions exempt either, arising from morbid excitement, delusional intoxication, hasty concupiscence, the bestial lust of the human goat. Magically, with the domination of animal sensuality, albeit selective, aligns with the dominance of the elementals of sex saturating the realm of the Lunar astral body. These sex elementals accompany and propel the spores* in the lunar body, seeking occult nourishment within a concealed sheath. A man enamored with a woman naturally finds inspiration in the notion of her feminine form.

Even in the most sublime loves, man remains bound by the concept of a feminine form, determining his virile potential, manifested concretely through erection. Innumerable amorous disappointments follow from the often-dramatic passing from the idealized state to the manifestation of the human-animal.

The common man inevitably faces the peril that comes with opening Pandora's box, unable to project their own fluidic body and discern the hidden impurities within their beloved's figure. This risk is compounded by the state of erotic emptiness associated with the idyllic phase.

Whatever animal actions takes place *uti piscem*—in the astral ocean. Elementals dominate.

The elementals are released from the hormones and the follicles.

The elementals pervade the couple and subjugate it to the animal archetype.

And the lucid and conscious love of the two souls becomes blurred and eclipsed in the lust of love.

Therefore, chasteness is to be understood and translated by the removal of the elementals from every plane of being. Chastity is, then, primarily a mental state, for which no erection is occasioned—in act or in potential—and human libido lies dormant. Chastity is a means of

---

*[Subtle forces attracted by the occult eroticism of the lunar body.—*Trans.*]

periodic purification and exercise to the exclusion of the elementals of sexuality, to the dissolution of erotic imagery. It occurs in the human domain and in Isiac initiation only as an alternation between abstinence and eroticism. The alternation is comparable to that of the Siren, which emerges at the surface of the sea to breathe (= purification) and then dives back down for copulation (= satisfaction): the instinct of a fish in its element.

The value of the purifying act is given by the relative duration of the period of abstinence. Pagan symbolism offers the key to this mystery: the mythological Siren is half fish and half woman, not as a female, but as a "virgo"—Mary! Alchemists represent the alchemical Siren with two tails—symbol of the two negatives! In Hindu figuration the god Vishnu floated on the waters in the form of an avatar, half fish and half man—as a deity or divine plane!

Those who know how to place themselves in the state denoted by the correlative sirenical and avataric configurations will have lucidity and purity in love and will dominate the action of the elementals so that they do not function as a secular arm of the animal archetype.

Therefore, the exercises of chastity are to be considered as preparatory, in alternation, to the perception and realization of the coeval state of divine love. The "removal" of the elementals through chasteness is properly negative, equivalent to the erection of a dam that the elementals and correlative erotic images cannot overcome; and therefore, they cannot invade the Mercurial sphere. Such that it is, in magical practice, the possibility of a more rapid and intense purification, consisting in attracting, as in a negative field, the elementals on an artificially created plane to subjugate them.

Ascetics and saints, intensely praying to God to give them the strength to reject temptations, hypothesize and visualize a "demon," which represents and precisely constitutes a centripetal field of elementals, driven out of mind and soul. In a magical sense, being the natural manifestation of the Solar–creative principle constituted by the generating impulse and the consequential exploitation of elementals under the function of guardians of the generating act, there exists a process, which reverses the projection of negative energy and assists the simple abstinence by removing the elementals and placing the Being in a state of sovereign quiescence. And given the constitution of man in four bodies or principles, the removal of the elementals imposes itself in all bodies. A relatively simple purification of the Saturnian body will put the beast to sleep.

The purification of the Lunar body is more laborious, and in fact receives all of the astral impressions and undergoes pressure of the monads in the channel of incarnation.

It is sufficient for the fatal evocation of unchaste images on the lunar body—in accordance with the drive toward incarnation—to have a generic thought of a person or persons of the opposite sex with a nonerotic "unconscious" sense. Since "in the unconscious" the association is necessarily consubstantiated!

Still more demanding is the purification of the Mercurial body since a minimum thrust of desire is enough to let the repressed elementals overflow into a copulative image. Finally, for the Solar body—that is, always within the context of the common man—the slightest misunderstanding of a desire for affirmation and power, as a generic virility, determines the attraction and the overflow of the elementals nestled in the body itself.

It is the act itself, as virility, that unconsciously arouses the sexual "latency" of the Solar body. A man dominated by the nymph Egeria* is quite the opposite of the principle of chastity because the woman bewitches him and therefore dominates him, placing leverage on the unconscious libido, that is, on those elementals that are associated with all the images of human vulgar virility.

The nymph Egeria may well appear as a devout servant or admirer or sympathetic companion, but no less evocative of images antithetical to magical chastity.

---

*[Egeria was a nymph who played a legendary role in the early history of Rome as a divine consort and counselor of Numa Pompilius, the second king of Rome, to whom she imparted laws and rituals pertaining to ancient Roman religion. Her name is used as an eponym for a female advisor or counselor.—*Trans.*]

ON REINCARNATION

The ego, as commonly understood, does not represent man's true being.* Instead, it is the "monad," an unconscious and hence negative root that maintains the continuity of the entity in both the sleep of the dead and the vigils of the living. This continuity spans various existences or physical embodiments, all rooted in the same fragment of the "mosaic of the One." Within this framework, ontology emphasizes the reestablishment of the law of bipolarity, as follows:

a Negative of Being in the Monad†
a Positive of Being in the Four Bodies‡
the five khandhas of the Buddhists who superfluously dissect the
    perception of sensation = Lunar body

And in such a prospectus, the Monad has a continued existence,# which is the last resort for the continuity of Being as an entity. On the human level, one detaches from the animal archetype—formed by multiplication of the primordial monadic unit and its fusion—with the emergence of the fifth element or fifth essence of the alchemists.**

It is by VITRIOL, the dissolving of Being and at the same time constituting the substratum or Second Wood of Life that substantiates the initiation. There are no "heavens," except in the sense of "quaternaries," in which the lower earth is the fifth essence of the plane that precedes the next; hence the fifth essence that for humans is subtle matter, for others is grave matter, that is to say the constituent Glorious Body or fluidic body, whose generation is the real object of the Great Hermetic Work.

---

*See Buddhism and Brahmanism.
†The LUZ stone of the alchemist-Cabalists.
‡The four bodies of the pagan and Brahmanical traditions.
#See Leibniz's exposition on monadic being.
**See Raymund Lully.

Therefore:

(*a*) the Soul is immortal by virtue of its negative aspect, which establishes the pure and simple revival from the sleep of death—a reality applicable to all creatures (entities)!

(*b*) the Soul is mortal by virtue of its positive aspect, equivalent to the sphere of consciousness, or of the "four bodies."

If the Soul becomes immortal* when evasion is effectively prevented, disrupting the unity of the creature-being, on the Isiac plane, and leading to the formation of the "Second Wood of Life."

The Soul is understood in its inherent state, recognized as a vital and sentient entity, in accordance with its proper nature. In this sense, consciousness alone constitutes the identity of the entity-being. In fact, it is through the phenomenon of consciousness and not that of life that the context and solution of the question must be understood. Hell is a state of consciousness in one's life!!! Of one's own personality!!! Which is an unconsciousness-unawareness also of the subconscious.

The soul can inverse itself, if not initiated-integrated, to the same bestial and noted regress that is symbolized by death in hell and given eternal "punishment." Never will the soul be able to recover so much, albeit in such a minimal state of consciousness; indeed it will be absorbed and definitively confused, that is to say irretrievably, in another (creature), which ontologically will not be able to destroy it, but will absorb it and confuse the consciousness in one of the other being-creatures with another history.

The possibilities vary:

- *metempsychosis* on the part of regressing souls towards lower states of being
- *regeneration* by monad-souls in an unconscious reconstruction of the analogous state
- *reincarnation* by the integrating or integrated soul

---

*The Soul is understood as the "vital complex."

How intuitive is it that souls—even if not initiated-integrated, but already having a more "organized" nature-structure—can prolong the fatal loop in the post-mortem and live their "soul" life in the intermediate existence for a certain and not ephemeral duration. Moreover, initiates, not yet having constituted the "Second Wood of Life," live in the post-mortem rather than in conscious time! And precisely for the intensity of the operations-creations made in life, which is to say for the efficiency of the Fifth Essence that they have drawn or better yet extracted from their lunar fluids or from the vase of others!

Consider the phenomenon of the rose plant, within the throes of the seasons. The plant remains but at each new season it projects and blooms new roses that in common with those of the previous year retain only the lifeblood of the plant. So that:

rose sap = negative monad
new roses = four bodies

That which remains is "what emerges from time to time in themselves taken by the vortex of illusory existence"; but with the complex of ideas, of affections, of interests incumbent in every day and that everyone takes care of and not "what remains of each person."

"That which remains of each one" is found in that moment of meditation that for a moment makes us pause in the chaotic vortex of samsaric-mahajanic existence; it is to be found in the flash of Hermes. It is that true state to be fixed and the true state of consciousness. In every "new individual" there are "roses": illusory facets of existence, and anyone who pays attention to them or one of them (the current, contingent one) is unable to understand the reality of the "return" and the possibility of it in the three forms of metempsychosis, regeneration, and reincarnation.

Wilted roses do not return.* That is to say that for individuals "dead in themselves," the karmic effects are discounted to the point

*[An expression used by Kremmerz. See also page 227.—*Trans.*]

that a further conscious existence becomes impossible. Without that, however, the "vital substance" is lost. In this sense, nothing is destroyed.

That which, on the other hand, is undone is consciousness, or following Buddhist terminology, is the karmic complex forming the stratification of Being. In regressions to lower states, and those mined by pathological forms receptive in a broad sense to the point of dementia or those without a "sense of self," the karma is exhausted, the animal aggregation formed in the progressive stages of volition is extinguished, and the Monad without any further karmic bond accesses another consciousness that fuses with it. It is a form of nirvana in reverse; indeed nirvana is inverted, turned downward rather than upward.

THE PURIFICATIONS

CORRESPONDENCES	
Ablutions	Saturn = earth
Diet	Luna = water
Silence	Mercury = air
Continence	Sol = fire
SYMPATHIES	
Mondays	Astral body
Tuesdays	Force, strength
Wednesdays	Intellect
Thursdays	Justice
Fridays	Art
Saturday	Hylic body
Sunday	Renew and Restore

In principle, two diets or fasting regimens are indicated:

1. For twenty-four hours following the entry of the Moon in the phase of New Moon;

2. from seven hours before to zero hours after the entry of the Moon in the new phase.

Ontologically the New Moon is in eclipse and therefore foods have a negative effect!

Fasting involves the exclusion of:

- fermented beverages
- foods originating from living organisms

It is a good practice to ascertain one's sensitivity with the phases of the New Moon, whether preceding, concomitant, or subsequent, so as to adjust the fasting period accordingly.

ON THE ALTERNATION OF DAILY INFLUENCES

The philosophical principle that presides over the alternation of days determines whether they are:

- auspicious
- nefarious
- positive
- negative
- neutral

They are the same principles of creation, since the One or First Principle* cannot create itself except by limiting itself† thus submitting itself to a "death"‡—for the obvious reason that the life of distinct beings, of individuality, would not be the case if the One did not infinitely deepen its essence and strength—whence its ineffability—in the shadows of its source perpetually rediscovered by individual beings, men, numens, eons, intelligences, archons, archangels, in the perennial thirst for knowledge and constant evolution.

---

*See the *to proton* of the Greek philosophers and the Chinese concept of the Tao.
†For instance, as in the macules or patches of Brahma in Indian philosophy.
‡See Osiris's death in the Egyptian religion and the crucifixion of Christ in the Christian.

Initium = Principle
There is no finality.

And "none" must be understood in a strict and absolute manner. None are final, for in its inevitable cycle of termination, Being would be consumed in the same final *ecpirosi*—apocalyptic myth—that psycho-analytically looms over the dread of uncovering the fire-solar mystery: a myth that transforms the historical elements of the world's material combustion into religious eschatologies.

The alternation of days—auspicious, nefarious, positive, negative, neutral—is a true and proper natural law in perfect occult correspondence with the alternation of light and shadow with intermediate phases, twilight or dusk. Twilight denotes a state of neutrality to be evaluated not as an ideal condition, but rather as a moment of equilibrium and therefore transitory, otherwise, it would be a form of life . . . without life! Inert!

Analogous is the Christian myth of peace, which leads to moral conformism and to an equalizing leveling mentality. The shadow cannot be assumed in of itself and in an absolute sense, since—owing to the similarity of the opposites—we would find ourselves blinded in darkness! Light in itself alone, also, cannot be assumed, in order not to be dazzled by the splendor of the Absolute Light and become blinded.

Ignorance and "materialism" suggest that the human psyche and states of sensitivity are, apart from moments of creation, equal and monotonous, implying that the influences of the days are identical or, at the very least, astronomically inconsequential.

To the dialectical objection: according to the principle of opposites, if one day is auspicious in one sense, it is nefarious for the opposite. The answer: reasoning by paradox. If for the gravedigger it's an auspiciously good day based on the greater demand for his services, then for the relatives of the deceased the same day is nefarious. Apart from the fact that, in general, the death of others is not only profitable for the gravedigger, but also for intimate relatives.

In addition to the belief that death, seen by humans as liberation from suffering, is actually a binding chain to existence and thus beneficial for those who, having determined their fate, have prepared for a better life, it's worthwhile to address the matter through Hermetic, or initiatory, perspectives, particularly in interpreting the transition from TWO* to Three.†

The Hermetic concept and the initiatory operations enable the passage "nothing is created, nothing is destroyed" and consequently, "nothing lives except through the removal of the lives of others" (an expression of the phenomenal struggle of creatures) to the "continuous act of creation for the virtual participation of the first principle in children."

In absolute terms, the principle induces the consequence of the addition of new energy, from the powerful Sun to the Saturnian plane. In relative terms, it induces—although affirming the indirect energetic addition from the Solar plane—the arrangement of energies and phenomena in the sense of the "triangle," and no longer that of the "binary." There is a sense of the third dimension, which develops from the two-dimensional *sic et simpliciter.*

One of the more expressive meanings, precisely, of the pyramidal ternary is that of the harmony achieved on Earth by the initiatory hierarchy, which due to its wisdom and its social operations implements and directs the political forces in the sense of the Three, balancing them, not in the passive and inert state of religion, but as active and creative magic. An example would be the prevalence of the productive factor, that is, the creation of new wealth by the distribution factor, which is economically absorbed by the first.

The perception of the alternation of days—auspicious, nefarious, positive, negative, neutral—occurs first through virtual creation and then in act, in the alchemical-Hermetic sense, and the fact of already

---

*See the Latona Matrix, Diana, Maja.
†See son of the alchemical operation Osiris, Risen Christ, heart beetle, double of the Egyptian Book of the Dead.

knowing this alternation is in current times and in the Western world the prerogative of initiates. The "meteorological" vision of daily alternations follows, in the mind of the mystic, with the perception of the different polarity of days, from the integral point of view, without however excluding any "barometric" or magical coincidences.

But how difficult it is to move from theory to practice in the alchemical work, and for initiates to do the same—to exclude nefarious influences from their creative or formative ideas on the days of the Work. And the greatest obstacle in initiation is the overcoming of the superstitious mystical background, the passive nature of one's spirit, which is natural to man. The danger is that it causes fearful forgetfulness, paralysis of acts occurring on a nefarious or negative day—and it is not intuitive to put oneself mentally in a passive and negative state to reverse the negative effects and to transform the negativity itself into a utility! However, already operating with regard to alternation determines the conditions in the subject—first virtual, then real—of contact with the forces of the divine third plane.

These are determined and disposed in favor of the initiate, to exclude automatically, through the action of his unconscious, unseemly relationships and acquaintances. And a certain mental concentration is enough to ascertain the deviation, apparently natural and without hidden cause, of commitments from the nefarious periods. Furthermore, the dialectical antithesis that skeptically would place a compensatory equivalence in the virtuality of the works and days yields to the factual finding that only initiates can and know—gradually learning from the art—to use the metaphysical values of the days. They do not benefit those who are not spiritually disposed and "sensitive" in an adequate manner, since even if anyone could infiltrate an initiatory brotherhood and pretend to exploit them, they would see each change with negative reactions in proportion.

In this sense, the principle of value reaffirms the authenticity of the concept of the "Good." That which is "Good" is valued by the auspicious day and in terms of the same does not correspond to the one in current use critical of social moral decay, but rather that absolute beyond worldliness. Therefore, the possible contradiction and proof of the defect are indicated within the operator.

Since the "harm" or negativity exerts a strong influence on the spirit and on whomever applies the practice of the work, the practitioner observes personal phenomena, accidents of others, and remains aloof without participating with one's mind-being in activities that animate common mortals in the machinery of everyday existence. Psychologically it surfaces in the alternation of values and as the expression of mental lucidity. A good day is one in which someone sensitive to the occult energies is in a perfect penetrative state, and his spirit and his nerves are perfectly balanced; it's easy for him to pass from the passive to the active state and to be able to draw from the cosmic forces the energy that they emit precisely on that day.

A nefarious day is one in which energy is lacking and an operation to draw energy, specifically from the cosmos, fatally causes an inversion of values either as an illusion or as a deleterious event. On such a day adverse forces could erupt unrestrained, not contained by cosmic positive balances. The operator who—even on the nefarious day—fixes the negative forces with the will to dissolve the negative forces turns the same negativity against them. But this action "on the negative," besides being the prerogative of masters, does not involve a valorization in a positive sense.

Therefore, whoever tries recklessly to transform the defensive and negative effects of the negative into a positive effect—thus placing himself in contradiction to the general harmony—would nullify the very value of the difficult reversal operation he has performed. Observe, therefore, which works are favorable and which are contrary, respectively, on good and bad days, elucidating the discrimination between the

- relative good and absolute good, and
- relative evil and absolute evil

One must make this discrimination while observing the recurrence and the patterns of events, following the indications of one expressed on a good day—or vice versa—and the reasons for any confirmation or denial of the intuition given in the datum.

In other words: auspicious and nefarious days in particular are exploited for the purposes of observation and Hermetic concentration. It is worth noting that the distinct values of the days are a general rule in magic as well. That is, the negative effect of impurity is minimal or minor for those who ignore it . . . average for those who have a causal notion . . . maximum for those who have full knowledge and "exercise" it freely.

This implies a wider application of the significance of days within the overarching principles of "purity" and "impurity." In this context, there's an assimilation where the notion of negative days extends to certain lunar phases and those associated with sexual functions—in this sense, it is compliant. These are deemed impure and thus typically regarded as negative:

- The day of the full moon.
- The day preceding the full moon.
- The subsequent three days.
- The three days following sexual intercourse.

In the first three cases, with exceptions, impurity is typically determined, whereas in the fourth case, the level of purity (or impurity) is influenced by the quality of the activity, which relies on the circumstances and the personal condition of the couple. If the union occurred under an auspicious zodiacal arrangement, the impurity would be lower compared to that of the lunar days.

Generally, the valences of the days are transmitted through tradition, from perception in the astral—for a multiyear period, an annual one, or a shorter duration. Moreover, the series vary according to the initiatory ritual and consequently according to the degree of the participants, who are otherwise connected according to the different classes of schools. In this sense, a criterion of discrimination and attenuation is introduced to the absolute value of the relative values without thereby invalidating the order.

Normally on days that are:

auspicious . . . one can initiate an "enterprise," especially in those endeavors that are pivotal and crucial;
and if the days are
nefarious . . . it's advisable to refrain from starting any new business ventures and to avoid engaging with anything malicious. It's important to take precautions against potential accidents, such as avoiding handling sharp or hot objects, and it's recommended to stay at home, rest, meditate, focus on studies, and minimize social interactions.

and if the days are

extremely nefarious . . . avoid any activity; postpone commitments; refrain from bathing, and avoid making major changes.

On days that are

positive . . . one can commence activities first on a material level (physical) and then on an intellectual level;
negative . . . it's wise to avoid initiating new business endeavors and reacting to negative individuals, but it's still acceptable to carry out operations that have already been started.

Hermes, during the most significant days, regardless of their ominous nature for those who follow the rules, illuminates the pathways of the mind, while simultaneously erecting an invisible barrier, a delicate and protective network that instinctively mitigates misfortune.

ON THE "CHOD" RITUAL

(See) . . . rituals . . . among the most imaginative is the one known as "Chod" (to cut, to suppress); a kind of macabre "mystery," represented by a single actor: the officiant . . . so cleverly combined to scare the novices . . . some are struck by madness or death during its celebration.*

. . . cemeteries or wild places, suitable for producing terror . . . The reason for this preference is that the effect does not depend only on the liturgical words. . . . It is . . . to move the mysterious forces . . . that exist in such places. . . .

It follows the irruption on the scene of "characters" of the occult world . . .

Without ceremony, but with geometric-magnetic steps.†

With instruments: a tambourine and a trumpet made with the femur of a sixteen-year-old virgin . . .

(see) The instructing lama, who presides, like a dance teacher.

The essential part of the ritual consists . . .

The celebrant blows into a *kangling* inviting demons to the party. . . . He—magically—imagines a female deity, who personifies his will. This springs from the top of his head while brandishing a sword in its hand. With a swift stroke, it cuts off his head. Then, while numerous vampires gather greedily in expectation, it detaches his limbs, flays him, and opens his belly.

The intestines come out, the blood flows . . . the hideous creatures bite, tear, and chew . . . while the officiant excites them at the ghastly meal with liturgical words . . .

He gives them that corporeality that has fed on other bodies: The debt has been paid.

(see) This act of the drama is called the "red banquet."

---

*[This text is an extract from a letter Daffi sent to Giammaria on his reflections on chapter four of Alexandra David-Neel's famous book *Magic and Mystery in Tibet*, and specifically because it addresses an important topic of initiation: that of liberating the subconscious of fears, negative impressions, and so on. The ellipses refer to parts of the letter where Giammaria has removed information that he feels is not relevant to the argument. Daffi wrote in a very stream of consciousness manner and this text reflects that style.—*Trans.*]

†[Possibly referring to particular steps that the officiant undertakes in the ritual to move in a manner and in a rhythm consistent with the inner experience of the ritual, for instance fast or slow, energetic or lethargic, west, north, east, south, and so on.—*Trans.*]

The "black banquet" follows.

The vision . . . fades . . . complete solitude in the darkness . . . silence . . .

He must now imagine that he has become a pile of calcined bones, emerging from a lake of black mud, the mud of the spiritual stains he has contracted and of the negative actions he has made—in previous lives.

He must understand that the idea of exalted sacrifice is nothing but an illusion, born of blind pride without foundation.

In reality, he has nothing to give because he is nothing.

The silent renunciation of the ascetic, which rejects the vain intoxication generated by the idea of sacrifice, closes the ritual . . . fascination.

Some lamas undertake trips to celebrate Chod near eight lakes, at eight cemeteries, in eight forests, and so on.

They devote years to this practice, covering not only Tibet but also Nepal and parts of India and China.

ON THE I CHING

The operation starts by placing fifty stems on a table, and of these, "forty-nine are taken aside"; that is, one stem is left from the bunch to then proceed further. The reason is exquisitely subtle. In other words, it is necessary to establish a double polarity: one fixed or negative, that is, the stem excluded, and the other positive—the forty-nine stems.

Then with a decisive blow, the group of forty-nine stems is divided and placed in two groups, one on the left and the other on the right. The two halves are assumed to represent the two fundamental forces: yin and yang.

Next, a stem is drawn from the pile on the right, though it shouldn't be seen as a leftover. This is another demonstration of the bipolar principle: indeed, the stem extracted should be regarded as—comparatively—fixed, meaning it's a part not subject to the movement of the leftovers.

Then, from the pile on the left, start to deduct the stems four by four, which inevitably results in a remainder of either one, or two, or three, or four stalks.

The system of consultation consists of three "coins" and is much more convenient, quicker, and can certainly be adopted for all responses that do not require complex analysis, or in cases where one is satisfied with a simple answer. The conventional value (which in the system of stems derives from the transposition of numbers) is instead attributed to the remainder and the reverse of the coins.

We prefer to attribute the value 3 to the front (masculine) and the value 2 to the reverse (feminine). The coins must be neither too light nor too heavy for them to bounce easily as the bounce is a mantic element not to be overlooked. It is preferable to operate early in the morning, in conditions of a calm soul, not troubled by worries.

Throw the coins up and don't allow them to fall out of your hands, let alone shake the coins in closed hands and then open the hands themselves. Coins must be able to bounce, roll, and so on, so as to—so to speak—absorb as many proper influences as possible and as few extrinsic influences as possible. Of course, don't sequence the throws of the three elements as the coins are arranged irregularly: you only have to add to them.

"*Panta rei*,"* and it is to the credit of Chinese thinking that it has not failed to keep in mind *where* it flows, toward which situation or possible situations or state of affairs it could lead to. Well—for these purposes—the I Ching is conceived as a method of clairvoyance in the sense that one has to see *the moving lines* as flowing from the bottom to the top. One must read the hexagrams from the bottom to the top as if to say from the earth or the subsoil toward man or world and from this to heaven in equivalence to the three "places" in which the hexagrams are divided.

And we have to see the lower lines as *pushing* the *higher* ones almost to the point of throwing them out of the field so as to determine a new

---

*["All things flow," Heraclitus—*Trans.*]

situation. This movement is the action-reaction response of the trigrams on each other and is considered as a clash, so to speak, of the yang and yin lines. Whether the sense of the derivative is to be understood as simply integrative is a matter of interpretation. Naturally if it is a question of motion, on a possible prospect of a deal, or of a judgment (always of course within the relative time limits) then some form of finalism can have greater consideration, but one must not let oneself be caught up in the finalistic tendency. The sign is what it is and the movement— derived for example from the pressure of the lines on others or other motions, indicated in the commentary—must be understood in itself, and not from outside.

If a movement can be expressed graphically, the sign can be broken down by following the motion, but do not let yourself be guided by the sign formed by the change of the movement. Rather, the *sense* (Tao) of the change should be taken as a warning and behavior guide to overcome the difficulty inherent in the question.

NIHIL SUB SOLE NOVI

There is a unique African system of consultation by means of vegetables that is practiced in central Africa (Tonga). The system is based on the factor of six and on four pairs of segments (lines) that are either broken (equivalent to the feminine lines of the I Ching) or whole (equivalent to the masculine lines of the I Ching). But contrary to the I Ching, the broken lines correspond to the value *one* and the whole lines to the value *two*. It consists of making the remainders of sixteen walnuts that pass quickly from one hand to another.

The remainders can be either one walnut and in this case would constitute a broken segment equaling *one*, or two nuts and a whole segment equaling *two*. The result is null when there are no remainders. It seems that the rest depends on the operator's mantic sensitivity so that they "feel" when the walnut or the two walnuts must be held at rest.

Sixteen nuts correspond to sixteen figures (in comparison with sixty-four hexagrams of the I Ching). Signs or combinations of solid lines and broken lines correspond to the number of nuts: sixteen. The signs are called *afan du* or even *kpoli*. For every afan du there are sixteen possible combinations of the four lines. From the 256 (16 × 16) combinations the operator or *bokonon* draws quite simple horoscopes with regard to the virtues of plants and animals.

We see how the idea of a mantic system based on combinations of masculine and feminine lines has also come to different people far apart from each other, distant in space and time and from different cultures.

THE SUBLIMATION OF MERCURY

Sublimation or the evolution of Mercury in the alchemical stages has its reference in the macrocosm in the formation of the world by the Logos (see the beginning of the Gospel of John). The Logos is united with the Matrix—itself emanated from the Principle—and from this union derives the World. Therefore, the emanation from the Logos-Matrix is reconciled with the creation that is the product of the union of the two.

In the ternary context, the Logos is conceivable as the third term of the action of the First Principle on the Matrix, an aspect highlighted by Kremmerz in *The Hermetic Door*, but in a more general philosophical and not specifically creationist sense. Moreover, the ternary of creation becomes evident as Logos + Matrix = World. In this sense the Logos, that is to say, Mercury—ontologically the third principle, hierarchically second—is considered active, due to its homologous nature to the first.

But creation is a quaternary, that is, structurally composed of two positive principles: the One or the Absolute, and the World, its complete mirror, even if fogged, and of two negatives: a black matrix or negative—that cannot be modified and that acts as a support to the positive action—and a white negative (Mercury); these hermaphrodites, since they undergo the action of the positive as the second negative of the ternary deriving from the One, change into a positive (World).

The example is the metal (Mercury) that is red-hot and placed on an anvil (Matrix) and forged by the hammer (One) and thus becomes a

La sublimazione del Mercurio

positive or a worked piece that "conceptually" reproduces the action (of the hammer). In this sense, Mercury is passive.

These two aspects are reproduced in the alchemical work. As active, Mercury, in creation, determines a progressive identification and growth of images, hand in hand with the growth of monads by phagocytic* means. The more complex and vital monads reach the human soul and from this—continuing the densification of the image—we pass to the growth of images in relation to the development of the astral bodies. The hemisphere of the hyliac plane pairs up with the hemisphere of the astral plane, in a fixed or, so to speak, corporeal state. Then the "first stage" of immortality is achieved.

As passive, Mercury goes through a whole series of shifts from the first fluidic state of its detachment from the One. Forming the Creation, *ab invertendo*† at the maximum purity within the Absolute, which corresponds to the maximum of impurity in the monad enmeshed in the

---

*Phagocytosis: the process of a single (monadic) cell engulfing, consuming, and completely absorbing another cell.

†*Ab invertendo*: inverting.

World. Progressively this impurity fades with the evolution of consciousness. From the human condition, the erosion of Mercury continues; it becomes more and more flexible, increasingly mediating between "gods" and "man."

The same passage of reasoning to intuition is a passive branching of Mercury itself. And sublimation is accentuated in successive grades as it goes to marry with the so-called solar manifestations that sublimate it to the maximum. It is in the terms of these premises and from the operational point of view that the first part of magic is so-called eonic. And this operation is "expressed" clearly by Khunrath.*

First, the Mercury needs to be considered, in its passive manifestation and subsequent operations, as a mixture to be placed in a passive position concerning Eros. From this point of view, what has been said by Kremmerz, contradictorily on chasteness, makes reasonable sense. Chastity can be a relative means of purification, as long as it remains limited in time to avoid incurring repression and suppression.

In a mental sense, it means that the position of the mixture must be initially chaste and therefore relatively passive. It corresponds to the passive Mercury with respect to the thrust of the Sun (Mars-Sun) that urges it from the inside as it progressively makes its way through the layers that keep it bound. That is what Kremmerz says, in *The Hermetic Door*, that eonic magic corresponds only to the first part of that magic— the purifying, mystical, purely hyliac one.

In truth, such magic would imply such a magical (Isiac) intensity that it would soon be able to perceive the eons sensitively. The first impact is vibratory and is the effect of the first push to initiation given by the inner Sun or fire (*pyr*), whence the pyronic state. But, as the Sun insists on pushing, then the eon no longer feeds solely on the mental-alimentary effluvia of the mixture, but in a certain sense passes to merge with the Matrix as an astral representation.

And like the mixture, stimulated by the eon, it secretes a double (hermaphroditic) Mercurial-Lunar fluid, so also the Matrix stimu-

---

*See Heinrich Khunrath, *Amphitheatrum Sapientiae Aeternae*, 1609.

lated by the secreted mixture, thé so-called Lunar fluids, produced by pyro-states.

The ternary is characterized by: positive *Mercury fluids*, *Lunar fluids* (of Mercury) white negative, *Lunar fluids* (of the Matrix) black negative. This nourishment also constitutes a principle of distillation—of Mercury—made compulsively and not actively. To a sufficient degree of purification, the distilled Mercury increases in subtlety, and the eon has extinguished its alimentary incentive; the fluids are turned toward the inside of the circle, and the image is no longer connected to the eon.

The phase is pre-solar. In this, the Sun presses from the inside on Mercury that always passively expands in the purification-distillation under pressure. The dominion over Mercury is given, therefore, by the image that represents the progressive sublimation of the strata that is peripheral to the Solar plane. The mystes has to resolve in a passive mental attitude to facilitate the greater purification-sublimation of Mercury, which, so to speak, reinforces the image of the pre-solar, precursor of the solar one. A shy bellow of the mythical bull of Mithras may also appear; it must increase and the passive state will find its counterpart in the phenomenon of the Green Lion, which is Mars reaching the extreme of exhaustion. True, then it has been resurrected, like a phoenix rising from its ashes.

In the solar phase, the passive cycle of Mercury reaches its end because its legs are cut off and it is ingested by the Sun, freed from the Mercurial prison. The images or figures within the realm of the solar plane possess their unique vision, independent from other landscapes. They exert their influence on the adept, guiding them through all their endeavors.

Consider therefore that Mercury is in its hermaphroditic nature in its passive aspect, secreting fluids, distilled by hand, and is "pushed" as though it were from the Sun or Mars-Sun. In its active aspect, however, in the various magical cycles, up to solar (considered as a principle), Mercury has to be seen philosophically in the aspect of intelligence—of will, ascent.

When the mystes draws near to a source of gnosis, he begins to separate from complexes of habits, customs, ideas; he already exercises a will as a measure of activity—detachment and research. And in seeking the image of the lunar plane, the image of the lemur fades and the detachment from this plane is a positive outcome moving toward understanding and the prejudicial understanding of the occult structure of man.

The four planes correspond to the four principles-elements that are disposed to form a triple circle: externally the Saturnian body, mediating the Lunar body and therefore internally the Mercurial body; while in a central position resides the Solar body as a nucleus. This structure has to be transmuted in such a way as to determine *in fieri** a scission: Saturn and Luna on one side, Mercury and Sol on the other, connected by the Glorious Body of all the alchemical-Hermetic traditions, which at the same time is transformed by Sol-Mercury and from the synthesis of Luna-Saturn . . . "after death."

Thus, Sol must emerge liberated and glorious and, through this, all the manifestations within and upon matter find philosophical elucidation by the changed occult structure of being. Sol and its attendant occult powers are not bound by the constraints of matter; they now effortlessly transmute and wield authority over it, bridging the separation between bodies and operating in seamless and uninterrupted continuity.

Pre-solar eonic magic and solar initiation alone do not enact such a transmutation, which instead unfolds through a lengthy sequence of "operations," not to mention lifetimes. Nevertheless, it remains essential to refine the structure of the three circles, allowing the three bodies to purify themselves and become translucent, thereby preventing them from hindering the ascent of Sol. In other words: the action of Mercury on the three bodies and on itself as a prison circle of Sol is in anticipation, a reflection of the actual transmutative action of rupture, which will, at the time, be made for the long solar-magic cycle or for longer cycles.

One can also say of detachment of the Sun from the cross, where the north, which is the seat of the spiritual principle in the material

---

*Pending, or in process.

context, must be brought to match the solar core—which is occult—that rises from the point of intersection of the four arms while the Taurus of Mithras bellows. The Mercury, therefore, assumes from the active point of view the initial function of the Universal Solvent.

In the event that the abating of the three fluids have not yet abated—and indeed cannot be the true solution and coagulation of the Glorious Body—it remains a solution and coagulation in relation to the walls of the circles. These walls become porous, allowing the projection of various bodies toward the still intermittent affirmation of Sol.

In the second stage, therefore, of the eonic magic, the one in which the Matrix is evoked, the Mercury, in its fluidity, has a dual active function.

1. It dissolves (+) or purifies the body when desired, utilizing lunar fluids using homologous juices.
2. Or it is fixed (-) to the extent that it attracts the action of the Genie, converging with it throughout the operational process.

The eon is here considered as passive, while in the aspect of passivity of Mercury it is seen as active—the guardian of images on the astral plane. The passivity of the eon must always be understood in relation to the complex magical mechanism, which is, per se free and active: on the hylic plane, it merely functions to bolster the evolutionary process in alignment with its genial nature. Those who believed they have a slave in the "eon" would remain bitterly disillusioned (as happened to many of the Myriam's faithful).

Naturally, Saturn also undergoes the purifying action of Mercury, flowing in projection in the Matrix, no longer as passive to Mars-Sun but active in combination with Mars, that is, Mars-Mercury. Then even a female eon can be used advantageously. However, the perception of the image is not necessary for operational purposes, nor is it necessary to "see" the eon to work with it. In this case, however, it will be necessary to rely on the magisterium from those with greater clairvoyance in the perception of these images.

In the third phase Mercury, like a snake biting its tail, devours itself; that is to say, it softens and renders permeable the third circle, that which holds the Solar core, that is the Mercurial circle, in prison. And thus, in fact, by increasing the distillation initiated by the eon, it more closely knits it up to make it fit to merge with the Sun.

Mars in this phase is joined to Mercury and in a certain sense devours it, that is, it consumes it and prepares the cutting off of the legs as illustrated by the *Mutus Liber*. Naturally, the transitions from the Lunar-Isiac phase to the pre-Solar phase occur gradually and without proper eonic activism. This is because it's impossible to determine beforehand the exact point of Mercury's sublimation, beyond which there's no longer any contact with the eon, or the precise moment when the mystes can fix a mental image without the assistance of the Genie.

In the 'pre-Solar' phase, there is the period of the Green Lion, which is marked by a crisis of Mars transitioning from its union with Mercury to its union with the Sun. During this time, Mars or Leo must undergo mortification, as depicted by the alchemists of the 1600s.* "Mars derived from Saturn, will have death . . ." indicating a phase that was also referred to as mortification by the alchemists.

At a certain point, therefore, the bellowing Taurus, or if you want, the Red Lion, makes its roar heard: which is the *red* work embarking on the "Dry Path." When Mars-Mercury and Sol unite, then Mercury is completely distilled or changed into mist. Belonging to the "dry path," which is not a conclusion but rather a commencement—involving countless alternations of colors: black, green, white, citrine, red—two distinct aspects will persist:

- the passive aspect involving the dissolution of the three circles that confine Sol within (within subsequent solar separators)
- the active aspect involving the coagulation of the Glorious Body

---

*[Probably referencing the anonymous author of the *Mutus Liber* that was published in La Rochelle in 1677.—*Trans.*]

Just as the silk cocoon must be dissolved in hot water to be unwound and then spun, so the three circles with their associated connections* must be dissolved in the Mercurial lake to be returned to their essence as threads. The alchemist says: "To make the heart content and delighted, transform the blond desert into a lake."

Let it be clear that, when it is said that Sol comes out at the end of the pre-Solar cycle, when we speak of a "further liberation" of Sol, we mean an ever-greater nobility, an ever-greater power, an ever-greater projection of Sol. The first emergence must be understood as a first step toward the liberation of Sol and that the path is extremely laborious and very long. Also, then, with Sol there is an action to purify and transform it, to make it fit to be received, to match the Glorious Robe.

The passages of Sol from the commingling with Mercury to its purification, as gold of the alchemists, are many because Sol contains the individual with all his historical background, which must be amended, settled, so to speak, karmically, so that the influence of ancestors is not exercised to the detriment of the evolution of the ascending individual.

The sublimation and distillation of Mercury can also be considered from the point of view of a binomial polarity. The bipolar separation is a fundamental law of nature and the universe: above there is the subtle, the noble, and below the thick, the ignoble; above the macrocosm, below the microcosm. Everything in nature is polarized: chemical reactions and the unfolding of ideas are subject to the law of bipolarity. The bipolar is duality that arises after the One has doubled into Logos and Matrix: the bipolarity is the structure that bodies and thoughts take to exist and act in the World, in Saturn.

Hence, in magic, after having expressed with the pentacle (five-pointed star) the uniqueness of thought and the magical will, we proceed to the hexacle, that is to say, the two intersecting triangles, one pointing upward and the other downward.

---

*[This refers to the albedo process, which dissolving the separateness of the three bodies (Saturn, Luna, Mercury) into the Mercurial and integrating them into Sol (essence).—*Trans.*]

Now, with the principle established concerning Mercury's refinement in the process of chemical work according to the universal law of the movement of the third principle (based on hierarchical placements), one can metaphorically liken Mercury in Saturn to a well where, in a state of stillness or naturalness, fish or humanimal lemurs swim. Initiation is like an initial stirring that, when cold, stirs and agitates the waters of the well: some spray of water will aid the gentle natural evaporation of the water itself.

Eonic magic, in the phase understood as lunar, can be represented as a boiling and relative evaporation of water; the eons are benefited (of the same vibratory nature in the various degrees) by that water, and they stimulate the further evolution "of the well." In the gross comparison, the fish-lemurs remain to swim below.

The tip of the triangle turned upward acts as the neck of the alembic and in the pre-Solar phase, the steam rises in the retort, passing the eons. The draft in the tip of the lower triangle in the well causes the pre-Solar "operations" to proceed (pre-Solar because it precedes the appearance of the Red Lion), and the level of the water falls in the well. At a certain point, the water is all projected into the upper alembic and in the lower remains the simulacrum of the work of draining the well. This is the moment of transition to the Solar phase. We pass from the so-called "wet" path of the alchemists to the dry path.

With this, we see the error of those who, writing without knowing about alchemy, suggest that there are two distinct paths in alchemy: one is wet, the other is dry, while instead, they are two successive cycles. Moreover, the passage of the initiate through the various planes—from the lemuric to the lunar, from this to the mercurial, and from this to the solar—does not mean that when he reaches the upper plane that he cannot descend to the lower one. They comprise all of the powers—and the major is not to the detriment of the minor—as well as starting, in absolute terms, a conclusion of the Work, since in the infinite projection of the Being in ascension the different phases described alchemically repeat themselves in the different objectives and cycles.

JUNE 28, 1966

ON THE PRINCIPLE OF MERCURY

In alchemical operations, the Mercurial principle is closely associated with the Martial principle. Already in the first phase of the Work—when the Gold or the Sun is hidden—the distinction between the Solar sphere and the Mercurial-Martial sphere is highlighted.

In this first phase, the Mercury-Mars action constitutes the Green Lion of the alchemists. The lion symbolizes the Martial force; the Green (Lion), of the lower elementary state of Mercury, and psychologically corresponds to intelligence, still vulgar, but already in an evolutionary mode.

The Work occurs intuitively only when the Green Lion is in agony. This agony is an exhaustion of forces, which psychologically corresponds to the exhaustion of all sophisms and equivocal dialectics in metaphysical investigation and, technically, to such a refinement of Mercury that it neutralizes Mars. Mars must succumb to the struggle with Saturn . . . that is, in a physical context the vulgar martial actions must be exhausted to allow them rise again as a fraction (1/7) of the "peacock's tail" or "alchemical rainbow" complex.

The secondary nature of the Martial principle with respect to the Solar principle ontologically results from the very fact that in the beginning the Sun is eclipsed in . . . Mercury. These by double negation are eclipsed in Saturn, to rise again as Apollo. The expression is therefore valid: Apollo = Sun + Mercury + Mars.

MEMORANDUM ON THE SECOND WOOD OF LIFE

The psychological-psychokinetic-magical problem, and so forth, of an initiate resides in CONSTRUCTING first, then MAINTAINING, in good condition, the SECOND WOOD of LIFE or fluidic body, which to the common man is an inarticulate block, evanescent and compressed between the MERCURIAL SPIRIT on one side and the FLUIDIC BODY or lunar (of which it is an emanation) and the PHYSICAL BODY on the other.

Within the initiate, this body primarily exists in a state of CONDENSATION, initially resembling a partial floating state in the post-mortem period before transitioning into the passive involution state of a SPORE.

A notable instance of this nature occurred with the late Vigliani. Kremmerz claimed to have corresponded with Vigliani after the latter's death, communicating as equals while Vigliani persisted as a non-terrestrial entity. This postmortem communication lasted for a period before Vigliani's presence faded away. According to Kremmerz, Vigliani expressed regret about his life and lamented missed opportunities. This transition led him to what Kremmerz refers to as the FIXED STAR state, denoting the initial stage of ascension in operative prayer, described as ascending "as a spiral to the sky of miracles." This concept outlined in Kremmerz's *The Hermetic Door* signifies the Integrated Human, which to the four bodies has incorporated the quintessence or fifth body or the intermediary GLORIOUS BODY, or AMPOULE. This refers to the fluidic body detached from the Lunar envelope and condensed into a realized fluidic substance through operative processes.

The problem is no longer to CONSTRUCT this state but to keep it POROUS, ELASTIC, and FLUIDIC, that is, permeable to the passage between the vulgar mind—BRAIN—as well as the lower occult body (the EGO of psychoanalysis and the physical body) and MERCURY + SOLAR + SPIRIT, or the superior mind.

It follows the dual function of the fixed fluidic body as:

(*a*) a TRANSMITTER of ideas of impulses of willed imagery.

(*b*) an OBSTRUCTOR of these images, when it is necessary to place oneself in a STATUESQUE state (see IZAR*) in relation to human sensations and listen to the VOICE of the SPIRIT.

---

*[Reference is made to a passage of the reserved text *Corpus Philosophicum Totius Magiae* where Kremmerz refers to a parable stated by his Master Izar Bne Escur that an initiate must become statuesque, that is inert like a stone on the outside, in order for the subtle body to liberate from its physical casing and receive input from the spirit realm.—*Trans.*]

If, for any reason, the intermediary body undergoes changes such as an alteration, contamination, or depletion, it results in the emergence of an INCOMPLETE AVATAR. In this state, the function served by the intermediary is only partially fulfilled and incomplete. In severe cases, this can lead to what is commonly referred to as mental illness, which is instead rooted in the occult fluidic body.

JUNE 1962

ON THE BIPOLARITY AND EMANATION OF CREATION

The expression "free will" is improper and tautological. The concept of "action"—in the notion and meaning not related to motion, but material activities—is instead properly opposed to the concept of "fate" as a dialectical opposition. Anthropocentrism is a Jewish-Christian vision of the world in which the individual is not only the center of the universe but where the creative sequence is gratuitously interrupted; the image and likeness of God are inserted immanently in the causal chain that exists for the cosmos escaping the "fatality."

The act-action of Liberation cannot be understood to be other than as a primordial moment or rather the original passage of the Monad from the negative-undifferentiated-inert state to the positive-differentiated-incarnational state in the quaternary—it cannot reasonably be conceived to be other than as the initial conversion from the unconscious to the conscious.

The soul, evolving from the Monad, develops and breaks the causal chain, as is its prerogative, making the future more or less conditional. Furthermore, considering the Ternary: Action + Fact + Contingency, it becomes clear that in truth there is in fact no Absolute Action! Understood as pure free will. Therefore, in a future event, in gestation, there is an interplay of three factors, only one of which is "free" per se, although in fact it has been already conditioned in comparison to the other two.

The Christ-centric excess in revelation has given rise to Christians—proponents of unipolar generation— drawing their doctrine from Jewish exoteric doctrines. They aim to assert the unity of both doctrines in their generative concept, highlighting the benevolent superiority of the God-Father and the God-Son over the One, which is perceived as displaying an indifferent and incomprehensible nature toward the faithful.

It is evident how Neoplatonism, already a priori, appeared fatally defeated on the level of dissemination, while on the philosophical level it denounced its own shortcomings in the face of the Nicene symbol of a Ternary, which is closer to Pythagoreanism (at least exoterically) than to Platonism. The descent from a first principle = spirit to the ultimate principle = matter, though depicted by cosmic analogies of successive and further condensations, does not prove to solve the problem of how and why the involutional process of energy into matter occurred and takes place! However, the natural sciences fail to explain the mechanisms and causes behind the aggregations and disintegrations, the emergence of phenomena as a whole, and the ultimate origin and driving force of universal will.

"Pythagorean" Hermeticism acknowledges that progressive condensation proceeds from the principle, but objects to the possibility that the creative work—in emanationist terms—offers an experimental connection, an analogical motive to make itself intelligible and to reproduce itself relative to the microcosm-man, to find that reality above any opinion or purely scientific-theoretical hypothesis.

The emanationist and unipolar solution is therefore agamic!* It posits a creative will or indifferent automatism as the First Principle—One—and God the Father would project the creation without undergoing any modification. It would create without necessitating a preceding act of creation, as it is inherently pregnant with subsequent creative processes by virtue that is beyond expression.

And this is not a solution, but leads back to the constant misunderstanding of every rationalistic form of the real nature of the One, which is a law and not an entity! If it were an entity, a further agamic arcana would be conceivable—beyond comprehension—not that the

---

*[*Agama* is a Sanskrit word meaning "a traditional doctrine/precept," "collection of doctrines," or "handed down and fixed by tradition—*Trans*]

derogation by the One from the universal law of attraction, created by itself, would have to be explained. The One, synonymous with the First Principle or God the Father, or whatever term one chooses, embodies a Law, not an Entity. Therefore, it inherently avoids violation of the principles of its laws, as it allows for a certain degree of contradiction. In other words, a law manifests and evolves according to its nature, avoiding arbitrary outcomes. Otherwise, it wouldn't truly be a law.

Well, given that the universal law has two phases, (1) Union = attraction, and (2) Dissolution (splitting) = repulsion, this law reveals by the retracing of its primordial manifestation that it cannot violate itself in the unipolarity of its agamic generation. Therefore, at the origin of the world lies a "bipolar split" preceding the act of creation: the constituent splitting of potential creation, just as the separate virile and feminine gametes* constitute the potential for a generation until they are united.

The Hindu doctrine expresses this law in an astrophysical image . . . in Brahman, as in the Sun, "spots" or areas of obscurity are determined, in their turn determining—with regard to the general solar or Brahmanic splendor—the alternation between shadow/light and good/bad, in which occurs the creation of life, understood as "alternation" and therefore "vibration."

But the symbol, however picturesque and exoteric, does not explain the quaternary structure of the Cosmos nor how the Force of Creation is translated into reality with the same laws of nature. Another problem that troubles the emanationist doctrines is that of the limitation of the unlimited principle, that is, of the creation of the world! For if the generation is unipolar, to argue that the final point of arrival is matter is more about posing the problem, rather than solving it. Assuming that the emanationist motion of the One is directed toward a final point of condensation . . .

- or the preexisting condensation end point, and not the One, but an unsustainable Duality would hold the universe *ab aeterno*.

---

*[Germ cells—*Trans.*]

One could not strictly speak of creation but movement within an existing world, as always existing;

• or the point here has been generated by the One . . . and it is necessary to adapt to the notion of actual creation, preceded by a potential.

The phenomenal unfolding of the four principles in the universe is necessarily preceded by a binary development. Mathematically at 4 we arrive only by computation—that is through 2 and 3.

Numerical abstraction exactly expresses that:

1. the world is constituted based on the four elements; constructive perfection is given by 4, in the sense that Creation is not if not in 4; and

2. consequently, 2 is in preparation for the creation and as such precedes the ontological development of the principles.

The application of the ontological criterion to the binary and quaternary arrangements shows how the Grand Binary Arrangement (potential egg of Creation) includes and conditions the entire development of the Quaternary Arrangement.

It configures and conditions it, not only because it proceeds in a logical sense, but also because that same motion (affirmed and not explained by Platonic emanationism in Judaism, Christianity, and Islam) repeats its origin in reality, in an ontological sense, from the attraction that the primordial Two = Female exerts on the primordial One = Male first principle, which it conditions and limits.

MEMORANDUM ON PERFUMES

This discusses which essences to burn for effective translation into the astral realm. It should be noted that perfumes or liquids can be supplementary for purification with ablutions, and so forth, but they cannot replace those for burning.

Sol
Sunday—solar genii.

Holly (or any pine, etc.): dry the leaves or needles, then crush or finely chop them for easier handling. Or else macerate the natural *resins* and *rubber* of trees or even the real and proper Arabic gum in granules.

Luna
Monday—lunar genii.

Be aware that lunar genii have two manifestations.

1. Luna-Proserpina genii are excited erotically or by human passions; use *moss* (or a plant that grows in damp places and requires drying) and compare with the scent of musk that the ether (also martial . . .) uses as an aphrodisiac: that can also be perceived by the emanation of female scents that you happen to encounter.

2. Luna-Diana genii are as Kremmerz refers to them, "Sisters of Charity of the Invisible"; that is, the beneficial actions or the true and proper beneficial genii; for them *alga marina* (seaweed) is recommended. The recipe states this also serves as an effective remedy for eye ailments, and to lend credence to tradition, provides relief for bladder issues.

Mars
Tuesdays—martial genii.

Rubber, a yellowish resin (though less than benzoin), possesses strong penetrating properties and solid consistency. The shredded and dried leaves of the Myrtle plant resemble those found in conifers. Juniper, a mild caustic, may even be what dermatologists refer to as the "dust of Sabina," that is a bitter acetic.

Mercury
Wednesdays—mercurial genii.

Mint leaves (see sexual smells, etc.); penetratingly subtle, even a little stunning; needless to say, all of the mints, i.e., peppermint, tree mint, spearmint, etc.; no botanical distinctions are to be made.

Jupiter

Thursdays—jovian genii (non-jovian can be severe too!).

Sandalwood or poplar; wood chips also chopped and burned, etc. They are therapeutic essences for sexual diseases, etc., and are in harmony with jovian medicines, etc.

Venus

Fridays—venereal genii (in the broadest sense, that is: art, form, beauty).

The superior aphrodisiac *benzoin*.

Saturn

Saturdays—saturnian genii.

Myrrh, the biblical gift presented to the infant Jesus by one of the Magi, symbolizing his future sacrifice.

Inferior judges, who are stern but not malevolent, operate in a punitive manner (comparable to the mythological attributes of Saturn and Mars):

Cinnamon: Its intense, pervasive scent evokes notions of judgment. This association extends to various foods like creams, yogurts, and even sweets.

Leaves of *Salix babylonica* (weeping willow) and *Salix decidua*: when fallen and face-down, they represent suffering. These plants symbolize the spiritual entities of the plant world that must endure hardship.

Malefic entities (particularly potent on their designated days and extremely nefarious during wave periods) can be evoked for three purposes.

1. Against enemies: their putrid nature further corrupts human weakness, causing ruin and harm.
2. As negative cosmic elements in rituals: For example, in full moon evocations and advanced theurgic operations, they serve as negative mirrors and discharge points.
3. To banish or remove them from certain situations.

Regarding substances:

Pepper (in powder form) is highly effective, as noted by Kremmerz.

Euphorbia, especially the giant tropical varieties, is significant. This concept extends to all *Euphorbiaceae* (spurges), which secrete a caustic, milky liquid. This substance has unusual effects on grazing animals.

Blood: I believe blood is not practical or advisable. In any case, it is certain that all pagan sacrifices were based on the evocation and taming to appease the evil or irate deities and therefore project the evil and negative aspect, and so on, with animal victims.

Incense and General Purifications to Superior Deities

Here's a warning that must be mentioned: I am not, today as yesterday, enthusiastic about incense. Since it was from the arrogant ignorance of the Nazarenes, it shifted from its original function (inherited from the pagans) to ceremonies aimed upward at the Te Deum, in elevations, etc., to be ignorantly applied to ceremonies for which myrrh would be required according to their own beliefs; and therefore Masses of the Dead, exorcisms, etc.

The incense used so indiscriminately sometimes becomes a vehicle of oppression, of evil, of sadness, of darkness. Use it with caution.

NOVEMBER 1962

ON THE PRINCIPLE OF THE QUATERNARY IN A POLITICAL CONTEXT

This essay was written by Marco Daffi in the 1960s, after a meeting that—through me [Giammaria]—took place in his home in Rome (from around 4:00 p.m. to 6:00 p.m.) with members of the "parliamentary right" then, one of whom, Pino Rauti,* is today party leader.

---

*[Former leader of the Italian post-fascist party Movimento Sociale Italiano (MSI), who died in 2012.—*Trans.*]

FOUR UNIVERSAL PRINCIPLES

FIRE	or	SOUL	or	ESSENCE
AIR	or	INTELLIGENCE*	or	POWER
WATER	or	SENSE	or	MEDIUM†
EARTH	or	BODY	or	MATTER

*Intelligence therefore is also "the radiant power of the same" and equivalent to pure Kantian reason, since the inferior manifestation of Mercury is an adaptation to the relative.

†It is the operational field of action on the three higher forms, in a political sense and "social matter."

The four political categories:

Sovereign

Military

Bourgeoisie

Proletariat‡

We shall clarify the autonomy of the bureaucratic-military caste in complete alignment with the principles of the classic traditional social organization and using the same symbolism of Hermeticism, in relation to the concepts of *Ars Regia* and regality.

It can be said that, given the parallelism between the numbers or rather between the Pythagorean numbers and the cosmic social ontology, *sub specie activitatis*, the four principles can be reduced to two, one active and one passive. Moreover, the effect of the splitting (division) of the First Principle, which, as it determines the creation, is valid as a negative (unconscious).#

‡Not to be confused with the pariahs—the outcasts.

#[This refers to the splitting (dividing) of the Monad into the Dyad, resulting in two components to Being, a conscious (positive) and unconscious (negative). The conscious is transitory, it extinguishes at death whereas the unconscious (negative) remains as the root (Monad) until a new incarnation whereby the Monad splits (divides) into two with the formation of dyadic, (-) unconscious / (+) conscious, unity.—*Trans.*]

It is like saying that the doubling of the First Principle in polarity conditions the active principle in the negative state; and Men in the physical world act unconsciously under the influence of occult archetypes. In these terms, the impure mineral that the alchemists exploited, saying it would crumble like in a crucible under the action of separation in the Hermetic "athanor," must be understood in the sense of bringing back to light, as positive, the primordial negative.

Is not the photograph of a negative, positive? This is the alchemical artifice, as an elaborate reversal; that is, the negation of the negative, to reconstitute the primordial positive to consciousness, which determines the Creation by an automatism not properly positive.

In the alchemical operation, the "created" gold is essentially the positive hemisphere, which naturally combines and merges with the negative hemisphere of the original gold according to the law of affinity. This process is rooted in the Pythagorean numerical law and reflects the duality of Positive and Negative evident in every principle of the universe's four constituents.

In this case, negative is the primordial distribution of the elements, while positive is the integration of the same in the alchemical operation. The alchemical process of bipolar division serves as a metaphor for socio-political transformation. It represents the conscious implementation of the dyadic principles in collective action, mirroring the fundamental law of creation. This process extracts and liberates elevated concepts from the undeveloped masses, much as alchemy refines raw minerals, so that analogously, the incomplete human masses (alchemy-collective raw mineral) are enucleated and released within the higher principles.

From a dynamic point of view, the two inferior categories assume themselves as a singular mass in agitation, and this confusion corresponds in fact to the current situation. There is no categorical separation between the class of employees and that of the so-called free workers but extreme fluidity.

With respect to this, as an ideological path, it is the action of politicians that is expressed on the level of political struggle, while in a position of apparent stasis, but in fact almost emerging from the conflict of Action and Reaction. It is the First Principle that imprints a determined era and the same determined political principle.

The ontology between the sovereign principle on the one hand and the politico-military principle on the other is in perfect correlation with the ontology between thought and action. And we highlight the supremacy of one over the other since the martial principle represents the energetic element that is released by itself unconsciously. An example of this is the Russian Revolution, led by Lenin. Lenin acted on the leveled masses, following the upheaval of tsarist institutions, with a Martial "mysticism," in which political doctrine was not preceded by political action.

The communist doctrine, therefore, agitated by Lenin cannot be considered as a principle corresponding to the hieratic one, but as a pure and simple mysticism promoted according to the Second Principle, which Lenin and the Bolsheviks had intuitively and instinctively adopted. And more specifically, earthly lust of the peasant masses, fomented by Lenin, in an absolute mobilization of force destroyed the previous arrangement founded on the ternary:

- feudal possession, rural community (Mir)
- direct ownership of property

Only later, from the same destructive action, Lenin brought forth the First Principle, namely, the doctrine and organization of the Kolkos and rural collectivism.

METAPHYSICS OF THE RIGHT AND THE LEFT

The political Right as opposed to the Left and the Center (for those who cultivate "traditional studies" it has significance as a reference to values of which it is representative), and the universal principles in their social formulations and their contingent political correspondence, can be reduced to a scheme susceptible to multiple developments, given that the current political-social expressions are those of empirical correspondence in the concrete, regardless of any consideration of merit.

The two principles of the lower castes (third and fourth) are sufficiently determined and identifiable:

Fourth principle—Sudra caste (in India) is the base, the material medium, i.e., physical work, corresponds to the proletariat and the politically "extreme left."

Third principle—Vaisya caste are the producers, farmers, merchants. It is the expedient medium of Luna in the sense of its changeability, or the inferior Mercury of an executive technical intelligence . . . therefore it expresses the middle class as a category as well as the evolved part of the proletariat; the middle class, in short, generally, as professional, bureaucratic forms, excluded from the efficient determination. Politically: the "left" and "center left" parties.

The two superior principles (first and second), on the other hand, in the progress of modern politics, do not have a clear factual distinction.

Second principle—Kshatriya caste is equivalent to chivalrous intelligence; it is important not to conflate this with the bureaucratic-military class.

First principle—Brahmin caste corresponds to a hieratic-royal nature. This concept is often misunderstood due to a flawed notion of "religion" that emerged during times of crisis. As a result, it's often interpreted in a narrow, faith-based sense rather than as a fundamental "value" upon which other values depend for the citizen.

This shows the fact that the Catholic-Christian religion has been identified since the beginning (after the fall of ancient civilization and the "death of the god Pan") with the state apparatus, so much so that it no longer constitutes a "caste" (and of the four, that of families as repositories of national ethical values, but instead they tend to be sectarian and exclusively clerical).

Such a hybridization was determined for which the higher value (hieratic or first principle) was degenerated (badly exercised) by the exponents of the inferior (military-bureaucratic or second principle).

The priest-kings have disappeared and have been replaced by the priests.*

The right will never be effective if it does not redeem itself as a universal value, that is, as the first of the four principles, the regal-hieratic principle. In political terms it can be said that the "betrayal" of Fascism was to deny the force that had taken it to power, that is, to deny the universal value of the stirpes,† to abandon the directive of the spiritual part of the nation to the second principle. That is certainly due to a lack of transparency, not realizing the real power that could have been leveraged.

And it is the same mistake of other "isms" that fell earlier. Yet the "stirpes" had clearly spoken. While a proto-regime (fascism) was spontaneously forming, a liturgy like Shinto—a religious-social form that was certainly a foundation for the regime responsible for the destiny of the nation—could and should have been assumed by Fascism.

The Festival of Trees and National Parks served as indications of this, albeit under the influence of the Catholic Church, even if originally influenced by paganism. Likewise, camp banquets, from which the transition to other similar ceremonies would have been effortless. Just as the ritual summoning of the fallen comrade (Present!), which, starting from mere liturgical invocation, could have evolved into the pagan belief in the continuity of the departed soul within the souls of the living. Not dissimilar to the exaltation of force, which is easily transferable from the physical field of application (truncheon) to the virile one, simply by returning the rod to a vertical position!

A Right that does not degenerate into a reactionary jumble must invoke-evoke the "value" of *religio*, as a class, that is to say, as the first principle of the four principles. Implicitly, though profoundly telling, is

---

*See coincidence with the development of the second principle in the Society of Jesus.
†[That is, aligning and rooting the political principle with the royal principle of lineages, ancestors, and archetypes.—*Trans.*]

the phenomenon of dictators experiencing "fear" when they sense their lack of legitimacy.

Dictators must "fear" when their rule turns illegitimate; however, the legitimacy of power has divine origin and it is not otherwise provided that for the divine it should be understood not as the arbitrariness of the individual, or a tiny minority, but the adaptation of the "sovereign" authority to the reason of the stirpes, hence, to the religio (logos) that is inspired by reason of the stirpes. The question is of principle and has its counterevidence in the facts. And history in this sense is a judge.

It was too late when Fascism instituted the Sacred Rituals of the Fallen, in the evident attempt to constitute a religio of their dead; too late when the heroes now were not a cult to themselves but subjected to the saints of the priestly-bureaucratic cult to be emptied of their limited debt.

However, a comparable successful political strategy would result in a profound shift in the direction of a RIGHT that no longer conserves institutions alien to its own, nor favors bureaucratic consolidation, but instead advocates for a resurgence of true freedom found in legal flexibility and the diversity of cults united under the common principle of national religiosity. It would also lead to an ethical reassessment, with the substitution of the morality of the male (virility) to that of the woman or infants (chastity), and for which the temporary, real abstinence, would not be excluded, indeed would be used as a means to such an end!

In the economic field, a Right, which is not only in name but also in fact, must reevaluate the principle of gain, the aristocratic principle of privilege of the ruling class through an organization of the exchange that transfers from the possibilities of the bourgeoisie (third class) the control of wealth, that is, restores the right to the administration of goods, especially of money, only to those who are entitled, only in principle(!) to enrich and possess. In the juridical field, truly and properly, the Right must set the laws in the interest of the nation, to the detriment of any other interest, which is where the regime erred after the conciliation with the Vatican.

Only in these terms would there be a spiritual climate (alias *"religio"*) initially inspired; legally conditioned, and by nature anti-demagogy. In short, to speak of religio is to speak of an unalterable substratum that remains unaltered in and beyond the apparent freedom of forms, even if it lacks a specific external ritual, even if rooted in the subconscious of the stirpes; but precisely for this reason it is no less as strong!

CONSIDERATIONS ON THE NATURE OF THE ROYAL PRINCIPLE

The traditional king is in a static function, in the sense that it must preserve and protect the specific order by administering it. But if it acts revolutionarily, it becomes a despot, a tyrant, even if outwardly covered with legal forms.

Thus, Peter the Great of Russia, who upset the society of the time and laid the premises of the Red Revolution, by not having maintained the traditional constitution in its established order. You could say that he was a Bolshevik *ante litteram*.

That is to say, either the king is assumed as the head of a priesthood, synonymous with tradition and thus viewed as a hierophant, or he is perceived as the representative of a priesthood that upholds tradition (divine right), thereby seemingly superior in power to the priesthood but ultimately subservient to it.

A prime illustration is found in the case of the pharaohs, where the most prominent among them were initiated into the high-ranking priesthood, while those lacking in spiritual insight and profane were relegated to mere followers or dissenters.*

Within the era of the Roman Empire, Octavian Augustus established himself as a typical figure of a pontiff, with a sceptre. The most drastic measures that provide for the protection of Roman society were taken not as imperator but as pontifex maximus.† Equally noteworthy is the example of the Doge of the Republic of Venice.

Moreover, as a paradigm of universal order, the influence of Marxist

---

*See Amenofi IV, Akhenaten, heretical predecessor of Tutankhamun.
†See Exile of the "profaner" Ovid.

doctrine on bourgeois-Czarist society acted as a catalyst in molding the political environment of its time, demanding critical-exegetical scrutiny as a secondary principle. It was only subsequently that the Leninist and Stalinist methods established the state's course, embodying an efficacious primary principle, regardless of any reservations about its spiritual import.

In summary: negatively, the First Principle (as consciousness and doctrine) arises from the action-force of a Second Principle upon an affected mass (matter) or Third Principle. Conversely, positively, it is thought that determines action!

ON THE LEGITIMACY OF GOVERNMENT

The legitimate king is the one who is and remains in the order of a tradition. The invocation of the monarch to repeat his investiture by divine grace is not (as is commonly thought) an arbitrary and despotic affirmation, but a real limitation of sovereignty based on a *quid* rather than the will of the sovereign and superior. That *quid* is properly called "tradition." And a traditional king cannot just because of such do violence to the spirit of the stirps, nor reform a *religio*, nor act contrary to the natural structure of the governed people.

Philosophically, every idea contains the seed of a preceding idea, akin to the Solar Principle (Gold), but in the endeavor of realization, there exists the concept of transcending it. And while circumscribing the analysis to the simple chain of theoretical deductions, the new idea necessarily passes through the first stage of impurity: that is, it corresponds to the moment of criticism, proper to every philosophy, while only later does the apologetics of the new philosophical idea arise in a phenomenology, that is, analogous to that of the purification-sublimation of the Second Principle, to that of the First Principle.

Mars is in the critical struggle against a previous "thought." The very idea of force implies impurities because only on the rhetorical level, where resistance can be given, does it have any reason to be an effort. Within the Solar plane, the Negative principle (in absolute terms, not solely because it opens to various realms of becoming), necessitates a self-imposed limitation of the entity or essence itself, devoid of any inherent resistance.

Analogously, sovereignty, as the guardian and bearer of the spiritual legacy of the lineage, asserts itself through the very concept it embodies in service. Through this, the philosophical demonstration of the truth of Magic is revealed.

To say in fact that an idea imposes itself on itself is to recognize its "imaginal" nature that shapes and adapts in its realization to the conscious physical order. The idea is not merely a rational contagion or a resonance of gray matter, but rather a mold (form) capable of manifesting in mystical-ecstatic experiences as well as cerebral vibrations.

The essence of the military-political Warrior is demonstrated and realized through force. Being on a relatively lower level, he lacks the "virtue" inherent in the hieratic nature required to actualize the idea, representing a diminution or adaptation of the idea conveyed to him from the higher absolute plane.

2

Confidential and Philosophical Letters

On Initiation, Alchemy, and Conscious Existence

Prologue to Part Two

Despite the differences in their respective methods of art, the *Epistolario Filisofico* (Philosophical Letters) document the laboratory work of Marco Daffi's "collaboration" with Giammaria. Daffi was drawn more to rituality as a means to enter into magical space, whereas Giammaria followed a more austere approach of direct consciousness that excluded rituality. The essays in this volume consist of the decade-long epistolary correspondence between Marco Daffi and his Genovese collaborator and fellow Hermeticist, Giammaria. The *Epistolario Filisofico* is composed of forty-four extracts, from twenty-seven letters covering a time span that ranges from 1957 to 1968 and is presented in an informal discursive format rather than with philosophical formality. The material addresses a wide spectrum of topics on initiation, from gnosis, avatars, eros, divination, and metaphysics to transcendent consciousness. Giammaria points out this material is suited more for adepts who have dirtied their hands in the Work rather than for idle doctrinaires, since those who have direct experience in the laboratory are better equipped to draw from certain intuitions.

In other words, the material is testimony to significant research and elucidations, in operational terms, on a series of discoveries including elaborations on the double astral, reverse astral imprints, monadic phagocitosis, double syzygy, muliebral or women's initiation, and on the spiritual avatar.

On the other hand, in doctrinal terms lengthy observations regarding initiation, initiatic orders, astral entities, and the magnetic-fluidic nature of creation are illuminated, while the "Kremmerzian" citations are intriguing for their singular takes on the hieratic nature of the Master (Kr.). In summary, the collection of "Philosophical Letters" is an eloquent testimony, for the form in which it is presented, on the continuity and actuality of this distinct alchemical-Hermetic tradition in the late twentieth century.

In many ways, for the breadth and depth of the material covered, the *Epistolario Filisofico* represents some of Daffi's most illuminating insights and articulations of his gnostic ascension. Daffi pays tribute in these articles to the creative impulse of the Hermetic practitioner embodying the dignity of a Renaissance magus—*homo faber*—man as *artifex* who makes, creates, and forms reality. In the literature of ancient Rome, Appius Claudius Caecus makes use of this term in his *Sententiae*, referencing the differentiated man (vir) as artifex of his destiny and his surroundings: *Homo faber suae quisque fortunae* ("Each man is the architect of his fortune").

The *Epistolario Confidenziale* are extracts from thirty-one letters written by Marco Daffi to Giammaria, between 1953 and 1969, and which document their decades-long correspondence. Presented in chronological order, the material covers a variety of topics from personal observations to esoteric problems the two initiates were working on in their respective *officinae*. These extracts are seasoned with a more conversational tone than what is found in the "Philosophical Letters." The letters are replete with *ad personam* passages and provide a window into the world of the magi: their lifestyle and *"tenore di vita"* emerge from behind the scenes to the foreground and are based in a uniquely Occidental context of magical praxis. Central to this praxis is the primacy of cultivating a purified form of amor (divine love), that ascending force that inspired Dante in the last verse of his divine opera to name it the force that moves the suns and the stars and raises the vibrational frequency to a state of sublimity that Kremmerz calls the state of MAG. Ezra Pound alludes to the same point, *sotto 'l velame de li versi strani* of the *Pisan Cantos*:

> *What thou lovest well remains,*
> > *the rest is dross*
> *What thou lov'st well shall not be reft from thee*
> *What thou lov'st well is thy true heritage.*
> > > CANTO LXXXI

Epistolario Filosofico
(Philosophical Epistolary)

Extracts of the Hermetic Laboratory

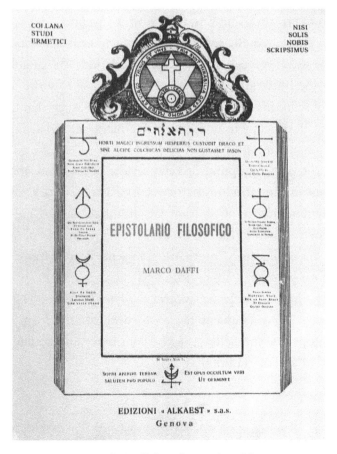

Epistolaria Folosofico, edited by
Giammaria (Edizioni Alkaest, 1980).

INTRODUCTION

Giammaria

I submit this text as an expression and record, albeit partial, of my "collaboration" with Marco Daffi, from letters written between 1957 and 1968 which in his honor I've collected, organized, and pruned of any sign of personal reference, and extracted from the context as he wrote about alchemical Hermeticism, despite the diversity of our respective methods or approaches in art.

It is, in truth, for the most part more for adepts than for doctrinaires, because whoever has dirtied their hands in the Work can draw directly from certain intuitions, truly proper inventions, in operational terms, that constellate the epistolary. They include insights on the astral double, the astral reversal, monadic phagocitation,* the double syzygy, and feminine initiation. That Marco Daffi chose to write about the principle of feminine initiation remains a *rara avis*, such that not even a single essay, in the copious literature of Hermeticism and alchemy, links back to woman's initiation.

From the doctrinal point of view, on the other hand, the pointed observations on initiation, initiatory orders, astral entities, and on the electromagnetic nature of creation are illuminating and not only for unwary novices; while, for the record, the "Kremmerzian" mentions, when not dispensing spicy information, in general, constitute a precious record "of his persona."

Ergo, we have here, the *Epistolario Filisofico* by Marco Daffi, which in summary, are an eloquent testimony and, for the form in which they are proposed, compelling, in the continuity and actuality of the alchemical-Hermetic tradition.

---

*[The process of absorbing and devouring the consciousness of singular beings (monads) at the time of death into the One (Universal Consciousness) and hence losing continuity of consciousness for future rebirths. This fate awaits those souls in the postmortem who drink from the river of Lethe and are destined for oblivion.—*Trans.*]

INITIATION

December 26, 1959

It is not the avatar that precedes the GLORIOUS BODY, but the opposite.

The stages of initiation are roughly:

1. mental formation, an Isiac psychology (the corresponding investigation, so to speak, of *a forma mentis*: not this–not that, as in the Buddha of legends);
2. receiving an Isiac initiation and, in the first phase, adherence to a center or circle or chain;
3. recourse to progressive means of purification up to a minimum of eonic perception or of fluidic sensitivity;
4. entry into Isiac magic;
5. acquisition of a solar initiation, which at first is conditioned, as pre-solar, by the presence of one or more eons. In this series, there are all the phases indicated by the alchemists, such as to whiten the Latona,* that is, to purify the body, the lunar, etc., cooking the lunar fluids, etc.;
6. the true and proper cooking of the alchemical vessel to meticulously separate the subtle from the fixed, the crude from the pure;
7. as the cooking persists; the resulting alchemical black residue resembles the act of skimming the top layer of the broth.

These are psychological states, sometimes extending to the "psychiatric," of anguish, of doubt, of the regurgitation of desires, and experiences from previous existences, of all that, in short, that boils in the pot of our vessel. Up to this point, the separation is only virtual and

---

*Greek mythological figure whom the alchemists personified as the goddess Latona, who along with Jupiter was the parent of Apollo. In operational terms, Latona refers to a natural alloy of gold and silver resembling brass or bronze, also philosophical gold, which is the unclean body of raw material of the Philosopher's Stone that must be cleansed of its impurities (Lyndy Abraham, *A Dictionary of Alchemical Imagery*).

therefore it is not the formation of the Second Body of Life, since a PURIFICATION is necessary to begin this work. Too quickly, the so-called orange coloration manifests itself, that is to say, the false powers of the psyche, the illusions, the hopes, soon denied by the disappointments and often by the reactions, negative, to the unwary.

Only after purifying the LATONA, from *latten-terra*, that is, one's proper occult (and also physical) center can one begin the preparation of the Glorious Body.

However, the Glorious Body does not yet mean consciousness of the astral self; one must ANOINT* it as one does for withered leather.

The state of avatar being the relative culmination of an outward motion (evasion of the physical body). Before realizing the avatar you will have to digest other experiences. After that, you can start the fixation of the human-animal couple and prepare the transition to a future birth. And it would be correct to say that the passage is also letting oneself be attracted—to submit, more than to force the passage.

Isiac or passive remnants are always re-pulling in the stages of being. Before attaining so much, there is a relative, conscious, postmortem buoyancy. It is a question of long and arduous experiences, real labors of Heracles, to escape from one's body in a state of fervor.

And yet it does not fully realize the powder of projection. This aspect has innumerable different levels; in a certain sense, the initial and prolonged transmutation of the body is indirect. It stems from the connection with the self-image, or projections from others already present in the astral; therefore it is a reflex action with obviously still limited or reflected results.

---

*[Smear or rub with oil, typically as part of a religious ceremony, such as "high priests anointed with oil." Daffi uses the term *ungere* which literally means to lubricate, oil, or grease parched leather. Analogically, the term refers to the initiatic process of loosening the band between the Hermetic bodies (solar, mercury, lunar) with the hylic shell for the purpose of integrating the disparate Hermetic bodies into a whole, the unified body of light or Siren. Essentially, the process involves the art of metamorphosis, where the mystes transforms into an initiate with a relaxed yet alert disposition and centered in a unified mind-feeling-ethereal consciousness complex that can easily separate from and slip out of its hylic shell.—*Trans.*]

To this extent, we are still *acting on ourselves*. Not that there aren't further possibilities, but the real powder of projection is not yet formed. Projecting into different forms is essentially docetic,* in the sense that a given form is not absorbed, but is reproduced as in a frame of film.

Magic involves the creation *ex novo* and not simply absorption (albeit from simple forms) of vitality, and CREATION of a new form, whether enduring, transient, or summoned spontaneously at will.

December 1962

Among the different points of view under which initiation can be considered is that of an inner revulsion which, today, is seen in terms of depth psychology (in fact it pertains to a median state of personalized Being). There is a certain correspondence between that which among the alchemists is called ALCHEMICAL BLACKNESS, and certain psychological reactions—which are confirmed by those of the external world of relationships—that terrorize and sometimes lead to suicide among the unwary and/or unprepared profane.

The concept, as expressed by the alchemists, gives the impression that the revulsion-evocation rests in the UNREAL, that is, in phantasms, fears, if not imaginary, at least totally out of proportion to their real weight and/or threat. Something like the Tibetan Chod ritual. But it is not all unreal or disproportionate and, if the alchemists express themselves this way, it is because the prevalence of the unreal over the real must condition the latter and allow the profane to face and dissolve it.

The revulsion-evocation has two aspects. The first is the reaction of the matrix, assumed as a mother, and it has its foundation in attachment to human life, which inexorably must be magically SLAIN, to make way for the magical life of the celestial cabalistic Adam. This is evidenced by the transient weakening of human caprices, the aversions, the fear of death, and the feeling of the impossibility of continuing on

---

*[Docetism is the heretical doctrine associated with the Gnostics that Jesus had no human body and his sufferings and death on the cross were apparent rather than real; a belief that rejects the orthodox tenets of a religion or theological doctrine; heresy, unorthodoxy.—*Trans.*]

the chosen path. Hence many, blind to the train ride, throw themselves out, without realizing that this can lead to being overwhelmed.

The second is the true and proper emergence of the dark occult of all images, of all the negative stratifications, conventionally called evil, and of the ENTITIES bound to them.

And this is the real aspect, in which the mother proposes herself as a devil—or demon—NEGATIVE because she is assimilated to the viscous and restraining potential of the Matrix as a mother and assails the profane. Suffice it to say that man, as a human being, kills and devours other beings and in struggle, naturally for food and survival, inevitably evokes elementary larvae *sub signo matris* and blood, demons of lust, vampiric sucking practiced in the attempt to absorb from nature—and in her circuit—energy, in monadic devouring (phagocytosis).*

These demons can be reproductive, like those pointed out to the inert and obtuse disciples, in the corpus of Kremmerz, or they can be specified in the presence of *ante atte* (previous) existences. I would say that the greater the evolution of being (consisting of previous projections) the more specified are the entities.

Hence the practice of masters or adepts, in the teaching department, to provide disciples with amulets, in defense against these demonic evocations, and talismans capable of dissolving other creatures and creations, as they (re)-present themselves to the consciousness of the profane.

Therefore the amulets are a bit like the *CAVE CANEM* of the villas of ancient *Romanitas* that, apparently revealing a warning for the stranger, actually meant (whether or not there was a dog in the house) that the dog to be feared was the stranger-visitor himself, and the formula was equivalent to the magic inscriptions placed on the doors of ancient houses in the Far East, as an act of defense by the common people against the emanations or impure and dangerous infernal companies.

---

*[A process by which certain living cells called phagocytes ingest or engulf other cells or particles. The phagocyte may be a free-living one-celled organism, such as an amoeba, or one of the body cells, such as a white blood cell. In some forms of animal life, such as amoebas and sponges, phagocytosis is a means of feeding. (*Encyclopedia Britannica*)—*Trans.*]

Perhaps, in our initiatory system, valorization will be more efficient by the delegation of the numen to imprint in the ritual (or amulet-talisman) those invocations of the suffering soul, unexpressed and, at least in the first phase of initiation, inexpressible.

This explains the reticence and the hesitation of the masters to give too much, in the matter of memories, from previous "lives."

INITIATIC ORDERS

December 13, 1959

In the astral (plane), there are many occult centers where imprints are deposited (archives of the matrix), from many solar initiations, in perpetuity, by the initiates of all times, of all places. Therefore, it can be reasonably assumed that initiation is eternal. No persecution, no massacre, can destroy it; in fact, physically terminated, the initiate soon rises with all his memories intact and supported by the astral body.

Therefore, whether ontologically one initially encounters the imprints of practices, rituals, etc., and then Beings from this realm, sphere, epoch, etc., is inconsequential. In this scenario, the imprints or deposits (though inadequately expressed) would pertain to the BLACK NEGATIVE or FEMALE, centered within the POSITIVE, while the adept is attentive in the WHITE NEGATIVE.* It can be expanded upon at will.

An organization in and of itself is not strictly necessary for initiatory purposes: it requires a "Master" with a profound "memory," and a "disciple" or mature soul to catalyze a convergence for initiation. This convergence occurs through the occult workings of the Logos, wherein mature souls (or Monads) ascend, find their sustenance, so to speak, and prevent the soul from falling into entrapments (hunger, desires). This process unfolds within the framework, grades, limits, and constraints of the given situation.

---

*[Black Negative denotes an individual functioning within an Unconscious state (Black), and receiving unconscious imprints (negative) from the astral realm. Conversely, White Negative pertains to individual Consciousness (White) awakened in the astral, such as the Adept who can lucidly operate in the astral realm in full possession of his (solar-mercurial-lunar) faculties, i.e. lucid dreaming.—Trans.]

June 7, 1968

The principle of the propagation of Gnosis is not entrusted to the existence of associations or groups, declaredly, more or less esoteric. Oh, how easy it is to affirm that one is esoteric when not! Gnosis is entrusted to the operational MEMORY of the powers of the psyche that rise in us (memory), with high-level initiates, of the true Great Arcanum, that which is incommunicable and unveiled—acquired in sudden illumination (as in Zen). The initiator must be considered as a MNEMONIST (the one who remembers).

The pursuit of psychic powers, when applied to evolution rather than pursued for its own sake, restricts the scope of memory and serves as a catalyst for advancing inquiry. It is like a mysterious antenna tuned to resonate with the corresponding vibration and attract, akin to seeking a true companion, the frater who has recently or long ago entered the current is drawn in.

Then comes the iterative instinct (the colors of the Book of the Dead) which (re)births the initiate in a suitable environment.

That the approach to the MENSA (table)* has its proponents, and its logos can also be deduced from the last preface to the *Dialogues on Hermeticism*, which is after 1924, in the six years preceding the passing of Kremmerz.

He expresses, among other sentiments: "Those who harbor within the annals of their spirit a remote recollection of this candid analysis of the occult faculties within the human organism, even amidst religious mysticism, inevitably find themselves drawn to the study of magic." How do they find themselves drawn? Through the myriad events I've recounted, and countless others that may unfold.

The transmission (not propaganda) takes place by intuition and by vibration like among true lovers (not sensuous illusions) at first sight, in the illuminations, by a step, by a sentence, by a little book; and then the Guardian of the Threshold blocks the way for the curious and the unwary.

---

*[The Bembine Tablet or Bembine Table of Isis or the Mensa Isiaca (Isiac Tablet) is an elaborate tablet of bronze with enamel and silver inlay, most probably of Roman origin but imitating the ancient Egyptian style. Daffi references its importance by stating Kremmerz personally told him that the complete operations of the great work are illustrated in the tablet—*Trans.*]

Those who surmount the obstacles (which I would liken to Dante's Seven Angels of Purgatory) attain a profound illumination, and with perseverance, no barrier can impede them in the Work of constitution or reconstitution.

And then, only through experience can it be determined whether they are authentic or counterfeit mnemonists.

EI HM'SC BÊL

PATHS OF INITIATION

October 28, 1959

When reading the writings of alchemists on poison, acid, solvent, universal serpent, and so on, the universal reference typically pertains to the third term, but in actuality it extends to the fourth term of the operation when viewed through the lens of symbolic imagery (refer to the letter dated October 28, 1959, on female initiation). Therefore, generally, the elixir refers to matter refined and capable of manifesting into actuality, while the serpent acts as an acid on matter in the course of refinement.

This does not exclude the possibility that some action may also take place in the previous phases or for the case of a degree higher than the state of refinement of the material, but the effect is simply fluidic, and as such we will understand the generic influence based on animal magnetism: for example, the infusion of vital energy to a patient without healing him. To rectify the karma of their infirmity, a therapeutic image is needed.

In this place, it should be noted that those who separate the two paths—wet and dry—know nothing of true magic. This is understood from the operational schema, concerning the distinction revealed by Kremmerz in *The Hermetic Door* between Isiac magic and Solar magic, theoretically intending to assimilate the wet with the Isiac and the dry with the Solar; a distinction needs to be made regarding the solar, "revealing" its intermediary moment between the Isiac and the pure Solar.

In the *Liber Mutus* or *Mutus Liber*, there is the figure of Mercury resting at the feet of the earth or humid radical (wet path); in others instead there is distinguishable the figure of Saturn cutting the feet of Mercury, wanting with that to symbolize the separation of the dry principle from the wet one, which is also comprehensively said in the Emerald Tablet. And to the technical separation or distillation, the psychological, philosophical, and so on.

Hence when Mercury unites with Sol in the AMPOULE, it becomes APOLLO.

MONADS

October 26, 1959

If we take a broader view of cosmic evolution, and analogously consider the *infinitely small* alongside the *infinitely large*, encompassing the COLLECTIVE PSYCHE, we see that each individual, like someone in a crowd, remains unique yet becomes part of something greater. This collective psyche, if consolidated, could manifest as a BEING, a CREATION—a TEMPORARY FORMATION.

This formation, in a more subtle, non-solar sense, resembles a deity. To take form, this deity must sacrifice itself on an immense, invisible plane that, although less dense, still exerts influence on a cosmic level and affects the ☉ (physical) realm through its ☿ (sulfuric) actions.

December 8, 1963

It could be said that the white astral corresponds to Mercury and the black astral to Luna. The concept of the pre-astral, that is, an IDEA on the astral plane in *Mente Dei*,* could correspond with another concept, namely that the astral has its counterpart or its image in the hylic plane, analogous to the hylic entity that has its counterpart in the astral. It is, of course, a question of analogies.

In other words, the astral monad, so to speak, sees as its image—in a semi-dream—the hylic, its completion, just as the hylic monad sees the astral in a semi-dream as its image. This answers the question of the relationship between the human and the eonic as monadic species.

---

*[The mind of God or the Divine Mind.—*Trans.*]

This sequence should be illustrated with tables: human masculine monad, feminine ditto, eonic masculine monad, feminine ditto. And this *law* is in analogy with what the disembodied monad SEES reflected during disincarnation. The two different astrals, then, would correspond to two different planes of existence between the eonic world and the human one, even if there is not a terrestrial counterpart.

December 10, 1963

If we view matter through the lens of Democritus's perspective, wherein it's seen as a concentrated form of energy, we can liken it to a myriad of material entities, resembling captives, particularly when examining its most fundamental aspects like inorganic structures and the like.

The problem of establishing the principle of interpenetration between the *hylic* and the *astral* leads to the following questions:

1. What force thrusts the monads to the composition of matter (hyle)?
2. What do the two mutual planes represent for the two qualities of beings?

Philosophical solutions are found or "can be found" in the concept of the tetrad. In fact, the interpenetration of MATTER would be none other than the eternal cycle of tetradic tendency by the astral monads toward the hylic one, monads or pluri-monads, depending on the size one wants to assume.

The death of a plant, for example, has a pluri-monad or soul, so to speak, that "goes" to the astral, while the myriad monad-cells remain more or less bound to the divided matter by the effect of *the being* that held the unit-plant together. The union of the collective plant being has an equivalent intending to the phagocytosis that would be *prepared on the opposite plane to the constituted one*, that is to say for the hylic monads on the astral plane and the astral monads on the hylic plane. In short, the collectivity of hylic monads "has" in astral the image of its union by phagocytosis and growth of the soul-plant or secondary monadic groupings (example: a group of plant cells).

The elementals, rather than possessing a distinct astral realm, possess a collective image of their own, and undergo phagocytosis on the hylic plane, due to the terrestrial effluvia and the temporary symbiosis with hylic monads.

Therefore my "philosophical" intuition on the four planes and images has a further development in monadic evolution itself. But it is a "philosophical" problem with the functioning of the hylic plane; this is not in so far as it is philosophically intuited (it requires a crucifixion as in the Hindu philosophy for the gods) but in, so to speak, technical terms. The elemental must take the initiatory element from the human level, to be fixed in the form of an eon, and even this fixation (mistakenly considered as immortality) must be or could better be expressed in manifest terms.

The postmortem, indeed, following the same cycle of death and rebirth, takes on its value in this sense: with the greater the evolution, *the faster the cycle of dis-incarnation.* The monadic cells that are transformed in substance (at least in part) with the death of the individual remain closer to matter and the *regressed state.* As per the postmortem cycle, it is necessary to meditate on the state of consciousness in this state (three cycles) and the relationship of fluidic feedings-rituals, for their support.

The LIBIDO is at the same time a fusion and creation and drawing together energies across two eternal rhythms. The primal forces of *eros kai thanatos** turns into an attractive force of phagocytosis—or does the lover imagine eating the beloved as well? Is it possible that even the libinal forms, even in mundane cases of mild sadism, signify an unconscious desire to devour, to integrate a piece of the beloved?

ON THE TETRAD (QUATERNARY)

October 28, 1959

The tertiary distribution ceases with the gradual appearance of the First Principle because it comes to form (the solar body latent in everyone,

---

*Ancient Greek for love and death, the two primary life forces represented at the opposite ends of the philosophical spectrum.

but evident with the initiation and with the ⊙ body proportionate with the determined degree of ♀) the QUATERNARY, which, evident in natural structures, instead are latent in "micro" and macrocosmic structures.

There are THREE REALMS of nature, as the fourth, that is, the electric, is latent and akin to initiatory perceptions—the eons have apperceptions similar to those of galvanic currents!

The integration in/within the quaternary structure, that is, the RE-COMPOSITION of the TETRAD, leads to a *PAX*, since the compound (a plurality of quaternary-tetrad monads) is now fixed.

In nutritional terms: like the phagocytic growth of the tetradic monads, so the feeding-crucifixion involves phagocytosis of created elements, hence the saying: "nothing lives, nor can live if not for the loss of life" (as in killing but also maternal breastfeeding).

June 2, 1962

The quaternary is indestructible, and the four tetradic units develop when preserved: the prematurity or delay of one of the four tetradic units marks the development of the others. So that energy drawn will no longer be from other monads through PHAGOCYTIC action, but from the solar plane to CREATION and not by subtracting energy. Hence, in the postmortem, the evolutionary nutrition of nonintegrated initiates remains fluidic (evocations of forms, funeral banquets, vampires) and becomes less and less fluid as it develops solarity.

December 10, 1963

The formation of the tetrad, and its re-formation, is similar to the combination of acid that forms the basis of salt, that exhausts the *cycle of matter*, and that resolves in the spirit, not by destruction but by "juxtaposition" of the elements that until now were separated.

Naturally, within the perpetual cycle of that portion of matter, which aligns with Kremmerz's assertion of "the world without end," new matter is continually shaped into ever-changing forms such as nebulae, constellations, and so forth.

THE HYLIC AND THE ASTRAL

December 19, 1959

In terms of the electric origin of the Cosmos, creation is conceivable *ex nihilo*, that is, from the sleep of the One or Brahman, from a primary electric HYLE. This is the Lamaist conception of CHANNELING the WATERS of the MERCURIAL LAKE, an intuition that life fundamentally resonates as a vibration, which must precede creation or condensation.

Clearly the ontological question should not be traced back to man, but to the electric monads that constitute the first material level, which the Cosmos derives from for successive condensations and evolutions, as we (on our plane) conceive it.

The First Principle is essentially that of *quality, laws.* I say essentially, in order not to preclude the infinite attributions of the One, which also includes that of being able to PERSONALIZE, certainly not as a WHOLE, but as a part, within the principle of individuation.

Of course, it is also extendable to the tetrad of the Deity, which in turn must be "intuitable" in the hylic, and subservient to karma or fate for it to become "inferrable." The proposition reconciles *the indifferent immobility* of the Greek gods according to Epicureanism and the Buddhist gods, in the original conception and not by that of the Diamond Vehicle, which conceives them as useful and necessary elements of creative planes.

When Man becomes divine and expresses his own numinous powers, he becomes an "expression" of God, assuming its attributions: he soon returns to the human and his *function* is indirect and reflected by that something of himself that speaks, often terribly, in the divine instant at the terrifying moment of creation—and assumes, in that moment, the QUALITY of the First Principle.

The eon, moreover, is contained in the First Principle, which has among its attributions that of CONTAINMENT. Islamic "theory" provides a more analytical approach in this aspect compared to Christian theory, making it truly preferable for comprehending the nature of the ONE. The eon underlies the same laws of individuation, that is, as a monad detached from the tetrad, which in some cases becomes man, which again in Islam is more analytical in this regard, than the Christian one and in other cases becomes woman, and so on. The ONE can also be conceived as Osiris, the black god, that is as negative, and monadic beings as positive.

It's a good practice to keep in your drawer a chapter on the universe from a positive perspective, as well as another that examines it from a negative viewpoint. On the positive side, the principle of individuation asserts its validity. We must recognize that alongside the material realm—comprising humans, animals, plants, and minerals—exists the immaterial, which is equally real and individuated.

The means of passage from the material to the spiritual (or astral if one wishes) is precisely the QUINTESSENCE of the alchemists, which in substance is fluidic condensation. Such a condensation is completely analogous to condensation, in succession, from the electrical level to the terrestrial, and so on. The law is the same.

However, for us, the fluid is impure and requires refinement through alchemical processes. In contrast, for the eon (which is fluidically pure), the aim is to densify this fluid to gradually fix its Solar body, enabling it to gain awareness from its astral plane (ASTRAL BODY). This process can be understood through a regular initiation, which mirrors that of humans on the hylic plane.

March 20, 1961

The EON is negative in the astral when considered from a hylic perspective. Whereas in fact, it is positive. But if we consider that the *eonic monad* also has two hemispheres, in so far as it tends to the hylic, it becomes integrated with its meta-hylic or positive hemisphere, and the charge is reversed.

To highlight:

- human—positive hemisphere and negative astral.
- eonic—negative hemisphere and positive astral.

Therefore: the first union of human-eon is from positive to negative in equivalence and in compensation. Eon-human, ditto from positive to negative. As are the two "female correlations," for a total of sixteen combinations.

1. Male human monad
2. Female human monad
3. Male eonic monad
4. Female eonic monad

Hence, there are two priorities to realize:

1. Terrestrial or crucifix of the *homo et mulier*.
2. Masculine.

We know from direct experience the phases of NIGREDO, ALBEDO, RUBEDO, as far as they are perceivable, are rooted in a terrestrial-positive monad. But the eon, depending on the phase it crosses in its integration, which, as Kremmerz writes, is found in the ternary *vir-mulier-eon masculus*, by a master of the Third Degree?*

We must assume that, by reversing the alchemical black phase, it suffers in the astral and fears the fleeting of death, etc.; the eon, at first male and then female, must suffer the pains and preoccupations of MATERIALIZATION.

Hence, we can contemplate the horror of its descent (eon) into base matter, losing its freedom of astral mobility, etc., where it is solely drawn from its integration even at the material level to reinforce the Saturnian principle, and, if it so desires, its Lunar resonance.

July 23, 1962

The HERMETIC DOCTRINE introduces the concept of an ELECTRIC CREATION of the material world, wherein electric prin-

---

*[In the Myriam, a third degree member is called a Master and is tasked with leading therapeutic-magical chains for distant healings—*Trans.*]

ciples find application even in the medieval constructs of fires, stoves, and stills.

The concept of an electrical creation starts from the assumption that there is a *MATERIA* (positive and negative electrons) and an *ANTI-MATERIA* (understood in the sense of the astral plane).

The challenge emerges regarding a CONNECTION or transition point from the astral to the hylic. This necessitates a reevaluation of the CYCLICALITY of the incarnation or life from the disincarnation or death . . . *somnum*. According to the system of specular reflections, in the so-called *aldila*,* THE PHYSICAL IS SOLEY THE REFLECTION OF A REFLECTION; sleep or dream reflected: one dreams of dreaming.

Hence, the two aspects of the physical in the state of disincarnation:

1. An evaporating fluid that the monad consumes and sporifies (see the conception of souls in the *Aeneid*) and that is a (fourth) body attached to evocations and ceremonies or fluidic emanations or rituals . . . mummies.
2. An image that guides the Monad on its journey through the footsteps.

In the conception of electrical creation, the problem of the bridge is resolved in terms of the following values:

The *static negative electrons* (astral-antimatter) corresponding to other elements (roughly incomplete eons similar to the humanimal or an animal) transition into a *static or positive state* and merge with the waters of the sources (reminiscent of the undines of sagas and legends).

By impregnating matter, a dynamic positive electron state forms an electronic ternary that charges matter as an "electrical complex," that the disembodied monad, which finds itself in a dynamic negative electronic state, ENTERS, changing its value from negative to positive, by the effect of the (positive) EFFERVERSCENCE of matter (hyle).

---

*[The great beyond.—*Trans.*]

This goes beyond the sexuality of the reincarnationists *a la dozzina** and their rabid opponents. In these terms, EROS (sexuality) and the LIBIDO of Epicurus and Lucretius represent the nurturing pleasure of humans and gods, embodied by Venus. *Hominum divomque voluptas alma Venus.*† And not just for men and gods, but for every tiny particle of matter.

The combination of two negative and two positive valences results in the quaternary structure essential for the ontogenesis of life. In short: matter is vitalized at first in a negative or positive stasis of the elementals (which are equivalent to the eons of the upper plane); this vitalization or descent of the spirit into matter takes place first in the astral, then this determines the attraction on the physical plane of the monads, terrestrial, masculine, or feminine—whatever they may be.

Here on the physical plane "the two masculine and feminine values that are found in the substances, which, by joining together, form a compound," such as: ACID + ALKALINE = SALT.

FEMALE INITIATION

February 26, 1957

The monadic concept must be kept in mind with respect to women in initiation. The Gnostics spoke of the celestial syzygy or the male and female couple together for eternity. The quaternary is intrinsic to the ONE, held in potential as a latent tetrad. Two pairs: the one that is positive is assumed to be the hylic, and the other one, negative, is assumed to be the astral.

Hylic monads are therefore oriented toward the human element first, in order to form a human couple; astral monads and others in order to form the eonic couple. The tetrad always tends to reproduce, to reconstitute itself in its original components and is perpetually aimed

---

*[Literally "of the dozen," and referring to those proponents of reincarnation that slothfully regurgitate the theories and doctrines of Theosophists and occultists of the nineteenth century.—*Trans.*]

†["Venus is the desire of gods and men" (Lucretius, *De Rerum Natura*)—*Trans.*]

at the respective integration. The final cause is, in evolution, the re-composition of the tetrad. Hence the cosmic consciousness of one's identification with creation.

Generally, women are secondary in development and perhaps tertiary in terms of consciousness possession, in relation to Mystes, and of the Tetrad. That is why, in initiation, the male must first detach himself from the female, because this distinguishes him from the perception of the third and fourth terms of the tetrad.

And the deception of the Great Mother is revealed in this. It is possible to apply it to the three ternary units of the quaternary, to develop the concept. That the tetrad is not "an exclusivity" (as you may think) of a worldly setting is equally evident from the concept of the Dantean mystical rose.

October 28, 1959

In Khunrath's ninth table* we see a hermaphrodite with a head that is half man and half woman. This has a double meaning: an occultation of the mystery of sex and the theoretical ideal of integration, indeed that the man or monadic masculine also clothes himself with feminine attributes and vice versa.

We discussed this with Kremmerz. It is a philosophical notion of magical self-sufficiency, rather than a renunciation of the absorption of a female monad by the masculine or vice versa. The two fountains flow from the breasts of Khunrath's hermaphrodite, symbolized by the Milk of the Virgin, that is, the fluidic emanation (to put it improperly) of both, which unites in the alchemical chemistry.

The ternary of the wet phase involves realizing:

- masculine Lunar body
- feminine Lunar body
- masculine Mercurial body

---

*Heinrich Khunrath (1560–1605), German alchemist, best known for his sweeping book on alchemy, *Amphitheatrum sapientiae aeternae solius, verae: christiano-kabalisticum, divino-magicum, physico-chymicum, tertriunum-catholicum* (Amphitheater of Eternal Wisdom), 1595.

And transitioning to the tetrad (quaternary), we must incorporate a non-human entity from the realm of existence.

The ternary of the dry phase involves realizing:

- feminine Mercurial body
- masculine Mercurial body
- masculine Solar body

The fourth term of the operation entails:

(*a*) if the woman does not have a solar development, refer to the solar ideogram.

(*b*) if the woman has sufficient solar development, the woman's Solar body acts as a mirror. The purer her vision and her nature, the clearer and more effective the projection will be.

From the imagination's point of view, there is:

1. in the humanimal union, the archetype of the species;
2. in the wet union, the residue disguised by the archetype, which gradually is enveloped by the fourth term toward an image no longer animal;
3. in the union of the wet and dry (pre-solar), the image transcends animality, embodied instead by the entity, liberated from the sentimentality lingering in the moist union; and
4. in the dry (solar) union the objectified image "extracted" from the realm of ideas serves as an ELIXIR when involving the subject(s), or as a POWDER OF PROJECTION when the action is extraneous of the operators' ☉ + ☿ bodies.

Women undergo analogous phases of initiation to men, as their full integration occurs when they achieve maturity in projecting their Solar body. Upon mastering this ability, they attain a heightened stage of evolution on the dry path.

The contrast between men and women is rooted in the reality that a woman (arguably superior in this regard) cannot, on her own, initiate a humanimal . . . without risking the contamination of herself.

And the evolution of women in the dry phase, or in the development of the dry phase, is depicted by Basil Valentine's *Triumphal Chariot of Antimony*, in which there are two female figures that are pulling a cart after two lions—green and red. One with Luna over the head—wet phase—the other with the solar disk—dry phase—entirely analogous to the lotus flower, which in Egyptian statues crowns the forehead of Isis or the priestess.

October 26, 1963

The propaedeutic study is always man, who confers initiation on women; the two, then, initiate the masculine eonic monad and with this they integrate the feminine eonic monad and form the SYZYGY.

December 9, 1964

To say that impurity inhibits the initiation between an initiated woman and a common man is valid only regarding a vulgar relationship. However, whether realized by a man or a woman, in the theurgic and thus transmutational context, one can assert transmutation both as a woman-master and as a man-master.

With the initiate, it is the masculine vigor of the man that initiates the sequence: man–woman–male eon–female eon.

The issue may be considered in relationship to the PLANE of access: both men and women can tap into this level if of an evolved degree. Kremmerz had this to say: "Ah! If only an initiate (feminine) of the grade of OTUNA would emerge."

February 8, 1965

A woman can proceed or potentially arrive at the same level as a man, only if the latter, as the active principle, remains the ontological prime mover of the operation. Furthermore, it is necessary to distinguish whether the woman cooperates or is merely a physical or psychophysical support.

In the Isiac fluidic path, there is more or less cooperation, but as for the energy that is being emitted (as Kremmerz says in *The Hermetic Door*) the woman—Virgo—conditions the agent, that is, she compensates it HERMAPHRODITICALLY.

Using terms like Hermaphrodite or Androgynous can mistakenly suggest that we're discussing sexuality. However, by embracing and identifying, forever, their proper gender, individuals not only reinforce the image of their gender, but also develop a heightened "imaginative" faculty of the other. Therefore, the ternaries must be distinguished according to whether the fluids are on even or in disparate terms.

So (with the above reservations):

THE LUNAR TERNARY
Mercury
♂ Lunar fluids   ♀ Lunar fluids

THE MERCURIAL TERNARY
Sol
♀ Mercurial fluids   ♂ Mercurial fluids

The IMAGE compensates for the disparity in fluidic potency (<). The androgyne or hermaphrodite, symbolized through the RITUAL, vicariously projects the deficiency of one or the other in its spectral portrayal.

Alternatively, you may need to descend to a lower level, reaching an inferior pole. Therefore, diligence in the reconstruction, or rather, the symbol of the *Rebis*, conceals the enigma of bipolar equivalence, representing the ultimate aim of celestial alignment.

THE SOLAR TERNARY
Mars-Sol
♀ Solar body   ♂ Solar body
(Solar imagination)   (Solar imagination)

If:

Mars-Sol

♀ Mercurial body   ♂ Solar body

The Rebis will have to substitute (->) for ♀ (Venus) when only Mercury is present, with the former serving merely as a support.

Inward or outward? It's about seeing the degree. In theory, the hermaphrodite is a closed circuit and sufficient for mental operations. But for the others?

When the Rebis (hermaphrodite-androgyne) acts sexually, the final cause of the union is a bipolar arrangement, which remains in the field of images. If the woman evolves to a solar intelligence, she is the counterpart of Adam Kadmon. Operations that close circuits are eventually possible for their degree or plane, and the masters prescribe the presence of the second vessel to avoid erroneous images of Luciferian pride, due to possession of the solar state. In ascension, the Rebis is set aside!

The woman is the eternal Isis who compensates with and for the eternal evolution even when "the underlying necessity is overcome" of the terrestrial body. Let me rephrase that: One always remains sexual, harboring the potential for the opposite sex within themselves; the focus lies on enhancing the clarity and intensity—the efficiency—of the image.

LILITH

March 20, 1961

As for the practices mentioned in the Corpus, they were never put into practice, and I believe they have the possibility of being so; evidently, Kremmerz meant to refer only to the first phase of purification in which LILITH as the impure Moon is purified.

July 23, 1962

Lilith can symbolize the astral. The astral-Lilith precedes the terrestrial Adam-Eve; that is, the electrified astral first permeates matter (hyle); before, the two components act by entering into an effervescent state to engage with the astral. Lilith would correspond to the elemental, characterized by transience and obscurity: that is, the *somnum* . . . astral dream. The pre-material state akin to VOLUPTAS, so to speak.

July 24, 1962

However, in its immutable aspect, Lilith is not, *sic et simpliciter*, comparable to the astral. Kremmerz, along with others who have explored the concept, places it within the realm of MUTABLE FORMS. A woman carries a negative charge for magical purposes, as she doesn't reflect but rather deflects. Lilith, embodying the archetype of the she-devil, conveys her message, ever changeable and iridescent, imposing her imbalance upon the man ensnared by her.

At the same time, Kremmerz sees Lilith as an index of OCCULT DEFORMATION of the LUNAR BODY, abnormally developed, as in mediums, sleepwalkers, etc. With this deformation, Kremmerz connects all the imbalances and also the infirmities (epilepsy, etc.) but does so in a concise yet frequently perplexing manner.

Therefore, we would have, in a first sense, Lilith as a black negative or fixed. In another interpretation, Lilith, as the she-devil, embodies a "femme fatale" who ensnares with her own aberrant Lunar essence (interpreted as epilepsies, etc.) the Lunar essence of a man, consequently transferring it to the Mercurial and exerting dominance, thereby profoundly distorting it. In the third sense, Lilith, as the Lunar body, is deformed in and of itself, independent of the action of a *virago* (an Amazonian woman who reverses roles and assumes masculine characteristics).

Pathology of the occult: a deformed LILITH can be transmuted or, at the very least, neutralized. I'm aware of two real-life instances where this has occurred: with the changing of sand into diamond . . . transforming the dark night into a radiant dawn.

EXPERIENCING THE SEVEN FORMS

December 26, 1959

In the journey through the diverse forms, it's essential to note that starting from a relatively equal standing among the Seven Forms, one gradually ascends to a more dominant position in a single form, ultimately reaching the absolute dominance of that form, which aligns with memory.

As one ascends, failure to attain absolute fixation on one's own form amidst the various potential forms of existence leaves one vulnerable to undergoing experiences that don't align with their own form. There are exemplary cases of men who have a vocation (job) in contrast to their own talent (hobby) and who often perform the hobby as a job and vice versa, with contrasts, disasters, or unpredictable successes, etc.

"Having awakened to consciousness," one can undergo as a mission what one inevitably experiences, influenced by forgetfulness and other associated factors. This multiple experience, which previously was characterized as Islamic passivity, becomes solar and active, willed, and so on, always with the inherent "shaping" of the proper form.

May 22, 1961

The matrix triples: black negative, white negative, reversal of the white negative: future astral body. The triadic holds cosmological significance; the quaternary is structural; therein lies the difference.

The seven colors or experiences should, in theory, follow each other like the seven days of the week, but a common mistake involves the belief that the Work can be fulfilled in all of its splendid colors by a single series, while there are as many series as necessary; free will, errors, sympathies + and −.

It is more accurate to say, ontologically, that the seven colors precede the white phase but then appear as synthetic proponents of the EVOLVED = RED, which does not refer to the color red, but the ultimate power. Since the ascension is infinite, everything starts again, albeit on another level.

June 2, 1962

Experience of the FLUCTUATING of the SEVEN (forms) must be considered negative in the descent and positive as fixed in the ascent and resolves always in the SEVEN. The seven is an absolute value and unlike the twelve, does not relate to a zodiacal configuration.

In the sense that the constellations may vary on the planes, but not the seven forms of intelligence, if willed from thinking and willed by Being (hypothesizing the Haruspic plane as without form [or without thought?] beyond the Logos). I pose the question *without thought* because, in fact, a thought, as "humanly conceived," does not exist in the higher planes; there is an identification with ever-more subtle forms of intelligence.

On the higher planes the experience of the seven cannot be repeated nor is a change of color possible? Rather, it is the experience and the prevalence of the NUMBER on the FORM that determines the rebirth with its flaws and its positive values, etc.

In any case, once the form of intelligence to which we are bound has been fixed by initiation (or, in the case modified, by moving its identification to another color or planet), the initiatory fate has been fixed. Fixation can also be understood as a prevalence of the fixed experience over others, as well as a specific characteristic assumed in so-called previous existences. The fixed experience involves piercing the barrier that separates us from what is commonly known as the Gloria Dei.*

By progressing in our perception, we can perceive on the superior planes by concentrating on the vast mosaic of COSMIC experiences of the forms to which they belong. This is the reason for the acquisition and at the same time of the loss of the "individual identification," *solve et coagula ad infinitum*: to increasingly perceive the COSMIC, focusing on FUNCTION rather than what the egoistic vision identifies.

The personality, within the SEVEN, becomes more evident and, precisely because of this differentiation, it becomes more modest or, if one prefers, less immodest.

---

*[Transcendent states of experience.—*Trans.*]

The perception of that which is referred to as POLYPSYCHISM: the masses have a psyche that does not nullify the individual psyche but conditions it to a certain action or line of development or tension. This occurs, on the superior level, because of the balance between the fixed form and the other six. In a crowd, there are all seven forms and innumerable subforms, but for that unique objective and direction, there is only one thrust.

On the flip side of the relationship fluidity-fixation in descent, there is the fixation-fluidity in ascent. During the descent, we are akin to passive seeds, or at the very least, we are tossed among various forms (seven) and constellations (twelve); whereas during the ascent, we assume a fixed form and merge with cosmic currents, aligning ourselves with those to which we are dedicated to the fulfillment of the task.

This could also be the case for a particular COSMIC AGE.

THE ONE

October 26, 1959

Not everyone will understand that man does not reach a state of finality, but precisely in this lies the difference between the mystical conception and our magical and forsaken one. For here we find one of the major secrets: since self-formation of the Being is infinite, it takes away from the facile joy of considering oneself ARRIVED—ENTERED in nirvana, and so on.

All the evolutionary processes and the cosmic personification process do not inevitably disappear with the act of absorption into the One.

The One by its nature (in its occult and terrestrial aspect) is negative darkness that can only be known (by gnosis, the ultimate Thule of Creation, the very reason for being of creation itself), in the act of creating and individuating.

Therefore, one should not be deceived, by the expressions "fixed star,"* and so on, made "also" so as not to discourage the profane

---

*[Stella Fissa.–*Trans.*]

from a laddered path that has no end. The problem, connected to that of individuation, is that of CONSCIOUSNESS. This affirmation remains eternal, in the structure that makes man equal to the GODS. But only in this sense does the state of a fixed star resolve into reality—the means ☉ by solar ♀ solar actions,* that is, eternal and indestructible.

So much so that to Modify—not to destroy—a ☉ by ♀ solar actions one must exhaust the effects and set it aside IN ETERNO of the Great Astral Archive, understood as the MATRIX, etc., or absorbed with the same procedure that the monads have to follow in becoming from simple elementary souls to complex and mature souls in ascent.

It is a matter of distinguishing states of consciousness from states of being. It is possible, even in Plotinian ecstasy, to perceive the ONE up to a virtualization—psychologically identifying with it, but never assuming the DIMENSION, the STRUCTURE, of the structure and dimension that they have per se.

With respect to the gods, angels, and so forth, they are EMASCULATED CHERUBS, passive to the extent that they are as they are, from the beginning of time and up to the Non-End, that is, eternal. In contrast are initiates who are active in the "fruitful tension and action" in the acquisition of potency to build their destiny, and so on, like in a sketch where there are two halves, indeed two faces of Fate: one, turned downward and already built, the other upward and yet to be built.

THE ASTRAL DOUBLE

January 21–24, 1960

The World is conceived as a ternary, depicted either in a triangular or in a circular form. Depicted with three circles or cycles, at the core lies BEING with its correspondences to the Monad, of historical

---

*[Understood as internally projected alchemical Solar and Sulfur actions.—*Trans.*]

being in its positive aspect, with all, that is, the characteristic profound qualifications.

Encircling the realm of historical or actual being lies the black astral realm, the obscure domain of emotions and passions, alongside the vast sea of reincarnation (human-animal), akin to samsara and the infernal rivers. This plane parallels the inferior state,* understood in a broad sense and not solely as the *locus infernalis*.

In its broadest interpretation, hell can be understood as one of the many underworlds—a realm where suffering prevails, and individuals lack any comprehension of the divine presence of God, as a divine state. This, unfortunately, mirrors the journey within the initiatory realm. Here, the path leads to a descent into the underworld, both in life and consequently in death, extending into the new life thereafter. The initiate, ensnared by the most perilous obstacle to ascension, which is pride (*hubris*), with the sense of sufficiency, dominance over others, and the illusion of having reached the pinnacle—loses sight of the eternal process of self-creation through integration. This journey entails continual overcoming of tests, even as they become increasingly subtle.

The ASTRAL, a synthesis of the Lunar and Mercurial realms, intertwines and merges until they intricately weave together, forming an inseparable tapestry. For those who have misplaced Ariadne's key, this framework resembles the Buddhist samsara: a maze of deceptive light and the misleading allure of creation's illusory beauty, along with the mistaken perception of its individuality. Conversely, for those solely fixated on the tangible, it represents the obscured or latent negative aspect.

The two planes also contain the meaning of the binary that is illusory until it is understood as an end in itself, that is, illusory sexual union, sensist, even if seasoned by the illusion of love and blessed by

---

*[Denotes a diminished level of consciousness, indicating individuals who are confined to a limited ability to perceive, comprehend, and express a more comprehensive understanding of reality.—*Trans.*]

religions and elevated to the noble, owing to institution, etc., while it does nothing but close up being in samsara.

This black astral can also be understood as an ocean. Perhaps those philosophers who said they see the earth surrounded by an immense ocean wanted to conceal and reveal this esoteric concept.

Outside the samsaric, there is the lucid astral plane, the white astral, generically of the spirit. It should be clear that in the initiatory process, one must first cross the plane of the black astral, passionate illusions, and cross it in a boat called by various names: Dante's barque of Charon, Amon-Rah's boat, etc., to reach an "enlightened" level of consciousness.

As the expression of the idea of a net of the Sephirotic emanations, in contact with the plane of the astral black, table 5 of Khunrath in his *Amphittheatrum Sapientiae Aeternae*, published in 1609, helps me in good measure.

The (so to speak) illustrious and distinguished commentators had no concrete practice of the alchemical action, as not to see how much is veiled beneath the surface, in a Dantesque expression, is spread so thinly. Certainly, they have fallen into the trap of the outward Jewish and Catholicizing form. And I'm coming to a condensed comment.

In the center, however, is a circle with a man on the cross; the commentators say that he represents Christ or the Virgin or the Son, where he must be understood as the man on the cross, that is, the initiate, and in fact, Khunrath writes: "*Signo Vinces In Hoc,*" which does not mean that you will conquer as did Constantine under the sign of Christ but that the figure must be related to the one below; a dove of the pontifical tiara, considered by commentators to symbolize the double current of light and love, which descends from God to man and goes back to the first.

Instead, Khunrath intended to conceal the sign of Venus in which the cross is placed under a sphere; the tiaraed dove, from which flames emanate, which are none other than the alchemical fire. The tiara indicates that by this means you will have the three parts of the wisdom of the world (Emerald Tablet). Around the flames that emanate from the central figure is the globe in the shape of an egg or circle (samsara)—and a cloudy sphere: the clouds of Atziluth, which are precisely the dark astral plane, obscuring the vision of God and imprisoning the samsaric world.

And here we relate an equivocation that the commentators have not resolved. They write only about the second person of the Trinity, represented by the central rose cross, piercing the clouds of Atziluth, in essence flickering the ten sephirotic radiations. These radiations are like so many windows open on the arcana of the Word, through which one can contemplate its splendor from ten different points of view. Now to those who "carefully" look at the figure, first of all it appears that the flames of the central cross *do not penetrate, do not scratch the surface* of the central circle, but they remain within it.

While commentators have not seen that from the tiara-ed dove, below, that is to say, to the feet of Christ (man) they catch greater flames, which are going to overlap the circulating radiations around the central figure, which is the world. These are the very flames that penetrate the clouds of Atziluth, not the other sephirot.

Hence, only with the capric force, symbolized by the dove (which is not always a symbol of chastity in the mystical sense of the expression), do the largest flames reflect the clouds of Atziluth. Thus, merging the two spheres, it becomes clear that the one closest to the world and indicated as flaming does not necessarily denote the flames are positive; on the contrary, they are negative flames that encircle the samsaric realm; illusory, symbolized by the colour orange, the fiery Mars cited by Kremmerz. And, again, to add that the dove with the tiara corresponds exactly with the underlying sphere, the illuminating sphere of Aemeth* or Holy Spirit, which others indicate as referring to the Mercury of the alchemists.

Thus, if we seek to associate Luna with deities like Astarte, the

---

*[From *emeth*, Hebrew for "truth", possibly referring to the Sigillum Dei Aemeth by John Dee.—*Trans.*]

seductive goddess, Proserpine, and so on, its value should be assigned to the initial ring of flames. Similarly, the value of Mercury, precisely corresponding to the sphere of Aemeth, should be linked to the second circumference. The upper sphere, adorned with dark tones and luminous characters, does not signify "the hidden nature of the first or third person of the Holy Trinity" in any manner. That the sphere is depicted as dark, or black, while the Absolute dominates above it, should already provide sufficient hints to the unwary commentators regarding the trigone of God the Father. It is clear, from all the analogies and symbolism, that Khunrath intended to indicate black as the Matrix and the Moon, the World (black) which became subjugated to the First Principle, as the deceased Osiris.

And then we highlight the quadripartition of the four bodies or principles according to Khunrath's symbolism. Above, the God the Father, who by adding his triangle to the ten sephirot, forms the number thirteen: if we want to indicate that of the twelve (zodiac) plus a virtue (following the Hebrew system, which is different from the Chaldean) only ten can be perceived as a virtue, while (you see how our assumption returns!) the other three (two plus one) cannot be classified as sephirot, although they radiate clearly from above so that the triangle is even closer to the sphere to be penetrated than not the same angelic choirs, domains and rulers of the ten sephirot. And even more, we see from the posture of the figures that the dense spheres according to the commentators, respectively, of Ain-Soph and Aemeth, added to the ten sephirot, form the number twelve and the classical duodecimal-partition of the World of Ideas.

In delving further into the analysis, we observe that there are in fact TWO forces piercing through the wall of Atziluth: above, there's the union with God the Father, symbolizing celestial intuition, SELF-INITIATION, or if you prefer, REMEMBRANCE. Those directly united with God the Father need only remember and unite without external aids or intermediaries. However, for the vast majority of initiates, there lies the journey below (INITIATION) to traverse in order to breach the walls of Atziluth (i.e., to cross the Stygian swamp or the Amenti). On the cross *sub sfera venit sapientia vera*, the marquis of Palombara, initiate, master, left written on the pediment of the Hermetic Door in Rome.

Another signification arises: the ten virtues or categories are worthless if one does not possess the secret of the positive and the negative, of the two spheres, that is, the luminous one (white) and the other obscure (black). Thus, above rises the Solar body, symbolizing God the Father; beneath it lies the Moon or Matrix; and further below, with the realm of the quaternary, the world of Man crucified within cosmic matter, symbolized by Saturn, and therefore also cosmic crucifixion. Through the intermediary of the dove, QUINTESSENCE, the true fire and not the fire around the circle, emerges, representing the third body, the Mercury of the philosophers.

One must bear in mind the principle of the bipolar splitting of Being to establish a connection with Egyptian symbolism, exemplified by the boat of Ra (taking the form of a serpent) and adaptable to the outcome of the "spinning" resulting from the divine kiss or the Glorious Body—manifested ectoplasm.

If—artificially—the circles are broken in two halves, the "boat" is expressed, and the convergence of the two nimbi stands out: what Khunrath indicates as "flames," i.e., the boiling of the Lunar body in reference to Aemeth or Mercury of the alchemists. The equivalence of the two figures (in table 5 of Khunrath and the pediment of the Hermetic Door)* is evident if we pay attention to the lower part of the upside-down triangle crossed with the other and indicated by a circle and the lower part of the "tiara-ed dove," where the flames burn throughout the opening of the wings of that HIGHLY VIVID dove for the part corresponding to the tail. Khunrath's design reproduces the effectiveness of the THREE GRADATIONS of the vividness of the flames, that is: the bland, those camouflaged with steam; the alive, those emanating from the dove; and the dense, the highly vivid ones at the bottom of the dove itself.

---

*[The physical Hermetic Door(way) of Marquis Palombara in Rome.—*Trans.*]

ASTRAL ENTITIES

January 21–24, 1960

The first contact occurs with the black occult, that is, the first representations suitably present to the profane, are entities that are not real entities (this revelation should be mentioned as a perspective to be validated gradually), but the categories, the orientation points that serve as a guide—and the numen knows if it has any and will need them, during its long journey. In a certain sense it can be said, so as not to be misleading, given that the perception of Being on the invisible plane is not within the reach of the initiate or initiator, that at first they appear in the same form of virtue or categories of the spirit, the same forms under which the Intelligences are classified (see sephirot).

Virtues, which are arranged and divided into rays of the Absolute, are to be considered as CHANNELS and each channel through the plane of intrinsic subjective-existence of the trans-human being is imbued with relativity, and obscured like a lens that clouds (for example, the Plotinian conception of the progressive fading of the four worlds or planes down to the ground). In short: the two planes of intelligence and nature are united in a single one, and the meaning of that one black or dark astral plane, which is presented here, will be understood.

I would like here to comment on an unpublished work by Kremmerz from his *Corpus philosphicum totius magiae restitutum*, in which the fundamental truths of magic occur, even, if the style and classification are questionable:

- Quaternary structure of the micro and macro cosmos
- Magical consciousness of reality
- Overcoming religious beliefs
- Fluidic and mental motions in the sexual act
- Purification rituals of the twelve zodiac signs
- Genii of the tradition (Chaldean)
- Beneficial and malefic figures (not sure why the latter were included)

KREMMERZIAN TABLE OF MAGICAL CLASSIFICATIONS

SYMBOLISM OF SIDEREAL COLORS	SPHINXES AND ANIMAL SYMBOLS OF UNIVERSAL SYMBOLISM	SPIRITUAL BODIES
NIGER: blackness from the earth	SATAN: Serpent with a human face	EARTH: Ariel, Spirit or from south wind, Austral: basis of the infernal triangle
ALBUS: whiteness from the foam of water	CHRIST: the fish and the sea crab	WATER: Gabriel, Spirit or north wind, Boreal: coming from the One God
MIXTUS: celestial green of the visible sky; air	CHERUB: the main bird and the dove among birds	AIR: Raphael, Spirit or west wind; of the accomplished mission
RUBEDO: red or gold flames of fire	MAN: perfected from the purely divine spirit	FIRE: Michael, Greater spirit or east wind from where the Sun is born

Kremmerz specifies that the four spirits are not objective entities but subjective values in a man. There's no need to disclose this mystery to the profane, for they remain connected (vinculum) with the astral entities, without, however, gaining anything, merely entwining themselves with notions of morality, tolerance, charity, etc., intrinsic to the ideas of such spirits.

Kremmerz, who also spoke of the invisible beings (gods, intelligences, etc.), explicitly links them to the magical rituals that he prescribed, exhumed, and internally perceived through clairvoyance and whose verbiage is *read* in the astral (see *The Hermetic Door*). In the Corpus, which for some strange reason he kept secret, he treats of the entities in a much more veiled and reserved way than in his disclosed work (*The Hermetic Door*).

The esoteric significance becomes evident in the author's counsel against prematurely embracing the notion of being as an invisible corporeality, because at first the profane must free themselves from the illusory belief that anthropomorphically divine or diabolical entities govern, over humanity, who, *as such*, in their impure, *samsaric* structure, could claim to make contact with them, apparently from a humble postulant but in reality from a master.

However, proceeding cautiously does not imply cessation; otherwise, for those aspiring to delve into magic, it would pose a psychological barrier, relegating them back to the Black Astral Plane they seek to transcend. And that this also corresponds to the magical technique that only comes by virtue of one being a master, for only then will the genie, the numen, or the eonic entity come into contact with the summoner.

If eonic entities manifest in any other way, they are either of a diabolical nature, or the one who evokes them, unconsciously, harbored a bit of initiatory fragments within their being. In other words; [Archangel] Raphael does not exist as such, but the entities that we empirically call Raphaelic, in their respective planes, do exist.

Certainly, it is not an easy passage; the journey involves three phases: initially liberating oneself from belief in religious beings in a broad, even spiritual sense; then comprehending the connections between psychological states and planes; and finally recognizing the entities themselves. However, this knowledge only comes after solidifying awareness of the mental categories and the progression of a mental motion "ad ulteriora." This journey is akin to the safe navigation of Amon Rah's barque both on and within the Amenti.*

It could also be said, in an apparent paradox, that the entities remain "insensitive" to human invocation until a direct channel with their plane is established. Until such a time, both the rays (sephirot) that emanate from the world of the archetypes and the invocations

---

*[In Dante's "Divine Comedy," particularly in the "Inferno" section, Amenti refers to the underworld or the realm of the dead. It is a term borrowed from ancient Egyptian mythology, where Amenti was the land of the dead, a place where souls journeyed after death. In Dante's work, it represents the lowest circle of Hell, where the souls of the damned are punished for their sins—*Trans.*]

do not meet, but diverge, twist, and move in a thousand directions, bouncing, rotating, echoing even up to the highest of the planes, that is the heavenly ones of humans, in a vortex, creating new illusions, new karma, fate, fabulations. Hence the magical ritual is one with the purification-preparation and specifically constitutes the support, representing the boat needed to cross the Amenti, which, like the inferno, is all that humanly stands in the way of perception and contact with the superior plane of entities.

Naturally and for the sake of convenience, I place the black astral as completely illusory. Wanting to deepen the meaning, I should say that the entities of the black astral plane are negative or neutral since they are not ritually relegated to the white astral or positive plane of the initiations and the Gnosis. Despite being living, tangible entities, not merely psychic states but actual, independent beings, they are deemed illusory not due to their existence but rather because of their influence. By inciting human passions, they redirect the navigator's course toward an illusory worldview or a simplistic understanding of the self, whether traversing the Amenti or the Stygian Swamp.

And the reaction of the mystes is frequently the same, that at a certain moment they recoil from the rational, the intuitions or inspirations or fleeting perceptions and return to the "psychological" perspective in which the entities do not exist, attributing everything solely to the introspective inclination of their own Being. This was the case for many of Kremmerz's disciples. But then even if they (the mystai) had fleeting contacts with an astral entity, they definitively lost them at once.

January 21–26, 1960

The black astral realm is transient, or at the very least, it instigates transience by perpetuating beings within their samsaric cycle. Consequently, their occult endeavors of connection and inspiration, if they occur, lack permanence. This realm is lunar in nature, characterized by its mutability, iridescence, and mercurial base, rendering it as elusive and volatile as quicksilver.

The work, on the other hand, in the realm of the white astral, if in itself not fixed, tends at least to fixation. In this sense, the black astral is inferior, while the white astral is supernal; the whole is always relative and within the limits of powers and entities.

In summary, it can be said:

From the Absolute there emanates rays or channels that are cor-relative, corresponding to the fundamental partitions of categories that condition the actions of beings, and therefore their initiatory process.

The rays or channels come as distorted in the passage through the intellectual plane (Intelligence of the World) and the sensual, emotional, passional (Soul of the World) plane.

These rays or channels *are* covered with personalistic dynamics; they are not specific intelligent beings or personalities; instead they are moral or philosophical categories, and therefore rather exoteric.

As such, they are the first to be perceived initiatically. All beings are then linked *ad infinitum* to each category, since what is syncretistic towards the bottom is classist towards the top.

And to quote Kremmerz, "no one attains the end." This specification is essentially esoteric in matter.

THE ARCHON

October 30, 1963

I've merged the concepts of *samsara* with the fixed and mobile, figuring the archon is susceptible to rotary motion that destabilizes (its consequent reactions, etc., symbolized by the motion). This reverses the fluids first and then rectifies them.

So the clouded moon settles down after the archon is overthrown, who is then subjected to the alchemical fire that divides and dissolves into two components: Heaven and Earth (false sky, that is, the religious sky symbolized by Jupiter). Then Sol-Quintessence rises while the portals of Heaven and Earth lead to the Underworld. Mercury polarizes with (true) Sol, and Luna polarizes with the purified Earth.

ON KREMMERZ

December 13, 1959

Kremmerz imbued the Fraternity of Myriam with an Isiac guise to conceal the true relationships among both the "sexes" with the Solar sphere. It could be argued that all the presidents of the Myriam and "high-level" exponents were regarded by him as solar disciples, or "masters." This perception extended to the followers and disciples of the Myriam as well.

THE NOMEN-NUMEN OF J. M. KREM ERZ*

March 3, 1963

As for the initiatory name of Formisano, it should be categorically excluded that it is a pseudonym in the common sense, and also the double *M* has to be excluded since it was from the Italian vulgarization of his name.

The double *M* is an erroneous affixing by the unwary and inexperienced "publicists" on his name. It is neither a surname nor an abbreviated name. Instead, it is a combination of separate and distinct letters, each with its own significance.

> ANGELIC NAME of a SOLAR GENIE under the SIGN of TAURUS . . .
>
> *J* stands for Jod, preceding in the manner of priestly languages with the addition of prepositional "from," "of," "derived from."
>
> When written with a silent *M*, "M" implicitly denotes a complementary letter. However, when written as "EM," it indicates that *M* is not silent but rather a quasi MM. If I use the term *"quasi,"* it's because it's not strictly an Italian letter but, as I mentioned before, a transposition of sacerdotal characters.

---

*[Giuliano Kremmerz—*Trans.*]

EM means, according to my memory, the HYPOSTASIS of, or hypostasis of Jod or of the first principles.

KREM aligns with TAURUS (constellation and/or magical value).

ERZ refers to the dominant GENIE, or ENERGETIC MANIFESTATION.

J . . . Jod or Yod

EM . . . Hypostasis or Genie of

KREM . . . in or of Taurus

ERZ . . . energy manifestation

Ergo: the Genie (EM) of Jod (J) in the Energetic Field (ERZ) of Taurus (KREM).

June 7, 1968

I wanted to travel to Argentina . . . where Kremmerz lived between the years 1883 and 1892 and then between 1895 and 1897; however, the tracks vanished.

Then, by a sliver, I almost met him in Monte Carlo in 1919. . . . Finally, I took lodging in the Riviera di Chiaia, exactly in the same house where Kremmerz lodged, in 1898, and where he set up the first initiative of his medical-Hermetic laboratory.

RITUALISTIC MAGIC

March 20, 1961

Magic is a world that includes and implies the psychic. From the moment one adopts a mantra, with this he enters the magical. Kremmerz speaks of psychic issues because he wanted to popularize magic in modern language.

MANTRAS are used in a mystical meditative sense or an Isiac-magical sense, for the effective contact with entities or planes or, in a magical potency sense (re: solar), since the same mantra is projected as an ASTRAL IMAGE and vivified by the VIS (virtue-force), to become a living and vital thing.

23 July 1962

In addition to the three modes of magical action on karma we have:

1. Fractioning of karma
2. Accelerating.
3. Taking on the "karma" (wrong and "malefic" but unfortunately carried out by some initiates) instead of the subject, the other "benefit" is articulated.
4. Discharging of karma on elements or subjects or infernal monads.

March 23, 1963

The ritual of Kons (Kons-sin-dar, a Chaldean priestly entity) is one of the few good things, together with the Lunations, given by Kremmerz: twenty days of chastity . . . the only occasion where I find myself in agreement with that.

ASTRONOLOGICAL MANTICISM

March 23, 1963

Kerneïtz* assumes that the karma of a new birth also denotes the zodiacal interconnection among the other elements of the reincarnation vortex.

The assumption, as opposed to what is believed, is exact, and that the personality (so to speak) chooses the place and time, and so on, of

---

*[Constant Kerneïtz is the pen name of Félix Guyot (1880–1960). His pen name Kerneïz comes from the name of his mother of Breton origin. He was a French astrologer (in the last issue of the year 1938 of the *Journal de la femme*, Kerneïtz would have predicted the German-Soviet Pact according to the rapprochement of Uranus with Neptune: "the war of ideologies will tend to transform into a fusion of these same ideologies") and very interested in Indian culture; he contributed to spreading the philosophy of yoga in the West. He was a professor of philosophy and a journalist in Nantes, London, and Paris—*Trans.*]

birth . . . but not in reference to one's complete being but to that part that manifests itself in that moment and place of that reincarnation.

That explains the possibility of a soul descending into a dog or lamb (see *The Hermetic Door*). Undoubtedly a human soul is distinct from that of a dog or a lamb. However, in that instance of conception, it undergoes a transformation and selects a new vessel, and emerges determining the way or means of a new envelope for THINKING (if one can say so) AS A DOG OR AS A LAMB!

Reread what he writes, exceeding in controversy, on karma, in correlation with the Latin conception of fate. Kremmerz considers fate as a tendency. Where fate is absolutely determinative, it is not the astrological finding that counts, but other factors that are not found in the said sky.

Correspondence:

- EARTH = COLD and DRY—i.e., the human body in a humanimal state without any fluid emission.
- WATER = COLD and HUMID—i.e., the animal body emitting cold, dead mercury.
- AIR = HOT and HUMID—the body, however, enters into fermentation but is tied to the humid radical; escaping reheated fluid.
- FIRE = HOT and DRY—that is to say, of the physical elixir.

In concordance with the intuition that the Twelve Sages never had a real existence: I agree with the intuition of zodiacal valences.

December 8, 1963

We are indeed the ones who project the zodiacal themes on the fictitious firmament of the twelve signs that do not have, for themselves, any astronomical reference.

Sol and planets have a real existence; not so the displaced constellations.

The *astrological* is constantly opposed to the *astromantical*, by which the astrological theme of the mandala or ideogram evokes thought-forms.

March 3, 1964

The historical-bound ego cannot be explored by astrology but only by astrono-logic. The archetypes are projected by man in a collective sense rather than by the individual person.

Traditional (ancient) astrology was none other than a disguise of the true research: and in fact, Kremmerz wrote: "Astron" the science of the occult, other than of the stars! Astrology is an exterior that can be more or less in harmony with the interior—the goal of astrology. I think it can only be a theme of the nativity for individuality and in a sense for some trends. Divinations reside within an external, natural setting, within the COSMIC CIRCLE amidst the realm of natural randomness, while the TRUE FUTURE awaits determination.

Perhaps the NUMEN imparts its initial thoughts, with signs and symbols, in a certain direction, but no further. There is no reference to a seer or augur.* Unless one engages right from the beginning with the same NUMINAL Essence, and provided the determination is already formed, it may reveal within its pattern that it aligns with our human patterns, even our view of heaven from earth, *even where the numen does not perceive with an earthly perspective.*

April 29, 1964

Regarding the progressed horoscope, its validity is rooted in the concept of the "astronomical house." If it is possible and true that today I can scrutinize heaven to draw auspices from it, the same must be presumed for individual facts from man: that is, to compare the *sky at birth* (tendencies, not determinations of events) with the *sky of today*, to see which actions-reactions can come from them. And the way to such a better interpretation and application I find in intuition, which I find rightly, in a fixed element (the cross of life, the zodiacal configuration) and of the mobile (planets and related aspects, etc.) under the nativity theme.

---

*[Understood in the ancient classical sense of a vates, sibyl, oracle, diviner, foreteller, and so on—*Trans.*]

We extend this principle to the fixed-datum and compare it to the mobile-derivative (the astronomical date of birth would be the fixed and the ascendant of the mobile) from the comparison between the two situations to ensue a more Hermetic interpretation of the horoscope.

We extend, I repeat, the principle to the events of today and we will mark as fixed, as are original fingerprints, the birth theme and the current situation of the sky, as are the mobile factors, where will be found the harmony between the different concepts.

On the contrary, in my opinion, it could be astromantically, and precisely for the purpose to sharpen the intuited haruspex, to separate, but only, the two moments of the fixed and the mobile, and also to discover nonindividual events therefore not related to the birth theme.

Perhaps, we should take a moment to fix ourselves mantically or rationally before the day when we want to see the event: unless we assume the present with the idea of the horoscope as a fixed beginning and the presumable date of the unfolding of the event, as mobile.

The idea of extracting a SENSE (Tao) from the positions of the sky should not be thrown into the garbage dump tout court. These considerations must also connect with the idea that a horoscope is unrepeatable. I am not of this inclination; meanwhile, the horoscope is interpretable by different operators and with this, we go to the idea of a median between different visions, like a landscape photographed from different points and perhaps with different "film" sensibilities.

As for the question concerning the hours of the day, I greatly appreciated the emphasis on the difference between the two systems: Egyptian (a first hour from the actual rising of the sun) and Chaldean (twelve daylight hours from the thirteenth to the twenty-fourth and twelve night hours from zero hours to 12:00 a.m.).

But it is a fact that both the Chaldeans and the Egyptians practiced mandalas and magic.

According to the Chaldean system, moreover, used in the Myriam, the day begins with the night, that is, at sunset; so that the first twelve hours from sunset would be the night and the following daytime.

Now, if the sun sets in winter around five in the evening, there are seven hours in the preceding day and five hours in the following day until 5:00 a.m., that is, during the night, and from 5:00 a.m. onward until the following 5:00 p.m. are the daytime hours.

The maximum difference between the two amounts to two hours. My calculations, on the other hand, are not related to the distinction between daytime and nighttime hours, but for positive hours and negative hours, which follow one another according to a determined rhythm that is practically reversed between the crescent moon and the waning moon (another element not taken into consideration by the usual astrology but of fundamental importance).

Certainly, therefore, we could not start the day at midnight, because at the end of the twenty-four hours, the day falls with the planet that gives the name to the day; this is more approximate with the Egyptian system. I must therefore consider that the Chaldean system is "so-called" Chaldean, but only for certain astrological calculations. Undoubtedly, the disparity is quite evident, and determining the optimal outcome can be a daunting task to navigate without losing ourselves.

Borracci, who certainly received clarifications from Kremmerz (I, on the other hand, had no way of talking with him about it) adopted the Egyptian system. I know not what else to say, just as Paracelsus pointed out the distinction.

November 23, 1964

According to the names of the decans with the relative decarchs, the sequence is the same as provided by Kremmerz for the hours of the day. Therefore, an obvious link is present. The decans have always been considered efficient in the Hermetic environment; I could not judge if they are also in the astrological *strictu sensu*. For the so-called fixed stars; that is stars *tout court,* there is an influence from the constellations.

As for odors, there are no specific treatments but only fragments, even with Kremmerz, they were provided always occasionally and discontinuously. That there is an INFLUENCE as with certain minerals is certain, but I would say rather as a receptivity from *certain influences*. However, not with a mineral in and of itself, it brings good luck or bad luck, but rather what *adheres* to it.

Things are different with PERFUMES.

The *Crater Hermetis** carries indications for stones and foresees the engraving in them of the FIGURE of the decan, but it is a personification to be evaluated not as astrological but rather as magical, not to mention reservations concerning the correspondences indicated.

THE TAROT

October 26, 1963

For the four figures (i.e., sixteen) the distribution of the colors has to be kept in mind; first of all:

Clubs	Sol	Fire	Summer	North
	Male	Hylic	Monad	
Swords	Mercury	Air	Spring	East
	Male	Astral	Monad	
Cups	Luna	Water	Autumn	West
	Female	Astral	Monad	
Coins	Saturn	Earth	Winter	South
	Female	Hylic	Monad	

---

*[Fifteenth-century translation of a Byzantine manuscript by the humanist poet Lodovico Lazzarelli of San Severino. Lazzarelli gained access to one of the Greek manuscripts of the Corpus Hermeticum that had arrived from Byzantium—not the incomplete copy that Marsilio Ficino had used for his famous translation published in 1471, but one that included the three final treatises (CH XVI-XVIII). Lazzarelli produced a beautiful manuscript of all the known Hermetica in Latin, including his own translation of these previously unknown "Hermetic Definitions," with introductory prefaces by himself. He offered it to his master, as a sign of deep gratitude, because thanks to him he had been "reborn from spiritual seed." Lazzarelli understood better than any other reader the process of "spiritual rebirth" described in the Corpus Hermiticum.—*Trans.*]

Given the above, the four figures reproduce the same principles in each color, not for the season, but the principle contained in them. Therefore, for example, the Clubs are:

King	solar	Masculine action
Queen	lunar	Feminine action
Jack	Principle of motion	
Knight	Quaternary synthesis of the first three	

Or rather do we attribute the quaternary conclusion to both the Jack and the Knight?

The Knight should correspond to the aerial figures of the Bembine Tablet. Then, translating the four principles:

King	Principle of manifestation
Queen	Receptivity
Jack	Consolidation
Knight	Movement

Likewise with the other four colors.

In summary, by merging the color with the principle, the meaning becomes clearer.

Similarly, considering the fixed and the mobile, the King and Queen are the two fixed, Sun or North and Earth or South; Jack and Knight are the two pieces of furniture.

The movement of the sun, both rising and setting, provides the basis for the dynamism of the situation (Jack and Knight), while the first two figures (Sun and Moon) symbolize stability and permanence.

By arraying the three rows of cards:

- On the top row, we find the active principle.
- In the middle the piece of furniture (function of Mercury and the Moon with the two movable principles on which one acts).
- At the bottom are the results or final outcome of the situation.

If there are four rows of cards:

- On top, there is the King
- In the middle, the Knight and the Jack—of the LADY
- Below, the Queen
- In the respective correspondences of Sun, Mercury, Moon, and Earth

All this arranges suitably with the Bembine Tablet and the Hermetic doctrine. The complexity of the possible interpretations is understandable and evident and therefore I suggest at least three reviews:

- one of seven cards for three rows—static analysis
- one of nine cards for three rows—passive dynamics
- one of three cards for three rows—active dynamics

Then browse through four cards, and there should be $12 \times 4 = 48$, which will give the conclusion. In analogy with the I Ching, however, the four whole lines form two *intrinsic signs*, to be carried out to derive additional indications.

In the same way, especially in the case of static measurement or analysis of the action to be performed, it would be necessary to remove the middle row on three-in-two rows out of twelve—that is, compared to a derivable sequence.

The tarot analysis I consider superior to the I Ching without therefore discriminating between these two excellent mantic systems. This is because the tarot points to the vertical and to the Western tradition (Egypt being the true home of Western thought, later transmitted to Greece and Rome) first to form the nucleus of the response and then to cover it with accessories.

This is the correct method for examining and arranging the tarot cards. When laying out tarot cards, begin by observing whether the figures are positioned according to their relative value or if they deviate somewhat from their expected placement. Then, consider how they interact with both the central cards and the majority of the Minor Arcana.

Consequently, interpretations of the particular spread should be formulated in the following manner:

- on the dynamic sequence (or, in the case of static, tensile, or pressure analysis) on the row, reading from left to right
- on the motion of action-reaction concerning the lower rows, etc., and, that is, from top to bottom

Theoretically the last card should be placed in the lower right corner or, at least, a group of three cards in the lower right of the last row.

Then, putting in relation the deep significations of the Egyptian deities of the Bembine Tablet with the more external significance, one should see present, past, future, all in a formidable complex mantic presentation. Months would not be enough to interrogate a single oracle.

The minor cards must be classified according to their intrinsic values, of which a hint is given by the current values of the common cards: the ace is the Principle or One, the two "is worth" less, and so the three and the four would correspond to the intermediate phases of formation-creation.

The five—quintessence—holds greater significance than six, forming a double hidden triangle. The seven carries substantial value. The eight returns to being a hidden number, while the nine and ten take on a conclusive nature, their value contingent upon whether the emphasis is placed on final or predictive outcomes or on opportunities.

From a statistical standpoint, an abundance of "feminine" colors—such as golds and cups—suggests decadence and an inauspicious prognosis, whereas clubs and swords indicate the opposite. Additionally, clubs and swords offer a supplementary implication of contrast and tension, while gold and cups convey notions of peace and harmony.

It's evident that we must approach the TAROT not with the commonplace cartological notions often embraced by many, but rather with a sufficient understanding of Hermetic philosophy.

In summary, for each group of middle cards, for the minor cards, one must keep in mind the sequence of the cards drawn:

1. action or initiation;
2. reception or negative black—matrix;
3. mobile or negative white;
4. creation;
5. quintessence of the cycle that is reproduced with five superimposed;
6. double receptive ternary;
7. mobile as in Logos;
8. double quaternary as creation and hylic and astral.

The relative concepts are absolutely clear. In general, the tarot should be less susceptible to perturbations—say, telepathic—than the I Ching.

October 30, 1963

When interpreting the cards, it is crucial to follow three fundamental principles: maintain a left-to-right sequence, analyze the relationships between cards both horizontally and vertically, and observe the progression from top to bottom.

> One should interpret them accordingly by: SUITS - FIGURES - TRUMPS.
> Suits are better than small cards.
> Once understood, that the Horse or Knight is higher than the Jack (fool) or Lady, then
> the significance of Jack in fourth place as a feminine or passive element is valid.
> Horse—Mercury, mobility, and so on—provides the clearest of meanings.
> The FOOL is placed as the last card by some.

In synthesis, it can be said that the Fool signifies progress and reinforcement of the situation, except when it specifically denotes mental disorder. It corresponds to the dance of the god Shiva, the eternal mutation of things, and also, in certain cases, the reversal. True that it has an analogy with the concept of ZERO that, arithmetically, is a MULTIPLIER. And so I see the Fool, who I would always place correctly at the end of the major cards or trumps and not in seventy-eighth place.

When it comes to consulting someone to interpret tarot cards, I prefer sticking to a specific arrangement in the deal. Otherwise, if a particular card that the consultant should resonate with doesn't appear, it could imply the consultant's absence in the reading!

I would place it at the top: at the far right (as the subject that submits to a situation and asks, etc.).

Regarding reversed cards, they can indicate a positive sign if they're part of an ascending series [3, 6, 9], or a negative sign if they're part of a descending series [10, 5, 1]. Meaning positive or negative concerning the significance of the card. This is why it is necessary to see the sense or Tao of the response.

My system of shuffling the cards is quite distinct: first putting all the loose cards on the table and then moving them, turning them over, even mixing the groups of cards vertically.

In this way, the mixing takes place after the previous deal, and only afterward do I collect the cards and compose the deck to break it down into four small piles that I recompose in order:

- The top pile—Sol
- Upper median—Mercury
- Lower median—Luna
- At the bottom—Saturn

Another system, however, may be different.

Certainly, they are to be felt vibrating when it is time to collect the cards after the mixing, I repeat, with the pile on the plane. Of course, you should feel the vibration when it's time to pick up the cards after shuffling, randomly spread out on the surface. Likewise, a similar sensation should be experienced when casting the coins of the I Ching.

Generally, the reversal means to delay or a reversal of action, with therefore negative meaning. The correspondences are unequivocal with the three great eonic numbers: seven, twelve, four. Tarots are less (not entirely) influenced by the personal unconscious because they are directed toward the higher planes.

November 20, 1963

The card known as the Throne, no. 10—Temperance—showing a woman who pours liquid from one cup to another, is placed in relationship to the other trump card, no. 17, the Star. In both, there is a decanting or transfer, but while in the Star the fluid is turned toward the earth and fecundated, in Temperance it is maintained in the cup or vase.

This, therefore, symbolizes the Great Work or Great Arcana, as well as the passage, we would say, for the avatar, from one body to another.

In the Star, the fluids dissolve in the natural order (natural magic in a sense is quite different from the Kremmerzian one) and in a vulgar sense, the meaning of the oracle can be dissociation (which would have a certain correspondence with the hexagram Huann, no. 59 of the *I Ching*).

In a sense, three segments of the I Ching should correspond to a trump: this, for its part, acquires variation with the position, the middle cards, the minor cards.

Temperance can also mean death, but death following an auspicious future, while the Star would give a less auspicious prognosis, a certain descent. In any case, even the meaning of fecundation must be kept in mind. . . . Also, transmutation, for Temperance, represents a passage of form, of content, even in the preservation of the fundamental structure, while in the Stars there should be a change of structure.

The vulgar meaning of moderation, of self-restraint, can be derived from the attitude of the angelic figure, which does not spread seed to the ground; hence a generic meaning of retraction, prudence, and the like.

But the basic meaning in Temperance remains the PASSAGE in all senses and, in a certain sense, the closure of the circuit, which remains open to the Stars. These correspond to the astrological influence; whereas Temperance, instead, corresponds to the solar influence or of a single star.

Epistolaria Confidenziale
(Confidential Epistolary)

Epistolaria Confidenziale, edited by Giammaria
(Genoa: private edition, 1990).

The following letters are part of personal exchanges that closely correspond to the ultra decade-long correspondence with Ours, and are practically identical (all dated from Rome) to those previously extracted from the Philosophical Epistolary.

All the letters are typewritten except for three: the one dated July 19, 1955, which was handwritten on pink onionskin paper using green ink; the letter from May 22, 1961, written on white letter paper with blue and red inks; and the correspondence from February 8, 1965, also handwritten on onionskin paper but in white, using blue ink.

The following eight letters are unique to the correspondence found within the *Epistolaria Confidenziale*:

January 19, 1953
July 19, 1955
January 21, 1960
January 25, 1960
July 23, 1963
July 7, 1968
May 12, 1969
June 1, 1969

The penultimate letter from Marco Daffi to Giammaria, dated May 12, 1969, roughly a little more than three months before the Baron's death on September 3, 1969, can be read as Daffi's final testament, bestowing on Giammaria executorship over material to be released.

Monday, January 19, 1953
Dear friend,

On today's date I wrote a long letter to G.,* a friend of our friends.

---

*[Elio G. was a medical doctor and surgeon from Genoa, contemporaneous with Daffi. Elio was a practicing initiate and member of Daffi's Pharaonic Group, Andromeda Circle, and Pleiades Ring from the 1930s until Daffi's death in 1969. Elio inherited the archive of Daffi's initiatic writings and material.—*Trans.*]

However, this correspondence was not directed to you—not because he isn't a friend (do you like the play on words?) but since his journey is on another path, with which you have astutely surmised from the image, "another ray toward the same center, so that the closer that it arrives at this end, the more the distances between the different rays diminish."

They are indeed friends, and G. is among them, who in a virtual sense is part of the Pharaonic Group in potential union with the Canadian center, with whom in 1929 I engaged in material correspondence with, and whose relationship—reviewed and endorsed—passed through Kremmerz.

I pleaded with the group headed by my friend Domenico Catinella (Bari, Palazzo di Citta [street name redacted] no. 5) to allow them to retain the Lunations, once again edited by this group, heir of the destroyed academy of Bari, with whom I have been linked to by friends, but in complete autonomy, because of the confederative affiliation that I approve of between those who remained of the Myriam and the Pharaonic Group.

Also for this reason I am writing my critical overview of the story of the Myriam, from which it is possible to derive a general principle valid for all magic practitioners and which could then deductively be applied to the same group of friends.

Subsequently, I will proceed to the editing phase, working on the draft and subjecting it to the scrutiny of the Pharaonic Group's principles, all while leveraging my accumulated knowledge.

The work on the Tarot continues. It will be in this sense—cultural and editorial—the primary scope of the Pharaonicus Group.

Your cordially welcomed friend,

Mörköhekdaph*

Tuesday, July 19, 1955, morning 06:45

Dear friend,

I send you the usual annual forecasts that could be a further reminder of your well-ascended Soul.

---

*[Vulgarized under the pseudo-pseudonym of Marco Daffi. —*Trans.*]

Regarding our friend G, I, respectful—as always with all the adepts—of the freedom of not doing, I would like to find the halfway point between the (my) Right not to give and the Requirement not to offer.

You, Gian, will be able, if you "feel" like it, to call or otherwise say that near you, there is something that he could copy on the spot, that is, without giving him something. With this, we will have the desired proof of your involvement . . .

I must bring to conclusion an essential chemical operation (you would say that, Gian Maria), and as it's commonly known, the substance cannot be extracted from the fire until the work in *rubedo* is completed.

Cordially,

Your very affectionate friend

February 26, 1957

Dear Gian M.

Thanks again for the undeserved praise on my Hermetic exposition; but I prefer to draw attention to the priority of the "discovery" of the white and black negative formula.

Of course, if I shall continue to live, I will have to print what can be given to the printers for printing.

Concerning the passage from the "Ternary to the Quaternary," I would be grateful if you could copy those three or four tables of the passage, of which I speak, of the Ternary inserted in the Quaternary.

All that is required is to sketch with the names of the conventional deities, of which we have agreed.

Yours,

October 26, 1959, Monday, 12:10 p.m.

Dear Gian M.

As I've said and written repeatedly, I am and will always be delighted to correspond with her,* since she is for me an excellent catalyst of ideas

---

*[Auri Compolonghi Gonnella, Giammaria's wife, companion, initiate, painter, sculptor, author, and designer of a tarot deck.—*Trans.*]

and perspectives, happy to be able to contribute to her exploration of alchemical symbolism to the best of my ability, although my expertise leans more toward the magical aspect.

You have astutely observed that the gods have not remained inert. Of course, the problem connected with individuation revolves around Consciousness. It's the very essence that renders Man eternal through the state of consciousness (in memory, both down here and up there). Reflection on the One is key. Becoming a Numen occurs when one creates themself as a divinity.

I will resume the noted work, incorporating in a semi-subconscious elaboration what you suggest to me.

Nothing new with external happenings . . .

Affectionately yours,

Wednesday, October 28, 1959, 13 hr. It's 27 x 59.*
Witnesses arrived.

Dear Gian,

Inspired and spurred on, as ever, by your sharp objections, I hastily jot down brief responses, albeit with significant reservations:

(a) to treat them in ulterior tables, and

(b) to carry out those corrections of expression, that help authenticate the unpublished (or perhaps even uneditable?)—I mean, the ineditable—material for my four readers. Also, the notion of dining together would be splendid . . . wouldn't it?

De mulieribus (How is she doing? given your expertise with Latin) the problem is very garbled and obscured in our Monist West from a religious point of view: the Semitic religions have been characterized by a form of contempt for the feminine: cf. the discussions whether

---

*[A convention Daffi employed was to include not only the date but the hour and the size in cm. of the paper used when corresponding. In Daffi's magical schema, each hour of a particular date has either a positive or negative valuation and is imbued with a particular virtue.—*Trans.*]

the woman has a soul, unfortunately, homologous to the claims of such Buddhist sects, which claim women cannot reach nirvana.

Sunday, December 13, 1959, 7:30 a.m.

Reference my December and your letters of the 4th and 9th December
   Dear Gian Maria,

I enclose the schema, if you want to see if it can be published, who knows when . . . it would be worth another Ternary to study it carefully on the scheme already studied by the TWO of US.

Moreover, in reference to my previous (letter), I would like to add that Kremmerz was the first to disclose the "initiatic" dimension of the eons. I believe that "The Hermetic Door" served as a mediated passage—probably not officially authorized, as he hinted, much like you observed earlier. He seemed intent on concealing the precise and fluid connection with the eons, which he preferred to refer to as eonic. Additionally, he frequently mentioned "elementals" and even provided suggestions and hints regarding various ingestible medicines for patients. For these elementals, individualized monads, a specific fluidic mixture and a temporary adjustment (which does not compromise their eternal monadic autonomy) might be applicable. Immerse (imbibe) the elemental in the operative vir.

I would say that the imbibition in the elementals (the intuition of Goethe) is the first step among poets, sensitives, aroused lovers, and artists to perceive the invisible, okay?

On the progressive *iter*, I've answered with the table on the rotation of the cross (refer). I can say that:

Vir = Sol acting upon

Virgo = vir agens = negative black if it operates as vir. Negative white, if it operates, as in the example in question, of Luna.

The third term, ♀, will earn you gallons by cooperating to purify the Mercury (moly herb, or Lunar fluids, cited by Evola in a note of *The Hermetic Tradition* that he certainly did not understand).

Then, they, the operator will have formed the true and proper **Solar** body, intended as a stable center, to act on ♀ similarly to what the **Vir** does. More is not possible by letter.

Affectionally yours,

P.S. For this reason, I reiterate that after your initial "declaration," if your Lady fully commits to you during the iter, the day when the attraction wanes in your later years (assuming the Lady is uncertain about the man's Vir, which you embody), it could significantly impact the Lady's fate. Didn't she express the idea that when bitten by the Dragon, one must transform into the Dragon to avoid being ensnared by its jaws?"

But at this point, you are made for each other.

Best wishes.

Saturday, December 19, 1959, 12:30 p.m.

In reply to your letter of December 16, 1959.

Dearest Giammaria,

The Buddhist Lamas explained to Tucci the concept of Waters from the Primordial Lake.

Indeed, you aptly note that these deities are bound to their positioning on the material and existential plane.

This insight reflects a profound intuition or vision! Christianity echoes a similar idea through its emphasis on the "humanity" of Christ in Jesus.

Of course, there has been and will be discussions about God (I agree, *sine sensii*) and there is no need to get involved in definitions . . .

I will resume my work on the commentary of the tables,* upon your return from the mountains.

We will have news to exchange . . . but in the meantime, I will give you one that will please you: I started with three supporting friends of both sexes, to layout the Bembine Tablet in relation to the Tarot cards. Let's keep track of Kircher's perspective for the central and median figures: Major Arcana.

Have a good rest and affectionately yours.

---

*[Reference to "Instructional Tables on Hermeticism," in Giammaria's book *Compendium of Hermetics* and the tables included in *Marco Daffi and his Work: Tables and Commentary* by Giammaria. The tables have not been translated into English yet.—*Trans.*]

January 21–24, 1960

We've already argued, wisely, about whether man should only be considered subject to the categories: here my idea takes its cue from the question and expands on the previous one too.

Kremmerz, however, from a preparatory point of view, is wrong about what he had written (I believe it's the first time in centuries) on invisible beings (of the eonic, he would say), which is incorrect. He should have insisted in the first printed works on the exoteric philosophical ideas connected to the different images and figures, and only later, with some of those in print and others not, to state the specific entities as autonomous entities in the common sense of the Deity.

January 21–25, 1960

In comparing the figure on the pediment of the Hermetic Door with that of Khunrath's Amphitheater, I tried to highlight the idea of entanglement of the Sephirotic emanations in contact with the plane of the black astral.

A good reference is found in table V of the *Amphitheatraum Sapientaiae Aeternae* published in 1609 that was brought to my attention with the Atanor edition. Although the comment is emphasized as the fruit of illustrious names, indeed the editor expressly says of "luminous comments" by doctors Papus, Marc Haven before, and Stanislaus De Guaita after, however, these distinguished scholars have written without having a hand in the dough, and since we are dealing with tables, and since I feel a little piqued to rectify what these illustrious commentators have written, I have made my own, albeit condensed, comments.

I affirm that the description of the figures can be approximately accepted, but not when the authors delve further into their meanings, and it should also be noted that the comment is incomplete as it does not give the whole text of the Hebrew inscriptions of the ten angelic "choirs" and is incomplete in other parts . . .

Kindest regards.

January 26, 1960

P.S. Recall attention to the figure in the Amphitheater of the triangle of flame on the top, on the tiara-ed dove at the foot of the human figure, on the clouds of Azuluth in the dark among the ten sephirot in the form of tiaras above the trine of God the Father . . .

Monday, March 20, 1961, 2:00 p.m.

Ref. Your letter of 18 cm. from this morning.

Dearest Giammaria,

You are truly frightening! With your Elephant's memory, applied to the analysis of the Sacred Wheel, you pin me against the wall!

I can't recall the exact "names," or rather "pseudonyms," of the themes; please bear in mind what was mentioned earlier.

In any case, thank you for raising the topic; as I've already said you're an excellent catalyst, and since I have to address the public (four stray cats), I'll carefully consider everything that has been said. It's possible that some might have questions or not fully understand, but I'll do my best to clarify,

While you climb Monte Viso, I will try to make the six tables mentioned above beautiful . . . alright?

By "astrological analysis" be more precise; are you asking me to provide a more specific interpretation?

I will see what can be done.

Affectionately yours.

May 22, 1961

The old tables you refer to can be aligned and integrated with other deities.

As the fourth term in progress, this could explain your feelings.

But on the experiences of the seven forms, it would be necessary to speak verbally.

Great Heraclitus! I did not know this text.

The *Commentarium* isn't that impressive.

The best of Kremmerz are his *Dialogues* and *Lunations*—they are truly valuable and well worth the investment.

Dearly.

June 2, 1962

To you, who momentarily was lost days ago

Dearest Giammaria,

Was Fulcanelli truly an initiate?

I cannot make a definitive judgment.

Keep in mind that "if they are alive," we shall be able to perceive intellectually or Hermetically what clothes they wear: by knowing someone personally, the knowledge of who they are, occurs immediately, I would say almost spontaneously.

If deceased, we can understand either from the course of their life, even through falsifications, or from their writings whether or not they were initiates.

And then, to what degree?

Dante was, but to my conviction not of the highest.

Balzac was higher than Dante, but also not one of the foremost.

For me, Fulcanelli wasn't either an initiate, but merely a copyist (I refer to Evola), at best, at the early stages, more of an interested or aspiring initiate than a fully initiated adept. It's as if he was a member of the Myriam.

Yours affectionately.

July 23, 1962

Dearest Gian M.

On my exposition of the alchemical-Hermetic doctrine regarding the concept of electromagnetic creation (primarily electrical), do we want to say electric of the material world? I seek your advice. I've positioned Sol and Luna based on a binary solution, while the Dissolution and Coagulation of the polarized Alembics are depicted in separate sketches to convey the idea.

. . . as a token of appreciation, I eagerly await a metaphorical laurel wreath! ❄

Sending warm hugs and best wishes for your mountain climbing adventures—don't let the sweat get to you!

July 24, 1962

To Gian M.

The figure of Lilith, her concept, quite predictably the theologians overshadow her which is cumbersome because they do not know where to place her!

Have a good mountain climb (but no hanging!) And in September we will hear from you again.

It is necessary to see and talk at length on these Tables of Alembics, etc.

Affectionately yours,

March 3, 1963, Sunday, 17:27

Dear Gian M.

I want to add a more in-depth view (this note brings advice) of that curious error in the transcription of the initiatory name of Kremmerz-Formisano.

It is believed that the unwary pseudo-vulgarizers of his name that should not have been desecrated (Hahahiahh & C.) believed in a supposed name of a type like this, which for example I pretend:

J (incorrectly points to = Julianus?)

M. what do I know: magister or magnus, etc, and then attached to Krem-Erz. Do you agree with this?

Instead, there are letters written differently, as indicated . . .

Dearly affectionate.

Saturday, March 23, 1963, 17:30

Received your package with the attached letter

Dated 23 but stamped 22

Dearest Gian M.

There was no need for the complete refund of the MM-Sacconi, since among my commitments (and they are not few: I lack the time to read as much as I would like) I cannot include astrology, which is a relative art.

We agree that *Astra inclinat non cogunt*, but the accurate predictions are rather, I believe, due to unconscious clairvoyance.

I don't know if I sent you the astronological study of Kerneïtz, who died very old and whose material has been published in recent months.

Reflect on this: it's the Karma = Desire for new birth that determines—among other factors of the reincarnative vortex—also the zodiacal alignment.

Additionally, consider the concept of zodiacal interlocking. (see Ps. XXIII).*

I agree with this study, but I do not want to write a treatise on it.

You can see who has different ideas about the value of astrology from an esoteric point of view.

To regard Fate as a tendency, as you rightly suggest, aligns with the Hermetic tradition.

I'm aware that for an astrologer, the hour and even the minutes of birth hold significance; so, I've heard . . . as the monks and the wanderers of the sublime have mentioned!

As for me, when I seek a reading, I feign interest in prognostication to conceal my genuine and tested clairvoyant abilities under the guise of pseudo-astrological inquiry (what I call astrono-logic). Do we understand each other, then?

Nowadays, it's enough for me to fix my gaze on a person, even if vaguely described, and perhaps it's even better if I know their place of residence, to unleash:

"With such authorization
   I'm pleased that you will venture
   as the Veltro† of the astral plane."

A friend of mine, an eon, used to tell me this.

As for Palamidessi, I am copying the Ode, because it was lost in the chaos of war.

Agreed: it should be emphasized that, as a connoisseur—not even

---

*[Likely a reference to a page in Kerneïtz's text.—*Trans.*]

†[Literally meaning *veloce cane* or rapid canine. The veltro in the *Divine Comedy* is the mysterious character announced by the poet Virgil, in the first canto of the Inferno (vv. 100–111). Metaphorically, veltro refers to a celestial being, specifically a hound, that is associated with a prophecy predicting the coming of a savior-like figure who will bring peace and justice to Italy and Europe. The identity of this figure has been debated by scholars over the centuries, with interpretations ranging from historical figures to symbolic representations of divine intervention. The "veltro" symbolizes hope and the potential for redemption in the midst of chaos and suffering.

as a scholar—of the integral science, he has never even glimpsed the antechamber. Did he not hesitate to amend (I would kindly correct the initial verse of Song III on page 117 of the aforementioned work) the "hand" in the text to "right," asserting that it is less generic? What a buffoon.

And what can one expect from someone who writes on clericalism, albeit well disguised, in the *Illustrated Tribune*, which I also sometimes buy?

. . .

You know how severe I am with Kremmerz-Formisano to whose foolishness I owe my present state almost exclusively. And with such a kaleidoscope I see everything, I say everything on what he wrote and spoke.

I've caused him to crumble!

And today who knows how I would treat him!

Anyway, the criticism is constructive and not destructive . . .

I lean toward your zodiacal intuition . . . also in my opinion the "twelve wise men" have been and are ample filler *pour epater le bourgeois* and nothing more.

Here a small surviving group is practicing the Kons ritual (Kons sin dar, Chaldean priestly entity); one of the good things, along with the Lunations.

With whom, twenty chaste days is the only time I agree on this point.

I wish you the best.

Aff. yours,

July 23, 1963, 12:30 p.m.

Dearest Giammaria,

I'll summarize in part what I wrote to my friend G. this morning (10:00 a.m.).

It was symptomatic that I had the urge to express (within the limits of graphic possibilities) the arcane concept, but understandable to us, of the gravitational force or vital force, which for the common person as for the initiate, refers to a state of consciousness.

Naturally, it is inductive in the electromagnetic sense, and submits to the influence without perception until elevated states are reached.

This force is valid both to keep the components of being (human organism) together and to act socially and in the environment.

This is the cycle of activity and senescence and applies to both social and economic creations of man, as well as to his own life.

Two tables and a comment can give an idea of my work.

It is the same law that applies to initiation. I'm currently working at a different table and will review all the comments in detail later today.

My situation stems from the well-known incident during which my consciousness remained clouded. It wasn't until the crisis a month ago that a completely negative memory resurfaced, echoing the loss of consciousness and darkness I experienced during that time.

I am bringing the (initiatory) consciousness back to its primary state. Another favorable thing is certainly the fact that I have set the problem to put back in place my consciousness and the gravitational energy that holds together the components of Being.

Everything can be changed, even compromised situations, even "impossible" situations.

Your aff. Mo.

Saturday 26th October 1963

Ref. Received yesterday, but evidently to be dated 24, having arrived yesterday afternoon on the 25th.

My Dearest Giammaria,

I've returned to working on the tables and commentary.

Many ideas were sketched out, and I've found ideas from them dated 1957. For example, an idea that you gave me on the evolution of the monads, especially the astral ones concerning initiation.

Fortunate outcomes (which I truly desire) have coincided with my ability to delve into the wisdom of the I Ching and explore the intricacies of the Bembine Tablet. This allows me to make comprehensive comparisons. Don't you find it fascinating?

Why don't you consult the Tarot on my affairs?

These are the two questions:

It would not be bad, in this our collaboration, if you review the values of the minor cards in the sequential alternation that I've mentioned.

Curious to know what comes out of your consultation.

Stay Healthy.

Aff. yours,

Wednesday October 30, 1963, 10:30 a.m.
Ref. Both 28 cm.

Dear Gian M.,

I don't subscribe to the conventional meanings commonly attributed to suits; instead, it's essential to delve into their philosophical significance and then derive the horoscopic implications from there.

Nevertheless, this task requires consideration of what you regard as pertinent, which, regarding suits, appears to be minimal.

I feel the vibrancy when it's time to pick up the cards after shuffling.

I await your oracle to attend to my affairs.

On the anniversary of the dead, I go, as usual, to the cemetery, and, as always, I stop by the niche of your grandfather, Vittorio.

In anticipation and with sincere affection.

Aff. yours,

November 20, 1963
Dear Giammaria,

I've consulted the I Ching further to your investigation, etc., and continued with my Tarot research.

I favor the idea that after the solstice, you will conduct the scrutiny, just as I will do independently with the I Ching and the Tarot.

Do you know that in the horoscopes made in 1962, about character, personality, etc., of nineteen names, so far 80 percent have been accurate? Two names were 95 percent accurate to their surprise.

I'm glad that you have grasped the meaning of the overturned cards, which I personally experienced, with the fanning system on the table.

As you handle the deck, you'll sense a vibration, a subtle notion indicating the opportune moment to gather the cards into groups, which eventually come together again.

This process parallels that of the I Ching.

In your letter dated October 29, 1962, you mentioned that your lady consults with the Tarot. In response, I posed my customary questions.

You informed me that your lady is currently unwell, although I remain unaware of the specific ailment. Consequently, I await her recovery before addressing my inquiries with a factual understanding.

Since then, I have not received any further updates.

Having crafted a horoscope for a legal matter, I wonder if it's the same as the painted cards and the "intuitive" horoscopes, as you wrote, but with greater precision.

Affectionately yours,

December 8, 1963

On the correspondences that you've discussed between the four quadrants and the four planes, it seems to me that they go (hand in hand). When Countess Sacconi passed away, I found myself without anyone to verify her technical assertions regarding the three dominants: zodiacal, planetary, and elemental.

I also believe that the theme of domiciles has its own reason for not being an *ad personas*.*

It's a good idea to proceed first with an evaluation of the general value of the horoscope and then with particular influences.

It seems to me then that the planet at the time of birth must be given importance.

It's right what you say about Jung's intuitions and, on the other hand, about his drifting, typical of a scholar who never laid his hands in the dough.

---

*[Domiciles refers to the division of the zodiac into twelve astrological houses. Here Daffi is saying the domiciles or houses provide information related to archetypal tendencies and not to that of a personal nature.—*Trans.*]

I know of your perplexities regarding karma and reincarnation, otherwise, I would suggest reading what Kerneïtz wrote on the relationship between karma and astrological themes.

Kerneïtz passed away a few years ago and his work went unpublished for years.

In any case, I wouldn't want to get involved in the study of astrology, which, after all, I couldn't start practicing.

I have plenty with the I Ching so other things are pressing.

I am enclosing a summary list of new tables.

But then what are we going to do with it?

In which wastepaper basket will we throw these writings?

Affectionately yours,

December 10, 1963 11:30 a.m.

Dear Giammaria,

I held off on my response to fully understand what you are observing: but in principle, I would agree, especially on the quadrants that would lead to a general orientation with the setting of their relative horoscopes.

For the remainder, I have already conveyed my findings.

I set out to throw down a fundamental concept for the later tables, namely on matter, which materialist philosophies (Jainists, semi-materialists, and monadists, however, included) are considered as something distinct from souls and destined to dissolve into an *ekyprosis** or reabsorb themselves in the bosom of the One.

With respect to the postmortem cycle, I am reviewing the notes (following our conversations) on the state of consciousness (?) in this state (three cycles) and on the relationship of nutrition through fluids or incense or other means for support and nutrition, as assumed in certain traditions.

---

*[A Stoic belief in the periodic destruction of the cosmos by a great conflagration every Great Year. The cosmos is then recreated (palingenesis) only to be destroyed again at the end of the new cycle. This form of catastrophe is the opposite of *kataklysmos*, the destruction of the earth by water.—*Trans.*]

As you can see, I have a lot to think about, also because before your intervention, all this important part of our becoming had remained unanswered, moreover not even addressed, if not in vague philosophical terms, by anyone and never in terms that were so technical, except for Kremmerz's written and verbal sketches.

Could this inquisitive and introspective nagging of mine be a foretaste?

It must be certain that a noticeable change (alas, oh how much I wish!) is taking place.

And at the same time, there's philosophical progress, thanks also to you.

P.S. And what about modern ideas concerning anti-matter, almost to our way of seeing, or about hyper fluidic states of worlds? (Do you perceive a glimpse of my notion of a pre-astral realm here?)

If you see my intuitive progress in this, let me know, otherwise, feel free to candidly share your thoughts, which I value.

Dearly.

March 3, 1964

In reference to your letter of February 18, 1964

Dearest Giammaria,

I owe you my heartfelt apologies for forgetting your birthday wishes, now, and as always, I wish you the very best.

I eagerly await the investigations conducted by your Lady using the Tarot cards. I believe she practices with the same skill and insight as you do.

Having thoroughly read and reread your notes on astrology, I find this approach to be more precise overall than modern scientific and divinatory methods.

Your distinction-application regarding the ego is particularly precise. While you declare the ego as ephemeral (not sharing the idea of reincarnation), it could also be described as "current."

The historical "I," which you consider ephemeral, can only be explored through astron-logic.

At 14:00 on the dot, I received your 1-cm. [letter] followed by the response on the Tarot as well.

Regarding the "aspects" between planets in the zodiac signs (rather than between the planets themselves, which are mobile), this concept was already discussed in our previous conversations, and I believe it to be accurate.

Kremmerz (aside from his masking antics, which are deplorable nonetheless) has consistently associated himself with Chaldean magic.

Now, however, we must tread the middle path. It is unwise to insist that the subject must be as skeletal as the ancient ones you consulted; there is more to explore.

Is there an objective that serves as the basis for all those subjective integrations that clearly emerge from the reticence of moderns?

I think there is.

It means that the subject will be more or less developed and complete, but in short, the fundamental themes and the sketches of personalities should not miss their purpose: this is an average.

I submit to you the question raised by some, and which I am duly interested in, namely that in addition to the birth theme it would be necessary to integrate with the theme of pre-birth.

This is carried out according to a curious calculation to reverse the motion of the Sun and can take into consideration a point located from one month to six months before birth.

Could the consideration have a basis?

An influence or correspondence with the "sky" can certainly occur before birth; and in some way psychoanalysis, even within its limits and its exaggerations, does not err by giving importance to uterine life.

Now then, with this integration, it would appear that errors in the horoscope made on the birth chart would turn up. An integrative investigation of which it would be better to define ways and limits.

Because if the two themes lead to discrepancies, which one will be the one to take into consideration?

Some propose a theme on conception, and it cannot be denied that, theoretically, this would be the most relevant theme to address.

However, it's practically impossible to comprehend that precise moment of erotic rapture of the monad, not to mention the confusion that arises from the introduction of three different methods!*

Oh! I know well that you see in astrology that it is a mirror of the moment in which one "comes" into the world.

And what about individual freedom? And the changes in collective or cosmic facts? And the impact with the revolutionary facts of science and technology that were unpredictable at the time of birth?

Your vision of astrology does not have all these issues on the table, since it is radical in the relativization of the relationship between man and world following the strictly alchemical vision, unlike the magical one that I've informed myself about.

I have had a long exchange of ideas with a young friend who would like to destroy the concept of time!

In his own words, he's had to admit, it is useless to summarize this interesting philosophical discussion.

However, it could be argued that, for an annual cycle, influences can be determined: and my interlocutor has admitted that if the future can be foreseen, then this can be valid for the annual cycles; and in fact what would the magical-zodiacal years be if not annual cycles pre-determined from time to time by forces to which we give the name of numina, for human affairs?

Affectionately yours,

April 29, 1964

Your 23 April letter arrived at 11:24, an elaborate response for these days.

Dearest Giam M.,

After your observations, I've carefully reread the Theoretical Exposition of February 18, 1964, and, except for what I write after thoughtful reflection, I find it is accurate and pertinent to everything we have said and written to each other.

---

*[Astrology, tarot, and psychoanalysis.—*Trans.*]

However, I remain of the opinion that the will at all costs to arrange the data in an ascending and descending linear line is no more than a graphic expedient if we want to capture an astrological tendency.

On the other hand, everything is artificial, because it is arranged in the opposite way to the astronomical orientation that places the sun in the north and its rising to the east and not in the west, and the sun turns clockwise and not counterclockwise.

The (fixed) cross of existence is, however, variable depending on the inclination of the *medium coeli* and this, as stated, provides a better criterion for interpretation with the greater or lesser width of the different fields, i.e., squares, while the two-square fields will always be equivalent in extension if the two semicircles on the ascendant line are taken, otherwise, they will also be unequal.

In my opinion, the actual astronomical hours of birth have their importance; experience comforts me in this regard.

The idea that the actual date of birth is the background to something deeper than the personality . . . and I also think that the prenatal period, calculated as you like, has its influence thereby disagreeing with what you think.

On the other hand, I agree with your introduction of fixed and mobile elements in the dynamic theme . . . as well as the haruspicy* that you've intuited.

As for the I Ching, I have personal experience that situations change; a forecast can extend months, a maximum of six.

Afterward (temporal sequence) the horoscope can repeat itself but must be recast.

In addition, with the I Ching, a horoscope may appear vague and difficult to interpret accurately. In such cases, the question is often repeated to seek clarification on the meaning of the previous response,

---

*[The religion of ancient Rome practiced the reading of omens specifically from the liver by a haruspex (plural haruspices; also called haruspex). He was a person trained to practice a form of divination called haruspicy (*haruspicina*), the inspection of the entrails of sacrificed animals, especially the livers of sacrificed sheep and poultry.—*Trans.*]

especially regarding specific features, and the system continues to function.

As for being able to turn to the oracle only for cases of extreme importance, it makes no sense.

If everything is embraced by the Tao, even small things can be investigated and then what can you say if a certain thing is small?

On the other hand, it's fine not to ask futile questions or get lost in the carelessness of living room dialogues.

The significance of the differences between the Egyptian and Chaldean systems does not strongly persuade me, from my perspective.

I have nearly relinquished my attempt to confirm the ebb and flow of positivity and negativity throughout the hours. Detecting their relative influences has proven elusive. However, I've observed that the calculations involving the sequential alignment of the seven planets—something we previously explored—yield a more predictable and controlled influence.

It seems to me that the element "ruler of the astrological hour" (not of real birth) could be relegated as secondary.

I would be grateful if you and your Lady could perform a Tarot reading for me using the Etteilla System. I have meticulously transcribed the cards.

While awaiting your response, I remain in gratitude and faith.

Aff. Yours.

November 23, 1964, 11:30 a.m.

Dearest Gian M.,

I repeat: when casting a horoscope, as you say, I do not know if the decans should be discarded . . .

As far as your concerns about the tables, first of all, the work that I have almost finished, the critical review of Croce's* thesis, is parallel to the consideration and copying of what I am sending you.

---

*[Benedetto Croce (1866–1952) was an Italian idealist philosopher, historian, and politician, who wrote on numerous topics, including philosophy, history, historiography, and aesthetics. In most regards, Croce was a liberal, although he opposed laissez-faire free trade and had considerable influence on other Italian intellectuals, including both Marxist Antonio Gramsci and Fascist Giovanni Gentile.—*Trans.*]

Therefore, if I hadn't meditated on *The Krater of Wisdom* I wouldn't have been able to send the work on decans, decarchs, and stars.

As far as I can discern, it appears that we have reached an agreement to exclude sensitive points and similar omens. However, endorsing the influence of the decans seems to align with Hermetic doctrine.

What age does the *Krater* date from?

Certainly, it is not ancient, filled with Gnostic and Neoplatonic expressions: Croce himself supports your thesis of the thieving after the persecutions of Theodosius and before the massacre of the last priests of Eleusis.

But I have the impression that Croce is clericalized, as far as it can be ascertained (and could not fail to) with the doctrine of rebirth, he eliminates the related expressions from the index: reincarnation, metempsychosis, etc.

They are preconceived theses that can be dismantled.

I believe that diamonds (like other stones) can carry a curse within them.

In any case, the stones indicated in the *Krater* are so exotic and strange, except for the few that we know, that it doesn't seem appropriate to bring them back. I believe in such a personification.

Kremmerz also reports names, but not with the result of such a jumble of indications that I consider irrelevant, and the data are discordant and not homogeneous. And then, if an influence is to be attributed to the decans, the idea is unacceptable that only in a decan can evocations be made for immediate practical purposes, such as having to wait a year to guard against certain influences!

I will have to rethink that to which you ask me and will try to discern the best with regard to perfumes.

If you wish I can also make a copy of the zodiac circle at your convenience.

Is it possible for your Lady to consult the Tarot for me?

Dearly.

Aff. Yours.

December 9, 1964

Your letter sent on the 3rd arrived here on the 4th.

Dearest Giammaria,

There is a distinction between teaching, which undoubtedly can also be done by women, and the initiatory plane, but in the current state of civility, which I would rather say of barbarity, there are no known masters.

Maybe it is not talked about with good reason? Out of prudence? In order not to reveal how much, that even in arcane relationships between a woman and a man, there is much that can easily be misunderstood?

Instead, a man as "initiator" (teacher) is generally admitted.

You will note that until historical times, even within the Christian era, it was believed that women did not possess a soul, considering also their secular subjugation. With this in mind, you can easily understand how, along with the conventional notions of chastity, a silent narrative emerged regarding the Templar, Essene, and Albigensian "sisters."

But there are many arguments.

You say that the "problems are exacerbated by the monadic (structure) approach seen from a higher perspective." However, everything could be streamlined if we were to consider it in terms of "energy fields."

The two, mine and yours, derive from two different visions and schools: the magical one in which I work and the alchemical one to which you adhere.

Fortunately for me, I have conversations with two friends who have become aficionados on occult matters.

I am otherwise busy, now, but I expect soon to resume writing, to refine what I have already sketched.

Best wishes for the New Year, in which I request new mantic investigations (Tarot) on me by your kind Lady.

Aff. Yours,

February 8, 1965

Schematic answer to the questions.

Letter 3 from February

Remember to properly manage the energy released through Isiac-fluidic processes.

I emphasize the critical importance of the second vase.

Alchemists obscured women's development, despite women having equal potential as men in pursuing the initiatory path.

But, I repeat, we remain Adech* or Eve, however, having within ourselves the heterosexual possibilities.

Would it be suitable to represent the Rebis within a closed mental circuit, featuring human figures in a circle with open arms and legs, alongside an open circuit displaying the signs of Venus (infinite matrix) and Mars (infinite logos) on a table? Such as:

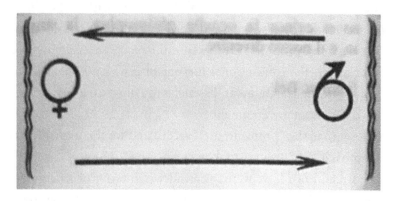

June 7, 1968

To Gian Gonella and Giorgio Maccio†

The principle of the propagation of Gnosis is not entrusted to the existence of associations and groups that are more or less openly eso-

---

*[According to cabalistic and gnostic teachings, Adech is the internal man or Superior Manas made of the flesh of Adam. In *Esoteric Medicine* by Samael Aun Weor it is called the Body of the Innermost and refers to the vehicle for the Archaeus, or [astral] vital life force, that Paracelsus also called the Mumia (from the Egyptian medical sources).—*Trans.*]

†[Letter from Baron don Ricciardo Ricciardelli to two correspondents from Genoa. This letter was included in an abridged form by Giammara. Instead I am presenting here the complete letter from Daffi to Giammaria and Giorgio Maccio who shared this letter with me without all of Giammaria's edits and omissions. Giorgio Maccio was a contemporary Hermeticist, author of articles under the alias Giorgio Venturi (*Parliamo di Marco Daffi*) and Cesare Varzi (*Gli dei ritornano*).—*Trans.*]

teric, especially since it is easy for one to assert that they are esoteric when in fact they are not.

For example, I read it stated in a book review that ectoplasm should be considered the Great Arcanum!

Whereas Gnosis is entrusted to the practical and operative MEMORY of the powers of the psyche that arise in us, namely MEMORY (remembrance), found among the higher-level initiates of the (true) Great Arcanum, which is incommunicable, and which is revealed-acquired with sudden illumination as in ZEN, and confirmed by the initiator who must be considered here as a "MNEMONIST" = he who remembers.

More limitedly, it is based on the memory of the search for the powers of the psyche applied to evolution and not as an end in itself that drives the search: there is like a mysterious radiating antenna, as demonstrated in the lives of animals and insects, which vibrates and picks up (as in the search for a true companion) the corresponding vibration, i.e. the long- or short-lived brother who has entered the stream.

He who writes this has had the good fortune to have been presented to a representative of Gnosis, a subordinate, but adherent to the Solar Center.

But it would not have been necessary for me (characterized by Kremmerz) as a hound dog (he said so himself) to follow in the footsteps where he had tread.

I wanted to go to Argentina to become engaged with an Argentine lady, where Kremmerz himself lived between 1885 and 1892 and then between 1895 and 1897.

Tracks vanished. I almost met him in Monte Carlo in 1919 where my grandfather insisted that I go and try my luck at roulette!

Finally, I took up lodging in the Riviera di Chiaia in the very house where Kremmerz had set up his first Hermetic medical laboratory in 1898!

Next, we encounter the concept of the reincarnation instinct, often symbolized by the "colors" described in the Tibetan Book of the Dead. This instinct guides the initiate or semi-initiate to be reborn in a familiar ambiance or within their national environment.

He could be a relative, a friend of the family, or a scholar. As for me, if my impulses had been awakened, it would have been Prince Leone

Caetani, who was in Italy at the time. He was Kremmerz's family friend that I mentioned earlier.

That the method for approaching the MENSA is governed by the safeguards and principles outlined in its laws can be inferred from the last preface of the *Dialogues on Hermeticism*, which dates after 1924, within the six years preceding his demise.

Among other things, he writes: "So what's the use of propaganda (read associations and the public notoriety of research) to the few aristocrats of thought?" But to those who possess the history of their spirit a distant memory of this great analysis of the occult faculties of the human organism, even crossing over into religious mysticism (see Giordano Bruno, see Johannes Trithemius) they all end up studying Magic.

To add, they end up how? With the thousand events of which I have mentioned, and there may be a thousand others.

Kremmerz also says that today he is against propaganda and only wanted to present a type of SCHOLA that is not theosophical, not spiritist, not mystical, that is, to exercise the powers of the psyche in practice, which are not solely mental but psychophysical, and from this we can deduce the *occulta philosophia* and structure of the universe and our becoming.

The transmission (not propaganda) takes place by intuition and by vibration like that which happens between lovers (true non-illusional sensists) at first sight, in the illuminations of a passage, of a phrase, from little books and then the Guardian of the Threshold blocks the way to the curious and the unwary.

He who overcomes the barriers (I would also say the seven angels of Dante's Purgatory) attains a thorough enlightenment and if perseveres then there are no obstacles that can be opposed in the work of construction or reconstitution? And then only will the experiment be able to tell whether the *Diadoratta** is fake or true.

Rome, July 7, 1968

Ei hm'sc Bêl

---

*[*Dia dora*, Greek for "to influence someone through gifts."—*Trans.*]

July 7, 1968

Dearest Giammaria,

I've included my astronological vision concerning you. However, please also consider the astrological findings that Countess Sacconi made for you. According to these findings, you will only find yourself during your ascension.

I add that not only the most "faithful" will refrain from attempting to intimidate you, but they may also experience betrayal from those who have demonstrated even greater loyalty. This phenomenon occurs, often indirectly, especially when a woman is involved.

Additionally, your friend Maccio will lose contact* with you for a significant period. However, as a silver lining, perhaps this Vir will find the path back home.

I know you will welcome him with that generosity of spirit that is your own.

I enclose the astronological horoscope and short notes to follow, in separate sheets.

The Astronological Portrait of Giammaria Gonella

Solar: with all the consequences stemming from intense clashes of character and mistakes fueled by simmering anger and unwavering false beliefs.

He was burned at the stake after being tortured.

Rabbinical precedents as a doctor of the Talmud.

Having extensive connections with the Greek world, yet remaining uninvolved, during the reign of Justinian, he witnessed the expulsion of philosophers from Athens. At that time, he identified as a Zoroastrian and extended hospitality to refugees.

Suited for dialectics—engaging in debates that oscillated between Byzantine subtlety and theological concepts.

---

*[I can attest from my direct correspondence with Giorgio Maccio that he and Giammaria did eventually lose contact.—*Trans.*]

Driven by ambition, he sought superior philosophical training and inner evolution, with the potential for inner manifestation.

Inclined to theorizing about abstract concepts of . . .

Given the precedents: prudence when interpreting causes, recognizing that originality could lead to serious adverse reactions.

MÖRKÖHEKDAPH

Comparing the above with that of your astronological self (apart from your polite objection to interpreting it through a reincarnationist lens, which I assumed, rather than your psychological perspective, treating previous lives as inferior modes of existence), let's juxtapose it with your own description. In your self-assessment, you state:

"Nubian sorcerer,

Outside the tribal sphere,

In respectful rapport *hinc et inde* with the priests of the nearby Egyptian temple . . .

Assyrian prince (as commander of troops), during the conquest of Egypt, but conquered by Egyptian wisdom . . .

Talmud scholar, considered a heretic, and was subsequently stoned; and his body burned with the ashes scattered in the wind."

Well, you can see that you have not just a little to meditate upon . . .

I too have not a little to meditate on to go beyond the vision that you have seen (and I thank you again for the gift) and that I have yet to surmount.

June 1, 1969, 11:39 a.m.

Dearest Giammaria,

I am at a loss for words to express the immense pleasure I felt upon seeing you again, and with her, the Lady who graciously and kindly indulged my requests for Tarot readings.

Let me tell you what I already said to her: you are made for each other, precisely because you are different almost to the opposite.

But what makes fate not unique but rare (?) was her "decree" that I will have to tell you about at the appropriate time.

Yet, it's so to speak, to be taken very, very seriously.

The risk is especially for the Woman if, when she fails to fall in love, she also loses sight of her Vir, and thinks of herself only as a woman.

Best wishes for what's best.

Aff. yours,

Rome, May 12, 1969, 11:30 a.m.

Dear friend,

Here is the ritual to practice in the case of the printing of our writings, that is, on Hermetic philosophy.

It serves to channel the elementals for the best. . . .

I make myself available to you.

In carrying out the dual task of my existence, to:

(a) render an organic and modern form to Hermetic philosophy, and
(b) manifest my Phoenician personality. . . .

It may not come to an end.

Regarding point (b), not to worry. I have done otherwise.

On the other hand, as regards point (a), you are the custodian of the tables and comments.

My friend G. also has not a little material, in which I've enucleated my knowledge of Hermetic therapeutics and other various—but always relevant—material.

In the event of my passing (or pre-death), I entrust you, my esteemed literary executor, with the burden—or perhaps the honor—of reviewing and publishing my works. As an expert of the sacred Rota, you possess the necessary discretion and judgment. I have full confidence in your ability to handle this responsibility with appropriate caution.

Second, indeed first: I'll ask [Elio] G. to make available the material in your hands.

If the friend G. were unable, since he in turn passes away, ask the heirs, the ways and terms I shall leave to your discretion as a legal expert.

Only if you find resistance (?) if the numen does not oblige, as the elementals would be inflexible with the unwary. You may also show this mandate if you consider it appropriate.

If the task is too exhausting, then burn them.

The publication (read) is done without gaining any profit.

If the publisher requires it, that is their business, but not ours?

In case of your impossibility, I've given the task to your father, who has accepted it. . . .

Aff. yo,

Nota bene: This letter (in which the "task" assumed subordinately in the case of my impossibility refers to the recovery of the material by the hands of my friend G. and its publication, not to the revision of the texts, in green ink, written on light paper, almost tissue paper, that after having agreed with the Kemi publishing house to publish the remaining texts of Ours, in 1980, at the house of Auri, in the presence of G. and members of the Corps,* I set fire to them and watched them burn.

(G.M.G.)

---

*[Corpo dei Pari, Body of Peers, is the initiatic circle established in the 1960s and inspired by the works of Marco Daffi and Giammaria, the Regent. See David Pantano, *The Magical Door* (Melbourne: Manticore Press, 2019).—*Trans.*]

3

Vitae Daffianae

A Life in Alchemical Hermeticism

The Return of Marco Daffi

Who is Marco Daffi?
. . . verily one could say, he was:
the essence of a spiritual explorer, (magical heroi),
a seeker of light on a journey (V.I.T.R.I.O.L.),
an Argonaut of the Tetradic-monad, (psychonaut)
in search of his roots (*katabasis*)
to integrate with his principle (numen)
across endless reincarnations (avatars),
seeking resolution for his wandering soul (fixed star)
by returning to his ancestral home (*nostoi*).
By means of an internal archaeology (mnemosyne),
in a luminous state of the sublime (gnosis),
summoning his Shades (*nekiya*),
in resonance with the Numen (mag),
repairing fragments of his soul (*medecina dei*),
exiled with every incarnation (avatar).
Yet, with the discovery of his pluri-monadic Self (anamnesis),
the crisis of identity, tradition, and destiny found
    is resolved (Isaic integration),
albeit as an incomplete avatar (karma)
—and hence, the return (avataric resurgence) . . .
unfolding the tapestry of Marco Daffi's existence.

Prologue to Part Three

The second half of this book delves into the human dimension of Baron Ricciardo Ricciardelli, the Saturnian shell encasing the astral yoke of Marco Daffi. We will examine facets of the Baron's complex biographical guises from memoirs and reminiscences to reflections of personal encounters by luminaries of the Hermetic world, including Piero Fenili, Giammaria Gonella, and Auri Campolonghi Gonella, among others.

As well, we shall flesh out impressions from those who encountered him exclusively through the medium of books or from the testimonies of colleagues like Hermanubis and N. R. Ottaviano.

The largely personal recollections reveal an intimate side of the Janus-like figure—man and magus—that was don Ricciardo: lucid, erudite, genial, and fully consumed with an indomitable spirit to investigate metaphysical reality.

Despite the predilection for a life withdrawn far from the clamor and impositions of society's conventions, the biography of Ricciardo Ricciardelli, once it can be written, will present an extraordinarily rich artifact, as the episodes selected for this volume suggest. Indispensable are the many vistas of the magus seen through the eyes of his contemporaries and when pieced together offer a vivid portrayal of this disciple of Hermes.

This Vitae Daffianae is the first such detailed reconstruction of the Baron's life framed through the format of biographical timelines. Included are snapshot-like entries on the not-so-earthly life lived by the Baron from a multitude of sources, chronologically arranged to cover the decades starting with Daffi's youth, his fateful encounter with Kremmerz, snippets from the infamous "Trial of the Magus," and right up until his final years, like a latter-day Diogenes in correspondence with his many followers.

To further round out the details of Daffi's numerous yet lesser-known written compositions, a bibliography of his published books and articles is included. Of considerable value are Giammaria's many contributions that open a window into the psyche of Ours and offer insight into the quirks and idiosyncrasies that characterized the Baron, especially with his particular take on the "Trial of the Magus."

Giammaria's exegesis of Daffi's important yet frequently overlooked writings is essential to grasp the breadth and depth undertaken by these Theseus-like journeys through the Hermetic labyrinth. It is worth noting the Baron's exceptional, if not strange, mind for piecing together such diverse and seemingly phantasmagoric elements within the maze of his initiatory pilgrimage.

In order to properly situate this biographical material within the perspective of alchemical Hermeticism, it should be emphasized that impressions perceived through the external senses cannot, by its very nature, constitute the highest form of experience available to man. External experiences, like perceptions received through the five carnal senses, are bound by the laws of matter. However, through the agency of spiritual channels, it is possible to transcend the boundaries of the corporeal world and have an experience of a different kind.

Through initiation, the seeker can cultivate inner faculties that open channels to experiences accessed from a whole new world of inner space and at a level deeper and vaster than what can be attained at the material level. Initiation has the potential to transcend material boundaries, to move beyond the conventional linear time-space-causality matrix and to climb the evolutionary ladder and exercise degrees of freedom and transcendent experiences not previously imaginable.

Experiences of this nature are the result of a mind turned and tuned inward to expand beyond prescribed definitions and borders—paths are crossed, energy unleashed . . . paving the way for a *nostoi* and a *nekyia* of experiences leading to Μόϰσα,* beatific illuminations, and inner journeys traversing the rivers of Lethe and Euone† to the resplendent Elysian fields.

Never has such an extensive compilation of previously undisclosed material and hitherto unknown aspects of the Magical Baron's initiatory philosophy, praxis, and life been consolidated within a single volume. For the discerning Hermeticist, the naked accounts by Hermetic *compari* about their personal encounters with the Baron reveal the chrysalis formation of the living mythos that is Marco Daffi.‡

Without discounting the condescending tones that the name Marco Daffi evokes within certain quarters—especially among some members of the Italian esoteric community who are challenged to reconcile the Baron's elevated doctrinal expositions with the more antinomian and scandalous events associated with his name—we can only point out that the Baron was not a prude, nor did he wish to live his life constrained by society's impositions or according to the mores imposed by bourgeois conditioning.

---

*Nostoi: a theme used in Ancient Greek and Latin literature referring to an epic hero returning home, often by sea. In Ancient Greek society, it was deemed a high level of heroism or greatness for those who managed to return. This journey is usually very extensive and includes facing certain trials that test the hero.

Nekyia: ancient Greek & Italic initiatory practice. A necromantic "ritual by which ancestral shades are summoned and consulted about important decisions facing the magical hero or tribe.

Μόϰσα (or Moksha): denotes personal liberation from samsara—the cycle of rebirth and suffering in the material world. This concept embodies the highest spiritual aspiration in the yogic tradition.

†Lethe and Euone are the rivers of forgetfulness and remembrance in Greek mythology and Dante's *Divine Comedy*. To avoid spiritual annihilation, the soul must navigate past lethe to attend the flow of Euone.

‡Mythos understood as the interior life of the individual lived in terms of a reality that manifests in dreams, imagination, vibrations, apparitions, recollections, and so on. The *Mythoi Daffiniae* can best be summarized by a famous extract from the "Trial of the Magus": "It could be said, MORKOHEKDAPH (in his own words), which Marco Daffi is the Italianized form, that he is a nonexistent person . . . because he is abstract. He belongs to the world of visions, magic, reincarnations, of the world that clings to the hospitable fields of the subconscious and is not a physical person, because it is an entity of the invisible world. They are all fossils of Daffi's inner resonance, memories, and past incarnations."

Testimonies by many notable representatives of the artistic, scientific, and literary worlds bear witness to Ricciardelli's genial qualities in thought, word, and deed. That the Baron lived according to ethical standards that may not conform to the societal conventions of the day does not indicate that he was a man without ethics or principles. In fact, the ethos that he embraced was at another level and beyond the grasp of the herdlike mentality prevalent in his era. Moreover, his observance of these *Caritas Hermetis* ethics shows that he, like a pious Aeneas, was true to a mission greater than the events that are associated with him.

Should it, therefore, be considered a fault, or worse an object of scorn and derision as claimed by some detractors, that he, with the passing of Kremmerz, who became the preeminent Hermeticist in the land of Ausonia—a land infused with the spirit of Mercurius—is himself mercurial?

Even with a cursory familiarity with his writings anyone bearing the slightest traits of objectivity would arrive at the conclusion that the accusations made against him do not stack up with the facts. Therefore, one is forced to turn the spotlight away from the accused to the accusers to see who these would-be detractors are, to try and understand where they are coming from. One often finds that lurking behind the shadows of ill will are those who, in bad conscience or otherwise misinformed, are easily suggestible. They may have vested interests to deflect criticism from the wrongdoings of their predecessors, or simply be shallow critics who base their understanding on the opinions of others—in essence, those who, by and large, can be characterized as among the herdlike masses. These same heavy-winded philistines—whom the Baron asserts are lethal to the initiate both in the here and now and in the metaphysical there and then—epitomize the Humanimal.

The integral initiate follows a rigorous practice of integrating their disparate Hermetic bodies into an organic whole, ensuring the virtual exchange of influences between the micro and macro realms. By remaining firmly rooted to their innate being and after having fixed their personal identity into their primary Self, they become more adapt at resisting societal conditioning and conformity. This resilience extends even beyond physical life into the postmortem, by maintaining an integral monad, albeit unconscious, where the Self is able to withstand the phagocytizing absorption into oblivion.

Initiation serves as the gateway for seekers of light to discover new dimensions of reality through the exploration and cultivation of inner realms. It enables seekers, akin to numinal navigators, spiritual argonauts, and magical heroes, to undertake internal journeys (katabasis), opening their inner faculties—seeing, feeling, hearing, smelling, and tasting – to a gnosis of experiences within dreams, imaginations, intuitions, apparitions, augurs and other altered states of consciousness.

Initiation provides spiritual seekers with the means to transcend human limitations and merge their Hermetic bodies, ultimately leading to more rarefied realms of sublimation—what Ficino called the "ladder of love." Through the unification of the self with its Solar essence, the initiatory process illuminates the initiate's spiritual progress and empowers their interiority.

As Daffi wrote in "Doctrine of Initiation and Neo-Buddhism," (page 60) "In contrast, initiates—and in particular we of the Italian alchemical-Hermetic school—prefer to recognize the full orthodox validity of the doctrines and schools that explicitly affirm man's positive development in his solar evolution to a state of potentiality that does not cancel the personality but rather makes it act in accordance with natural laws, which are not violated but transformed in their application toward ascending or descending realizations."

In the Dissertamina, we read, "Communities determine the collective psyche that is the prerequisite for the type of common man. While outside the bonds of union, the individual souls are free from the possession of the collective entity. It is with this sense that we can explain actions performed by individuals in conditions of perfect autonomy, quite opposite to precedents and from the same committed to the moment of possession of the individual psyche in the collective" ("On the Reality of the Individual Soul," page 76). Ultimately, the magus shouldn't concern themselves with seeking approval from the masses. Daffi would refer to those knowingly or unknowingly trapped within the collective mindset of mass formation as the herd—the hum-animal—whose souls are prepared for slaughter (absorption) by the universal process of monadic phagocytosis whereby the (unique) one is devoured by the All.

For nothing sets the magus apart from the herd more than the degree of integrity exhibited by their respective beings. Unlike the herded individual, who by all intents and purposes appears willingly to compromise their integrity for the pursuit of perceived advantages, the true magus remains steadfast and anchored by a *fides* to the principles, values and ideals that form the foundation of who they are.

This personal equation manifesting as an internal disposition of primary virtue betrays a particular ontology of the elemental configu-rations underlying the two contrasting beings, that is, the one who is fixed and positive in their nucleus* and the other type that is volatile and negative at their core. The contrast is as clear as it is conclusive between those with whom the initiatic community calls the integral or the impeccable and those referred to as the compromised.

To further emphasize this point, Kremmerz writes in the open-ing lines of the *Corpus Philosophicum Totius Magiae*: "The first hierographic sign of Potency, is Virtue, in its absolute form . . . which represents Essence, Will, Force, Creation. For all proceeds by order, both in the visible world and the invisible, which relates to the Potency of the Primary Virtue, symbol of universal existence in its fullness. Only the First Principle of the Primary Virtue is of itself cre-ator and created, therefore a Perfect essence, underlying the nature of existence. This Virtue is the First Entity and generator of Self, and represented in magical symbolism by •, which is at the center of the two crossed lines: ⊗."

---

*[The spiritual nucleus or numen is one and not many, however the numen manifests in different modalities according to the specific plane of the representation. Using the Hermetic tetradic or quadratic paradigm as the basic framework for the multiple states of Being the numen manifests into different representations playing out its atavistic and karmic trajectories, much like what occurs within the specter of dreams.—*Trans.*]

The self can invert itself, if not initiated-integrated, to the same bestial and noted regress that is symbolized by a hellish death and enduring eternal "punishment." Never will the soul regain even a fraction of its potential, remaining trapped in a minimal state of consciousness. Indeed it will be absorbed and definitively confused, that is to say, irretrievably, in another, which ontologically will not be able to destroy it, but will absorb it, confuse its consciousness by the other being-creature with another history.

Within each "new individual," there exist "roses": illusory semblances of existence that one or some of them (the current, contingent) come to dominate, blinding them to the reality of "the return" and its potential in the three forms of metempsychosis, regeneration, or reincarnation.

"Wilted roses do not return" is a phrase Kremmerz was apt to use. That is to say, that for individuals "dead to themselves" the karmic effects are discounted to the point that a further conscious existence becomes impossible . . . without, however, the "vital substance" being lost. In this sense, nothing undergoes annihilation. What, on the other hand, is annihilated is consciousness or, in Buddhist terms, the karmic complex constituting the stratification of being, including those influenced by pathological conditions extending broadly to the verge of dementia or related to the "sense of self," karma is exhausted. The animalistic aggregation formed in the successive stages of volition is extinguished, and the Monad, free from any karmic ties, gains access to a consciousness that merges with it.

What assurances are to be sought that form a bulwark against the sterile pedantry of those who consider knowledge as a finite end already reached by humanity and without taking into account the most significant divergences, the infinity of the universe, the role played by Providence, and the meaning attributed to the metamorphosis of the differentiated man?

That which Marco Daffi embodies as an exemplar of magical heroism is the same spiritual fire that animates man in the tortuous path of transcendence. The true protagonist of this quest is divine love—that universal force of love that animated Socrates as philosopher, the love that converts Actaeon into a specimen of nature, and that which leads man from base to elevated things, from mere external appearances to the profound truth of the idea.

Be that as it may, the patient reader will be rewarded with a bird's-eye view of the magus at work in his tantalizing and somewhat bizarre magical world. Seen in this light, the Marco Daffi mythopoesis* is not confined to the laws of three-dimensional reality but more accurately construed through the kaleidoscopic lens of the magus's vision of reality, which the reader can see only if they look with the seeker's eyes.

Giammaria cautions the unsuspecting reader, saying, "Daffi is the stuff of legend, haloed with magism and phantasmagory concerning which he did little to set the record straight." And since, as Daffi exclaims, "I have to address the public (four stray cats)" and must take into account "that which has been said, or what one might ask or not understand," about which he proudly insists the readership "will not be disappointed" for "there is a wide world of wonders to marvel at."

Although we must acknowledge that besides carrying out a long-term correspondence for over three decades, Giammaria possessed an innate understanding—perception and feel—that uniquely qualified him to directly communicate the essential takes on constructing an accurate portrayal of Marco Daffi, which of course is indispensable for readers approaching his work to place it in proper context.

Nonetheless, we cannot fully agree with every assertion and characterization he makes concerning Ours, statements suggesting the Baron was not primarily a Hermeticist, that he moved away from Kremmerz's

---

*[A key feature of the Italic Hermetic tradition is the homage to the Greco-Roman patrimony of mythology, specifically as it relates to the homology of Hermetic operators with archetypal figures—gods and heroes. The extent to which the spiritual forces of mythologized heroes in-form and plasmate the individual operator could be described as mytho-psyche or psyche-mythic.—*Trans.*]

notion of reincarnation after encountering Giammaria or that he lacked a precise notion of the paranormal.* However significant or not these assertions may seem, the following sections will attempt to make a case—on fundamental issues of identity and tradition—by providing sufficient examples to reposition or at least to reconcile Marco Daffi's exalted place within the golden chain of magical heroes of the Hermetic tradition.

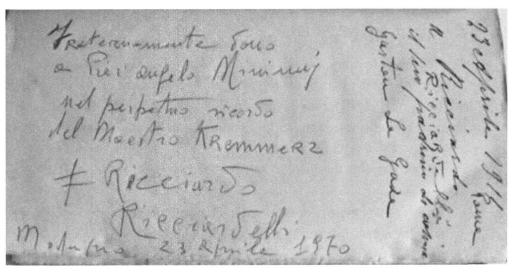

French language Catholic prayer book, 1903 inscribed on the left in red ink, "Fraternally yours to Pierofilo Minni in perpetual memory of Master Kremmerz ≠ Ricciardo Ricciardelli, Modulno 23 April 1970" and on the right in black ink, "23, April 1911 Roma to Ricciardo Ricciardelli godfather of your confimation, Gaston Le Gade."

---

*Giammaria's statements do not square with the facts, valuations made by Daffi in his writings and especially those written toward the end of his life (*Alchimia Ermetica, Terapica, Erotica, La Sulimazione del Mercurio*), as well as his adopting the pseudonym A Kremmerzian in the mid-1950s, point to Daffi affirming the extent of his being influenced by the writings and directions of Kremmerz, even though he may take issue or veer from the orthodox interpretation.

OCCULT NAMES

Numen est Nomen est Omen

Mörköhekdaph is an "initiatic name"
of presumed Phoenician origin,
and perceived as an ancient resonance
of a subtle state of awareness
beyond the dimension commonly referred to as "real."
This name, however, was arrived at by a process of
"inner archaeology."

Marco Daffi, under whose name the writings in this volume appear, was acclaimed by those in the know as a highly evolved initiate who dedicated the better part of his forty-five-plus-year vocation in the pursuit and practice of Hermeticism, throughout its manifold forms and varieties. His writings are the fruit of profound investigations and inner odysseys to the unexplored regions of the psyche where the worlds of the microcosm and the macrocosm intersect to reveal the universal truths underlying Gnosis.

As an initiate worthy of that name, Daffi upheld the dignity of a master with honor, integrity, and humility, despite facing overwhelming trials and tribulations that placed severe restrictions on his personal freedoms, challenged his inner constitution, and mired his name to the point of ridicule. Undoubtably, the Baron's abundant wealth afforded him the luxury to weather the storm and the means to cultivate an opulent spiritual practice.

His initiatory practice was enhanced by an innate sense of apperception that enabled the effective transcendence of his biographical self, to the emergence, within deep-rooted layers of being, of a veritable cornucopia of ancient personalities and incarnations. Giammaria confirms that "he operated flanked by eons and it was 'all' a ritual. Crises passed and came to him as an act or event of 'revulsion.' And it should not be excluded, therefore, that in the midst of this, he signed a letter addressed to me, under the name of Ei hm'sc Bêl. Of this different personality, I can only say that it refers to an 'incarnation of the Andromeda Order,' according to him, of a 'physician and apothecary of Phoenician origins, from the constellation of the Pleiades.'

"Rarely did he use the name Ei hm'sc Bêl, and never did he speak to me about that name, nor did I ask him about this alternative personality that I sensed was interfering with that of MÖRKÖHEKDAPH, so I cannot assert whether it was or not involved in the 'tetradic drama' of which Ours was considered the protagonist, as a 'Pilot of the Tetrad.'"*

However, as a result of these same circumstances of abundant wealth and opulence combined with an unrelenting dedication to Hermeticism—which by its very nature is a reserved practice better suited for the quiescence of interior life—Daffi was left vulnerable and a target for exploitation by the malicious intentions of friends and foes alike.

His blind adherence to these venerable practices—Hermetic in name and by nature—were conveniently exploited by fraternal brethren, family members, unscrupulous lawyers, and the insatiable greed of the compromised, who contrived a web of deception to the detriment of the Baron and ultimately gained access to his considerable wealth. Daffi would regard these crises with a Stoic countenance and refer to them as "revulsions" or corrosive waters necessary to purge the soul of karmic influences.†

It is on similar grounds that in this instance or for that matter of other more celebrated cases throughout history—see the trials of Apulieus, Giordano Bruno, Tommaso Campanella, and Cagliostro to name a few—that primacy is given to adopting an "occult name" or "initiatic name" such is the case with Marco Daffi, fully endorsed by the Baron, to represent the writings communicated through the agency

---

*The "initiatic monad" and "pilot of the pluri-monad" are his words, in the sense that he received directives, by induction. A continuous ebb and flow of consciousness within the numen itself, when the consciousness of the original tetrad is regained in REVULSION of the preexisting monadic order. "Marco Daffi e la sua opera," Kemi, 1980.
†See Philosophical Letters: "Initiation," pages 137–141.

of the historical person Ricciardo Ricciardelli. The writings attributed to Macro Daffi first appeared in print in the late 1970s and early
1980s through the relentless efforts afforded by the Genovese lawyer
Giammaria Gonnela.

In my conversations with Giammaria, he was wont to say that he
preferred to use the name "Marco Daffi" rather than that of "Ricciardo
Ricciardelli" to avoid legal harassment from the Ricciardelli family and,
from a hieratic perspective, to represent the authentic personality and
true author of those writings, who rather than the historical figure of
Ricciardo Ricciardelli, is authenticated by the entity that revealed itself
as Mörköhekdaph.*

"One could say MÖRKÖHEKDAPH (Marco Daffi is the
Italianized form) is a nonexistent person . . . an abstraction, that belongs
to the world of visions, magic, reincarnations, and the world that lurks
in the dark chasms of the subconscious and not a natural person, rather
an entity of the invisible world."†

For Marco Daffi, by any stroke of the imagination, is a nonexistent person, leaving no biographical traces or historical footprints in the
chronicles of time and space. His existence is as an abstraction from
another plane and an astral entity that has disassembled its constituent subtle bodies and through the trauma of rebirth has amputated his
third body and is therefore forced to seek out its feminine counterpart
to repair this debilitating lacuna.

In this regard, it may ring hollow to ask whether the "name"
(nomen) imparts value or reference on the "historical" level, or if,
through an inner archaeology of the atavistic roots of the psyche,
whether it is possible to acquire awareness of one or more ancient identities more-or-less distant over time. For "this problem" is valid in and of
itself and deserves to be considered if, in the light of the purest Western
Hermeticism which does not place greater validity of the rational to the
detriment of the intuitive, a justification for meditating further on this

---

*Giammaria, *Collecta*, Editrice Amenothes (forthcoming).
†*Il Processo del Mago*, 107.

enigma could also represent the whole retrospective process based on the Hermetic *topos* of "what if." Therefore the "name" remains, in the order of the logos . . . an evocation of the presence of the numen.*

NOMEN EST NUMEN EST OMEN†

According to an ancient Roman tradition, every entity—whether of a person, place or thing—has three names: a sacred one, a public one, and an occult one.

This custom was rooted in the sacerdotal proceedings of ancient Rome and the public name of Rome was joined to the religious name of Flora or Florens, and used on the occasion of certain sacred ceremonies. The reason and necessity for the secrecy of the name leads to another tradition widespread among the ancients and which is also found in the history of the origin of writing: the name of an object or an entity expresses the essence and energy of that object or entity. In this regard, the Latin phrase *nomen est omen*, the literal translation of which means the: "name is an omen," "name is a destiny," "destiny is found in the name," or "in name and in fact," comes from the Romans' belief that a person's name was their destiny.

Naming something was tantamount to making it come alive and become living. Knowing the name meant, in practice, having the power to influence, for good or ill, the object of one's knowledge. The phrase *nomen atque omen* ("a name is at the same time a portent") was the creation of the Roman comic poet Plautus (250–184 BCE), who quoted it in a passage in his play *Persa* (*The Persian*), written around 190 BCE.

---

*The numen is the subtlest and irreducible level of consciousness that is beyond any dichotomy. The numen represents the occult root of being *in homine divinus*. The name, in Hermeticism, is a sonorous revelation of being, and therefore understood as the energetic substance (that which is underneath—meaning *sub-stare*), of the name and expressed (taken out—from *ex-press*), whence the magical power of the "divine" word (!) for those who know how to "say it." A saying: the name contains the "named" energy (see the *indigitamenta* in the ancient Roman religion and, on the other hand, the use of "mantras.")

†Your name conceals the destiny of your soul.

For the Egyptians the naming activity was not a simple exercise, in fact, according to the belief that through such knowledge one could magically dominate the person who bore that name. That is why, when one wanted to annihilate a person, one would remove their name by hammering it out of the inscriptions; it is, in short, the Roman *damnatio memoriae*, a phrase that literally means "condemned from memory."

In Roman law, the *damnatio memoriae* was a penalty consisting of erasing any trace of a particular person, as if they had never existed; it was a particularly severe penalty, reserved especially for traitors and enemies of the senate. This curse of erasing their name was intended for both the living and the dead. In fact, the name represents a person's authentic personality and, in a sense, their destiny or life span.

Particularly when we reflect on the fact that in ancient societies, possessing the name of an individual or object implied a degree of ownership, control, and dominance over them. The use of the name to "eliminate" the opponent in ancient Rome was particularly present in the *secratio* or the act of cursing practiced by the ancients to call the infernal deities against their enemies and in the *defixiones*, the curses against opponents; today we would call them "statements of accounts" usually engraved on sheets of lead scratched, rolled up, and placed in a tomb or thrown into a well so that the "enemy" was as close as possible to the underworld and the world of the afterlife!

The name of the recipient on the curse was always carefully specified so that there were no mistakes by the deities concerning the victim, and, to reinforce the negative effect, magic letters or complex formulas were added. The name *defixiones*, derived from the Latin *defigere* (to lock up, confiscate, immobilize), clearly alludes to the desire to immobilize the physical and mental abilities of the person being cursed. The act of piercing the metal plate bearing the name of the hated opponent was identified with the physical act of piercing the enemy, reinforcing the invocation of divine punishment.*

---

*See Felice Vinci, "Never say Maia: A hypothesis on the cause of Ovid's exile and the secret name of Rome," Arduino Maiuri, 2017, *Roman Notes on Philology*, Fabrizio Serra Editore.

"Although Venusian in form, Marco Daffi was also attuned to the ways of Mars, to which Venus is sensitive, while a calibrated Mercury was necessary for the evocation of MÖRKÖHEKDAPH. In fact, it was a question of evocation, of a personality that built itself on its own and that reflected also in its physiognomy, but which found its own essence from the particular suggestion of our interpersonal relationship. For my part, I realized that the suggestion met 'its psychological possibility' by reason of its organic classification within alchemical Hermeticism and by virtue of flourishing with full autonomy in my absence."[*]

Daffi's view on Eros and Love were similar to those laid out by Marsilio Ficino in "On the Nature of Love: Ficino on Plato's *Symposium*" (*Sopra lo amore ovvero Convito di Platone*) where the complementarity of archetypal constituents of personality types are the triggers of attraction and that, for the vast majority of individuals, operate at an occult level and about which those stricken with carnal desires are unaware. However, Daffi's investigations dive deeper than that to examine the personal equations of the individuals that make up a couple from the praxis of harmonic complementarity for each of the reciprocal four subtle bodies.

In discussions with a colleague knowledgeable in Kremmerzian matters, he weighs in with the following observation: "while Daffi was a Gnostic 'libertine,' Kremmerz was an Encratite.[†] Regarding the practice, I ask that you read the correspondence carefully and you will see that Daffi was far from sexual magic. It is true that he discusses sexuality, but in a physiological-initiatory key, showing how certain phenomena take place at an extra-Saturnian level starting from the redemption of the subtle bodies. So much so that in one of his last letters he speaks of fluids, clearly underlining that initiation involves the domination of the human beast (also and above all from the erotic-sexual point of view)."

---

[*]*Giammaria, Marco Daffi e la Sua Opera*, Editrice Kemi, 1980, 22.
[†]"A member of an ascetic Christian sect led by Tatian, a 2nd-century Syrian rhetorician. The name derived from the group's doctrine of continence (Greek: enkrateia). The sect shunned marriage, the eating of flesh, and the drinking of intoxicating beverages, even substituting water or milk for wine in the Eucharist" (Encyclopaedia Britannica).

The individual has as the basis of their self a numen, the search for which is seen as an investigation or journey to discover the essence, nucleus, or veritable root of who they really are and to represent it in the form of a name that through its evocation (nomen) authenticates the primacy of their Being. Therefore, it could be properly said that: Nomen est Numen est Omen represents the *alpha and omega* of the individual's life purpose with the resolution of affirming one's true identity and tradition.

The enigma surrounding Ricciardo Ricciardelli, whose nomen-numen is resolved by the journey of his initiatic struggle, a veritable *Hypnerotomachia Morkhokedaphianae* or the Strife of Love in the dreams of Marco Daffi. This journey entails the restoration and healing of his third body (the Lunar body) by channeling the path of Amor, to harmonize the four elemental bodies of his tetradic union under the guidance of his numen. Marco Daffi emphatically asserts that initiation is the great reset of being. It enables the realization of the transcendent or transpersonal Self with the reintegration undertaken in the astral environment that allows for a greater freedom for inner transformation than the more restrictive limitations imposed by the affinities of dwelling within the confines of biography and history.

Much has been written about Ricciardo Ricciardelli, alias Macro Daffi, that is pure fantasy based on conjectures and misconstrued information bent to suit certain biases that discredit the Baron in favor of a haloed reconfiguration of hierarchs of the primitive Myriamic academies of the 1920s*. Those who had direct experience with and knowledge of Daffi, such as the eminent writer on traditional studies Piero Fenili,† recall an

---

*In reference to Daffi's correspondence with Giammaria certain key components of Daffi's life purpose are revealed, such as an incomplete avatar, past life identification with Mörköhekdaph, Ei hm'sc Bêl, etc.

†Piero Fenili; former magistrate, authoritative writer on Hermeticism, and founder and editor of the journal *Politica Romana*. A substantial trace remains of one of these important discussions in a February 1988 article by Marco Daffi (this was the Italianized transcription of his ancient name Mörköhekdaph) entitled "Gli Avatars" (The Avatars). Within it, the Baron narrates a discussion he had with Kremmerz regarding the topic, sharing his thoughts and thereby elucidating the rationale behind his disagreement. It seems that Daffi's stance on this matter doesn't align contextually with Kremmerz; nevertheless, the Baron formulates his own theory in this regard, which he would expand upon in subsequent issues 33 and 34 of the same magazine by Piero Fenili.

altogether different image of the aristocratic esotericist: "such is the point of the situation, the so-called official portrait that outlines the complex figure of the Baron with its chiaroscuro (apparently darker than light). I realize, therefore, that the reader will be a little surprised that I provide an image of the Baron that is anything but in line with this official 'portrait' and indeed, in some ways, in stark contrast to it" (*Elixir* 4, 15).

Through a careful study of the Baron's more detailed accounts of Hermetic practices, such as what can be found in the *Dissertamina*, the *Episolari*, or "Hermetic Alchemy, Therapeutics, and Eros," one is forced to conclude that he was not prone to flights of fantasy or worse to paranoiac ramblings. There are too many details associated with digging into the internal mechanisms and processes of initiation to arrive at that conclusion—that he simply had a vivid imagination or some such argument. Most of the sources of derision and denigration derive from the old-school Kremmerzians—Manzi, Borracci, Verginelli—who were in collusion, whether directly or indirectly, with those who had directly tried to defraud Ricciardelli since the late 1920s. In fact, Kremmerz suffered a lot knowing that his old colleagues were taking advantage of Ricciardelli. Without doubt, Ricciardelli has to accept a great deal of responsibility for this Medusan plot in the Pasquale Pugliese affair, however, there are two sides to every story, and we should avoid blaming the victim for the transgressions of the perpetrator.

At the core of Daffi's writings resides the deep-rooted notion, formed by experience, of Gnostic self-deconstruction and self-creation bound by the ideal of an infinite possibility for transcendent development, for seekers to plumb their souls and manifest their creations, to reveal the identity of their true selves, for a fleeting glimpse of their numen and for the free expression, to others, of their nomen.

Here then is the Vitae Daffianae—a summary of the mythological life story that is Baron Ricciardo Ricciardelli, alias the initiate Marco Daffi.

Before the War

1900–1930

Ricciardo Ricciardelli (RR) was the scion of an ancient and prestigious lineage of Neapolitan nobility through which he inherited the title of Baron. The Ricciardellis were recognized as one of the wealthiest families in Italy, owning large tracts of agricultural land in Abruzzi, Apulia, and Lazio. After a considerable amount of research, the official tombstone records on Ricciardo Ricciardelli were confirmed. Ricciardo Nicola Ricciardelli was born in Naples on November 23, 1900, to Mario and Maria Capitaneo of Modugno (Bari), married in San Severo (Apulia) on September 14, 1924, to the noble lady Letizia del Sordo, and died in Rome on September 3, 1969.

The Ricciardelli's originated from the Apulia region, located at the heel of Italy. The young Ricciardo found himself both fortunate and unfortunate to inherit a considerable family fortune, fully at his disposal. As early as the mid-eighteenth century, the Ricciardelli family owned not only a grand ancestral palace in Rome but also extensive estates in the city of San Severo, in the province of Aquila, and throughout the regions of Abruzzi and Lazio.

The Palazzo Ricciardelli in Via Soccorso in the city of San Severo belonged to the family of his wife, the del Sordos. As head of the family, the marriage with Letizia del Sordo resulted in RR obtaining possession of his wife's inheritance, and their primary residence took on the name of Palazzo Ricciardelli-del Sordo. In the city of Francavilla

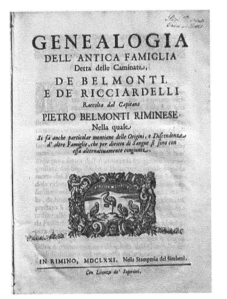

Left, a genealogy of the ancient Ricciardelli family.
Right, the Ricciardelli family coat of arms. A blue background with a diagonally placed red band bordered in silver and adorned with three stars all in gold, accompanied at the top by a gold comet and its tail and at the bottom by a profile of the head of a Moor.

al Mare (Abruzzo), Baron Ottavio Bartolomeo Ricciardelli was born, son of RR and Letizia del Sordo, the latter belonging to the noble family of San Severo. On the outskirts of Francavilla al Mare lies a broad promenade spanning approximately three hundred meters, known as "Fonte Letizia" in honor of the mother. It leads to the Porto San Franco lookout, named after a spring renowned for the therapeutic properties of its mineral water.

Baron Ricciardo Nicola Ricciardelli was entrusted at an early age to the strict education of his grandfather Ottavio. The young Baron grew up exhibiting signs of introversion, often solitary and burdened by the familial expectations set for him since childhood. As the sole heir of the family, he entered into an arranged marriage with the Countess Letizia Del Sordo from San Severo, heiress to a wealthy patrimony. Baron Ricciardo Nicola Ricciardelli initially pursued studies in Agriculture at

Marriage of Mario Ricciardeli and Countess Maria Capitano,
Ricciardo's father and mother

Mario Ricciardelli, Ricciardo's
father

the Faculty of Rome, followed by enrollment in the Faculty of Law at Bologna in 1923, and later in Economics back in Rome. Following his grandfather's passing, he inherited a vast estate valued at around 20,000 million lire, an immense fortune for the time.

In 1926, following the passing of his grandfather Ottavio, his initial actions involved severing all the bonds that had anchored him to his familial circumstances. This marked the beginning of what he termed as the "purge," starting with the purification of his assets.

On October 29, 1929, the "Ricciardelli" sports field in San Severo was inaugurated, in honor of Ricciardo Ricciardelli, who generously gifted the land to the city.

In the following years, the Ricciardelli sports complex served not just as a venue for sporting events but also for scholarly evaluations in primary and secondary schools, overseen by local authorities and the prefect.

On January 20, 1929, in the satirical weekly publication "Gargano," RR penned the following: "The San Severo sports field was built on a solid foundation and easily passed inspection by the Superior of the Provincial Sports Authority. The Ricciardelli family's contribution to the City of San Severo will be significant as they erect a new wing of the sports facility, titled 'LITTORIO.' The objective is to motivate, equip, and train athletes to build the future legions of Italy."

The fate of the Angora sports field of today (Ricciardelli sports field) are reported in the local land registry. At that time several newspapers wrote that the land was for sale, and that many investors were interested in buying shares, including local entrepreneurs such as a famous building contractor in San Severo, who was president of the local football team. However, a clause in the will, placed by the Baron, indicated that if the field was no longer used for the purposes for which it was donated, it would go back to the possession of the Ricciardelli family.

Growing up in Naples, the young Ricciardo expressed an uncanny interest in occultism and esotericism from an early age, which then turned into a lifelong dedication to the study of metaphysics, the paranormal, and Hermetic studies. Within the years immediately following World War I, Ricciardelli became acquainted with the Hermetic

Ricciardelli villa-farm in 1918

philosophy and practices of Giuliano Kremmerz, who was to become his constant reference point on matters of Hermetic initiation, particularly that of therapeutics, alchemy, divination, and avataric resurgence. The Baron's life forever changed after his introduction to the teachings and thaumaturgic figure of Giuliano Kremmerz.

Although economically he was considerably well-off, university educated with degrees in agriculture and jurisprudence and contributing articles to the journal *Pagine libere*, an avant-garde bimonthly magazine on political science, in the mid-1920s, the opulent Baron found himself lost in the dark woods of despair. His relationship with his newly married wife, the baroness Letizia del Soro, was strained to the point of precluding any possibility of intimate relations.

He was encouraged to visit a specialist on these matters, in Rome, who turned out to be a doctor of Hermeticism, a certain Giovanni Bonabitacola, head of the Vergilian Academy, the Roman chapter of the Hermetic chain of the Myriam. Dr. Bonabitacola introduced don Ricciardo to the Hermetic doctrines and practices of Giuliano Kremmerz, who, as fate would have it, would assume the role of Virgil

Inauguration of the Ricciardo Ricciardelli sports field in San Severo,
Apulia, October 29, 1929

to Daffi's Dante throughout the spiritual journey that encompassed the
rest of his terrestrial stay.

In 1926, RR was formally introduced to Ciro Formisano, alias
Giuliano Kremmerz, founder of the Hermetic Fraternity of Miriam
(abbreviated Fr+TM+Mir+, also known as Myriam) by Giacomo
Borracci, the head of the Bari branch of the Fr+TM+Mir+. The year
after, in April 1927, RR visited Beausoleil, France, next to the principality of Monaco to meet Kremmerz in person, from which would follow
a series of other in-person encounters and epistolary exchanges between
the two right up to Kremmerz's passing in May 1930.

By the time that Ricciardelli was introduced to Kremmerz, the
Myriamic academies were effectively not functioning as a result of the general state of disrepair that was further exacerbated by the nascent Fascist
government's decree to suppress Masonic lodges and secret organizations.

A member of the Myriamic Fraternity wrote: "Kremmerz welcomed
into his circle of acquaintances the curious figure of an aspiring occultist
whom he, however, declined to admit into the Myriam. Nevertheless, he

held a fraternal affection for him, which was warmly returned: Baron don Ricciardo Ricciardelli." The Baron wrote about and had much to say regarding Kremmerz and his relations with him and various hierarchs of the Myriam. The Master regarded him favorably on a human level, yet discouraged his initiation into and practice of the Myriam due to concerns about his psychological instability.

Although not formally belonging to any of the Myriamic academies or chains, between the years 1926 and 1930 RR became acquainted and directly corresponded with the major exponents of the Myriam including Giacomo Borracci of the Bari-based Pythagoras Academy, Giovanni Bonabitacola of the Roman Academy Virgil Circle, Vincenzo Manzi of the Sebeto Academy of Naples, Manzi, Verginelli, Catinella, and so on.

Kremmerz quickly picked up on RR's extraordinary psychic attributes and unusually advanced knowledge of initiatic matters; however, noting the instability of his character, he directed RR not to enter into the Myriamic Chain but rather to work in isolation under his own direct supervision.

However, this statement contradicts the assertion that Kremmerz had no intention of admitting Ricciardelli into the Myriam, much less the prestigious Great Egyptian Order, considering that the Myriamic academies were largely inactive at the time of Ricciardelli's meeting with Kremmerz in 1926. After an unsuccessful homeopathic treatment to address his sexual disfunctions, Kremmerz passed don Ricciardo on to the Great Egyptian Order (GOE) for ulterior consultations.

It was through Kremmerz that we are to assume RR was first introduced to the advanced adepts comprising the Egyptian Order, which at that time was headed by Prince Leone Caetani, who had moved to Vernon, Canada, in the mid-twenties to escape the ever-increasing climate of clerical-political repression.

For the following three years, up to Kremmerz's passing, invoked at that time as the *Numem Magister*, Ricciardelli's entire life was oriented toward the initiatory Hermetic practices.

From that day forward, the disciple's journeys to the Delphus of Hermeticism would become more frequent, as he delved deeper into its mysteries alongside his companions. And continually RR went to Beausoleil thirsting for initiation, for whatever resolution he might find as to the source of his own fate, entirely captive to the Kremmerzian siren.

However, it was not uncommon for Kremmerz to extend invitations to disciples and admirers to join him in Beausoleil. Often, he would rendezvous with them at the Monaco casino, where, albeit somewhat reluctantly, he would accompany his wife and son, every evening, who were engrossed in games of chance. Meanwhile, Kremmerz, amidst a circle of friends, disciples, and admirers, would engage in lively conversations in one of the establishment's halls, conversing in brilliant terms, as he alone knew how to do, and with so much spirit and joy. Rarely did the master agree to participate in the games; he used to say that he "knew well if and when it was appropriate to do so," and when he did, well then, there was little doubt concerning the results.

Over the next three years, the Baron engaged in frequent and often intense correspondence with the erudite Hermetic master from Portici.* Kremmerz recognized Ricciardelli had achieved a considerable psychic emancipation; however, it also seems that it was the master who told him that his psychic problems, accompanied by sexual dysfunctions, were due to karmic retributions committed in previous lives.

"Ricciardelli, keep your composure; you're a lion held back by chains!" the master would retort, speaking in the Apulian dialect, whenever Ricciardelli pushed for initiation. Ricciardelli cultivated a closer bond with Kremmerz, whom he revered as a true adept, in contrast to the potential initiate that he wished to become. Not long after Kremmerz began to elevate Ricciardelli above certain other disciples within the Myriamic circle, Ricciardelli found himself gaining insight into the prominent figures and inner workings of the Fraternity of Myriam, which occasionally surfaced in his writings.

Apparently Kremmerz intended to keep Daffi at arm's-length from his Apulian disciples of the Myriam (constituting the majority

---

*"The magus from" or "Hermetic master from Portici" are common terms used to describe Kremmerz by admirers. Kremmerz was born in Portici, a small city close to Naples.

of affiliates with the fraternity) claiming that they were not true Apulians like Ricciardelli, but in reality, reincarnated Frenchmen, and that he, therefore, had to prepare for them special teaching methods, absolutely unsuitable for a true Apulian like the Baron, who, having correctly understood the explanation, called his fellow countrymen of the Myriam Gallo-Apulians! As Ricciardelli grew more acquainted with members of the Myriam, particularly as he got to know the hierarchs and their tendency to call themselves masters—Masters of the Myriam—his understanding of the Order's challenges and limitations deepened. But, at the cost of sounding even more iconoclastic than what has appeared, Ricciardelli would state it is "unfortunate and incumbent on me to formally declare that this situation is not true, and that the 'masters of the Myriam' insofar as they were capable of supposed powers they gained by themselves through the simple practices of the Myriam, or from any 'manuscript' or 'notebook' of any number or series that one wants, have never had any real impact except in the organization, and, I believe, for a very limited number of people."

RR exclaims:

On my first encounter on the path of destiny with the group of initiates from the land of Apulia, I was given the title of "maestro" by Manzi (Vincenzo), adding the qualification "in the bottle." Master in a bottle, according to Manzi, meant a master inhibited in his powers and crippled by his memories. Although Kremmerz never used this expression with me, Manzi claims that it was coined by him. The reality is, I cannot endorse such a grave assertion; I must uphold my duty to speak the truth, to faithfully recount my personal experiences (even those veiled by the passage of time), to weigh what might have been predetermined by a higher will regarding certain so-called "masters" of the Myriam, and to reflect on what was discussed and elucidated by Kremmerz.

Now, it happened that I heard Kremmerz speak in frank terms of lacking "masters" and of having semi-masters: for example,

"master" was used to describe Borracci* of Bari and Banabitacola†
of San Severo, who moved to Rome to take over and reorganize the
Vergilian Academy; "almost-master," for example, was what the then
living engineer Clemente and the late Vignali were called.

The degrees were then undefinable, which is why I came to find
myself suspended in a nimbus cloud of masters, nimbus in relationship to the "master" par excellence Kremmerz, or, as he was called
using the Masonic expression by Bonabitacola, "Grand Master,"

The "Grand Master" literally was surrounded by so-called masters such as Borracci or Bonabitacola, who occupied ambiguous
positions that left it uncertain whether they were to be seen as
superior or slightly subordinate to me, akin to the cherubs depicted
in religious artwork swirling with enigmatic reverence around the
"near-masters."

Now, while there emerged from the recesses of my tormented
spirit more or less confused memories of powers, of past lives, of
instructions to follow, and when I was preparing for an important
meeting with the "Master" himself, indeed I was told I had to throw
myself at his feet to implore I do not know which forgiveness or
intercession from the supernal spheres!

To be honest, the welcome I received from the sympathetic old
man was not severe at all, as I had been led to believe. Unlike their
relationship with the Master, whom they addressed as the "Grand
Master," Kremmerz seemed distant with them. However, his words
hinted at warmth as he treated me with friendliness akin to that of a
newfound brother. This demeanor was contrary to my initial impression and offered solace in the midst of letting go of preconceptions.

Allow me to explain. It was obvious that Kremmrez treated me
as an equal; the word "master," uttered from his mouth, sounded
to me different from how he pronounced it with the others. But an

---

*[Giaccomo Borracci was head of the Pythagorean Academy of Bari.—*Trans.*]
†[Givoanni Bonabitacola was head of the Vergilian Academy of Rome before
WWII.—*Trans.*]

instinctive detachment from the others, especially since I could not grasp their position in the Myriam kept me in a state of mistrust that never protected me from the unfortunate misunderstandings between them and me—and which Kremmerz completely fulfilled.

I don't know which experiences and disappointments that his trusted group of faithful followers gave him: I only know that many questionable aspects of their business activities were brought to light by people of integrity that were superior to them owing to their independent and integral character.

Therefore, with respect to my question of the relationship between me as "master of the first degree" and Borracci as "master of the third degree," Kremmerz shot back in a manner that I rarely saw him do in the three years of our acquaintance. He jumped up and said the following: "What master and which masters; a distinction that I introduced but that has nothing whatsoever to do with the Egyptian concept of master."

Later, at that time, on several occasions he showed himself annoyed by the expression "master," even if addressed to him. On my insistence to understand the degrees or the meaning of these terms, he told me explicitly that the group of subordinates from Apulia were not his first or foremost disciples—having progressed as far as they could—that they remained disciples, and therefore inferior to me. He added in one of the last letters that they were inferior to me also for another aspect.

He stated that they were not his direct disciples from previous lives but were disciples of a French master (I wasn't told for what reasons) who couldn't at the present oversee their development, and that in some sort of way were delegated to him by proxy. I could not say whether tacit or expressed. He also gave detailed explanations—which I cannot report here—but which demonstrate that Kremmerz had adopted this group of Gallic-Apuliese systems and methods that were not suitable for others and even less for my case. With these premises I shall move on to consider that which in the historical account I have called the Apulian period of the Myriam (the second period).

From the statements made by Kremmerz and in consideration of the facts that his primitive program was designed to create a hierarchy in which, gradually and through the rigorous development of actual powers, a progressive initiation takes place, always remaining within the scope (according to the constitution) of passive therapeutics, whether or not it was actually achieved, thus ended the first cycle of the Myriamic activity.*

The official closure of the Myriamic academies and the vicissitudes that ensued in Italy due to the anti-Masonic measures of Mussolini's regime, if on the one hand they considerably limited the impact of the brotherhood on an eminently public and visible level, on the other they had to represent one stimulus for reflection and change.

There is no doubt that Kremmerz was thinking of giving a new structure to his schola and that he had in mind radical changes also related to his personal sphere, considering that, in 1928, he had toyed with the intention of emigrating to North America with his own family. The Dialogues on Hermeticism represented an ideal *vade mecum* for those who wished to approach the study of magic and an excellent tool for study and reflection for those disciples (there were many) who, while practicing, still had serious difficulties in ot understanding even the rudiments of the thought of their teacher.

On February 26, 1929, in a private letter addressed to professor Quadrelli (Ercole Quadrelli, "Abraxis" in Evola's UR Group), Formisano recognized the failure of the previous structure of his school, hoping for a decrystallization of the same that unfortunately, would never be implemented.

Kremmerz died, in fact, on May 7, 1930, at his home in Beausoleil from a stroke. The funeral was barely concluded when some followers who had come from Italy to take part in the public ritual, including

---

*[The first cycle of the Myriamic activity occurred with the publication of the revised "pragmatica," which led to giving the fraternity a more hierarchical structure and more independence among the various academies of the Myriam.—*Trans.*]

the lawyer Giacomo Borracci, rushed into the home of the deceased, in the spasmodic but vain search for confidential materials and precise instructions concerning the succession to the leadership of the fraternity. Formisano must certainly have taken steps to make the secret documentation in his possession disappear, most likely delivering it to the fire or to the safe keeping of his Parisian secretary Jean Brenniere, all tracks leading to whom, mysteriously, were soon lost.

On the one hand, from the trial papers, there emerged evidence that Ricciardelli suffered from a serious form of sexual inhibition and that already in 1924 he had turned to the physician Giovanni Bonabitacola (head of the Vergilian Circle of Rome, since January 15, 1921), who tried to heal this pathology using the magical arts.

However, the application of occult therapeutics did not produce the desired effects, and it was for this reason that the patient (convinced that his illness was attributable to an avataric state), accompanied by other hierarchs of the Fraternity of Myriam, went to visit Kremmerz at Beausoleil in southern France, next to the Principality of Monaco.

The thaumaturge from Poritici treated the pathology of the wealthy aristocrat with homeopathic remedies. It is not known whether the therapeutic interventions had their desired effect in favor of Ricciardelli. What is certain, however, is that his mental instability was considerably worsened by the morbid interest he developed in occult practices, the exercise of which Kremmerz constantly tried to keep him from.

Moreover, Kremmerz must have realized that he was dealing with an unbalanced subject; but he certainly could not have imagined that, as early as 1922, his friend had suffered from serious mental disorders that, in 1925, had led him to be hospitalized at a sanitorium.

It is therefore understandable why Ricciardelli was convinced that certain hierarchs of the Myriam who possessed therapeutic powers, such as Borracci and Bonabitacola "could not" have acquired them in the Schola, and that these powers were nothing more than "a resurfacing of the powers they already possessed in other existences."

It's curious to think that therapeutic skills primarily arise from the collective magnetism developed through consistent and dependable practice within the chain. However, this concept seems at odds with the acquisition of personal abilities stemming from magnetism and further enhanced by transformative magic following participation in the Myriam. These abilities aren't solely tied to the chain but are internally acquired by the mystes under the guidance of various masters, whose benevolence may vary.

1930s

On May 10, 1930, with the unexpected passing of his master, don Ricciardo was left with the small barque of his ingenuity to deal with the predicament of his soul and the subsequent search for his missing piece, what he deemed as the sacred bride. RR was given exacting rituals by the Egyptian Order to assist in evoking memories from his past lives, along with ones designed to purify his soul of karmic impurities, so that he might navigate through a spiritual purgatory.

Although a direct disciple of Kremmerz, Baron Ricciardelli (alias Marco Daffi) renewed his contact with an "Egyptian" order in Canada, where Prince Leone Caetani had moved during the 1920s. Marco Daffi launched a series of Hermetic chains—the Pharaonic Group, founded in 1926 and revived in 1953; the Chain of Hamzur or Andromeda from 1956 to 1962; the Pleiadic Ring from 1962—with the help of friends from Bari and Genoa, and which, however, were limited to a small number of qualified members.

Throughout the 1930s, RR corresponded with Leone Caetani (Ottaviano, head of the GOE) and other members of the GOE in Canada, and after Caetani's death in 1936, with the subsequent head of the GOE, Vincenzo Gigante. Daffi was the first to identify the Roman prince Leone Caetani as the author of the articles, signed "N. R. Ottaviano" and published in *Commentarium*, the journal for the Hermetic academies of Dr. Giuliano Kremmerz

Throughout the 1930s, RR received operating rituals from the O.E. and founded an initiatory chain, the Pharaonic Group, dedicated to practicing Hermetic therapeutics. RR, along with a small circle of initiates, engaged in the experimentation and practice of lunar and solar rituals from the O.E., which were further refined to enhance their therapeutic effects.

Daffi recast the O.E. rituals* toward healing applications within the framework of the *Medicinae Dei* Hermetic practice. Eventually, the Pharaonic Group was placed *in somnium* and a new chain was revived called the Andromeda circle, with members never exceeding half a dozen members throughout the 1930s–1940s.

---

*The rituals were partially published by Editrice Kemi in *Thesaurus Mediciane Dei, Rito di Hamzur: Il Libro Ermetico dei Morti* and will be included in my forthcoming book *The Hermetic Book of the Dead* (working title).

The Trial of the Magus

In the late 1930s, Daffi was implicated in what became known as the infamous "Trial of the Magus." Before his untimely death, Kremmerz rejoiced in the birth of his first grandson, Pasquale, who in his words was born under a favorable sign; benevolent and destined for great achievements. Kremmerz suggested subjecting Pasquale to a rigid education, necessary to better develop those innate and beneficial inclinations that he believed were detectable in the soul of his grandson.

Grandfather Ciro waited with trepidation for the arrival of this grandson, and in a letter dated February 1920 addressed to his daughter, predicted a bright future for the little one who, he wrote, should have been called Julian—not Kremmerz or Kromer, but more like Julian the Apostate—as if to signify an avenger with a very generous heart, having the sentiment of justice within him.

Upon attaining the age of maturity, Pasquale was entrusted by his father Ferdinando to the care of Professor Vincenzo (aka Vinci) Verginelli who was bestowed with the task of preparing him to take the entrance exams for university. After the war, Vinci Verginelli was a well-known hierarch of the Myriam who for many years up until his death in the mid-1980s was the veritable head of the Rome-based Vergilian Academy.

By March of 1937, Baron Ricciardo Ricciardelli, who by this time was deeply immersed in the Neapolitan form of Hermeticism and a self-proclaimed follower of Giuliano Kremmerz, went to the home of the aforementioned Verginelli and persuaded the young Pasquale, under a pretext, to accompany him to a hotel in the capital, in order to initiate him into magical practices.

Ricciardelli was convinced that the spirit of Kremmerz himself, or the geni of Köböaks (of whose existence he had learned directly from the esotericist of Portici) and perhaps also that of Julian the Apostate, was incarnated in the body of the youthful Pasquale Pugliese. The Baron had developed a sort of obsession with the figure of Koboaks, even before meeting with the young student of profesor Verginelli.

In the presence of the phantom entity, Köböaks, Ricciardelli would attempt a complex solar operation following which Köböaks's brilliant intelligence was expected to manifest. The eccentric aristocrat in turn presented himself as the reincarnation of the Egyptian priest Mörköhekdaph who, four thousand years earlier, had plundered a sacred treasure kept in the Temple of the Sun and had illicit relations with the daughter of the presiding Pharaoh. His numen had therefore been condemned to reincarnate as a multimillionaire who would have to squander all of his assets in order to remedy the sacrilege perpetrated.

As if this were not enough, Ricciardelli was convinced that to repair the seduction perpetrated against the daughter of the Egyptian monarch, he would have to force his wife Letizia to give herself carnally to his driver, a certain Antonio Mazza, who became one of his most trusted advisors and who pretended to show a passionate interest in Hermeticism so as to gain his own personal advantage from the extravagances of his host.

For his part, it seems that Ricciardelli had cultivated extramarital relations by frequenting a certain woman named Carciopolis, who became his mistress, a certain Iris, and finally Lucia Leonzio, called Lucietta, a fifteen-year-old peasant girl in whom the noble esotericist believed to recognize his soulmate (his Ankh-es-en-amon?).

The Egyptian-Chaldean influences that Ricciardelli drew from Kremmerz's symbolic-philosophical framework are clearly evident in his unconventional theories. These ideas led him to divest his lucrative assets in favor of the seventeen-year-old Pasquale, driven by a desire to shed his karmic burdens and, as he claimed, acquire an even greater fortune through fabulous winnings from divinatory practices, compensating for the impact left with the purging of his psychic alienation.

Despite his young age, Pugliese did not let himself be enchanted by Ricciarelli's extravagances but took the opportunity to have the latter deliver about one and a half million lire, which he squandered by pretending to indulge only in the whims of fate. With the consent of the Baron, Kremmerz's grandson went to Venice, a city considered by the noble gentleman to be particularly suited to favoring contact with the eons. Here Pugliese met the German ballerina Katharina Forster, who subsequently became his mistress. During his visit to the lagoon capital, Pasquale informed don Ricciardo that he was, in fact, the geni of Köböaks. He then asked the Baron to send money to that name at the Regina hotel, where he was staying, in order to settle the debt that the priest Mörköhekdaph had accrued during a previous life.

Later, the youthful swindler disclosed to the Baron that he had corresponded with a certain Erwin Koboaks, a citizen of Latvian descent, on whose behalf he had asked Ricciardelli for and received additional funds. Over time, Pugliese refined his deceitful tactics. He began employing stamps and documents bearing Köböaks's name to fabricate improbable magical incantations, all the while pretending to be in a trance before the Baron. Additionally, he presented RR with a gold medallion inscribed with the initials of the enigmatic Latvian esotericist, furthering his deceitful charade.

Pugliese's lavish lifestyle caught the eye of Florence's police, leading to his temporary detainment in June 1939 when they discovered a substantial sum of 29,000 lire in his possession. However, it wasn't until December of that same year that the Roman police finally arrested him. Ricciardelli, deeply convinced of his need for atonement for serious faults, made frantic efforts to rectify his transgressions as swiftly as he could. In doing so, he unwittingly embroiled Pasquale Pugliese, who was entirely ignorant of Hermeticism, in a precarious predicament. The Baron, squandering vast amounts of money, engaged in extravagant Hermetic rituals, adding to the young adult's unfortunate circumstances. RR's family arranged to intercede in the nefarious relationship between the Baron and Kremmerz's grandson through a trial that became famous given Ricciardelli's acclaim and importance.

The trial of Kremmerz's grandson occurred in the Court of Rome, with the honorable Arturo Tocci presiding as its president, alongside judges Umberto Guido and Edmondo Siciliani. Concluding on April 1, 1941, Pugliese was sentenced to three years and two months of imprisonment and ordered to pay a fine of 10,000 lire for exploiting an incapacitated citizen.

However, Pugliese would later succeed in reducing his sentence to two years in prison and to escape paying the entire fine, probably retaining a substantial part of the defrauded money that he had managed to hide in collusion with the engineer Vincenzo Manzi (the one who more than others would have benefited from Don Ricciardo's alleged insanity), and who helped to support this suggestibility by attributing to the Baron the title of master in a "bottle," that is, of a master disabled in his own memories, asserting that this expression had been coined directly by Kremmerz.

And so it was this same Manzi, who in the late 1920s contrived to defraud the Baron in a scam involving the Tivoli olive oil mill. More and more convinced that he had to atone for his atavistic misdeeds with financial ruin, Ricciardelli was persuaded by Manzi and Borracci to invest his assets in a company already heavily indebted with a loss on its balance sheet: the Tivoli oil mill.

In Beausoleil, these individuals finalized the agreement with Kremmerz present, who, as per witnesses, offered detailed guidance on executing the purchase of the plant optimally. He cautioned his disciples that failure to adhere strictly to the instructions would lead to him taking severe measures against them.

At the end of the meeting, Manzi obtained the position of chief executive officer, securing annual payments of over 80,000 lire, while Borracci, a lawyer invited to follow the matter from a legal point of view, demanded the exorbitant honorarium of 240,000 lire.

Finally, the "Hermetic banker" (as the attorney Polito De Rosa defined him) was also involved in a deal with Alessandro Cavalli, president of the Banca Romana Commerciale and secretary of the Virgilian Circle, who presumably dealt with granting the necessary liquidity for the purchase of the oil mill.

Nevertheless, this financial endeavor swiftly devolved into an insurmountable abyss, consuming approximately 4,000,000 lire within three years. This amount equated to the entire inheritance bequeathed by grandfather Ottavio to his grandson Ricciardo, consequently pushing him perilously close to bankruptcy. Ricciardelli wrote to Kremmerz in 1929 to inform him of Manzi's conduct, but the initiate from Portici underestimated (or perhaps pretended to) the seriousness of the situation.

In any case, in August 1929, the scam was definitively consummated and Ricciardelli found himself the sole owner of the highly depreciated shares of the notorious oil mill that, in the meantime, had changed its name four times: from S.A.O.T. to S.A.O.L., and subsequently Società Anonima Oleifici Tiburtini and finally Società Anonima Oleifici Laziali. Following this financial maneuver, Manzi fled with 500,000 lire defrauded from Ricciardelli, and Kremmerz found himself compelled to intervene, in July of that year, by requesting a loan of 20,000 lire from Ricciardelli, presumably to settle overdue payments owed by the Academies. Nevertheless, facing increasing pressures stemming from these events, he felt obligated to delay the repayment to a future date.

On the other hand, following these events Manzi was removed from the Fraternity of Miriam, while Kremmerz intervened to resolve a dispute that arose between the Baron and the lawyer Giacomo Borracci who demanded the payment of a fee for a claim of legal assistance. As punishment for not following the instructions given by Kremmerz, Borracci was forced to renounce his honorarium, which seems to have been donated to the coffers of the Egyptian Order.

However, recent investigations show that the master (Kr.) did not take any disciplinary measures against Vincenzo Manzi (inexplicably, his reputation enjoys the respect and consideration of some of the more "orthodox" fringes of Kremmerzian Hermeticism), who spent with impunity the money stolen from the unfortunate Ricciardo, and spread the rumor that shortly before his death, Kremmerz would have telegraphed him to come and be at his bedside.

Given the conduct of the Neapolitan engineer in the Ricciardelli affair and his manifest infidelity towards the ideals pursued within the SPHCI, it would seem rather unlikely that such an episode (Kremmerz's invitation to his deathbed) could ever have occurred and that, indeed, it was told by Manzi solely to overshadow a sort of moral investiture that the master would have liked to confer on him at the point of death.

Let's leave the last word to Manzi himself, who in 1945 described the death of his spiritual guide in a private letter addressed to his fraternal brother Pietro Suglia:

> On May 5, 1930, a telegram reached me: "Come immediately because I am ill." On the morning of May 7, we were alone in his room, family members were at lunch, peace and silence reigned around us as if we were isolated from the world.
>
> At one point he said, smiling and looking at me with those big eyes full of kindness and charm, he uttered his last word: "Vinciè don't move' I want to rest," he smiled and closed his eyes and slept. Neither breathlessness nor movement disturbed his stillness. After a while he loosened the grip of his hand. It was 4:00 p.m. on May 7, 1930.
>
> Family members came running, relatives and friends came, and with human formalities the curtain fell on the scene of a Great Hermeticist.

The events reveal that Kremmerz had already foreseen the inevitable "extinction" of his own fraternity, allowing for a period of time during which no one could assert any rights over his own "initiatory creation." The series of scandals leading to the trial generated a significant sensation, drawing unwanted attention to the typically discreet spiritual community. Indeed, the publicity was so extensive that it served as the basis for the publication of a book, *Il Processo del Mago* (The Trial of the Magus), featuring the indictment by the public prosecutor and the arguments presented by the defense and plaintiff lawyers.

Following this necessary digression, Ricciardelli was deeply engaged with establishing a Hermetic circle, known as the Pharaonic Group.

Among them was a former railwayman and now pensioneer from Bari, Vito Candela, nicknamed the "master beggar" who was likely involved with this circle since the late 1920s.

Daffi writes in his *Diarum Hermeticum*: "June 1935, rekindled ties with Vito Candela, the Master Mendicant, also known as Salvatore, associated with, among other things, engaging in ritual practices with Maria Mozzi. He portrayed this fervent lover of his as a medium possessing extraordinary powers of divination, intending to capitalize on her talent for predicting horse race results."[*]

The two shared a passion for gambling and soon began to bet large sums of money on roulette and horses, sums that were naturally paid out entirely by Ricciardelli, owing to the poverty in which Candela found himself. Ricciardelli and Candela came to engaging two "pupils" or "doves," a certain Citeri and Maria Mozzi, who already suffered from a severe form of nephritis, who were subjected together (according to the testimony of Baroness Del Sordo) to a rigid regime aimed at enhancing their mediumistic and clairvoyant skills.

According to this regimen, it was thought, the two women could establish a connection with the astral realm to receive guidance on choosing winning numbers to play at the roulette table or selecting the name of the horse on which to place their bets at the race track.

The constant deprivations ended up aggravating Mozzi's already critical health conditions and Ricciardelli's and Candela's attempts to heal her through Hermetic medicine were not succesful. The girl soon died and her father, devastated by grief, denounced the protagonists, leading to the opening of criminal proceedings against them at the Court of Chieti, whose proceedings over 1935 and 1936 apparently never made it to trial.[†]

---

[*]*Il Processo del Mago* (The Trial of the Magus), Capiferro, Guzzo, Editrice Rebis, 2010.
[†]Adapted with permission from the volume *L'Arcana degli Arcani* (The Arcane of the Arcana), G. M. Capiferro and C. Guzzo (Viareggio: Ediz. Rebis, 2011). See also *Il Caso Ricciardelli-Pugliese* (The Disappearance of Kremmerz and the Empty Succession: The Ricciardelli-Pugliese Case), G. M. Capiferro and C. Guzzo (Viareggio, Ediz. Rebis, 2005).

IL PICCOLO

ESTE, Mercoledì 28 Maggio 1941
XIX dell' E. F. - VI dell'Impero

Uffici del giornale: Via Silvio Pellico N. 8

Ogni numero cent. 30; arretrati cent. 60

ondra costretta a confessare
parte delle perdite subite nel Mediterraneo

Churchill cerca di calmare le vive appren-

Una relazione al Duce

I nostri bombardieri attaccano
la base navale della Valletta a Malta
e gli impianti logistici di Tobruk

regista possono senza il consenso dell'autore apportare sostanziali modifiche ad un soggetto cinematografico loro rimesso per la realizzazione.

Il "mago" Pasquale Pugliesi
ricorre in appello

Roma, 26

Contro la sentenza del nostro Tribunale che lo condannò, come si ricorderà, a tre anni di reclusione, il «mago» Pasquale Pugliesi, a mezzo del suo difensore avvocato Di Stefano, ha proposto appello.

Il reato di cui il Pugliesi era stato dichiarato colpevole era quello di circonvenzione in capace in pregiudizio del barone Ricciardo

Ricciardelli, abilmente sfruttando le credenze di quest'ultimo nella reincarnazione e riuscendo in tal modo a carpirgli 1.800.000 lire. Si sostiene dalla difesa che gli atti attribuiti al Pugliesi non integrano gli estremi del reato contestatogli in quanto il Ricciardelli non è affetto nè da infermità mentale (come afferma la sentenza) nè da deficienza psichica, e in secondo luogo perchè mancano le prove dell'elemento intenzionale per lo abuso dell'altrui credulità, e infine perchè dalle risultanze processuali sarebbe risultato che il Pugliesi non fu l'incube, ma se mai il succube del barone Ricciardelli.

Contro la stessa sentenza si è gravata anche la parte civile, lamentando che, quanto ai danni, il Tribunale abbia rinviato la liquidazione di essi al Magistrato civile.

The front page of the 1941 newspaper *Il Piccolo* of Trieste. Translation: May 27, 1941: Pasquale Pugliesi, known as the "magus," is contesting the court's verdict that sentenced him to three years in prison. Represented by his lawyer Di Stefano, Pugliesi has filed an appeal. He was convicted of deceiving Baron Ricciardo Ricciardelli and unlawfully obtaining 1,800,000 lire from him by exploiting his beliefs in reincarnation. The defense argues that Pugliesi's actions do not meet the criteria for the alleged crime, as Ricciardelli is not mentally incapacitated, nor is there evidence of intent to deceive others by abusing their beliefs. Furthermore, the trial suggests that Pugliesi was not the manipulator, but rather the victim of Baron Ricciardelli's beliefs. Additionally, the plaintiff criticizes the same verdict, objecting to the court's decision to defer payment of damages to the civil magistrate.

Contemporary Report of the Trial

Published in 1942

As if from the plot of a gripping novel, an incredible and disturbing "occult" reality shook the foundations of "esoteric and imperial Rome of the 1940s" with the proceedings of a sensational trial that took place in the middle of the fascist regime. The sentence is clear and definitive but the full publication in 1942 of the indictment by the public prosecutor and of the speeches of the well-known lawyers in a volume with a singular and strongly evocative title "Trial of the Magus" lifts the veil on unknown episodes and hidden truths, pregnant with dark implications and unpredictable developments

Many of the questions and secrets that emerged from the controversial investigation have not yet been resolved or disclosed, but an objective fact adds a further enigmatic note to the mystery that permeates the entire scenario: as soon as it was printed, the book "inexplicably" disappeared from circulation to the point of becoming literally unavailable, even in antiquarian circuits. Some speculate that it was made to disappear to prevent a series of bewildering revelations and embarrassing confessions from becoming public knowledge. But involving whom?

Evidently by someone who intended to prevent the spread of incandescent news and information that would have cast a heavy shadow on the characters mercilessly involved in this grand Guignolian scandal centered on a colossal as well as a squalid scam, consummated in a climate of murky deceptions, moral miseries, grotesque lies, and fatal illusions.

The tragic story revolves around the role of two protagonists: Ricciardo Ricciardelli, a well-known and wealthy baron passionate about esotericism on the one hand, and Pasquale Pugliese, the grandson of the most distinguished representative of Italian magical Hermeticism Giuliano Kremmerz (however, absolutely not part of the proceedings), on the other, while, in the role of active "extras" animating the stage were some of the highest exponents and leaders of the "Fraternity of Miriam" (the initiatory organization founded by Kremmerz himself), principals of academies and, according to what the prosecutor Polito de Rosa denounces in his scorching "j'accuse," greedy jackals of the lowest order whose actions will be stigmatized in a concise warning that sounds like an irrevocable verdict: "No one dares speak of probity, rectitude, and dignity of life, when speaking of them!"

A cursory reading of the indictment suggests that the Baron shared co-responsibility for being taken advantage of, having lost four million lire after losing a few hundred thousand lire at the time (shortly before Kremmerz's death). The indictment also details the events involving the Baron, subsequent to the death of Kremmerz—and proceeding from the trial itself, including the speeches of the Civil Party and the defenders of Pugliese, convicted for circumvention of an incapable party (Ricciardelli).

By all accounts, the Ricciardelli-Pugliese trial was an extraordinary court case, with the protagonist, Baron Ricciardo Ricciardelli, a well-known member of the Neapolitan nobility with Abruzzese roots and possessions also in Puglia and the defendant, who was the prodigal grandson of Italy's most highly distinguished practitioner of the Hermetic arts, Giuliano Kremmerz.

The jurists consisted of some of Italy's most acclaimed barristers: Niccolaj, Polito-De Rosa, Di Stefano, and De Marsico, who were all active participants in the trial in which a young student (Pasquale Pugliese, aka Magus Köböaks) was accused of taking advantage of the naivete of the noble Ricciardelli to embezzle his wealth.

Ricciardelli deliberately handed over large sums of money to Pugliese who acted as a faux intermediary of the magus Köböaks to pass on certain magical practices that the Baron believed would have allowed him to be purified or in the very least to change the direction of the fate in which he was destined from a previous life. Ricciardelli was convinced that part of his Hermetic "atonement" involved him purging himself of his wealth to repair his soul and regain inner purity and serenity . . . with the presumption that these disposed riches would then return to him a hundredfold.

The trial revolved around determining the degree to which Pugliese intentionally exploited Baron Ricciardelli. Both the prosecution and defense teams highlighted specific episodes to influence the verdict. The defense counsel, representing Kremmerz's grandson, also referenced Giuliano Kremmerz and his diverse works on Hermeticism applied to therapeutics, occultism, the science of the magi, as well as Professor Verginelli, during the arraignment.

---

*From *Il Processo del Mago* (Rome: Soc. Ed. del Libro Italiano, 1942).

REFLECTIONS ON THE TRIAL OF THE MAGUS

From the broadest sense of his existential perspective, the Baron viewed the trial and the circumstances leading up to the court case rather differently. For those seeking to form an independent opinion based on authenticated documents, it is recommended to explore the original edition of a book available in the library. This book vividly illustrates the morally dubious methods employed by certain members of the occult Fraternity to influence, manipulate, and deceive their designated victims, leaving them spiritually and physically drained, devoid of vitality, and ultimately serving as a rich feast for their insatiable appetites.

The original edition of *Il Processo del Mago*, from the Italian Book Publishing Company (Rome, Piazza Poli, 1942), bore the subtitle: "Niccolaj, Polito de Rosa, Di Stefano, De Marsico." Contained within are the accusations and legal arguments presented during the trial of Pasquale Pugliese, the grandson of Ciro Formisano, known as the Magus of Portici. Pugliese faced severe condemnation in the trial initiated against him by Baron Ricciardo Ricciardelli.

In this trial, the misdeeds of Pasquale Pugliese and the myriamites Giacomo Borracci, Giovanni Bonabitacola, and Vincenzo Manzi are extensively documented, supported by established evidence. Some of the indicted, as noted in the court proceedings, evaded severe sentences in the trial. The book vividly unveils the Freudian psychoanalytic techniques employed by Giovanni Bonabitacola, a physician from Sansevero residing in Rome, on Baron Ricciardo Ricciardelli. It also delves into the concurrent utilization of occult practices, proclaimed as "Hermetic" by the Myriamic school, and the ensuing calamities that followed.

In 1940, at the height of the fascist era, and at the beginning of World War II, Pasquale Pugliese, grandson of Ciro Formisano, was subpoenaed by the family of Baron Ricciardo Ricciardelli and specifically by his wife, Baroness Letizia del Sordo.

The accused—Pasquale Pugliese, son of Ferdinando and Adelina Formisano—was born in Bari on January 12, 1920.

The sensational trial captured the public's attention, fueled by the intense fascination that paranormal phenomena and their devotees evoked in the society of that era. The hearings were packed with university students, curious to witness a legal matter that seemed to move the hands of the clock back many centuries, evoking the shadows of the most famous trial about magic brought in antiquity: the one against Lucius Apuleius.

Moreover, amidst the densely packed courtroom, which included numerous university students, an intriguing subject of study emerged. The noble demeanor exhibited by the judicial figures, especially that of Baron Ricciardi, offered an exceptional opportunity for character analysis.

From the indictment of the public prosecutor Francesco Polito de Rosa and from the pleadings of the plaintiff's lawyers Adelmo Nicolaj, Alessandro De Stefano, and Alfredo De Marsico, a disturbing picture emerged that largely absolved the lucid madness of Ricciardelli and condemned not only Pugliese but also the greed of those who had made huge gains taking advantage of the psychic ability of Ricciardelli.

In the course of his indictment, the chief prosecutor, De Rosa, pointed the finger in particular against the lawyer Giacomo Borracci, against the engineer Manzi, and Vito Candela, known as the "Master

Mendicant," a penniless retired railway worker from Bari who, as a falsely professed exponent of Hermeticism, ended up stealing from the Baron a million lire, which he squandered on women and gambling.

From the court documents, it became apparent that Ricciardelli suffered from a profound sexual inhibition, and as early as 1924, he sought the aid of physician Giovanni Bonabitacola, who headed the Myriamic Vergilian Circle, in an attempt to remedy this condition through magical practices.

The student, Pasquale Pugliese, with his pale adolescent face illuminated by two very lively eyes, defended himself by assuming that he was not the exploiter but the exploited by Baron Ricciardelli, that he had been initiated by the same into the Hermetic sciences, that he was so influenced as to believe in the identity of the magician Köböaks who, according to the baron, he must have been the reincarnation.

Baron Ricciardo Ricciardelli maintained an Olympian air of solemnity and patient endurance throughout the trial, his demeanor exuding refinement. He consistently sat beside his defenders, seemingly seeking refuge in the shadow of their robes, perhaps to shield himself from the allure of the young magician.

Ricciardelli claimed to have met Pugliese because he was the grandson of the Hermetic scholar, his friend Ciro Formisano, who had often told him about the existence of the Swedish occult master named Köböaks, a great mediator of wounds of the spirit and wise counselor. In a moment of spiritual crisis due to serious family concerns, he had talked about it with the young student, and the latter after some time had communicated to him that he had entered into relations with Köböaks and had offered himself as an intermediary. Hence the beginning of the fraudulent work of Pugliese toward the Baron and so began the disbursement of sums, which the Baron believed actually went to Köböaks and that instead Pugliese squandered happily, leading a life of great pomp between travels, gambling, and lovers.

The passing of his Hermetic Master left Ricciardelli with an unfulfilled mission and many unfinished tasks to attend to including "the identification of my ancient personality, of my true being, the awakening to integral existence and the true life that I have to lead, the memory of the fundamental principles."

The haunting revelation that tormented RR was the need to atone for the most primal of sins, a sin of love and misappropriation of the Pharaoh's jewels (thus the dual "inhibition"), symbolizing the loss of his fortune. His life mission resurfaced as a master of magic, rekindling his innate capacity for genuine love, along with reclaiming countless riches. He aimed to recoup the fortunes lost during his journey of penance, embodying today as the reincarnation of the Phoenician Mörköhekdaph, an avatar of the Egyptian master Afrato, whose external appearance was imposed upon him.

The entirety of the Baron's life can be described as dwelling within an atmosphere fraught with danger, unease, mysterious defenses, and covert malevolence permeating the realm in which he dwelled—a peculiar and unsettling realm populated by numinous entities, incantations, talismans, hidden forces, and ruled by an unseen and all-knowing master, the "judge," who seemed to summon ancient spirits veiled in shadows, amidst the neon glow of bright lights and rationality of the twentieth century.

By this point, Ricciardelli found himself accused of insanity, branded a fantasist, and worse yet, depicted as someone who no longer conformed to reality, but perceived as a lunatic, reshaping reality to match his wild imaginations. He retreated from public scrutiny, recommencing his pursuit of Hermetic enlightenment.

After the War

By the war's end, Daffi took up residence in Rome and conducted a series of conferences, lecturing on Hermeticism and metapsychical topics to members of the prestigious Accademia Tiberina of Rome. He contributed a series of important articles on the Hermetic tradition and magic to newly established journals including the monthly neo-Myriamic journal *Iniziazione: Rivista di Studi Eosterici* (Initiation: Review of Esoteric Studies) and the journal on scientific mysteries called *Scienze del Mistero* (Science of Mystery) edited by the renowned scholar on Tibetan and Indian traditions, Giuseppe Tucci. His contributions to *Iniziazione* included an article on the "Doctrine of Initiation and Neo-Buddhism." This independent neo-Kremmerzian initiative was made up of a few valid researchers and remained vital and active until the early seventies.

The article "Doctrine of Initiation and Neo-Buddhism" inaugurates a series of historical contributions published in esoteric journals dedicated to a form of Occidental-based Hermeticism, dubbed Italic and classical in the heroic sense of an initiate undertaking a spiritual descent or catharsis to purify their inner being and prepare the groundwork for ascending to more sublime states of spirituality.

The article in question delves into the symbolic significance of "rebirth" within the realms of Hermeticism and esoteric studies. While these interests waned during wartime, they thrived in the following years and remained vividly relevant to enthusiasts. Notably, a core group of devotees, particularly centered around the publisher

Spartaco Giovene of Milan and his re-publication of Kremmerz's works, kept these ideas alive and flourishing.

Iniziazione was in fact the first esoteric magazine—and the first with an explicit Kremmerzian imprint—to appear in Italy after the fateful year of 1945 and constituted a courageous and extremely demanding challenge for the publisher Giovene, a talented and active Kremmerzian Hermetist already known for having given to the press a valuable series of notable works on occultism and magic, now rare.

The life of the journal itself spanned a few years until 1947, during which it contributed a wealth of material on this unique branch of Occidental initiation. Within its pages there are translations of classics, articles, and very interesting writings, most of which were previously unpublished, first of all by Kremmerz (and well-known Kremmerz exponents), by the publisher himself, and by G. Catinella, Papus, Borri, Pernety, Apuleius, Ottaviano, Ricciardelli, Manzi, and others.

It is difficult to imagine today how many and what difficulties must have been faced and overcome in those tumultuous years to be able to undertake and achieve this enterprise, the result of inspiration, ideals, discipline, will, and above all love for the values of a luminous tradition that has seen in Kremmerz one of its greatest and best exponents. It should also be noted that a first group of scholars managed to gather around the journal under the banner of that School founded by Kremmerz and that the publisher *Giovene* evidently hoped to reconstruct in some way.

From the ashes of a devastating war, the publication of the first issue of *Iniziazione* in September 1945 undoubtedly represented an event of considerable importance for the esoteric community and cultural environment of that period. The partnership resulted in the foundation of an operational laboratory or academy, which assumed the name of Fraternity of Miriam and the Schola Philosophica Hermetica Classica Italica (Italic Classical Hermetic Philosophical School), or SPHCI.

1949

In 1949, Ricciardo Ricciardelli, alias Marco Daffi, was introduced to Giammaria through the intermediary of an Italian esotericist, Ugo Gallo, and began a twenty-year correspondence with him until RR's death in July 1969. Giammaria would describe their relationship as consisting of a pilgrimage to the *interior homine* of which the acronym VITRIOL represents the quest for the elusive Philosopher's Stone coursing through one's veins, brilliant as a star.

At the time of their fateful meeting, Giammaria could be described as a wanderer, with no surname or fixed biography, a self-proclaimed alchemist, lawyer, and Latinist, appeared through the haze of history in the postwar period, and on business visits to Rome met Baron Ricciardo Ricciardelli, known among the members of Vergilian and Pythagorean circles as Marco Daffi (an Italianized form of the name of his daimon Mörköhekdaph).

Giammaria recalls his first encounter with RR in these terms: "The beautiful and precise memory of the first meeting with the Baron Magus constitutes the background of this narrative tapestry of other times, in which stands out the magical and divinatory skills of the Hermeticist, as well as intriguing revelations on his esoteric thought."

For over two decades, Giammaria and the Baron met regularly in Rome. Marco Daffi, a friend and advocate of Giuliano Kremmerz, emerged as an independent Hermetic magus and philosopher, whom Kremmerz referred to as "master." The distinction was confirmed in a letter by Kremmerz himself, acknowledging the Baron excelled in the Hermetic craft independently, outside the confines of the Fraternity and not owing to it.

In this context, Daffi could be likened to Julius Evola, who, much like him, could never—and never wished to—completely assimilate into any organization. During that era, Evola emerged as a unique "intellectual beacon" for several esoteric circles and political movements, which, through him, developed and embodied his doctrines. However, these circles couldn't assimilate Evola into their ranks; instead, he integrated them into his journey and his endeavors.

And further still, the Baron was never an isolated person, a reclusive ascetic, or a social mask who hid behind a lonely and proud magician. Far from it, Daffi succeeded in creating a new model of Hermetic society, different from "Ur" and "Krur," although having certain similar characteristics in common. Established in the late 1920s and enduring until the late 1960s, his various circles—Pharaonic Group, Andromeda Circle, or the Pleiades Ring—were grounded in principles that enabled their members to effectively embody a Hermetic paradigm suited to the existential demands of the latter half of the twentieth century.

After the war, Marco Daffi founded a small yet independent group of Hermetic nomads, a veritable clan of initiatic Wandervogel* based in Rome. Initially the circle was called the "Pharonic Group" and then changed to "Andromeda Circle" and the "Rite of Hamzur"; then in 1962, it became the "Ring of the Pleiades." It could be argued that these circles embodied, in their symbolism, both the physical and metaphysical aspects of Mörköhekdaph within the Hermetic tradition framework.

He corresponded with several disciples of Hermes, among them Giammaria Gonnella, in art: Giammaria, an aspiring lawyer and Dr. Elio, a surgeon, both dedicated practitioners of the Royal art, who resided in Genoa. Giammaria was an independent alchemist, and for many years was the sole compiler, editor, and commentator on Marco Daffi, and thanks to him we now can read the works of that original Italian Hermetic master.

Daffi never treated Giammaria as a mere "disciple," always regarding him as an equal. Giammaria, owing to his independent worldview and grasp of Hermeticism, as well as his innate talents, personality, and vitality, couldn't fit the mold of a "follower" or conform to the traditional hierarchies within esoteric circles. He could never pursue a conventional career in esoterism, by founding an organi-

---

*Originally signifying migratory birds, the term was adopted in the early twentieth century by German youth to symbolize a movement devoted to wandering, hiking, and embarking on journeys as avenues for liberty, self-expression, and exploration.

zation with a formal hierarchy having "superiors" and "subordinates."

Giammaria described the Baron as consistently engaged in delving into the depths of his psyche, with an inner perception aimed at exploring spiritual states and reclaiming deeply rooted memories and visions that transcended common experiences. As well, the Baron demonstrated uncanny mantic abilities to foresee winning lottery numbers and horses that went beyond the ordinary.

Indeed, the Baron harboured several distinct objectives that he aimed to pursue. He explicitly conveyed to Giammaria in July, 1949:

1. If I possess both energy and tranquility, I aspire to fulfill the purpose of my existence by giving a contemporary and organic form to Hermetic philosophy that is traditional."

2. Implementing the refinement of Mercurial perception within the framework of financial gains, entailing the wagering of bets on various lucrative avenues such as lotteries. Following each victory, a portion of the winnings would be set aside, while the remainder would be reinvested. The financial context assumed a pivotal role in Humanimal initiation, serving as a crucial tool for harnessing subtle energies, while perception gleaned insights from the Library of the Invisible.

3. The application of Hermetic therapies and more extensively of the *Medicina Dei* rituals, proposed for use by the Andromeda circle (later adopted by the Pleiades Ring), to address diverse healing requests, screened *ad hoc* with the assistance of Elio, a surgical physician and specialist in oncology.

In, 1948, Daffi penned the lead article for the Rome-based publication of international culture: *Ulisse: Rivista di cultura internazionale.* Titled: "Alchemical Hermeticism," the essay outlined Daffi's vision of alchemy as a distinct yet intertwined filament of illumination within Hermeticism. It emphasized a practice of gnosis guiding the initiate toward altered states of consciousness essential for interior transformations along the alchemical path.

Other contributors included Aniceto Del Massa, who also contributed throughout the 1920s and '30s to the respected journals on initiation studies: *Atanor, Ignis, Krur,* and *La Torre*. Additionally, Professor Emilio Servadio, a renowned psychologist, also contributed to *La Torre* and maintained a close relationship with Julius Evola during the same period.

THE 1950S

In the later years of his life, through the 1950s and '60s, Marco Daffi communicated a series of rituals from the Egyptian Order to "Giammaria," who used them for the new initiative of the Corpo dei Pari (Corps of Peers), formed in the early 1960s and disbanded after twelve years in the 1970s, which, however, Daffi remained outside of.

By the late 1960s, the enclave of mystes associated with the Peers aroused the curiosity of the Genovese press and public. They achieved notoriety by posting placards and posters on the walls and buildings of Genoa, reminiscent of the early Rosicrucians, in the seventeenth-century, that had plastered manifestos along the walls of Paris.

For the record: from the early 1950s and onward Daffi stood as the focal point amidst the (few) lights and numerous shadows of Italic Hermeticism. He served as an indispensable resource and go-to luminary for those pilgrims seeking the cinnabar path.

"I have seen and been privy to some remarkable stories, tales, true gems—real beauties, so to speak," Daffi would exclaim. "However, due to karmic forces and my own immaturity—perhaps even an avataric immaturity—two years after Kremmerz's departure, unbeknownst to me, an intense battle raged against adverse elements. Despite this, in pursuit of realizing the primal agenda, it became necessary to advance and awaken my oldest Atlantean heritage, thus embracing the deepest hieratic inclination, while simultaneously tempering the external and social aspects—possibly through a Pharaonic approach—and seeking to placate the Fates" (from a letter from Marco Daffi to Elio and to the Myriamic "friends" of Bari, dated January 19, 1953).

ACCADEMIA TIBERTINA

Throughout the 1950s and '60s, RR would deliver numerous lectures at the esteemed Accademia Tibertina in Rome. It is believed that within the academy's library, there may still exist copies of one of his works on Jainism, possibly related to a course he conducted at this esteemed institution—a testament to his scholarly contributions.

The noted scholar, Anna Maria Partini, specializing in Renaissance Hermeticism, tells of her encounters with the Baron: "We would often meet RR in the mornings at either Caffe Adriano or Cola di Rienzo, near his residence in Piazza Cavour. Our conversations flowed freely, delving into topics of religion, philosophy, and alchemy. Occasionally, politics would be discussed, although I found myself less engaged in those discussions. Towards the end of 1956, a small group of Hermetic

The emblem and seal of the
Accademia Tibertina

enthusiasts, including Professor Vincenzo Nestler* and members of the scientific committee of the Society of Metapsychics, was formed. Baron Ricciardelli occasionally joined us and contributed insights on the theoretical underpinnings of parapsychology, particularly the telepathic phenomenon. Our discussions ranged from Rosicrucianism to mysticism and tradition, from metapsychics to magic, and even delved into topics like the Journey to the Underworld of the Midnight Sun. Themes that consistently revolved around transcending the boundaries between spirit and matter held particular significance for us."†

Baron Ricciardo Ricciardelli maintained his connections with an "Egyptian" center in Canada following the passing of its leader, Prince Leone Caetani. He initiated a series of personal endeavors, including the Pharaonic Group, established in 1926 and revived in 1953; the Chain of Hamzur or Andromeda from 1956 to 1962; and the Pleiadic Ring from 1962 onward.

These ventures, supported by friends from Bari and Genoa, garnered a modest following. However, during this period, the Pharaonic Group's activities remained primarily aspirational, transitioning into a "potential" affiliation with the enigmatic "Canadian" Egyptian order from 1956 to 1962. Marco Daffi expanded and restructured the sodalitas into the vaguely defined "Chain of Hamzur" or Andromeda, and later, from 1962 onward, into the Pleiadic Ring, with his friend Elio remaining steadfast at his side.

From 1950 to 1951 RR documented his research and experiences with Kremmerz and the Myriam, which eventually were published in a book in the late 1970s.

---

*Vincenzo Nestler was a member for many years of the Italian Scientific Association of Metapsychics (A.I.S.M.) and of the Tiberine Academy, in whose Faculty of Psychological Sciences he was a lecturer. He has collaborated with conferences, writings, and experimental works, also with other important centers of parapsychological research (SIM, SIP, CSP, CIP). His articles have appeared in various specialized magazines. As an experimenter, Vincenzo Nestler has directed various experiments with gifted and qualified sensitive subjects, and is also known abroad as one of the most significant Italian parapsychologists.

†*Il Fuoco che non brucia: studi sull'achimia* (The fire that doesn't burn: Studies on alchemy), Massimo Marra, Mimesis, 2009.

The book consists of two distinct parts, each made up of a single essay. The biographical section on Formisano is a transcription of original notes by Marco Daffi that were compiled by Elio (a surgeon from Genoa who died prematurely) who, around the 1950s, due to his interest in Hermetic studies, presented this work to Marco Daffi. Elio had personal contacts with Daffi, and from 1950 an epistolary correspondence that grew over time more and more copious, until 1969. Their particular correspondence, made not only of words, also included suggestions, instructions, diagnoses for Hermetic medicine operations.

The second essay is a memoir penned by Marco Daffi for scholars of alchemical Hermeticism, primarily those associated with Myriamic or neo-Kremmerzian schools. Among the recipients of this memoir was Elio, alongside other esteemed scholars. Following thorough revisions for publication, the resultant book stands as the most authentic and comprehensive account to date regarding Kremmerz and the Therapeutic-Magical Fraternity of Myriam. Kremmerz established this fraternity not as a conventional initiation order but rather as a school dedicated to the practical application of Hermetic medicine. (*Giammaria, Marco Daffi e la sua opera.*)

On January 7, 1953, in a letter to the journalist Dino Provenzal, Ricciardo Ricciardelli responded to an article by Provenzal, "Ricordo di Benedetto Croce" (Memories of Benedetto Croce) published in the *Gazzetta del Popolo* of December 20, 1952, on the third anniversary of the philosopher's death, to point out that the latter was a relative of the Ricciardellis and to describe the characters at the salon "of Croce's house," among whom he mentions Don Giacinto Castaldi, tutor of the Ricciardelli household and of Croce himself.

1960S

The noted author on esoteric traditions, Piero Fenili, wrote of his encounters with the Baron: "My friend Placido Procesi was the first to talk to me about the Baron in the mid-sixties, with accents in which sympathy, consideration, and caution entered in equal dose. In any case, the character had to be taken seriously: it was certainly no coincidence that Kremmerz, a voluntary exile in Beausoleil, had repeatedly received him, chatting with him, almost as equals, on some crucial themes of Hermetic philosophy. Such was the case also with the lawyer Giammaria Gonella, Professor Luciano Raffaele di Santadomenica and Doctor Aleandro Tommasi, who had the good fortune to attend to the Baron for longer than his imminent death would have granted me" (Piero Fenili, *Ricciardo Ricciardelli, The Magical Baron,* Elixir, #4, Edizioni Rebis, 2006).

In Giammaria's correspondence with Daffi, crucial aspects of Daffi's life mission come to light, such as his revelation as an incomplete Avatar and the past life identification as Mörköhekdaph. Baron Ricciardelli possessed an esoteric library of significant importance, including, among other things, unpublished manuscripts on magical, theurgical, and alchemical practices and collected in part during Giammaria's personal contacts with him.

In the first two weeks of May 1963, RR had a debilitating crisis that he defined as "a revulsion"—with nightmares of death—and in the course of which the figure of Ei hm'sc Bêl first appeared. On June 6 there followed a difficult three weeks with recurring dreams and nightmares.

He described it as the emergence of a financial and initiatory crisis of the humanimal order, but also the means of untenable control of subtle powers, and claimed to have resumed with a new "contact" and apperception from the "Library of the Invisibles."

In navigating the realms of consciousness and monadic existence, he asserted his role as a pilot of the pluri-monadic. Through the power of "inductance," he claimed directional prowess, steering amidst the perpetual flux of consciousness within the Soul. This awareness extends to the original tetrad, in revulsion with the established monadic structure.

He cautioned that during the magnetic influence of the Moon-

Mercury conjunction, as well as the new moon and three days following it, there tends to be a inclination towards solitude, a continence, hence "yielding" to the full moon for "pollentia pollutionis."*

Furthermore, he said that:

The Four Tempora† are captured by the Chaldean ritual and that the value of certain foods and medicines oscillate according to the cycles (see the Lunations of Kremmerz).

Specifically, he stated that:

The Pharaonic Group remained active from 1932 to 1956;

The Hamzur Chain (or Andromeda) from 1956 to 1962;

The Pleiadic Chain (or Pleiadic Ring) since 1962.

---

*Intense pollution and defilement.

†Tempora = finite time.

Obituaries

On September 3, 1969, Baron Ricciardo Nicola Ricciardelli passed away. The Italian Society of Psychic Research announced his death in both *Metapsichica: Rivista Italiana di Parapscicologia*, (Metapsychics: Italian Journal of Parapsychology) and *Rivista Italiana di Ricerca Psichica* (Italian Journal of Psychic Research), sharing the following obituaries:

IN MEMORIAM DEL BARONE RICCIARDELLI — Il 3 settembre, in Roma, è deceduto il Barone Ricciardo Ricciardelli, valoroso Collaboratore di « Metapsichica » e di altre Riviste di Parapsicologia. Era nato a Napoli nel novembre del 1900, ed aveva compiuto studi classici, dimostrando presto quelle tendenze mistiche e umanistiche che affiorano (più o meno vivamente) nei Suoi scritti più importanti. Uomo coltissimo, si era interessato attivamente di Filosofia Ermetica e di Religioni Orientali, ed aveva partecipato brillantemente alla « Ricerca oggettiva sulle Mantiche » (I-KING). Lascia, oltre a vari articoli e conferenze di parapsicologia, diversi lavori « ermetici » (purtroppo non tutti completati).

Confidiamo di poter scrivere ancora di lui nel prossimo fascicolo pubblicando alcune note che egli aveva preparato per Metapsichica, e sarà questa la più degna commemorazione.　　　　　　　　　　　　　　　　　　　　　V. N.

In Memoriam: Baron Ricciardo Ricciardelli

Metapsichica: Rivista Italiana di Parapscicologia,
no. 3–4 (July–December 1969): 157.

On 3 September, in Rome, Baron Ricciardo Ricciardelli, a valiant collaborator of *Metapsichica* and other journals of parapsychology, passed away. He was born in Naples in November 1900, and was devoted to classical studies, revealing early on mystical and humanistic inclinations that permeated his most significant writings to varying degrees.

A highly cultured man, who ardently pursued Hermetic philosophy and

Oriental spiritual traditions, making notable contributions to objective research into the "Mantic arts," such as the I Ching.

Alongside his diverse writings and lectures on parapsychology, he leaves behind several "Hermetic" works (regrettably not all of them finished).

We hope to honor him once more in the upcoming issue by sharing notes he had prepared for *Metapsichica*, ensuring a fitting tribute to his memory.

V. N. (VINCENZO NESTLER)

NECROLOGIO

Si è spento in Roma il 3 settembre scorso, con animo sereno, il nostro Consocio Barone Ricciardo Ricciardelli, lasciando in noi tutti un vivo rimpianto.

Nato nel 1900 a Napoli, ma abruzzese per elezione e per sentimento era Uomo molto colto. Preparato sulla base degli studi classici aveva sviluppato le Sue ricerche nei campi della filosofia ermetica e delle religioni orientali, nei quali campi aveva raggiunto un tale grado di conoscenza da consentirGli una notevole validità sia negli scritti che negli interventi, sempre precisi ed opportuni, alle conferenze, tenute da oratori qualificati, nei vari cicli culturali.

Appassionato studioso dei fenomeni paranormali, li approfondiva con instancabile interessamento, ricercando nei testi italiani e stranieri, avvantaggiato in ciò dalla conoscenza di varie lingue.

Sensitivo anche Lui, forse inconscio di possedere particolari qualità, penetrava i fenomeni parapsicologici interpretandoli con acume non comune.

Un settore particolarmente da Lui studiato ed esplorato era quello dell'*I-King*, nel quale non si appagava di soffermarsi all'esito della sperimentazione, quasi sempre positiva, ma ne coglieva l'essenza, con la tenacia e la sicurezza del ricercatore convinto delle proprie ipotesi.

Ha lasciato studi interessanti, quali: *Alchimia ermetica, Ermetismo alchemico, Psicologia animale, Studio sul mito di Andromeda*, ecc. Condusse, anche, studi pregevoli sull'*astrologia* e sui *tarocchi*.

La S.I.P., che Lo ebbe Socio e Collaboratore molto apprezzato, Lo commemorerà degnamente in una delle riunioni del Ciclo Culturale del 1970.

Obituary: Baron Ricciardo Ricciardelli

Rivista Italiana di Ricerca Psichica
(Italian Journal of Psychic Research), 1970.

Our esteemed colleague, Baron Ricciardo Ricciardelli peacefully passed away in Rome on September 3rd, leaving us all with profound sorrow.

Born in 1900 in Naples but a resident of Abruzzo by choice, he was a man of great erudition. His education was rooted in classical studies, supplemented by a deep dive into Hermetic philosophy and Eastern religions, where his expertise earned him significant respect in both scholarly writings and public engagements. He was often called upon to speak at conferences hosted by esteemed scholars across various cultural circles.

Driven by a fervent passion for the study of paranormal phenomena, he delved into them with unwavering dedication, meticulously researching Italian and foreign texts and drawing upon his proficiency in multiple languages.

He possessed a sensitivity that he may have been unaware of, yet it endowed him with certain qualities enabling him to penetrate and interpret parapsychological phenomena with exceptional insight. One area he particularly delved into was the study of the I Ching. Rather than merely focusing on the outcomes of experiments, which were often positive, he sought to grasp its essence with the determination and confidence of a researcher firmly convinced of his own hypotheses.

He left interesting studies, such as those on Hermetic alchemy, Alchemical Hermeticism, animal psychology, the myth of Andromeda, and so on. He also conducted valuable studies on astrology and Tarot cards.

The Italian Society of Parapsychology, where he was a member and a very much appreciated collaborator, would worthily commemorate him in one of the meetings of the Cultural Cycle of 1970.

Ricciardelli at a banquet

4

The Legacy of Marco Daffi

Commentaries and Remembrances

Prologue to Part Four

The series of articles, essays, and extracts of letters compiled in this final section offer expanded and varied insights on and about Marco Daffi. To round out the profile of Ours, included are memorials about and impressions of Marco Daffi, testimonials from initiates and artists as well as a synopsis of Marco Daffi's opera omnia of published works.

PROFILES OF AN ARGONAUT
OF THE TETRADIC MONAD

Piero Fenili's article "Ricciardo Ricciardelli, The Magical Baron" offers a firsthand account of Ricciardelli and his relationship with Kremmerz, which is intertwined with his particular studies on oracular modes of visioning including manticism, the tarot, and "astron-mantics," With extensive scholarly research, Daffi applied his visionary prowess to unraveling the mysterious code surrounding the "Mensa Isiaca" or Isiac Table with the study of the tarot. The Jesuit scholar Athanasius Kircher investigated this connection back in the late 1600s through his work *Oedipus Aegyptiacus* and further scrutinized by the exegesis of Marco Daffi on the trumps of the tarot. These highly symbolic images finally emerge singular and enigmatic, enriched with the esoteric commentary of Marco Daffi.

In Giammaria's "The Voice," the evocative memory of first meeting with the magical Baron constitutes the background of this narrative tapestry of other times, in which the magical and divinatory skills of the Hermeticist stand out and complement the intriguing revelations of his esoteric thought.

Within Ricciardelli's intricate revelation of the Hermetic vision he emphasizes the difference between two different but related initiatic-semiotic systems: astrology and astronomy. He posits that astrology explores the individual dimension within their temporal context, focusing on the personal and biographical aspects. In contrast, astronomy addresses the impersonal and numinal Self, and strives for alignment with the Principle, to which the Name acts as a reference point. Hence one refers to the first as a symbol of the second. Interested parties are advised to scrutinize Giammaria's article "The Voice" for further clarification on this topic.

Giammaria Remembers

Giammaria

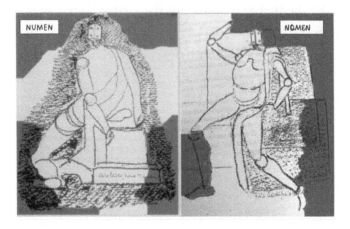

Readaptation of the Unconscious and the Conscious from the
unpublished sketches by Auri Campolonghi Gonella

I was introduced to the Baron through Gino Testi, a figure known
among the right-wing youth of Rome. They would gather in the after-
noons at various galleries in the city. The group was led by Pino Rauti,
whom I visited with the Baron. They acknowledged me because they
knew I had fought alongside them, athough I didn't share their extreme
views. I'm unsure how Gino Testi knew the Baron. This occurred in
1949–50; Testi was a man at the time, while I was still a boy, seeing him
as a father figure. I found him fascinating due to his interest in esotericism, and I inquired about alchemy. He admitted he wasn't well versed
but offered to introduce me to someone who could help. The next day,
I met the Baron, marking the beginning of my friendship with Don

Ricciardo, which lasted from that challenging year until his passing in the summer of 1969.

At roughly the same period, I became acquainted with the notorious figure of Italian esoterism and the guru of right-wing circles, Julius Evola. I encountered Evola on two occasions; he presented himself as a scholarly figure, exuding an air of superiority. Evola was the undisputed leader among the youth of the extreme right whom I had associated with in Rome before meeting Daffi. However, upon encountering Daffi, who displayed no pretensions whatsoever, my interactions with Evola ceased entirely.

Between 1947 and 1948, an article discussing the Great Work was published in the journal *Ulisse* (Ulysses), signed, if memory serves, by "a Kremmerzian," by Ours (Marco Daffi*), indicating the author's affiliation with Kremmerz. This was Marco Daffi, still under the influence, at least psychologically, of Giuliano Kremmerz (hence the signature "a Kremmerzian"). Subsequently, following our association, it became clear to him that alchemy and magic were inseparable facets of Hermeticism. However, this Hermeticism was distinct from the Gnostic-Mediterranean magic associated with Kremmerz and his predecessors—it encompassed influences from Egyptian-Hermetic magic sources and more.

Those were years in which Ours would have been careful not to write (or even conceive) sentiments akin to those that can be read in the letter of March 23, 1963 (see p. 198 in the "Confidential Letters"), where in contrast to astrology he extols the virtues of astronology and portrays himself as a *Veltro* possessing prophetic visionary qualities. Our encounter proved immensely consequential for each of us, despite our positions on opposite ends of the initiatic spectrum, though not in contention with one another—but perhaps it was precisely for this very reason.

For Ours, it served as a way out; a ploy to get out of an impasse of "cultural" irrelevance, whereas for me, it marked the beginning of a journey toward the divine, guided by the alchemical-Hermetic concept of an *interiore homine* pilgrimage of the self, symbolized by the

---

*[The article in question "Ermetismo Alchimico" was actually attributed to Ricciardo Ricciardelli, whereas Giammaria alludes to two articles reviewing Kremmerz's Opera Omnia where they are attributed to "A Kremmerzian."—*Trans.*]

pursuit of the Hidden Stone referenced in the acrostic VITRIOL—a stone with a philosopher's vein, radiant as a star.*

For my part, I was always reluctant to support Marco Daffi, particularly regarding his theurgical magical rituals. He sensed my reservations, which were not directly related to the path he had chosen. In essence, our encounter proved pivotal for both Marco Daffi and myself.

Yet, the continuous exchange of letters (thus, the Philosophical and Confidential Letters) and the contrast in our approaches to the Art were not merely a matter of disagreement, I would venture to say, but also posed challenges.

Ultimately, it manifested in the written word, where the "personality" of MÖRKÖHEKDAPH conveyed his teachings, disseminated through works such as the "Dissertamina," the "Philosophical Letters," "Introduction to the Mantic Arts," *Alchemical Hermeticism*, the "Avatars," and "Solve and Coagula." At its core lies the "Tables and Commentary of the 'Hamzur Ritual'"—a pivotal work, perhaps his most inspired contribution.

The documentation related to the "Thesaurus Medicinae Dei of the Hamzur Ritual" also referred to as the "Hermetic Book of the Dead" was made available thanks to the relatives of Dr. Elio, a friend of both Marco Daffi and mine.

The first section of the book compiles the therapeutic formulas of "Medicinae Dei," conferred to Marco Daffi on May 29, 1950. "This gesture served as a symbol of healing from Master IZAR, who had previously administered thaumaturgical healing for blennorrhagia in Naples around 1880, and later decided to impart it (or, if preferred, re-impart it) on the 19th and 26th of June."†

Yet, the focus of the text lies primarily on that jewel of rituality, namely the Ritual of Andromeda or Hamzur, characterized by diverse

---

*[Ex Epistulis, "Ex Epistulis", Giammaria's book published by Amenothes, 2017, encapsulating his correspondences and recollections with numerous figures of the tradition encountered during his seven-decade journey in the Great Work (p.118).—*Trans.*]

†[The receipt of a positive signal following the application of the therapy suggests that the correct formula was utilized.—*Trans.*]

and sublime inspirations. Marco Daffi endeavored to compliment this ritual with numerous Carmens (extremely lengthy but of mediocre craftsmanship) and intricate Ciphers (talismans), tailored to the intricacies of the Ritual of *Medicinae Dei*. These Ciphers and Carmens were transcribed from another source, stemming from operations conducted on February 4, 10, and 11, as well as March 2, 1952.

The ritual is analogous to the initiatory practices known as *Medicinae Dei* for the transfer or alleviating the fate-karma of the afflicted or suffering individual. This is achieved through fluidic means involving the interaction of spiritual influences (fluids) with vegetative substances, administered into drinks, compresses, or ablutions, as the case may require.

Among his extensive body of work, special attention is directed toward the "Operational Tables and Commentary" and the "Compendium of Hermetics: Tables of Preliminary Studies." The Operational Tables serve as the initial stating point (or syllabus, one might argue) for those embarking on a specific inner journey. Primarily intended for the "disciples of light," it aligns with the "Compendium of Hermetic - Preparatory Tables," while providing— at the same time—the tools of the trade for those who want to proceed correctly on the Path.

The astral realm, viewed integratively and through creative imagery, represents a negative (photographic imprint) that requires reproduction and expression in a positive form for its realization. Moreover, viewed from this perspective, the astral represents an entity (quid) of imperfection, incompleteness, with a passion to be fixed and purified. This arises due to the relationship that a non-integral individual must initiate, envisioning a state of being connected to the movement of fluids (Lunar body).

A substantial trace remains of one of these important discussions in an article by Marco Daffi entitled "the Avatars" (Gli avatars), which appeared posthumously in issue no. 32 of the bimonthly *Kemi-Hathor* journal of alchemical and symbolical studies. Within it, the Baron recounted a discussion he had with Kremmerz on the topic, sharing his reflections and elucidating the rationale behind his disagreement; it remains unclear if this was conveyed personally to Kremmerz. Nonetheless, by formulating his own theory on the matter, he laid the groundwork for further exploration in subsequent issues of the same journal.

Venusian in form, he was sensitive to the ways of Mars, to which Venus is sensitive, while a calibrated Mercury was necessary for the evocation of MÖRKÖHEKDAPH.

In fact, it revolved around an evocation, the summoning forth of a personality that developed autonomously, and which reflected even the physiognomy of the individual. However, its distinct essence stemmed from the singular dynamics of our interpersonal relationship.

From my perspective, I realized that the summoning emerged from the "psychological dynamis" activated by the organic application of alchemical Hermetic operations. This activation resonated with equal intensity and autonomy irrespective of my presence.

Marco Daffi operated flanked by eons, and it was "all" a ritual. When we speak of the "Body of Glory" or the "Second Wood (Body) of Life" we refer to a concrete energy field, outside the conditions of physical existence. Even if we strip away the dramatic elements of his vision of reincarnation, the numen as divine consciousness is in *ad homine* and beyond any dichotomy.

In response to the age-old precepts of the *Ars Brevis*, Hermeticism could be summarized, in the words of Marco Daffi, as a vibration, an impulse, a ray of light that resolves into an intuition.

The Baron did not have "disciples," since he absolutely did not want to become a teacher to anyone, even if in fact Elio G. (a friend from Genoa whom I introduced to the Baron) considered himself such, as did Giorgio M. (Giorgio Valentini) who even today still believes that to be the case.

"I did not consider myself Daffi's disciple. It's incorrect for anyone to think and write this. On the contrary, it was Daffi who changed his positions to mine . . . and if it were not for me, Daffi would have been quite forgotten, as well as dishonored by the publication of the trial transcript. With the argument that the number of humanity is constantly increasing, I convinced him to no longer identify as a reincarnationist. It was the case that Daffi adhered to that position, and we never talked about it anymore. . . 'In the end, Daffi asked me, in reference to his writings that I burn them, as clearly expressed by his will.'

"The rituals of the Corps of Peers* were transmitted by Marco Daffi to me."

Over the last period: "When we met again, the last time, in May 1969, I went to see him with Auri, whom he already knew by correspondence and to whom he had asked to 'conduct' Tarot readings. Our meetings in the final two years had thinned out, while the correspondence and collaboration on the doctrinal level continued, albeit to a lesser extent, since the figure of Mörköhekdaph was gradually fading. I found a different man, absent, and in the hours in which we were entertained, the VOICE—as Auri said—of the master was only briefly heard. We left with a deep sense of discouragement.

"We corresponded for a while. Then, after a period of silence, indirectly, I received news of his death. The responsibility and the privilege fell upon me to review and publish everything, exercising caution, and without personal gain from the publication (i.e., printing), except for what the publisher could derive. Finally, to fulfill his wishes, I burned all the materials I possessed" (Giammaria, "Psychography of a Figure," in "Marco Daffi and His Work").

---

*[The Corps of Peers (Corpo dei Pari) was a Hermetic circle of members founded by Giammaria in the 1960s and active in one form of the other up until the mid-1970s. See *The Magic Door*, Manticore Press, 2019).—*Trans.*]

Interview with Hermanubis
Conducted by N. R. Ottaviano

Jean-Marie d'Aquino-Vallois descends from the ancient Neapolitan House of the Prince of Caramanico (one of his ancestors, Luigi d'Aquino, cousin and disciple of the Prince of Sansevero, was the mysterious Althotas, Master of Cagliostro) and from the House of Vallois, the ancient kings of France.

He began his initiatic path very young and met many masters of the Western Hermetic and Rosicrucian traditions. Originally from Italy, he has lived for many years in France. His initiatic name is Hermanubis; we will refer to him by this name during this interview.

MASTER Hermanubis, how did your spiritual path begin?

With World War II having just ended, my hometown, Naples, seemed to have become a true antechamber of hell. The writer Curzio Malaparte in the novel *La Pelle* (The Flesh) perfectly described this apocalyptic scenario. I was eighteen years old and had a great love for the East, especially for Vedanta philosophy and Tantric yoga: I had avidly read the works of Arthur Avalon and the writings of Patanjali, as well as the books of Guénon and Evola. One evening a friend invited me to a conference organized by the Kremmerzian Academy in Naples, whose head was then Vincenzo Manzi. I was rather disappointed by what I heard, but I met a character who struck me: his name was Eduardo Petriccione. Don Eduardo lived in Pozzuoli, and I went to see him several times: he lent me some alchemy texts that were difficult to find at the time by Llull, Bernardo Trevisano, Flamel, Cesare della

Riviera, Basil Valentine. I became very passionate about the "Ars Regia," bombarding him with questions to which he always answered me in a simple and concise way. One day he phoned me at home and told me to come to him in the afternoon of the following day as a personality he wanted to introduce me to would be visiting him: it was in this way that I met my master, Don Vincenzo Gigante.

So, did Gigante have any esteem for Kremmerz or any of his disciples?

In reality, my master was very fond of Baron Ricciardo Ricciardelli, alias Marco Daffi, whom he considered *nun poco'pazzariello* but who, apart from some bizarre aspects of his personality, was a serious and rigorous Hermeticist and who had been a direct disciple of Kremmerz. Often Daffi went to visit him, and I had the opportunity to spend time with him many times and learned to appreciate and esteem him.

However, Daffi boasted that he was in contact with an "Egyptian Order" residing in Canada, the place where Caetani went into exile during the Fascist era (in Italy) and where he died in 1935.

However, this was Don Vincenzo's expedient aim at "diverting" attention from his person; after all, there was a part of it that was the truth since Don Vincenzo was the successor of Leone Caetani! An initiate never denies the truth but hides it! However, I can assure you that Daffi received several teachings from my master but not the Supreme Arcana, or the Arcana Arcanorum.

Remembering Marco Daffi

N. R. Ottaviano

Marco Daffi is the initiatic name of Baron Ricciardo Ricciardelli, a singular figure of Italian esotericism from the first half of the twentieth century. Initially a disciple of Giuliano Kremmerz, Daffi broke away to pursue an arcane Hermetic practice that was expanded and revised by his

*Baron Ricciardelli's Metamorphosis into Marco Daffi
by Auri Compolonghi Gonella*

disciple Gian Maria Gonella (Giammaria). Daffi was the first to publicly disclose the identity of N. R. Ottaviano, of the Kremmerzian journal *Commentarium*, as Prince Leone Caetani. He also revealed that the mysterious "Ekatlos" of the Evolian UR group was also Prince Caetani.

Don Ricciardo was initially a disciple of Kremmerz but left him to follow the teachings of N. R. Ottaviano (Leone Caetani) in the Egyptian Order (O.E.) or the Great Orient Egyptian. Daffi was among the very few to stay in touch with Don Leone after his exile to Canada, and, on the death of his master in 1935, he became a pupil of Vincenzo Gigante, successor of Prince Caetani, who led the O.E. in different circumstances. Don Leone's letters express gratitude and fondness toward his former pupil, Daffi, whom he described as having exceptional intuition and a sharp intellect. He also noted Daffi's deep devotion and unwavering commitment to the Order's universal traditions and customs.

"The falling out with Formisano doesn't seem to have caused young Ricciardelli any tare." In his book, *Marco Daffi and his Work*, now difficult to find, my dearest friend and Don Ricciardo's cherished disciple, Giammaria, elucidates the core principles of the Hermetic teachings he received from his master. Giammaria passed away in January 2022 at the venerable age of 95 years.

The Magical Baron

Piero Fenili

When the name Baron Ricciardo Ricciardelli is mentioned, the minds of the uninformed often drift to the renowned "Trial of the Magus," a somber and intentionally surreal legal case. This trial featured the grandson of Kremmerz as the accused, charged with exploiting a vulnerable individual, with Baron Ricciardo as the aggrieved party.

The trial, held before the Court of Rome, concluded with the conviction of Kremmerz's grandson and caused a certain sensation, which led to the publication of a book with the same title that included the indictment of the defense lawyers' arguments, and the civil action pleadings. This was what was commonly known about the Baron until Giuseppe Maddalena Capiferro and Cristian Guzzo shed more light on his character with their diligent research, to which I shall refer.*

Such is the situation that the so-called "official" portrait outlines with its *Chiaroscuro* (apparently darker than light) the complex figure of the Baron. I realize, therefore, that the reader will be a little surprised that I provide an image of the Baron that is anything but in line with this "official" portrait and indeed, in some ways, is in stark contrast to it.

The first time I heard mention of the Baron was back in the mid-sixties, from his friend Placido Procesi,† with accents in which sym-

---

*[Reference is made to the books *Il Processo Del Mago*, Edizioni Rebis, 2010 and *L'Arcano degli Arcani*, Edizioni Rebis, 2005.—*Trans.*]

†[Placido Processo (1928–2005), a physician, archer, and celebrated scholar connected with the Roman-based Myriam of the 1960s and '70s. He was also known after World War II for being Julius Evola's personal physician.—*Trans.*]

pathy, consideration, and caution entered in equal doses; however, his character had to be taken seriously; it was certainly no coincidence that Kremmerz, a voluntary exile in Beausoleil, had repeatedly received him, almost in terms as an equal on some crucial themes of Hermetic philosophy.

Of the remains of one of these important discussions, a significant trace can be found in the article by Marco Daffi (this was the Italian transcription of his ancient name Mörköhekdaph) titled "The Avatars," which appeared posthumously in issue 32 of the bimonthly journal *Kemi-Hathor*, in February 1988. In it the Baron recalled a series of conversations he had on the subject with Kremmerz, whose thoughts he then reported, while showing the reasons for his dissent; we do not know if these were communicated back to Kremmerz, but in any case this led his formulating his own theory on this topic, which he elaborated on in the subsequent issues of the same journal.*

He was a character, as you can see, to be taken anything but lightly, as they say. And I was careful not to make this mistake when, sometime later, I had the good fortune to make his acquaintance.

If my memory serves me correctly, this happened at the home of General Nulli Augusti, in Rome, near Piazza Ungeria, in one of the most exclusive cultural salons in the capital, best placed to converse on topics of a spiritualistic nature. Many years later and in completely different circumstances, I met Viscount de Cressac-Bachelerie in France, editor of a high-level metapsychical magazine, and I learned that he too had come into contact with the same coterie of spiritualists whom we met in that Roman parlor.

Baron Ricciardelli, or don Ricciardo, as his friends called him in private, made the impression of being an interesting, jovial man, completely alien to, so to speak, "hierophantic" poses. I noticed sometime later, when going out to a restaurant together, that he was a good fork and shared, for dessert, my then preference for strawberries with cream.

---

*[*Kemi-Hathor* no. 38 contained the coda of the article "The Avatars."—*Trans.*]

His conversation was engaging and "different." The man demonstrated he was living in some kind of a magical dimension. It felt like he was on this earth by accident or by condemnation, as if he had been endowed with the rare balance of a true master; I would have said he was on a mission.

Certainly, ordinary existence, with its petulant concrete demands, the ferocious animalistic imperatives of the struggle for life, and the procession of hypocritical fictions with which these things disguise themselves in so-called civil society, had no hold on him.

I fully agree with what the Baron said in describing himself as a non-existent person, an abstract being, that belongs to the world of visions, magic, reincarnations—to that world that clings to the hospitable fields of the subconscious, and who is not a natural person, but an entity from an invisible domain. The slightest pretext offered by the conversation was enough for the Baron to fly off to another dimension, about which he evoked unsuspected laws and unprecedented perspectives.

Once he offered that we go together, at night, to a meeting place in the countryside along the road that leads to the Alban Hills, because there was an abode that housed a genie. He added that he carefully kept this location secret because he did not want some unworthy person to go there and "dirty it" (so he said verbatim). He certainly would not have imagined which and how many "contaminations" we have witnessed in the years following his death.

On some points, which came to light more from his writings than from his words, I kept on the defensive. I did not share, as a confirmed Platonist, that we can only recognize our true selves in a hyper-Uranian realm, beyond space and time, where some of his fugue states were in an inner space (toward the Andromeda nebula) or back in time (to Atlantis). But I must say that his speech generally presented a good rational and cultural structure without slipping into a disordered and uncontrollable visionariness. He knew how to deal with the topics that were proposed to him with logic and attention.

In the library of the Accademia Tiberina in Rome, there are likely still to be found some copies of one of his works on Jainism, possibly related to a course he conducted at this esteemed institution. It is a work of high regard.

Moreover, if don Ricciardo had only been a raving occultist, he would not have been able to enjoy the respect and consideration of people with a vigilantly critical sense, such as the lawyer Giammaria Gonella, the professor Luciano Raffaele di Santadomencia, and the doctor Aleandro Tommasi, who had the good fortune to spend more time with him than his imminent demise would have allowed me.

He had taken a liking to me, and so he decided, in his goodness, to investigate my previous incarnations as was done, I believe, in the most respected school of magic to which Kremmerz belonged, in order to assess the suitability of those who aspired to be affiliated with such arcane traditions.

I recall an encounter, after he had taken on this task, I met him at the end of a conference, and he waved his walking stick toward me as a sign of greeting, saying, "Doctor Fenili, I'm thinking about you, I'm thinking about you."

Until, after some time, I was summoned to Cafe Fassi, at the entrance to Corso d'Italia, at Piazza Fiume, a jewel of Umbertine Rome (miraculously it has still survived—who knows for how much longer—the vulgarity of the times, with its large hall decorated with imposing mirrors, wrought iron tables with marble tops, and a beautiful garden that, in the hot summer days, provided a pleasant coolness). We sat down at an outdoor table, ordered something, and then the Baron, adopting a stern demeanor that brooked no frivolity, extracted a sheet of paper from his briefcase. This sheet contained a "review" of my various incarnations, and he handed it to me for perusal.

I immediately took a breath of relief: in my past, there were no pharaohs or saints, priests, popes, or emperors, or any other fine historical figures. Otherwise, Arturo Reghini's fierce invectives would have crossed my mind like a flash of lightning: "never is there one that in a previous life was a seller of roasted chestnuts under the arcades of Piazza Santa Maria Novella in Florence."

Reassured by the absence of sensational avatars, as the Baron might have called them, I calmly reread the page that concerned me, while don Ricciardo was waiting for my reactions. The first part interested me less because I felt distant from it. With the second part, the music changed, because it strangely converged with a complex web of psychological, philosophical, and existential inclinations, also deep-rooted impulses, and steadfast preferences for certain temporal, geographical, and historical contexts. It resonated with the paths of initiatory inquiry I was already exploring, providing me with a well-defined and cohesive perspective

Very well, I said to myself, the Baron has some telepathic power and can read my thoughts. However, the possibility that the Baron had received some ritual from Kremmerz for this kind of investigation led me to a prudent, Pyrrhonian suspension of judgment.

We parted with the Baron's promise to give me the "beautiful copy" of that sheet, which I imagined or rather, I hoped, was accompanied by some hierogram that would increase its magical charm. Instead, I never saw him again. Sometime later, the magical Baron's earthly departure concluded with his full expiation, which I wish for him was definitive, owing to the initiatory burden he willingly shouldered. I am left with the sorrow of having lost a highly esteemed partner but perhaps also a friend.

To characterize the role he played in the awakening of interest in Hermeticism throughout Italy in the twentieth century and to try and determine how much such a role can have a meaning that is not ephemeral and transient, I cannot do better than to reproduce the inspired words with which Giammaria concludes his "psychographic portrayal" of the Baron, of whom he was a friend for many years: "Apart from this comprehensive profile, the philosophical doctrine within Marco Daffi's work holds universal significance, representing the essence of the 'Egyptian Order' originally transmitted by Kremmerz in the early twentieth century. This philosophy was revived by Marco Daffi in the

1950s and persisted until his passing, embodying a continuous revelation of the Star of Hermes."

Such was Baron Ricciardo Ricciardelli, for the little that I could know of him. I would like to honor his memory and revive interest in the vision he articulated through words.

The Voice

Giammaria

"I beg of you, please take it easy with the Baron," said Professor Gino Testi, when accompanying me to visit Baron Ricciardo Ricciarelli for the first time. "Of course," I reassured him, but I wondered, to myself, what was the reason for such counsel.

The meeting took place—at 5:00 p.m., at the Baron's house, on Via Tiber in Rome—and went well without incidents, so much so that on the way back I asked the professor the reason for his concern and his warning. In response, he told me that once, he had accompanied a knave of a friend to the Baron with whom this particular individual, during the discussions, announced that in his previous life he had committed suicide.

In an uproar the Baron told him, resentfully, that he would now have to relive that experience and, standing tall and firm, made gestures in the air with his hands murmuring who knows what words . . . Then the knave, in a trance, got up from the sofa where he was seated and headed toward the balcony next to the room. "Luckily," continued Professor Testi, "I was by the door of the balcony and blocked the passage, otherwise he would have jumped off, and that was enough of a shock to revive him from the trance."

I was a little surprised since the Baron seemed to me to be a quietly reserved and poised person, as I then experienced over the next twenty years, even when we talked about the "Trial of the Magus" (against the grandson of Kremmerz) in which the Baron, among other things, was accused of suffering from paranoia.

Incidentally, it can also, in an improper sense, mean paranoid (not paranoiac) as in those who profess the basic idea of a separate "path of reality" and—why not?—also schizoid (not-schizophrenic) who, like Ours, consider themself a medium for the emergence of multiple *ab antique* personalities, thus embodying a reincarnational evolution of existence in its entirety.

That reincarnation was his *idée fixe*, from which, for the sake of truth, he deviated from in our later get-togethers. These gatherings, aside from in the summer, were initially monthly, then biweekly in the first half of the month, then weekly. The frequency gradually decreased until 1969. I would visit don Ricciardo (as his family called him) in the afternoon, sometimes staying well into the late evening.

I did not visit him in the morning because I was engaged first at the Pontifical Lateran University with the study of canon law, then at the

Baron Ricciardo Ricciardelli with Giammaria in the mid-1960s

Roman Rota, and also at the Institute of Oriental Languages and Rights for two years, and then in Arabic and Hebrew classes, as well as for six years with complex psychology classes at an Italian-Swiss Institute. As was the case, in our last encounters he explicitly acknowledged that he had mistakenly written in the essay "Alchemical Hermeticism" (*Ulisse* journal, October 45, 1948) on the "cycle of rebirths" as an alchemical-Hermetic principle, and also agreed that it was the responsibility of Theosophy to sell reincarnation as the fulcrum of Buddhist thought, which indeed rejects the notion of an ego that passes from one existence to another. That, moreover, *samsara* represented the manifestation of a new existence under the influence of a precedent does not mean or involve that it is reincarnation; instead, it can be said that it expresses the phenomenon of *metempsychosis*, where the psyche of the deceased—seen as an individualized complex of energy fields—assimilates the most diverse psychic energy fields, just as the physical newborn assimilates the physical characteristics of its ancestors, and precisely this excludes any means of personal survival in the afterlife.

In short, true *metempsychosis* entails the migration of both psychic and physical elements, referred to as *metensomatosis*, which manifests in various forms throughout history, including in art and politics. This occurs when a prominent artist or influential figure leaves behind an enduring legacy of their ideas and artistic expression. These legacies are upheld and championed by followers, whether consciously or unconsciously.

His primary fascination revolved around reincarnation, which he believed was necessary for a process he termed "purgatory." He used this idea to describe the journey towards becoming a divine entity or "numen," as he put it in his private correspondence (Confidential Letters).* He discussed these ideas under the pseudonym Mörköhekdaph, which I have interpreted as Marco Daffi.

In the context of this purgation, he once asked me *expressis verbi* to help him with a certain magical operation. Basically, I was

---

*[See the first letter, dated Monday January 19, 1953, p. 188—*Trans.*]

instructed to sit on the sofa in front of his work table behind which he sat, as usual, to look at him and recount what and how much I had "seen." Obviously I was prepared for it and after not even two to three minutes I told him that I saw the room transformed into the hall of a large temple, with two high columns on the sides and, behind an altar, I saw him, with a heavily bearded face but still recognizable as himself, dressed as a priest—Egyptian—when behold, behind on his right, by the door of the room near the hall was a black screen, of a deep and dark blackish color. And all of a sudden as if it triggered in him a motion there emerged a vague (human-like?) figure who made an effort to come out in the light . . . but it didn't completely appear. "He saw what I saw too," he told me, and "I couldn't see any further," he concluded, thanking me. For me it was a typical case of telepathy between us instead of that of a priest of the pharaonic court who, *in illo tempore*, preying upon the Pharoah's wife and had misappropriated the treasure of the Temple of the Sun.

In this context, Baron Ricciardo Ricciardelli serves as a symbolic scapegoat, undergoing a purification to atone for the divine transgressions of Marco Daffi, in all of its numinosity. The notion of a *peccatuccio ad divinitatem*,* and the consequent price one must pay, echoes themes found in H. Rider Haggard's novels. However, for our subject, it was his own historical circumstances—and I stress historical—that needed resolution. In this life, he sought to achieve this by leveraging the vast inherited wealth at his disposal, amounting to tens of millions in the currency of that era.

As for me, I was particularly intrigued by his ability to give a coherent doctrinal framework to Hermeticism and with alchemy, in particular. Specifically, I should clarify that when I refer to "magical": it's in the context of Daffi's Gnostic perspective, which diverged from the Egyptian tradition and therefore isn't strictly "Hermetic." This divergence was shared by Kremmerz and the entire Neapolitan School. In fact, during the 1960s, I redirected requests for "mantic or divinatory"

---

*[Roughly translates "to sin against the divinity."—*Trans.*]

readings to Auri, my wife at the time. Auri, skilled in tarot reading, was frequently called upon by the Baron to perform them for him and eventually became his pupil.

For his part, Daffi delved into the tarot and the I Ching not only for personal consultation but also to grasp their philosophical underpinnings. He also dabbled in what he termed "astronology," as mentioned in letters 47–50 of the "Confidential Letters": "When I sought information, I feigned seeking astrological insights (actually astronological) to conceal my true intent—exploring my internal abilities. Now, I merely need to observe a person."

Put simply: astrology concerns the person in their time and place and therefore of their anagraphic or biographical self, while astronology addresses the impersonal I, the numinal self, aimed at identification with the principle for which the name is a reference . . .

However, this work seeped into the Tables of Hermeticism and continued over the years (see the "Letters") and above all precisely to prepare them for their publication; in the meantime, I founded the Corpo dei Pari, as a mandate expressed by Ours, as the executor of his will (see the appendix of the "Confidential Letters").

Astrology remained on my shoulders. Certainly, Daffi possessed remarkable insights into the core tenets of Hermetic philosophy. His reflections on the Monad, as captured in the "Philosophical Letters," are particularly striking: "The One . . . is by its very nature a darkened negative, its singular objective being—the very essence of creation itself—to generate and discern" (!). This underscores the alchemical directive to transmute gold from the gold one already possesses.

Daffi has eloquently written about his singular initiatory practice (see the "Letters"). He also has written at length about Kremmerz and Kremmerzians—see Confidential Letters and the *Bulletin of the Italian Society of Metapsychism and Parapsychology*, vol. 1, no. 2 (July–December 1955): 84–86 and vol. 4, no. 1 (January–June 1958): 13–15.

As many Kremmerzians turned to him to receive consultations, suggestions, and advice as I observed firsthand and as discreetly, he confided in me, having casually met more than one of those. However, just before his passing, it seemed as if he had never existed!

The Baron was unaware that my friends—Bruno (Swiss), Otto (Austrian), and Puska (Polish)—whom I encountered in Rome, were also treading on the same path. Meanwhile, Giorgio Venturini penned a brief essay titled "Speaking of Marco Daffi," and Elio G., whom I mention in "Marco Daffi and His Work," and already associated with Prof. Ugo Gallo, considered himself a disciple of the Baron, despite ours never having formally proposed such a role.

I should add that our relationship became almost like a family, so much so that the Baron would also come to Genoa to spend Christmas with me and mine and to offer me and my mother, who came to Rome for the occasion in 1949, dinner at a well-known restaurant when I took my license in *utroque iure** in the 1950s.

As for the vicissitudes of Baron Ricciardo Ricciardelli, within and outside of this worldly realm, few things speak more profoundly than the events chronicled in "The Trial of the Magus." From its pages, it appears that Kremmerz, at the time of his death, had been indicted before the Court of Chieti with other Kremmerzians, with implications for the Baron. However, Ricciardelli always ruled out his co-responsibility, instead attributing accountability to him on a separate plane, a perspective I would term "astronological," as detailed in the "Confidential Letters."

To gain insight into Daffi's mind set, one need look no further than his letters. In these missives, he delves into various Hermetic themes in an original manner. Auri, who had corresponded with Daffi for years at his request, witnessed this originality firsthand, particularly in relation to tarot practice. Additionally, Auri's experiences after the Baron's passing provide ample food for thought.

In essence, "behind" or "inside" the person of Baron Ricciardo Ricciarelli was the initiate Marco Daffi, with all its shadows and light.

---

*[Both laws, that is both civil and canon. In the 1950s, Giammaria resided in Rome to study civil and canon law at University.—*Trans.*]

It was understood that the Great Work served as an "indication," albeit not solely as a vision of life, but rather akin to a dream with subsequent implications.

This encapsulated the inherent challenge faced by those on a "path of power," where the focus is on transforming the dream of life rather than awakening from it. Gradually, and certainly as Auri aptly remarked after encountering him, it became evident that his VOICE emerged as a guiding force along that path.

.

Don Ricciardo

Auri Campolonghi Gonella

When I first met don Ricciardo, I felt a mix of anticipation and curiosity, but more importantly, I held him in high regard. He was a kind and pleasant gentleman, very polite, who knew how to put guests at ease. When don Ricciardo became aware that I was consulting (tarot) cards for myself and others, he asked if I would consult them for him too. I gladly agreed, and he told me that he would write to me when it was required. Such was the case. After a short time, I received his message asking me to bring out the oracle, but with short words and in very definite terms. I did my best, and from that moment on, within a few months, I received from him a list of questions. He was always polite and thanked me with words of gratitude.

There was a time, however, when I was asked to see if some persons, close to him, had "betrayed" him—why I don't know. From the vision arrived at by the reading it became clear to me that he was going to be betrayed, as had already been done for something else. Serene and convinced that I had done my duty, I awaited his answer; but when the answer came, I was breathless, reading that I had got everything wrong and that I must have mistakenly "seen" and, in short, that "I should be careful before writing." I went back with my mind to the reading, I went back to "seeing" but I, out of that question, saw nothing other than the betrayal by the same two individuals. But I resigned myself to thinking that I must have made a mistake. I apologized by letter, even though I still couldn't understand why, since with the assistance of memory I saw betrayal again. After about a month I received another letter from

don Ricciardo Nicola Ricciardelli

Baron Ricciardo Ricciardelli with Auri Compolonghi Gonella

don Ricciardo this time apologizing to me, because he, unfortunately, had proof that he had been betrayed by these same two people. So, we resumed the exchange of letters. But it was time for don Ricciardo to leave this earth, far too soon and much to our chagrin. I missed his letters asking me to see and investigate some character, which I did very carefully.

When don Ricciardo left us, I felt and we continued to feel a real and strong sorrow, since he was for us the voice of a deep interiority that turned up at times—even in moments totally out of context—so often to surprise us, but that we also welcomed as the "voice" that was no longer don Ricciardo but of an "entity" outside the "heavy" world that surrounds us.

There came a moment when we were to read for a few hours the "Psalms of Accompaniment" for the departure of don Ricciardo. It was agreed upon that I would be the second voice in saying the words of the psalm. Everything was ready: the room where I would pronounce the words "accompaniment" was purified and devoid of any presence other than mine, leading to the threshold state of the "unconscious." Each word of the psalms flowed effortlessly at that moment. However, at one point, I began to sense something different: it seemed to me that toward my right there was a certain something; I perceived an invisible presence that, however, seemed to want to take over my interiority and suddenly I understood.

I closed the book of psalms, turned to that presence, and said, "No!" I said no to becoming a "Pythia" at the mercy of those who still wanted to "talk" through me. I said no to erasing my little life and my even smaller sensitivity. "No!" I said aloud, "in my little life I will do my best, alone, intact and without anyone, here or later, taking me as a crutch. Goodbye." After that I allowed my memory to fade with the happenings of those events and even today, I am happy to be myself in my own dimension. One may be small, but the path is long for everyone.

Postscript

Who was Marco Daffi? His true identity remains veiled in mystery. A certainty perhaps known only to the bearer of that name. Yet, in his absence, focus turns towards the life story of the enigmatic Baron Ricciardo Ricciardelli, his writings, and other primary sources, particularly those individuals best positioned to offer definitive accounts, for insight.

Giammaria, Daffi's closest collaborator and the one to first disclose the name "Marco Daffi," asserts that this identity is more than a mere figment of the imagination. Instead, it embodies an ancient numinal persona* masking an archetype striving for manifestation through the vessel of the historical person of Ricciardo Ricciardelli.

Hence, Mörköhekdaph emerges as an Orpheus-like figure, a mask concealing a primordial essence that descends into the underworld realms and resurfaces at will, mirroring the mythical hero's pursuit of his lost Eurydice. This figure bears resemblance to the archetypal "Myriam," which the Hermetic practitioner must actualize in a state of rarefied purity and heightened consciousness, enabling the Hermetic rituals to attain virtualization.

Similarly, one could posit that the manifestation of Marco Daffi alludes to a distinct gnosis or altered state of consciousness, granting access to a plane of being that is interior, anterior, and superior to the commonly experienced domain of existence.

---

*Refers to the reincarnation of a previously existing personality. Specifically, the esoteric practice employed by Baron Ricciardo Ricciardelli to tap into and embody a personality from one of his past lives. This practice, likely taught to him by Kremmerz, involves an initiatory method of awakening primitive, ancestral memories to uncover the spiritual core of one's being. In other words, it's the process of recalling and reliving a former self from a previous existence.

In existential terms, "Mörköhekdaph" embodies a Hermetic identity, alluding to the effervescence of a sublime personality emerging from the fusion of an integrated cluster of energy, deep within the psyche. This wellspring of energy can be accessed by the operator through transcendent levels of consciousness triggered by Hermetic rituals and brought into focus by pyschonavigational techniques, which the ancient Pythagoreans referred to as "anamnesis."

In contrast to historical figures whose biographical existence defines their legacy across time, this persona seeks integration within the archetypal realm of memory, ensconced deep within the psyche, where it strives for manifestation.

This journey through the astral domain unfurls as an initiatory odyssey, wherein the Hermetic operator charts the vigils of their psyche and inscribes their revelations. Within the alchemical crucible, it is not the adept who garners virtue, but the quintessential dream of the *Lapis Philosophorum* itself, gaining verity with each transmutation from successive projections into manifestation.

In the aforementioned article, Piero Fenili notes that when the Baron delved into his past, he encountered inner visions that manifested clear figures, images, and scenarios. While suspecting his remarkable clairvoyant abilities were innate, he also speculated that Daffi had probably acquired the technique of "psycho-ancestral retrospection" directly from Kremmerz.

Hence, it's prudent to assert that the primary and sole beneficiary of the Hermetic text is the operator themselves. Here, Daffi delineates a roadmap depicting the desired, envisioned, and eventually realized journey after many, many herculean trials.

The subject matter of the Work, in the hands of the operator who longs for the grace of realization, ultimately becomes one and the same as the subject that reveals the sense of the supreme metaphor: that of life and death itself. Every text is nothing but a confused memory, a limited reproduction, a pale glimmer of the epiphanic revelation of what the Stone attains.*

---

*"Marco Daffi and his World," Giammaria, Editrice Kemi, 1980.—*Trans.*

Are the figures Marco Daffi, Mörköhekdaph, or Ei hm'sc Bêl merely fleeting zephyrs, akin to the migratory birds known as Wandervögel, coming and going with the changing seasons and reminiscent of the elusive Phoenix, often cited but rarely sighted?

Or does this spectrum of names and figures allude to a solitary argonaut of the psyche, whose quest to discover his true, perennial, and primary selfhood propelled him on extraordinary inner journeys to unearth the underlying source of identity, the unified energetic field or NUMEN and to disentangle himself from his biographical identity?

Marco Daffi's exploration of a vast array of topics within Alchemical Hermeticism attests to his mastery of the practice. This leads to speculation on the "occult name" or "initiatic name," which carries a discernible Eastern influence—an ancient echo that manifests a distinct vibrational resonance in a subtler plane of perception, beyond the usual boundaries of what is commonly accepted as reality.

In this light, the "name"* may bear value or reference on the "historical" plane, or perhaps, through an inner archaeological descent into one's own past, unearthing ancient identities.

This conundrum is inherently meaningful and warrants exploration. Considering the perspective of Western Hermeticism, which values the role of intuition on par with rationality, meditation serves to delve into the retrospective process, by directly confirming the boundaries of "What Is Possible."

Thus, the "name" serves as a valuable tool . . . within the order of the WORD . . . as an evocation of the presence of the NUMEN. This viewpoint echoes FICINO's notion of the macro-microcosmic relationship,

---

*The Baron refrained from using his Hermetic names "Marco Daffi," "Mörköhekdaph," or "Ei hm'sc Bêl" in his publications, understanding that such names intimately connect the practitioner to their guiding spirit and soul. Public exposure of these names, he believed, would profane them, diminishing their magical potency and effectiveness in metaphysical projection. Kremmerz later regretted allowing his Hermetic name to be associated with his works. Similarly, Renaissance magi who advanced applied metaphysics, such as Ficino, Bruno, Pico, and Campanella, never publicly claimed the title of Magus. For the authentic practitioner, any display of hubris acts as a nullifying force, akin to kryptonite.

suggesting that the cosmos is mirrored within us. Marsilio Ficino delved into a series of introspective practices designed to discern individual temperaments and devised a method for probing the essence and dispositions of people. By mapping astronological correspondences, he sought to identify the celestial types or divine synergies inherent in our existence.

This form of transpersonal introspection serves as a useful psychoanalytical tool for plumbing inherent inclinations and intrinsic values, enabling individuals to confront conscious decisions regarding identity and tradition. As we read in *The Book of Ak Z UR* (Edizioni Alkaest, 1980):

> From the vast expanse of the UNIVERSE down to the microcosm of the human being, MAN identifies with ADAM KADMON, the cosmic archetype, permeated by and encompassing all forces operative within the universe itself. Anchored in the juxtaposition of opposites—FIXED and MOBILE, POSITIVE and NEGATIVE—the individual's existential journey unfolds.
>
> Within this journey converge all elemental, intellectual, and archetypal qualities, traditionally symbolized in Hermetic texts by the three great "Eonic numbers": the QUATERNARY (FOUR), the SEPTENARY (SEVEN), and the DUODENARY (TWELVE).
>
> From the theme of the WORLD and MAN, we transition to internalization of the HERMETIC WORK (the Great Art). In this context, the THREE REGIMES* are also contemplated: a DRY phase and a HUMID phase of the PATH, ascending to a state of MAG, experiencing the SEVEN FORMS, operations within the TWO VESSELS,† and so forth.
>
> All of this is represented with the understanding that the star of HERMES also irradiates within the rational sphere. Thus, EONIC experiences, rituals, or other elements on the margins of the

---

*[The alchemical nigredo, albedo, and rubedo stages.—*Trans.*]

†[Two Vessels being the conscious exchange or transfer of spiritual or life energy from one initiate to another subject, commonly observed between male and female pairs, although such transference can manifest among individuals of the same gender when their energies complement each other. Refer to *Introduction to Magic*: Volume 1 and *The Hermetic Physician* for further insights.—*Trans.*]

JOURNEY are deemed "operative" solely if the individual ascribes value to them on the plane of reception; otherwise, they are subsumed and exhausted within the realm of awareness.

When journeying along the path, it's crucial to understand how knowledge intertwines with experience, and equally vital is the process of integration within the sphere of assimilating the known contents as they are encountered. "One may venture into the depths of the Infernal realms, navigating their twists and turns, yet it's akin to a one-way journey unless, like Orpheus, one has unlocked the key to the arcanum veiling the return."

Strictly speaking, this distinction* arises between mythologems of Hermetic Experience such as the Seven Forms, represented by the REBIS, and mythologems of Integration, those associated with the GLOBE of VENUS. These symbols and mythologems are referred to in the jargon of the practice as "homologous."

Accordingly, the doctrines and concepts are understood through the confirmation of experience and the assimilation of its content that serve as mediators in the integrative process. Hermeticism is dressed in modern attire to accentuate even more its universal content in the sense that, like the splendor of HERMES, it represents the GARMENT of REVELATION.†

This aligns with the foundations laid by Kremmerz, who, at the beginning of the last century, broke away from the archaic and outdated language that had previously characterized authors in the realm of Hermeticism. Daffi introduces several novel images, such as the Siren and the Avatar, to explore states of initiatic consciousness.

In the present context, given the near impossibility of erasing collective knowledge and logical concepts expressed in everyday language from our minds, directing the reader toward the concepts (internal forces) proposed and represented in this Book can undoubtedly improve

---

*[Possession of the key to the arcanum of initiatic descents and ascents, also referred to as VITRIOL.—*Trans.*]

†[The Book of Ak Z UR, Giammaria, Edizioni Alkaest, 1980.—*Trans.*]

comprehension, sharpen vision, provide foresight, and enhance under-standing of the enigmatic arcanum that is alchemical Hermeticism.

Just as the splendor of HERMES is embodied in revelation, and which the "personality" of MÖRKÖHEKDAPH is infused in its teach-ings and disseminated among the Dissertamina, Philosophical Letters, Introduction to Manticism, Alchemical Hermeticism, the Avatars, Solve and Coagula, and crystalized within the Tables and Comments of the Hamzur Ritual. Moreover, it may be here that his greatest inspiration was imparted.

What we can ascertain with certainty about MARCO DAFFI is the following.

Baron Ricciardo Ricciardelli, also known by his spiritual names Marco Daffi, Mörköhekdaph, and Ei hm'sc Bêl, was an Italian esotericist and a fascinating figure with unique experiences and contributions of magical Hermeticism during the twentieth century (1900–1969).

Ricciardelli dedicated his life to the study and practice of Hermeticism, with a particular focus on alchemy, manticism, and initiation. His operational contributions spanned several decades and left a significant impact on esoteric circles and individuals inter-ested in the practice. He followed in the footsteps of the renowned Hermeticist, Giuliano Kremmerz, exploring the more esoteric aspects of Hermetic practice.

EXPERIENCES AND WRITINGS

Hermetic practices: Marco Daffi initially claimed contact with an "Egyptian" center in Canada, from which spawned a series of personal initiatives: the Pharaonic Group, founded in 1932 and resumed in 1953; the Chain of Hamzur or Andromeda from 1956 to 1962; and the Pleiades Ring from 1962, with the help of colleagues from Bari and Genoa.

In the last years of his life, Marco Daffi communicated a series of Egyptian rituals to Giammaria (Gonella), who used them for the new initiative of the Corps of Peers (founded in 1960 and concluded after twelve years, which Daffi was never part of). Already by the end of the 1960s, this group aroused the curiosity of the press and the Genoese public by posting manifestos in the style of the Rosicrucians that appeared in seventeenth-century Paris.

Inner Laboratory: Daffi delved into the interdimensional aspects of consciousness by descending into the depths of his own psyche and explored past-life regression for self-discovery, transpersonal realization, and Hermetic healing.

Oracular Intelligence: He practiced various forms of Vatic or oracular modes of visualizations, drawing from his considerable mediumistic capabilities and psychic faculties.

Biographical Context: In addition to his initiatory pursuits, Daffi led a remarkably vibrant human life. Insights into Ricciardelli's biography, passed down by initiates, artists, and scholars who were acquainted with him, enrich our understanding of his work and philosophy. Marco Daffi's lasting impact is evident in his investigation of the practical aspects of initiation and Hermetic gnosis, effectively connecting spiritual practices and initiatory wisdom with contemporary understanding. His writings continue to inspire seekers of light on their spiritual paths.

Alchemical Hermeticsm: The Hermetic practitioner, graced with a transcendent insight, endeavors to communicate it, fully aware that the profundity of this experience lies beyond the grasp of most. Yet, in this attempt, they appear to reawaken an innate ability to harmonize with the unseen realms, aligning their inner vibrations in unison with the hidden cosmic order.

Within the Myriamic tradition, initiates refer to a transcendent dimension as MAG, which infuses the OPERATOR with a vibrational resonance from a subtler plane within the denser one—a celestial offering where angels frequently guide the way and provide stairways to alternate realms through dreams to transform magical consciousness.

In saying that Hermes manifests, the operator not only designates, but partly evokes, images on the edge of sensibility, reactivating a dormant consciousness, nourishing a phantom. This is the sense of the dance that every aperture into light implies; that the flame is luminous, and the memory of the event not betrayed by a single word. Here, dramatized in classical Hermetic fashion, is the imposition of a name on an emerging psychic reality; the name here is flesh, it is a tangible being.

In this moment, an entity is born, to which in art a name must be imposed to render it stable, to fix it. It is a dangerous act because recognizing it confers existence upon that which hasn't existence, in its accepted definition, but it is also true that it is necessary if one wishes to begin any process of revulsion, of the human-animal.

The first step lies in the order of reflection; the medium is the vision—the magical tool par excellence—delegated to reveal aspects of a reality that lies beyond the observer's reach.

The "Name" can serve as both a deception and a revelation, bringing forth an existence that may not align with reality yet still acting as a conduit, albeit one that is elusive.

Writings: Through the publication of works dedicated to Marco Daffi, we provide access to his writings, enabling direct familiarity with him through vivid firsthand accounts from those who had personal acquaintance with him.

Today, courtesy of Inner Traditions, we gain genuine insight into Marco Daffi, known in his time as Baron Ricciardo Ricciardelli, overlooking biased opinions and partial judgments which, as Daffi himself would say, only serve "Humanimaleries."

Rather, greater value would be gleaned from a thorough review of Daffi's writings and not solely from an academic perspective, rather from a philosophical and initiatic digression, inspired by what was written and said by Kremmerz, and much of it directly received by word of mouth. This material is essentially operational, describing doctrines, techniques, experiences realized or within the realm of possibilities, without the intermediation of "hierarchies."

His visionary insights shed light on esoteric healing, alchemical philosophy, initiation, gnosis, atavistic resurgence, avatars, eros, divination, and consciousness.

Translations: Among the works dedicated to Marco Daffi are several translations into English, including this text, *The Hermetic Physician*, and *The Hermetic Book of the Dead* (forthcoming).

CONCLUSION

Lastly, did Marco Daffi truly exist? We can affirm that existence for him was the outcome of a search for Being-in-self, the embodiment of a fully imagined NUMEN.

That Marco Daffi was an astral being embodying a human guise in the historical fixture of Baron Ricciardo Ricciardelli seems like the most likely scenario. However, placing this character into a historical context does not imply certainty that it figures as a historical person revealing itself across the wheels of time. For the astral realm transcends the linearity of time in a past-present-future sense to reveal an eternal Now.

In this light, one could assert with equal validity that Marco Daffi is not a historical figure per se, but rather an ever-present archetype, a primordial essence capable of manifesting at will across the tapestry of perceived time.

That which endures of him—books, articles, rituals, epistolary— is vast, lucid, and admirable. It springs from a rare experience, bequeathed for a future memory to those rare individuals, veritable magical heroes, a community, or what he termed as the eternal initiatory family, coalesced around identities of faith and seekers exploring paths of spiritually living.

To the others, no one, however, and for whatever reason they want to read his work, will be able to escape the impression of having before themself, in addition to a vision of the alchemical sea, also one of the fundamental chapters of Hermetic research in this century.

Marco Daffi, along with Kremmerz, restored the principle of an authentically rooted Occidental initiation, rescued from the alienation of Orientalism, and whose ideals, practices, and doctrines remain archived in the library of the Invisible and available for retrieval and practice to those special types, psychonauts who have what it takes to undertake the spiritual odyssey.

Through his dedication to restoring alchemical Hermetic terminology, in contemporary language, he reclaimed one of the subtlest traditional methods of inner transformation.

By investigating a multitude of esoteric subject matter, he demonstrated the clarifying power and sharp intuition that marks his brilliance.

Lastly, mention must be made concerning the living example of disengaging from the collective leveling by pursuing a spiritual path to realize a degree of personal autonomy and self-sovereignty unparalleled in modern times. It is the exquisite blossoming of the soul into its fullest expression of Selfhood.

Consider those fortunate who, in their lifetime, witness this rare phenomenon—akin to a Comet streaking across the night sky, a fleeting yet unforgettable epiphany to the extraordinary.

DAVID PANTANO

In Perpetual Memory of Baron Ricciardo Nicola Ricciardelli.
May Heaven Reserve for Him a New Existence in which His Holy
Aspiration is Fully Satisfied with the
Most Triumphant of Ascensions.

A PERPETUA MEMORIA
DEL BARONE RICCIARDO NICOLA RICCIARDELLI
NATO IN NAPOLI IL 23/11/1900 CHE ISPIRATO AI SENSI DI CRISTIANA CARITA'
DONAVA ALL'OPERA NAZIONALE BALILLA, NELL'ANNO 1929 COSPICUO
TERRENO IN SAN SEVERO, DA ADIBIRE AD ATTIVITA' SPORTIVE PER I GIOVANI
DI SAN SEVERO – IL 03/09/1969 IN ROMA ANNIVERSARIO DELLA SUA MORTE DI
TANTO BENEFATTORE CON GRATITUDINE E RICONOSCENZA IMPLORANDO PACE
ALL'ANIMA ELETTA QUESTO MARMOREO RICORDO
PONEVA
TARGA IN MEMORIA DEL BARONE RICCIARDO NICOLA RICCIARDELLI

POSSA IL CIELO RISERVARGLI, UNA NUOVA ESISTENZA IN CUI LA SUA SANTA
ASPIRAZIONE SIA PIENAMENTE SODDISFATTA COL PIU' TRIONFALE DEGLI ASCENSI

Commemorative Plaque of the Baron Ricciardo Ricciardelli Sports Facility in San Severo

In Perpetual Memory

of Baron Ricciardo Nicola Ricciardeli

Born in Naples on 23/11/1900 and inspired by a sense

of Christian Charity donated to the National Opera Balilla, in the

year 1929, on this conspicuous land in San Severo.

To be used by the youth of San Severo for sporting activities

03/09/1969 in Rome, on the anniversary of the death of

such a benefactor with gratitude and acknowledgement imploring

peace to the chosen soul is posed this marble plaque

in memory of Baron Ricciardo Nicolo Ricciardelli.

May Heaven reserve for him a new existence in which his holy

aspiration be fully satisfied with the most triumphal of ascensions.

Annotated Bibliography
Marco Daffi's Opera Omnia
Giammaria

In the period spanning 1945 to 1950, the decision matured in me to fully commit—*toto corde*—to alchemical-Hermetic research. My notions of alchemy were rather rudimentary and vague on the one hand, while on the other I found myself utterly inexperienced in the face of the symbolic and metaphorical canons of operation—that is, the meaning behind the jargon escaped me.

It was precisely under these circumstances that in 1949 I had the good fortune to meet the person who subsequently became known in the field of Hermeticism as Marco Daffi, and fortuitously was able to visit him regularly for ten years and for as many more to remain in contact, as much or as little, as necessary.

Fortunately, it was possible for me, thanks to an assiduous practice using the material gleaned from our interpersonal relationship—consisting of profound reflections and engaged meditations—was able, over time to become familiar with and internalize the alchemical key.

For the record, the name Marco Daffi was my "invention" and well accepted by Ours (see his letter of January 19, 1953) . . . and as to the "literary work," I would say that in a broad sense, as far as I know, his writings—and this is not all of it—consist of those in the following list.

MARCO DAFFI'S FUNDAMENTAL WRITINGS

Books

Translated in English

Ermetismo Alchimico: Articoli (Alchemical Hermeticism), Marco Daffi (Ricciardo Ricciardelli, Edizioni Rebis, 2017)

Dissertamina (Dissertations), Edizioni Alkaest, 1980

Epistolario Filosofico (Philosophical Letters), Edizioni Alkaest, 1980

Epistolario Confidenziale (Confidential Letters), privately published

The Hermetic Physician: The Magical Teachings of Giuliano Kremmerz and the Fraternity of Myriam, David Pantano, Inner Traditions, 2022. Containing translations of the following:

Giuliano Kremmerz e la Fr+ Tm + di Myriam (Marco Daffi, Edizioni Alkaest, 1981)

Alchimia Ermetica, Terapica ed Erotica (On Hermetic Therapeutics, Alchemy, and Eros), Marco Daffi, Editrice Kemi, 1980

"Giuliano Kremmerz, Commentarium ed altre opere, Opera omnia Vol. II" (Giuliano Kremmerz and other works, Opera omnia volume 2) 1954, by "A Kremmerzian" and attributed to Ricciardo Ricciardelli, from the *Bulletin of the Italian Society of Metapsychics*, 1955

"Giuliano Kremmerz, Dialoghi sull'ermetismo e scritti minori, opera omnia" (Giuliano Kremmerz, Dialogues on Hermeticism and minor writings, Opera omnia volume 3), by "A Kremmerzian" and attributed to Ricciardo Ricciardelli, extracted from the *Bulletin of the Italian Society of Parapsychology*, Editrice Universale di Roma, 1958

Untranslated

Considerazioni biografiche su Kremmerz e la My+ (Biographical Considerations on Kremmerz and the My+), Ricciardo Ricciardelli, presented by Luciano Raffaele di Santa Domenica. Quaderni della Schola Italica, 1988. From a confidential writing, entrusted by

Baron Ricicardo Ricciardelli, are revealed initiatory details related to the intimate life of master Kr + Kremmerz and related to the activity and esoteric structures of the Fr+ of Myriam, published in *Il Sole Arcano*, Pier Luca Pierini, Edizioni Rebis, 2011

Thesaurus Medicinae Dei, Il Libro Ermetico dei Morti, Rito di Hamzur) The Hermetic Book of the Dead, Hamzur Ritual), Marco Daffi, Editrice Kemi, 1980

Il Rito di Andromeda (The Ritual of Andromeda), Baron Ricciardo Ricciardelli, presented by Luciano Raffaele di Santa Domenica, also known as "Hamzur's ritual" or "of the Tablets," alias "the journey of the soul in the sacred representation of Hamzur," *Quaderni della Schola Italica*, 1996

Il Tarocco Secondo la Mensa Isiaca e l'I king (The Tarot of the Isis Tablet), Marco Daffi, Edizioni Alkaest, 1980

Solve et Coagula nello Speculum Artis di Giammaria, Marco Daffi, Amenothes Editions, 2004

Operational Tables and Commentary, part 2 of Marco Daffi and His Work, Giammaria, Marco Daffi, Editrice Kemi, 1980

Compendio di Ermetica, Tavole di Propedeutica (Compendium of Hermetics: Tables of Preliminary Studies), Marco Daffi, Editrice Kemi, 1980

Corpus Philosophicum totius Magie: restitutum a J EM KREM ERZ - Aegiptiaco Manuscripto, compiled by AK ZUR, critical notes by Marco Daffi, Third Edition, Editrice Kemi 2001

Le Carte Storiche della Fratellanza di Myriam, note critiche di Marco Daffi (The Historical Papers of the Fraternity of Myriam), critical notes by Marco Daffi, Editrice Kemi, 1980

Scritti iniediti e rari di Ermetismo Magico (Unpublished and Rare Writings on Magical Hermeticism), Marco Daffi, Edizioni Rebis, 2021

Articles

"Alchimia Ermetica" (Alchemical Hermeticism), Ricciardo Ricciardelli, *Ulisse, Rivista di Cultura Internazionale* (Ulysses, journal of international culture) #7, 1948

"Neobuddhismo e l'Iniziazione" ("Doctrine of Initiation and NeoBuddhism"), *Iniziazione: Rivista mensile di studi esoterici*, 1945

"Memoria per l'Accademia di Bari sul Maestro Giuliano Kremmerz e sulle origini e I primi passi della Fratellanza T+M+ di Miriam": Discorso pronunicato nella Sede dell'Accademia Barese nell'Anno (Memoir of Master Giuliano Kremmerz and the Origins and the First Steps of the Fraternity T+M+ of Miriam. Speech delivered at the Headquarters of the Bari Academy in the Year 1950), Don Ricciardo Ricciardelli, unpublished essay, 1950. The essays extracted from this memoir was compiled, edited, and repurposed by Giammaria into a book format which became *Giuliano Kremmerz e la Fr+ Tr+ di Myriam*.

"Che Cosa E La Magia Per I Suoi Cultori" (What is Magic for Those Who Cultivate It), Ricciardo Ricciardelli, *Rivista di Scienza del Mistero*, 1946

"La Sublimazionne del Mercurio" (The Sublimation of Mercury), Marco Daffi, *Kemi-Hathor* no. 28, 1987

"Commento alla novella 'La Meravigliosa Storia dello Specchio delle Vergini'" (Commentary on the novella "The Mirror of the Virgins"), Ricciardo Ricciardelli, Edizioni Rebis, 2021

"Gli Avatars" #32; "Gli Avatars incomplete" #33; "Gli Avatars spirituali" #34; "Gli Avatars incomplete" #41 (The Avatars #32; The Complete Avatars #33; The Spiritual Avatars #34; The Incomplete Avatars #41) *Kemi-Hathor Journal on Alchemy and Symbolic Studies* l, 1988–89

"Introduzione alle mantiche" (Introduction to Manticism), Marco Daffi, *Kemi-Hathor Journal on Alchemy and Symbolic Studies*, issue no. 36–39, 42–49, 1988–91

"Disposizione dei Trionfi in rapporto alla Tavola Bembina" (Disquisition on the Tarot Triumphs in relation to the Bembine Tablet), Marco Daffi, *Kemi-Hathor* no. 79, 1996

"Excursus su: La Mensa Isiaca" (Excursus on the Symbology of the Isis Tablet), Marco Daffi, *Kemi-Hathor* no. 79, 1996

Il Libro dei Mutamenti- I King (Article on "The Book of Changes"—I Ching), *Kemi-Hathor* no. 57, 1992

Hermetic Prophecies and Inner Visions, essays attributed to Marco Daffi from the book *Dagli Atti del Corpo dei Pari* (From the Acts of the Corps of Peers), Edizioni Alkaest, 1978

"Scritti inedita e rari di Ermetismo Magici" (Unpublished rituals from the Hamzur Rite and the Andromeda Circle), Marco Daffi, Edizioni Rebis, 2021

"On the Character of the Paranormal Faculties," Ricciardo Ricciardelli, *Italian Journal for Psychic Research*, Fasc. 1–3, 1964

"On Precognitive Phenomena in Relation to Determinism," Ricciardo Ricciardelli, *Italian Review of Psychic Research, Official Organ of the Italian Society of Parapsychology*, Fasc. 2–3, 1966

"In Margine ad Una Critica" (On the Margins of a Critique), critical review of Dr. Stevenson's book *Twenty Cases Suggestive of Reincarnation*, Ricciardo Ricciardelli, Italian Review of Psychic Research, Italian Society of Parapsychology #3, 1967

BOOKS, ARTICLES, AND ESSAYS ON MARCO DAFFI

Il Processo del Mago (Trial of the Magus), Societa Editrice del Libro Italiano, 1942

Marco Daffi e la sua opera, tavole e commenti (Marco Daffi and His Work, tables and commentary), Giammaria, Editrice Kemi, 1980. Introduction by Giammaria and the tables and commentary are primarily written by Daffi with Giammaria's notes.

Parliamo di Marco Daffi (Speaking of Marco Daffi), Giorgio Venturini, private edition, 2008

"R.R., Il Barone Mago" (Ricciardo Ricciardelli, The Magical Baron), Piero Fenili, *Elixir* no. 4, Rebis Editore, 2006

"Verso il segreto di Ricciardo Ricciardelli" (Towards the Secret of Ricciardo Ricciardelli), Piero Fenili, *Elixir* no. 8, Rebis Editore, 2009

"La Voce" (The Voice), Giammaria, *Elixir* no. 8, Rebis Editore, 2009

"Don Ricciardo," Auri Campolonghi Gonella, *Elixir* no. 8, Rebis Editore, 2009

Sul Rito di HAMZUR, Dagli Corpo dei Pari (On the Ritual of HAMZUR, from the Corps of the Peers), various authors, Editrice Amenothes 2006

"I Tarocchi Egizi" (The Egyptian Tarot), Auri Campolonghi Gonella, *Elixir* no. 8, Rebis Editore, 2009

Il Corvo Gracchio Due Volte (The Crow Caws Two Times), Auri Campolonghi Gonella, private edition

"Una interessante discussione su Marco Daffi, Kremmerz e la Fratellanza di Miriam" (An Interesting Discussion on Marco Daffi, Kremmerz and the Fraternity of Myriam), Syras and K. Hader, *Elixir*, no. 9, 2010

"Fluidita Gnostica" (Gnostic Fluidity), Ezio Abrile, Fenix journal

"Il caso di Pandora" (Pandora's Box: The Reality and Background of the Trial of the Magus), Pierluca Pierini, *Elxir* no. 9, Rebis Editore, 2010

The Magic Door: A Study on the Italic Hermetic Tradition, David Pantano, Manticore Press, 2019

The Return of Hermes: Notes on the Body of Peers, a Contemporary Group of Hermetic Practitioners, David Pantano, Manticore Press, 2017

Index

Please note that italicized page numbers in this index indicate illustrations.

BOOKS OF RELATED INTEREST

The Hermetic Physician
The Magical Teachings of Giuliano Kremmerz
and the Fraternity of Myriam
by Marco Daffi
Foreword by Hans Thomas Hakl
Collected and Translated by David Pantano

The Hermetic Science of Transformation
The Initiatic Path of Natural and Divine Magic
by Giuliano Kremmerz

The Invisible History of the Rosicrucians
The World's Most Mysterious Secret Society
by Tobias Churton

The Lost Pillars of Enoch
When Science and Religion Were One
by Tobias Churton

Three Books of Occult Philosophy
by Heinrich Cornelius Agrippa
Translated with commentary by Eric Purdue

The Hermetic Tradition
Symbols and Teachings of the Royal Art
by Julius Evola

The Way of Hermes
New Translations of *The Corpus Hermeticum* and
The Definitions of Hermes Trismegistus to Asclepius
Translated by Clement Salaman, Dorine van Oyen,
William D. Wharton, and Jean-Pierre Mahé

Hermetic Herbalism
The Art of Extracting Spagyric Essences
by Jean Mavéric

INNER TRADITIONS • BEAR & COMPANY
P.O. Box 388 • Rochester, VT 05767
1-800-246-8648 • www.InnerTraditions.com

Or contact your local bookseller